THE VOYNICH PROJECT: NEPHILIM RISING
AN ΩMEGA FORCE THRILLER

By JAMES K. ROLLINS

THE VOYNICH PROJECT

This book is a work of fiction. The characters, organizations, and incidents are drawn from the author's imagination and are not to be construed as real. Any resemblance to actual events or persons, living or dead, is entirely coincidental.

Contact author at: voynichprojectjkrollins@yahoo.com

Published by Mainstream Publishing.
Chapter House UK
Pitfield
Kiln Farm
Milton Keynes
MK11 3LW

Library of Congress Cataloging-in-Publication Data

Rollins, James K.
The Voynich Project: Nephilim Rising an Omega Force Thriller
ISBN 960-8317-68-1

10 9 8 7 6 5 4 3 2 1

THE A TEAM MEETS THE FAIRIES

This novel is dedicated to the real heroes, the men and women of the U.S. Armed Forces, who lay their lives on the line ~~on a~~ daily ~~basis~~ to ensure our freedom.

↑ pile of newspapers

Play the VOYNICH QUEST by going to:
http//:voynichprojectjamesrollins.com

MS 408 - Voynich Manuskript

GENESIS 6:4 The Nephilim were on the earth in those days, and also afterward, when the sons of God came into the daughters of men, and they bore children to them.

The Nazis believed the Nephilim were the first great Aryan race of the "north." They attempted to restore this mystical race of Superbeings, whose offspring they christened the *Vril-ya* or *Sonnenkinder.* The Third Reich considered these children to be the fountainhead of the new master race.

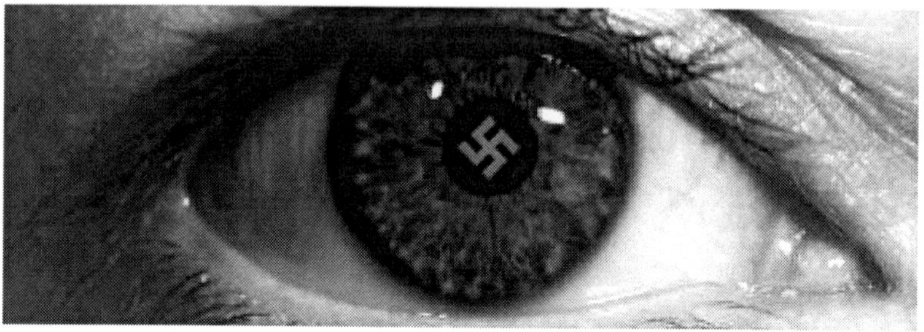

THE ΩMEGA TEAM:

Major Brody Devlin: Former State Dept. DSS and ex-Marine now agent in charge.
Sgt. Clint “Chewie” Raindancer: ex-SEAL and Native American.
Lt. Braxton: Former Justice Dept. Attorney—Nazi hunter.
Scout Thompson: Former computer hacker and DSS CIF, Computer Investigations and Forensics.
Sgt. Conners: Scotsman and former member of British RAF’s “Rock Apes Squadron.”
Madison Dare: Doctorates from Princeton in math and physics.
Bill Sorensen: Former DIA director of covert ops.

THE ENEMY:

Al-Dajjal: KGB trained assassin and neo-Nazi.
Heinrich von Gant: Head of the *Vril* Society and arms dealer.
Margot Gant: Mystery woman without a past. Brutally sadistic killer and masochist.
The Ice Axe: Bodyguard and hatchet man.

THE INDIGO CHILDREN:

Wendy/Noor El Alam: "Light of the World."

The Lost Boys: Peter, Gabriel, Johnboy, and Raji.

THE DAUGHTERS OF AWEN:

Dr. Blair Morgan Kelly: Renowned archaeologist and Celtic High Priestess.

Ginny Doolittle: Eccentric fairy-godmother-like protector.

(TEASER EXCERPT)

London

With her last ounce of strength, the girl shouldered her way through the door. The steady drizzle of rain felt cool and welcoming as she pounded across the rooftop. The cold evening air poured into her lungs as she ran. *Almost there*, she thought. *A few more feet and I'll be free.*

She stopped suddenly and inched her way toward the edge of the roof.

The wind rocked her as she stood blinking the rain from her eyes, arms outstretched and struggling to maintain her balance.

Looking down, she could dimly make out the blurred afterglow of headlights. The image brought a smile to her lips. It reminded her of fireflies swarming through the night.

From behind, the door burst open and slammed against the wall with a loud thud. Light from the stairwell shot across the rooftop, reaching for her.

She turned. A knot of dark figures spilled out of the doorway and stood silhouetted in the weak backwash of light.

Even in the grayness, she could recognize the outline of the tallest form, her blonde-white hair capturing the watery light. Her stature, her body language was unmistakable; it held the raw cruelty of a coiled whip. She could almost feel the black wind of Margot Gant's terror. Wendy's tummy was sick with fear. There were tears in her eyes, and she hated that.

The sound of another familiar voice, winded from the fast climb to the rooftop, sent panic shuddering through the girl.

"Time to come home, little one," Dr. Craven said.

She didn't answer.

Another figure at the doctor's side took a step forward.

The girl inched closer to the edge. Then Margot's arm shot outward, halting the other man's advance.

The blinding beam of a torch seared her eyes.

"Shut it off, *du wichser*!" Margot snapped.

When she turned to Wendy, her persona transformed instantly. Feigning a sweet, motherly voice, she said, "No one's going to harm you, darling."

Oh, bullocks you won't, Wendy thought.

As she spoke in soft, soothing tones, Margot's hand glided to the tranquilizer pistol tucked neatly in her waistband at the small of her back.

Somehow, Wendy sensed the weapon mean old Cruella was hiding; she could picture the cold black metal in her mind's eye.

But as she stood with her arms still extended, she felt as if the wind might waft her to safety. With half-closed lips, she began singing a nursery rhyme. "Rock a bye baby, in the tree tops. When the wind blows, the cradle will rock ..."

Wendy took another step. Wind tore across the rooftop, flaming her hair.

"When the bough breaks ..."

Wendy's eyes were closed tightly now, her eyelids heavy with memories as she rolled her head from side to side.

She took another step.

"NO!" Margot shouted as she dove forward.

Silent, graceful, and weightless as an angel, the eight-year-old girl disappeared before her eyes.

They stood at the edge, staring down at the street below.

Nervously peering over the ledge and shaking his head, the pasty-faced doctor at Margot's side said, "Can't make out the street from here, *ja*?" He took a step back, gave a sigh of relief. "For a moment there, I thought just maybe, our little bird could actually fly."

Margot's fiery eyes glared. She spun and backhanded the doctor hard across the cheek. "She *can* fly, you fool. That's the whole damned point!"

Kelly did all his feats upon,
The Devil's Looking-glass, a stone,
Where playing with him at Bo-peep,
He solved all problems ne'er so deep.

—Verse by Samuel Butler which is pasted to the underside of an obsidian mirror on display at the British Museum once used by Elizabethan alchemists John Dee and Edward Kelly.

Not all good comes from above.

—Motto of the Vril Society

"Nazis. I hate these guys."

—Indiana Jones

PROLOGUE

ABOARD THE ORIENT EXPRESS 1940

Its headlight spearing the darkness, its whistle shrieking, the night train to Istanbul screamed down the rails.

As the cars swayed beneath the engine's plume of smoke, Doctor Carl Jung was snuggled in the lower berth of his private compartment. His liver-spotted hands held a red leather-bound diary.

His mind drifted back to the previous day when he'd stood on the platform of the Vienna station.

The porter shouts, "All aboard."

But something tugs at Jung's senses. He spins around. The dark figure of a man in a trench coat materializes from behind a luggage cart. He is manhandling a beautiful woman in a blue dress toward the train.

In an instant, they vanish into a passenger car.

The shrill blast of the train's whistle as it rocketed into a tunnel jolted him from his reverie. Emerging from the blackness, the compartment was jarringly still. Then he heard it. His breath held tightly, his gaze tracked to the door.

The door handle made a faintly perceptible clicking sound, slowly began to turn, then stopped.

Jung made for the first-class compartment's sliding door and yanked it open.

No one.

He took a quick peek down the passageway, forcing a feeble smile at a prune-faced old woman with a dowager's hump who was gumming a lecherous smile as she hobbled toward him. He glanced to his left. The tassel of his Fez swaying as he sprinted away, a man in a crumpled suit slipped out of the car.

Jung's sixth sense drew his attention to the door's threshold. A folded letter addressed to him was lying at his feet. Snatching the note, he ducked into the compartment, taking great pains to securely lock the door behind him. He lowered the silk shade and with palsied hands unfolded the note.

> *Doktor, you are in grave danger. Trust no one. Beware of Der Vril! Kerim Bey, BROTHERHOOD OF LUXUR*

A soft rap at the door.

Jung tucked the note into his vest pocket and cracked the door. The young woman in the blue dress he'd seen earlier stood in the doorway. Her liquid brown eyes were haunting, glinting with a predatory heat. The form-hugging, off-the-shoulder blue dress elevated her beauty to a classic level.

Jung's keen eyes caught the thick swab of makeup beneath her left eye, and the ugly bruise it failed to completely conceal. Abruptly, her demeanor changed. Her eyes glistening with unspilled tears, she forced a fragile smile.

She stumbled, weaving a bit. Jung caught her arm, steadying her. "*Was ist los*?" he asked.

In a blur of motion, a tall man dressed in a trench coat stormed in, shouldering his way past the women and into the compartment.

With a violent shove, he pitched Jung across the room.

As the doctor lay sprawled on the sofa bed, his gaze cut to the woman, who stood trembling, her eyes downcast. "Shut the door," the attacker said in a breathless half whisper. She nodded weakly, struggled to close the sliding door, and locked it.

Peeking out from beneath the wide brim of a black fedora, the attacker's bulbous eyes fixed on Jung. As the man towered over Jung, the muzzle of a Luger .08 Parabellum pistol fisted in his meaty hand never wavered. The attacker bowed smartly and flashed a wicked grin as his heels came together with a perceptible click.

"Baron Rudolf von Sebottendorff at your service, *Doktor* Jung," he said in crisp German. "I apologize for calling unannounced at such a late hour, but I have no time for formalities. However, as amends for my rudeness …" The baron pulled a flask from his coat pocket and tossed it to the doctor. "You look like you could use a drink."

Jung unscrewed the cap, took a long pull. The brandy buoyed his spirits. Jung stared, unflinching. But the longer he stared, the stranger he began to feel. He felt woozy. Dark motes eeled at the corners of his eyes.

"It's not poison, I assure you," Sebottendorff explained, "merely a strong sedative. I do not have the stomach for such womanly methods. No, if it wasn't so messy, I would place the muzzle of this pistol next to your temple and blow that weak, arrogant brain out the other side of your skull. But there would be too many questions."

Jung tried to steel himself against the drug's effects. Instinctively, his hand crept across the bedcovers and groped for the diary. Finding it, he weakly clasped the book.

He matched the baron's stare, his eyes flashing contempt. Jung found his voice. "Your reputation precedes you, *Herr Glauer*. While you pretend to be an aristocrat, a gentleman, and the intellectual founder of the *Vril* Society, your actions scream loudly. You're nothing but a jack-booted Nazi thug! You may use whatever alias you wish, but you're no more a baron than I am."

Sebottendorff fingered his scarred cheek. "By decoding the Voynich manuscript, you know how to speed up the process. How to create a new master race of Nephilim," he explained, his eyes sparking madly. "You know how to unleash the maximum potential of the *Vril,* the secret life forces of creation. Hand me your magick diary, now!" As Jung fought to hold the diary, he felt Sebottendorff's strong, sausagelike fingers pry it from his grasp. Then darkness folded around him.

ISTANBUL

Kerim Bey pulled up the lapels of his crumpled suit coat against the biting wind. In the distance, he could make out the baron and the woman in blue, his *sister*. He'd ducked off the train and followed them from the station. He cursed as a gust of wind snatched at his Fez, and he grappled to square it securely back onto his head. His footfalls echoed in the mist-shrouded night as he crossed the cobblestone street in pursuit of his prey.

He quickened his pace, closing the distance. When he rounded the corner, he drew up short, ducked into the shadows.

Two street beggars sidled up alongside Baron von Sebottendorff and the woman, pacing them as they walked along the riverbank. Kerim Bey could make out their drunken catcalls as they taunted the baron.

Kerim Bey sprang out of the darkness and bolted toward them.

"Elena, run!" he shouted to his sister. She tried.

Without warning, one beggar grabbed Elena and roughly wrenched her toward himself, ripping her gown from her shoulder in the process.

The second man pounced on the baron.

They struggled.

Gunfire cracked.

The shot went wild.

The glint of cold steel flashed in the moonlight as the beggar's blade found the baron's shoulder. The baron's Luger clattered uselessly across the pavement.

Kerim Bey moved to his comrades' side. Disguised as rum-soaked beggars, they'd taken the baron by surprise. Kerim Bey stood squarely with his handgun leveled pointblank on Sebottendorff. As he kissed his sister lightly on the cheek and clasped her hand, he told his accomplices, "A good night's work. Get Elena away from here. I have a score to settle."

***

The full moon's reflection rippled across the dark surface of the Bosporus Strait, staring up at Baron von Sebottendorff like a summons to a watery grave. He clawed at his shoulder, struggling to remove the dagger that was buried to the hilt.

A gunshot echoed through the night as his kneecap exploded. Howling in pain, he looked up into the cruel eyes of the man in the Fez, who clutched a smoldering Mauser machine pistol. In his other hand, he held Dr. Jung's diary that he'd seized from the baron moments earlier.

Kerim Bey smiled dryly as he said in a harsh whisper, "That was merely to get your attention."

Sebottendorff's raged-filled eyes blazed. "You damnable *Untermenchen!* Give me back my diary. If it's money you want, name your price."

Kerim Bey moved closer, his eyes boring into the wounded beast. "I don't want your filthy money. I just want to send you back to Hell where you belong."

The baron's eyes flooded with terror. The air was lathered with the ripening stench of fear-sweat and urine.

"This is for my sister," Kerim Bey said, his steel-eyed gaze cold, his voice and hand steady.

The Mauser barked twice, filling the baron's gut with hot lead.

His jaw hinging wide, he stared in disbelief and terror at the bloodied front of his shirt. His hands flew to his stomach as he tumbled backward into the cold waters.

CHAPTER 1

Present Day:

Tell Brak Nagar, Syria

The Syrian Desert is a volcanic wasteland so hellish that it seems like the hungry burial ground of an ancient enemy, waiting to be fed.

Dawn crept in over the jagged horizon. Yousef stood alone, quaking with fear, sick with fright. Terror ripped through him like a big, shiny crosscut saw.

Shaitan himself, *al-Dajjal*, had come to this place. Soon he and his soldiers would soak the sand with blood. Innocent blood.

Soft as the tread of the desert wolf, the night wind that raced before the dawn was still. The roar of an approaching truck startled him. In the distance, pinpoints of light bobbed as the truck jostled across the rough terrain. Suddenly, its headlights loomed large and speared through the darkness—reaching for him.

Yousef wanted to warn them to turn back. He wanted to wave his arms frantically, to jump up and down and scream at the top of his lungs. But instead, with the muzzle of an AK-47 pressed against his spine, he waved the flashlight, signaling the coast was clear, luring them into a deathtrap.

The truck's passenger door, displaying the dust-caked logo of the British Archaeological Society, swung open. The passenger's face was hidden behind a *kafeeyeh*, a scarf that offered protection from the howling winds. The tall figure jumped to the ground and marched to the rear of the truck.

"*As salaam aleeikom, Doktari*," Yousef shouted shakily to the figure's back. The doctor didn't reply.

The morning's light was beginning to paint the night-clad desert and surrounding rock in an eerie radiance.

When Yousef reached the back of the truck, a rough voice rang out, demanding and cursing in vulgar Arabic that the workers be careful. "No, no, no. Stop it, right now. Put that down. That one first. *Allez*, that's right."

One of the workmen grunted and stood glaring.

"Sonofabitch, don't you dare give me attitude, Rafiq," Doctor Kelly said. "That's it … lift together. Allah be with you."

The doctor stood with one foot propped on the bumper, haranguing the men unloading the trucks like some crazed camel driver.

Although covered in sand from her dust-filmed riding boots, to her khaki slacks and matching bush jacket, Dr. Kelley's outfit couldn't disguise the sensual physicality of her, her aggressive beauty.

The majority of the cargo now unloaded, Dr. Blair Morgan Kelly removed her scarf and shook out her hair.

The AK-47 wielding soldier sucked in a sharp breath when Dr. Kelly bent at the waist to toss her mane of long, fulsome hair. She had hair like a wild horse's mane, deeply red-toned and nearly as tousled. She righted herself and tied the scarf around her neck.

She shrugged, nodding at the awestruck guard. "What's with the *mon* General here?" she asked Yousef. For a woman, her voice had a low, husky timbre that was as seductive as it was alluring, as if filtered through amber-colored whiskey and wisps of smoke. Her lips were full, her mouth sulky and demanding.

The man mumbled to himself in Arabic, stumbled backward, and made wide, frantic hand gestures at her.

Yousef smiled weakly. "He says you're the Harlot of Babylon. He's warding off the evil-eye."

Rolling her simmering sea-green eyes, she said, "Oh, puh-leez."

Yousef's smile faded quickly. He broke out in a cold sweat, swallowed hard. Furtively, he looked around the site. He was trying to hide his fear but imagined that Dr. Kelly could hear his knees knocking loudly, hear his heartbeat thundering like hooves against his rib cage.

Puzzled, she asked, "What's wrong, Yousef? You look like you're about to jump out of your skin."

The sharp crack of automatic weapons fire answered her.

* * *

Iraq-Syria Border

At 0400, twin Chinook helicopters lifted off from the classified desert ops base located west of Mosul, Iraq and headed for the border. In theory, the mission was similar to one launched by Special Forces at the beginning of Desert Storm.

Saddam Hussein was targeting Saudi Arabia and Israel with long range scud missiles. While the scuds were relatively ineffective, they were creating a terror-driven panic and intelligence reports believed they could be equipped with nerve gas such as sarin or a biological warfare agent like anthrax. Despite multiple bombing sorties, the mobile missile launchers were not being taken out. The Iraqis hid the launchers under bridges and in barns or substituted dummy mockups as open targets.

The decision was made to take out the Iraqi Command and Control Center just forty miles south of Baghdad.

Just like before, the Chinooks were filled with two ops teams. The first team would take out the target; the second would set up a protective perimeter.

But Major Brody Devlin knew this mission was entirely different. They were attempting a snatch and grab, an extraordinary rendition.

In plain terms this meant they were making an unauthorized apprehension/kidnapping of a citizen from a foreign country on foreign soil. The country was Syria, and the man was known as al-Dajjal, a ruthless ex-KGB agent who had become muscle for the Syrian regime. The joint private finding between POTUS, the President of the United States, and the UK's Prime Minister had labeled al-Dajjal as a bloodthirsty war criminal.

Rumors of genocide within Syria had been confirmed by local assets, including photos of bodies stacked in mass graves like cordwood, arms lashed together, and for the women and children, a much more *humane* end—a bullet to the back of the skull.

Major Devlin rode in the lead helo with the squad code-named Task Force Black. Since the findings were joint, so were the squads. The Brits supplied seasoned veterans, who were not currently on active duty, from the SAS—the Special Air Service—and the RAF's counter-terrorism ground troops, and a team from SBS, the Special Boat Service, the equivalent of Navy SEALS. Devlin, known as Brody by friends and fellow officers, commanded a team of operatives from a new branch of the DOD.

In the past, DELTA forces had supplied the much-needed manpower for both overt and covert paramilitary operations. But with too much publicity, combined with having had their role with the State Department usurped by the private firm BLACKWATER, the need arose for a new special response group: the ΩMEGA FORCE. ΩMEGA was the perfect designation for the unit. Since it was the last letter of the Greek alphabet, it symbolized the *last* resort.

The group was composed of ex-Special Forces personnel and a few *brainiacs,* as the regular grunts called them. Young academics from various sciences who worked under the cover of the Army's Future Combat Systems Division, or for that matter, any federal agency required for the mission.

"ETA to border, one minute, Major." Devlin heard the pilot's words through his headset.

Like before, the helicopters were flying in at low level beneath radar. Even though Devlin knew that Syrian airspace was as easy to penetrate as a horsefly winging through a tattered window screen since the Israelis and the Soviets had all but decimated the Syrian air-defense system, his gut lurched as they churned across the border.

Devlin decided that if *he* was nervous, so was his crew. "Alpha and Beta squads, systems and weapons checks," he barked into his mic. As both acknowledged, he wormed his way through the helo, making small talk with the troops and surveying the equipment.

Lieutenant Braxton, his second in command, scooted up beside him. "Just like old times, hey, Brody?"

Devlin smiled and nodded. "Whata we got from intel?"

Braxton nodded toward their communication specialist/geekizoid, Scout Thompson, whose fingers were flying over the keyboard of a field laptop.

Scout looked up. "We've got our eye in the sky, a Global Hawk, doing the recon, courtesy of Langley, and they report that the target is on the move again but heading into the northeastern sector as planned." Scout slid his wireframe glasses back to their proper resting place at the bridge of his nose.

Scout was the unit's resident techno wizard, late twenties, sandy mop of hair, with boyish good looks, some peach fuzz on his upper lip. "Satellite imagery shows our target's a sitting duck. Seems the asshole likes to parade around in a vintage black Mercedes convertible decked out with bumper flags like some freakin'—"

"Nazi?" Devlin broke in. "Hear he has a riding crop and sports a white silk scarf. He fancies himself as being Rommel, the Desert Fox."

Sgt. Conners, the Unit's ruddy-faced Scotsman, jumped in. "Well then … we'll kick his bloody arse back to Berlin, just like old General Monty did to Rommel."

Devlin cracked a smile and then shot the sergeant a stern look.

"Yes, sir. Minding me own business I am, sir," Conners replied, burying his head in field-stripping his weapon. Conners had come from the Royal Air Force's special unit called "the Rock Apes." And that was exactly what Conners looked like to Major Brody Devlin. With the abundance of coarse, black body hair covering his forearms and chest and his simian stance, he resembled a gorilla.

Devlin knew from his briefing that al-Dajjal's fascination with the Third Reich had a historical basis. His real name was thought to be Eric von Raeder. His father was Doctor Gregor von Raeder, a German zoologist and anthropologist who served as head of Heinrich Himmler's infamous *Deutsches Ahnenerbe, (Ahan-ner-ba)* or German Ancestral Heritage Society. It was a clever euphemism. Its true agenda included everything from barbaric human medical experimentation, to the investigation of the occult, and expeditions to remote corners of the world in search of archaeological evidence to support Himmler's theories of the origins of the Aryan master race.

His mother, Samira, was Iranian and a respected archaeologist in her own right. After the war, Gregor and Samira fled to Russia where he had been promised less interference with his research. Eric von Raeder had a keen mind and was educated in the finest universities Russia and the UK had to offer, which was sponsored by the KGB.

He traveled the world extensively with his mother, visiting many archaeological digs on her expedition. On one of these digs his mother was killed during an Israeli retaliation raid in Palestine. Since then, Eric had a deep hatred for Jews and of course their staunchest ally, the United States. After his mother's death, he converted to Islam and adopted the name Azrael al-Dajjal. He was initially a KGB operative specializing in the Middle East, due to his fluent command of Farsi and Arabic. But the lure of money made him a freelance consultant. *Consultant my ass*, Devlin thought. *Stone cold executioner was more like it.*

Devlin had a bad feeling about this mission and especially about their target. The man was intelligent and a brutal calculating butcher. Even his choice of a Muslim name made Devlin's blood run cold. Al-Dajjal was the Islamic name for the Devil, more specifically—the Anti-Christ—his spawn.

The pilot's voice squawked in Devlin's headset. "Major, I need you up front, ASAP!"

In the chopper's cockpit, Devlin studied the radar screen as the pilot pointed. "See that system moving right at us?

Devlin nodded. "Storm front?"

The pilot shook his head. "Dust storm, big-time. Came up outta nowhere. Really strange but this shit happens out here."

Devlin winced. "Damn it! Shouldn't Sat Recon have picked this up?"

The pilot shrugged. He was a displaced cowboy named Tex. "Shoulda, woulda, coulda, Major. All I know is she's one big mother and doing about … a hundred and twenty knots."

"We can't outrun it then?"

"Y'all think y' sittin' in a Raptor Jetfighter or somethin'? Well we ain't … this here Baby-Huey-sized whirlybird couldn't outrun my granny with a case uh the trots. I'm fixin' ta put—"

The chopper began to pitch and yaw violently, buffeted by gale-force winds. Tex shouted to the co-pilot, "Find a place to put 'er down and I mean … NOW!"

"Where are we?" Devlin managed.

"Smack dab in the middle uh bum fuckin' nowhere … or the seventh circle uh Hell for all I know. Better tell the boys ta strap in, we're goin' down steep and fast."

A blinding burst of light blasted the cockpit.

Devlin's hand flew to his eyes.

When his snow-blinded pupils finally managed to dilate enough to see again, he stared in awe.

Tentacles of blue-white lightning formed a tree of fire that snaked down the night and to the ground. The sky exploded again, spitting arcs of electrical discharge to the exact same target below.

A shaft of pale blue light suddenly pulsed from the ground where the lightning bolts appeared to have struck. Then the shaft shot skyward, growing in diameter and intensity.

"Whoa, Nelly," Tex stammered, his eyes seeming to glaze over the longer he stared. "Never seen nothin' like this. Just look at that sucker."

"Let's get a closer look," the co-pilot said, his voice wooden.

A frightening, almost seductive feeling swelled in Devlin's chest.

Glancing at the pilots, he could see that they were being affected, too. The pulsing rays throbbed like a beating heart. They were mesmerizing, pulling at your mind like some ghostly tractor beam.

The color was luminous, hypnotic.

Percussion caps of thunder detonated around them and Devlin saw that it appeared to shake the pilots out of their trance.

Devlin shook the cobwebs from his head.

In a blur of sound and motion, the twin helicopter swarmed past them, heading directly for the pulsing blue beam.

Tex screamed into his microphone. "ZEBRA TWO CHARLIE, from GROUP LEADER, pull back."

No response. Only the drone of high-pitched static.

"ZEBRA TWO CHARLIE, acknowledge … pull back, do not engage. Repeat … *do not engage*!"

Devlin and the pilots watched helplessly as the other helo disappeared into the throbbing cone of light.

CHAPTER 2

Dr. Blair Morgan Kelly had waited long and hard for this grant. Tell Brak Nagar was a dream come true for a thirty-something archaeologist like her. Originally discovered in the 1930's, the site was dated at 6000 BC, the late Neolithic age. Cuneiform tablets that resembled hen's scratching to the layman told of Tell Brak's bizarre history.

The *Tell,* or mound, was trapezoid-shaped and over a mile long. The site was pre-Akkadian. It predated Assyrian culture, the Babylonian dynasty and even the empire of Hammurabi the Lawgiver. It was the time of Sumer and Ur and later Chaldea, the time of wise magi and mystery. It was a time of magick and demons.

But the cuneiform tablets also told of a great catastrophe. The Brak Event.

It was this event and the Palace of Narim-Sin, grandson of the Sumerian King Sargon the Great, that Blair Kelly wanted to discover.

When she'd first pulled into the camp, she had a familiar saw-edged pain in her stomach. She dismissed it, writing it off as a case of nerves.

But now, as she and Yousef were being led by a group of yellow-toothed thugs, prodded along at gunpoint, she wished she'd learned to listen to her instincts.

This was her baby and she wasn't going to share it with some claim-jumping cretins, armed to the teeth or not.

The rocky terrain was uneven; she stumbled more than once and was jerked to her feet by rough hands. One thug in particular kept leering at her, raping her with his eyes. *If push comes to shove*, she reasoned, *I'll kill this bastard first.*

Yousef came to her defense, placing himself between her and the ogling thug. "Keep your filthy paws off her, *ya kalb*!" he shouted in Arabic.

When the guard grinned widely, he revealed a gold incisor tooth that winked in the sun's glare. He made a clucking sound while eyeing Blair from head to toe. "I'll do what I want with this *koos*."

Then he wheeled on Yousef, his lips skinned back like a rabid jackal. "Call me a filthy dog … will you?" He drove the muzzle of the submachine gun into Yousef's solar plexus and finished him off by swinging the butt of its stock to her defender's jaw. She heard the crack of bone as Yousef went out cold.

Reflexively, she kicked out, landing the edge of her boot hard against the thug's kneecap.

The thug squealed in pain, "*Ya sharmuta*!" Another guard came from behind and pinned her arms. The wounded brute hobbled toward her. He spat in her face and backhanded her across the face, splitting her lip.

Blair winced in agony but looked him squarely in the eye. "You kiss your mother with that mouth, *ibn haram?* Call me a dirty whore again and I'll feed your shriveled balls to the jackals, you bleedin' sod!"

He pressed closer, his rank breath streaming over her face, his beady eyes dancing. She grimaced and pulled back. His body odor was like roadkill.

"I will show you who is a sonofabitch. I'll make you pay for that later. When we're alone in my tent." The thug sneered and licked the outline of his lips as he ran a grimy finger up the front of her blouse, lingering at the deep valley of her breasts, then along her neck, finally tapping her swollen lips.

"*Waj a zibik!*" she shot back, sneering.

Apparently objecting strongly to her suggestion that he should come down with a good dose of the clap, he hit her again.

The salty taste of blood filled her mouth as they dragged her away from Yousef's crumpled body.

When they crested a hill, she stopped short. A few yards away, she could make out a long trench with a bulldozer parked at the end. A group of men, dressed in black tunics and billowing pants, trained their AK-47s on a small group of children who stood lined up on the ridge of the trench. Blair took a deep breath and fought back the hot bile rising in her throat.

A tall man stood in the center of the killers. He had a military bearing, his stance wide, his black German jack-boots spit shined, his black slacks and black leather jacket custom tailored. A white silk scarf slung loosely around his neck flamed in the wind.

As if sensing her presence, the man turned.

He cocked his head and gave a crooked grin. Arms extended as though surprised, he lowered them, slapping his thigh with a riding crop as he strode briskly toward her.

"*Doktor* Kelly, I presume," he said, bowing elegantly. "You will, I trust … pardon this little intrusion of mine on your dig. But I assure you, we are colleagues with a mutual goal."

The sex-maniac thug shoved her forward, knocking her to her knees. When she stood, she spat blood at the gorilla's feet.

The leader's smile turned razor thin, his eyes bristled with rage. Moving with the unnatural speed of a panther, he was on the thug in seconds.

He stood eye to eye with the apish brute. Slowly and methodically, he removed one glove, then the other.

"*Du archgesicht*!" In a blur, his right hand shot out, the leather glove slapping the thug's cheek. The thug winced as his hand flew to his face, where a bright red welt blossomed.

The leader turned and studied Blair's bruised face. Then, like a hawk, his head swiveled and he stood nose to nose with the man.

"You are a pig," he ranted in Arabic, spittle streaming from his mouth. Then he lapsed back into German. "This lady is our guest. You dishonor me with such brutish behavior."

He spun, locking his gaze on Blair, the mirrored lenses of his sunglasses blazing like hellfire in the desert sun's glare. He removed his sunglasses, revealing piercing cobalt-blue eyes, and began cleaning them with a silk handkerchief.

Switching to English, he said, "I trust you were not harmed, *Doktor* Kelly. My sincerest apologies for the savagery this lout has displayed." He proffered the silk hankie to her.

She nodded her thanks and dabbed at the trickle of blood creeping from the corner of her mouth.

Without waiting for her answer, he wheeled around. It happened so fast that Blair never saw the man draw his weapon. A loud report cracked the stillness and a gaping hole suddenly appeared in the thug's forehead. The asshole's head tilted back slightly, like he'd been slapped again, and he sunk to his knees in a heap.

Sunlight kicked off the gold-plated Walther PPK as the leader holstered his weapon.

As if nothing had happened, he finger-combed his long white-blond hair and gave a detached smile. He sauntered over, took her arm gently, and guided her toward the children. "There's someone that I would like you to meet, *Doktor*."

Blair studied him. This monster was an Aryan poster boy. That lantern jaw with a cleft chin, those icy blue eyes, that intelligent forehead.

But then she saw it.

Standing next to him, she noticed the jagged scar that crawled down his cheek, traversing his lip, which accounted for the perpetual crooked smile that seemed plastered to his face. It was as if some spiteful god, in the process of molding him from clay, had raked a finger across his cheek, branding him for eternity. She tried not to stare. He seemed to sense it and covered his mouth with his hand as he walked, pretending to be deep in thought.

When dealing with a sociopath, it was better to engage them than to show contempt, she'd read somewhere. She took a deep breath, licked her swollen lip. "I don't think we've been properly introduced."

He stiffened. "How absolutely unforgivable of me. I am known as Azrael al-Dajjal, my adopted Muslim name, of course. A princely one at that… wouldn't you agree?"

Trying desperately not to beetle her brows, she smiled.

He spoke in an affected Queen's English and laid on the charm with the practiced subtlety and casual off-handed manner of a true British gentleman. But this dime-store storm trooper was anything but.

"You realize, *Doktor*, that we share a mutual passion."

"Really? And what would that be? Riding boots?"

He laughed heartily. "I see not only are you a beautiful and intelligent woman, but you also have a highly cultivated sense of humor."

"I try."

"No … I was referring to my love of archaeology. Perhaps you have heard of my mother, Samira al-Bani?"

She pretended to puzzle on the name for a moment.

"Oh, you must mean Doctor von Raeder?"

He nodded and she could have sworn he blushed slightly. "That would be her married name, of course. My father being Herr von Raeder, the eminent zoologist."

"That's remarkable. As a graduate student I studied her work on the Babylonian digs. What was it she was searching for again? The Fountain of Youth?"

His eyes narrowed to points. "Oh, that silly rumor. She had a passing interest in all the myths of lost kingdoms … Thule, Shaballa, Lemuria. But she believed they all had some historical basis in fact."

"You don't share her passion for lost civilizations and mystic treasures, I take it?"

They had reached the children now, who stood cowering, eyes lowered out of fear more than respect.

He regarded her with caution. "To a degree. Troy was once thought to be only a legend until an amateur found the ruins of the city deep beneath the desert sands. Let's just say I'm on a scavenger hunt of sorts, shall we?" He turned toward the children and guided her to his side as he slowly moved down the row of tiny faces. Their ages varied. She guessed they ranged from about six to fourteen years old. As he passed each child, he reached out and cupped their chins, raising their faces toward him. He would look intently, reach into his pocket and hand them a sweet, then move on to the next.

Something in his manner sickened her. It was as if he were inspecting chickens in the bazaar, lifting a wing here, poking at the breast there.

"I've almost found it, you know," he offered casually. "The Temple of the Eye of Sin."

He'd said it so softly that, for a moment, she thought she hadn't heard him correctly.

He walked on, coming to the next to the last child. "We have unearthed a large monolith," he went on. "And in the center, like at the pyramids of Egypt, there is an eye-hole. As you know, the Pharaoh would peer through the eye-hole which focused his vision on Sirius, the Dog Star."

No ... she'd heard him correctly, all right. He'd found the temple.

He continued. "And you followed the vector of the eye-hole back to ..." his voice trailed off.

He drew up short at the last child, a young girl. When he raised her chin, unlike the others, she stared back knowingly, a look of confidence only possessed by a mature woman rather than a little girl. But the girl couldn't have been more than eight or nine years old. Her whole being seemed to shimmer with a brilliant but soft radiance. Her face held a classic beauty that graced temple frescos.

But it was the child's eyes that haunted Blair. Deep, luminous pools of indigo that held you with their intensity seemed to look into her soul. And although her skin tone was slightly dark, the girl had flaxen hair.

A cloud drifted past the sun, momentarily casting a long shadow across the barren landscape that surrounded them.

Al-Dajjal paused and turned his head toward the sky.

For a brief second, he looked as though his mind were miles and miles away, gazing upon some strange distant backdrop, another place, another time.

The shadow passed.

"Remarkable, is she not?" al-Dajjal said, excitement stitching his voice. He turned to the girl. "Fear not, child. No one means you any harm," he said softly in Arabic. Then he lapsed into German, shaking his head in appreciation and gently taking her hand.

"*Der Sonnenkinder. Der Vril-ya.* The future of the world lies in your tiny hand."

"What was that?" Blair asked, pretending she didn't speak German. But Blair was familiar with the terms. The Nazis believed that The Children of the Son, the Children of the Light, were the fountainhead of a new Aryan master race. And that the Sumerian civilization had been visited by the Anunnaki, the fallen angels of the Bible, who mated with Earth women and produced these special children—the Nephilim.

"Oh, pardon me, *Doktor*." He released the girl and turned to Blair. "I occasionally slip into the tongue of my fatherland. An eccentric habit, I suppose. I was merely thinking aloud what a beautiful *specimen* she is, so unique. A fine example of the Nephilim, the true Aryan bloodline."

The word specimen made Blair's skin crawl and ice-carved dominos topple down her spine. She had to keep her wits about her. *Remember girl*, she chided herself, *this guy's Dr. Josef Mengele, the angel of death in the flesh.*

Another man dressed in the dust covered and tattered clothes of a digger scrambled toward them. A thug blocked him with his rifle butt. Al-Dajjal turned and nodded. "You have news?" he asked in Arabic.

The man licked his chapped lips. His hands were palsied and one eye was milky with a cataract. "The entrance to the temple. We followed the path of the laser you positioned and … praise Allah … there it was!"

"Well, don't just stand there, lead on," al-Dajjal said as he took the hand of the little girl and followed. Glancing back over his shoulder, he called, "Come along, *Doktor*, you don't want to miss the show." With the young girl in tow, he marched off.

They'd climbed down the series of ladders and were now at the lowest level of the dig. Blair looked around, sizing up the work. She moved to the monolith and peered through the eye-hole, letting her gaze follow the path of the ruby laser beam that was aimed downward through the hole, pointing to the spot where the observer would have stood to look upon the constellation of …. *Damn, of course.* She moved to the spot. Looking skyward, she realized the eye-hole would have been focused on the thigh of Orion.

The polar stars held a fascination for the ancients because, unlike the other stars that changed their positions in the heavens after they died or sank each day, the Big Dipper and Orion's belt seemed to remain, revolving around a central axis.

"The similarity to the Egyptian sky worship is uncanny, don't you think, *Doktor*?"

Blair gave a long whistle and brushed the hair from her face. "Mind if I take a look at the entrance?"

He bowed. "Ladies first."

The slope to the entrance was still loosely packed fresh dirt, and she slid down as carefully as she could. Pulling a brush and flashlight from her bush jacket, she began dusting off the top of the entrance, which was still being cleared by the diggers.

Suddenly he was behind her, and she felt his hot sour breath on her neck. It made her squeamish, like the time in Brazil when a large python had coiled around her neck. She glanced over her shoulder. "There's an inscription here and it's Proto-Semitic."

He moved closer. "Here, let me hold the light."

She continued to brush carefully until the inscription was clear.

"Hold the light at an angle to give more shadow to the lettering, please."

As he did, the symbols jumped out from the surface.

From behind came his voice, raspy and thick. "The Temple of the Eye of Sin. *Mien Got*, we've found it!"

"Wait, there's more," she said, dusting the next column of symbols. These were different, a variation she wasn't familiar with. Then it came to her. They appeared to be a more bastardized Sumerian cuneiform script.

She read aloud. "Muu..ll..a Sa..ZU..ZU, Guardian of the twelve gates, keeper of the STARFIRE."

Behind her, a loud murmuring rose into a shrill chorus of wailing and howling, which turned to screams. She wheeled around to see the diggers scrambling out of the pit shouting, "*Mulla Sa ZU ZU!*" as they fought and clawed their way up the ladder like a frenzied troop of tree monkeys.

Then the distant sound of machine-gun fire layered over the screams of the diggers. The bastard had ordered his goons to execute the rest of the children. She glanced over and saw that the little girl was now at al-Dajjal's side. The child's eyes sparked with terror. She vowed to see him rot in Hell for this.

Then it suddenly seemed as though her wish may come true.

A first she felt a tiny tremor, then the ground beneath her feet seemed to shift; she widened her stance.

Reaching out, she grabbed the hand of the little girl and pulled her to her side. The rock face above began to crack and a large fissure erupted. It ran the full length of the cliff side, and began etching its way across the ground toward her.

Dust rained down on her, clotting the air.

The ground began to split open and a large crevasse began to form. Al-Dajjal cursed as he was knocked off his feet.

Without thinking, she merely reacted and leaped to her left, still clutching the girl in her arms. She fought her way to higher ground.

The gaping jaws of the crevasse leered back from below.

A sheet of rock crumbled to the right of the temple entrance.

When the cloud of dust lifted, a statue emerged from the mist like some demon rising from the Pit. Its head was like a bloated lizard with large, lidless eyes that stared outward menacingly. It had a large flat nose, high cheekbones, a low bulging forehead, and a gruesome mouth filled with razor-sharp tusklike teeth. From its gaping maw a small body dangled, half consumed, struggling to escape.

Symbols carved in stone beneath seemed to blaze in the sunlight. She translated it in her mind.

THE CORPSE SWALLOWER.

Her gaze flew back to the widening fissure below. Al-Dajjal was cursing and had pulled a long, wide-bladed dagger. Again and again he thrust the blade into the rock, trying desperately to gain purchase.

The cliff face gave way again and another wall of rock showered down, revealing a towering column.

Something glistened in the sun like glass.

She stood dumbfounded, staring at a large crystal or quartz skull. But it wasn't humanoid in shape. It had a bulbous head with gogglelike eyes, made of concentric circles.

Beneath her the rock was crumbling and she lost her footing. She began sliding faster into the mouth of the crack in the world. She was vaguely conscious of the girl's tiny hand. The girl's grip tightened and then came a new sensation; a lightness of being, a feeling of calmness washed over her.

She looked down and saw her feet suspended in midair. She raised her eyes and saw the sky, realized she was climbing toward it, flying higher and higher, until the hungry jaws of the pit lay far below.

She saw the girl at her side, glowing with an almost transparent blue-white haze. It wasn't frightening; it wasn't ghostly, but reassuring and pleasant.

Together they floated over the edge of the cliff and slowly began to descend. It was like some strange sort of high, a joyful rapture that she never wanted to end, this feeling that filled her now. But the ground was coming up beneath them. They touched down.

She gulped a deep breath and tried to compose herself, then turned toward the girl, her mouth gaping in astonishment. She didn't know why, but she asked in Arabic, "What is your name?" The little girl answered in English, "They call me … Noor E Alam." Her cheeks dimpled as a tiny giggle escaped from her lips. The girl's smile was beguiling.

"Okay, little miss Light of the World. What do you say we get the bloody hell outta here while the getting's good?"

Noor nodded and held her hand tightly.

Blair took a step and paused. "Don't suppose we could maybe fly?"

Noor E Alam smiled shyly and shook her head.

Blair blew out a long sigh. "Didn't think so. Come on, my bonny li'l *laeken*, we're a long way from home."

* * *

Below, a hand grappled around the hilt of a knife and al-Dajjal, the true demon of the pit, pulled upward, straining every fiber of his being, and crawled to safety.

The quake had subsided. He gained his feet and made his way to the pedestal. He reached out and lifted the crystal skull from its mooring.

CHAPTER 3

They had been on the ground about thirty minutes. The dust storm had howled over the squads, temporarily immobilizing them. It was the longest half hour Devlin had ever spent, locked in the cramped chopper with a team of restless men, wondering what had happened to the other team, their comrades.

The weather cleared.

"You raise 'em on the radio yet?" Devlin asked Scout.

Long-faced and somber, Scout shook his head. "Negative. All we're picking up is their distress beacon loud and clear. Command and Control hasn't had any luck either, but they've been apprised of the situation."

Tex had climbed into the rear. "Well … Major, let's take a look-see what we got."

Standing outside the chopper with Scout beside him, Devlin surveyed the trackless void that surrounded them. They weren't that far off course, but they may as well have been planted on the surface of the Moon.

Tex appeared at his side. "Blasted dern sand has mucked up the turbines."

Sergeant Conners was standing at the pilot's side. "Balled up royally, sir. We won't be goin' anywhere for at least an hour."

Devlin chewed his lower lip and glanced at the ridge.

"Scout, you put 'em due west over that hill?"

"Hard to say exactly 'cause they're too close to give you an accurate fix from the transponder. But that would be my best guess. We going after 'em, boss?"

A deep voice boomed from behind them.

"Damn straight, we are. Never leave 'em behind, sonny. " It was Clint "Chewie" Raindancer. He was a towering hulk, a Native American Indian with coal-black eyes that had a shiny clarity and directness. He had non-regulation long dark hair swept into a neat ponytail. His high-set cheekbones and hawkish nose gave him a noble appearance.

He'd been nicknamed Chewie because, although he could hold his liquor, just getting steely eyed and silent, he would suddenly let out a bellowing roar resembling Chewbacca, the hairy Wookiee from *Star Wars*. Once, that bestial war cry alone had been enough to make a pack of shit-faced bikers turn tail and run, rather than picking a bar fight with the unit.

Brody and the guys were at the bar. Chewie was leaning with his back against the bar rail, dressed in a sleeveless denim shirt, frayed at the shoulders. As he stood with his arms folded across his chest, his biceps flattened so they looked like horses' flanks.

A group of bikers was playing fast and loose with a leggy barmaid, hooting at her and shouting obscenities, playing grab ass as she threaded between tables.

Then things turned rough. A bearded biker grabbed her, hoisted her over his shoulder, and threw her onto the pool table. One pinned her down, while another climbed on top of her.

Chewie's deep voice called to the pack leader, who was looking on with an oily grin. "Let the lady up."

An icy stillness fell over the room as the two attacking bikers looked up. The pack leader strode slowly and deliberately toward the bar, never taking his eyes off Chewie. A motorcycle chain dangled from his hand and flapped against the pant leg of his soiled jeans. His beer gut jutted out from under his T-shirt, almost leading the way.

Without warning, the paunch-bellied biker with road-kill breath and a swastika tattooed to his forehead swung the Harley chain at Chewie. Blocking the jagged chain with his forearm, Chewie looped the chain around his arm and jerked.

The biker didn't have the brains to let go. Like a smack-down wrestler, Chewie stepped back and planted his feet. Holding tight to the chain with both hands and leaning backward, he whipped the biker in a tight circle. When he yanked the dizzied biker closer, Chewie let loose with his earsplitting war cry and head butted the fat jerk into next week.

The sight of their pack leader slumping in a heap and messing himself, combined with Chewie biting the cycle chain in two with his bare teeth, had been enough to convince the gang to rabbit.

As he stood staring at the big lug now, Brody Devlin scratched his chin and smiled.

Chewie pounded his chest with his bear paw of a hand.

"Ready to move out, sir."

Devlin nodded and turned. "Okay, Sergeant Conners, you and Tex get this bird up and running.

"Aye-aye, sir," Conners said in his thick Scottish brogue. "We've got yer back if the *bloidy* wogs show their ugly faces."

To Scout, Devlin said, "Get the Sat link up and humming and keep me appraised."

Pulling Braxton to the side, Devlin whispered, "Brax, this is a shit storm we're in. Those were experienced pilots and flyin' off like that makes no sense. It's bad juju. I feel it in these old bones. Set up a tight perimeter and keep a sharp lookout, will ya?"

"You got it, Skipper." He studied the ground for a moment, then looked up. "Figure those guys bought it?"

"Only one way I can think of to find out. Chewie and I are gonna do a little recon, see if we can find 'em. But keep trying to hit 'em on the radio."

The Chinook was a bull when it came to lifting supplies and vehicles, but the interior was too tight to accommodate a Land Rover when packed with the ops teams and equipment.

The terrain had been slowly rising as Devlin and Chewie walked. Cresting a hill, they could make out a track that led through a valley. A small *Wadi,* or river, snaked through it and led to a village nestled at the base of more barren hills.

Even though a two-man rescue mission was dangerous, they weren't your average soldiers. Because ΩMEGA was augmented by the Army's Future Combat Systems, they received the latest in hardware and weapons. Some of the stuff was right out of a science fiction novel and was still classified.

They had the latest stealth and communications technology. Their helmets used bone induction technology pioneered by research in providing hearing for the deaf. The human voice vibrated through the man's cranium, which was picked up and converted through the transmitter in the helmet's headliner. There was no need for a mic. Likewise, the incoming transmission was also conducted via the skull, so earphones were optional. The voice seemingly came from inside the soldier's head. It was a strictly hands-free communication system. A visor gave a real time display in both infrared and thermo-imaging.

Even their firepower was updated.

The Brits carried their usual Sig P226 sidearm, 40 mm grenade launchers and Milan anti-tank missile launchers, but they were, like his team, issued the new KRISS SUPER V 45. caliber submachine guns. Named after the deadly Indonesian sword with a flamelike blade, it was specially designed to reduce the buck factor, recoil and muzzle rise, but carried the wallop of a 45. round at 1100 rounds per minute, a solid man-stopper compared to the 9 mm.

They were on the outskirts of the village. The air reeked of ozone and something they couldn't identify.

Chewie snorted and scowled as he pointed up ahead. The shadow of a corpse was printed on the road, but there was no body. Devlin fought back the chill of horror that was stippling his forearms with gooseflesh as they passed through the deserted outskirts of the village.

Lining either side of the roadway, they saw the bloated carcasses of goats and chickens and livestock.

The silence that blanketed them was heavy.

Nothing moved.

"Biological weapons? Maybe Anthrax?" Devlin murmured.

Chewie shook his head. "CBWs didn't do this, Brody." Then he nodded toward the edge of the road.

Instantly, Devlin saw what he meant. Even the sparse vegetation was withered and wilted, lying limp and lifeless. Devlin knew that Anthrax wouldn't have scorched the plant life like this.

Chewie dropped to a knee and reached out; the plant crumbled between his fingers, leaving a residue like charcoal dust. He gained his feet and brushed his hand on his pant leg. Staring straight ahead, his tone grave, he said, "Death walks here."

The rocky landscape ahead sparkled as if it were littered with shards of glass.

They pressed on, eyes tracking left and right, their weapons at the ready.

When they got closer, Brody saw that the sparkling diamonds were actually the glistening husks of a host of dead locusts. Whatever this plague was it had even devoured the swarming insects in midflight.

Chewie drew up short and pointed with the muzzle of his submachine gun. A body, the first they'd seen, lay face-down in the earth, and it was like whatever had killed him had cut him down in his tracks.

Standing next to the corpse, Chewie rolled the man over with his foot. The gruesome face stared sightlessly; the eyes looked like they were cauterized, like they'd been gouged with a hot poker. The clothing was nothing but scorched, tattered rags. Charred flesh and a blackened tongue that lolled from between blistered lips greeted them.

Devlin dropped to a knee to examine the man. Since they had no surgical gloves, Devlin pulled his knife from its shoulder-hitched scabbard. Using the knife, he lifted the scorched shirt, exposing the corpse's chest, and pushed the tip of the blade gently against the flesh. It was mushy, as if the muscle and sinew and tissue had been half-eaten, digested by something feeding from within.

Devlin's stomach lurched. A pair of dog tags glimmered in the blazing sun. They identified the man as Corporal Collins a member of the SAS. Devlin's eyes tracked down to the man's regulation boots. *Should have caught that.*

He flipped over the dog tags that were lying in the center of the dead soldier's rib cage. Underneath, the skin was a natural flesh color, as though the metal had shielded it from some kind of radiation.

Devlin looked up and met Chewie's stare. The bear of a man stood silently, a pained look on his face. He knew they were both thinking the same thing. Find the rest of the unit, the survivors … and fast.

In the heart of the village, Devlin's uneasiness mounted as they combed the streets. As if the villagers had fled in panic, the door of every home stood wide open.

And for now, they could find no clues. Chewie was checking the buildings on the right, sneak-peeking around each doorway before entering, and then he would emerge shaking his head shortly later, signaling that he'd found no one.

Devlin searched the opposite side. He paused at one door, thinking he heard a sound.

He entered. The room reeked of strong garlic and tobacco. The first floor had a few sticks of well-worn furniture. He climbed the steep stairs to the second floor. At the rear of the house, a curtain was draped over the doorway. He could smell the aroma of food. The kitchen. Cautiously, Devlin pushed the curtain to the side with his free hand, while keeping the KRISS's muzzle aimed straight ahead.

An untouched meal lay on the table. The lamb stew had thickened. Why weren't there any flies infesting the abandoned plates? Where the hell was everyone? And how had they disappeared so quickly? The questions and the probable answers all pointed to one fact: whatever had happened struck every living thing and spared no one.

He was mulling over the facts as he made his way out of the house. He was so absorbed with the enigma he never saw the attacker coming.

The figure pounced, knocking Devlin to the ground. The man was on top of him.

Screaming curses like a madman.

Steely fingers tore into Devlin's throat; the attacker's thumbs were crushing down on his windpipe.

In a blurry haze, Devlin clasped his hands together, formed a V-shape with his forearms, and drove his arms upward. This focused the force of the blow against the weakest point of the death grip, the attacker's thumbs. When the madman's arms flung to the side, Devlin brought his clasped hands down hard against the bridge of the madman's nose.

Wailing in pain, the attacker rolled off.

A quick roll to the right and Devlin made it to his feet, still gasping for air. But the assailant had gained his feet, too. They stood squared off.

Devlin was looking into the crazed eyes of one of his own men. His devilishly twisted face distorted the soldier's appearance.

"Carter, it's me, for Chrissakes," Devlin shouted.

But Carter's eyes danced maniacally, like a rabid dog. Carter reached down and palmed his knife. He took one step and suddenly collapsed to the ground, writhing and convulsing like an epileptic, heels drumming the ground. Foam bubbled from his mouth. Slowly his head turned and his eyes regained their humanity, pleading desperately. A crow-like croak of sound came from his trembling lips. Steam rose from his uniform as it began to smolder. The stench of cooked flesh poured off his body.

A mantle of tiny blue flames ate through the fabric of his clothing.

Devlin stood dumbfounded. From the corner of his eye, he saw Chewie enter the frame and kneel at Carter's side. He whispered something that sounded like chanting as he rocked his head in rhythm to the words.

When Chewie reached out and took Carter's hand, the skin peeled away into his in a single piece.

Chewie winced and fought to stand.

Devlin moved to his side. "There's nothing we can do for him."

The stoic warrior nodded solemnly, his face dead-set with repressed emotion.

As though he also understood his fate, the naked, raw claw that was once Carter's hand waved them away.

They stood in silence for a moment.

Then panicked cries ripped the air.

They spun toward the sound. Chewie tore off ahead and shouted, "Brody, this way!"

Although in good shape, it was all Brody could do to keep up with Clint Raindancer. Once, over too many shots of Jack Daniels, Devlin asked him why he was called Raindancer. Chewie gave a sly grin and told him that the name meant a brave warrior who could run between the raindrops … untouched.

In the distance, he heard the tortured screams of men.

Gunfire cracked.

The ghost town and its empty windows seemed to laugh silently as they hurtled past. Like some house of mirrors, the buildings and pathways all began to look the same, as though the stone walls were shifting and revolving to create a never-ending maze. Devlin held tight on Chewie's ass, realizing the man was a natural tracker with a sixth sense for finding his quarry.

When they rounded a corner, the second Chinook loomed straight ahead. It was in the village square, and it looked like she'd made a soft landing.

The agonized screams culled from behind the chopper.

Chewie went right, Devlin went left.

When he rounded the helo, Devlin saw them. A tangled knot of men and women, dressed in tattered rags, were hunched over something.

Devlin spotted Chewie. He whispered softly, his helmet picking up his words and transmitting them to Chewie.

Like a panther, Chewie crept toward the huddled mass.

Looking past the squirming clump of bodies, Devlin stared in horror at the killing field. Syrian soldiers, their weapons clutched in a rigid death grip, were strewn everywhere across the ground.

A thin, blue haze still lingered.

The air choked his lungs with the odor of cordite from fresh gunfire, and the coppery tang of blood shot waves of queasiness through his gut.

His skin grew cold with terror.

Like a wolf catching scent of its prey, an old woman's head reared from the knot of bodies, and Devlin could have sworn the woman was actually sniffing the air.

Her head swiveled with unnatural speed.

Feral eyes locked on him.

Her whole face was wet with blood.

CHAPTER 4

Clinging tightly to the steering wheel of the Land Rover, Blair cursed as they rocketed across the desert. Behind her, a wake of dust churned across the landscape, marking their escape route. The wheel bucked in her grip. With Noor and Yousef at her side, the vehicle was tossed and jostled as she maneuvered the rough terrain.

She'd found Yousef stumbling down a hill, battered but alive. Opting for speed, she'd borrowed one of al-Dajjal's bodyguards' vehicles.

"Can't we go any faster?" Yousef pleaded anxiously as he twisted in the seat, frantically searching for their pursuers.

The sheen of sweat glistened on his face. His eyes were wide, terror stricken.

"I've got it floored. But I think the Desert Fox won't be on our heels. I nicked these from their vehicles." Reaching down, she hoisted a distributor cap and a knot of dangling wires and smiled.

"Look out!" Yousef shouted.

Cranking the wheel hard, they barely skirted around a large boulder.

Just as she was about to speak, a Land Rover roared into view, bearing down on them from her left. She caught a glimpse of the henchman perched behind the machine gun; sunlight glistened off his goggles as he fixed them in his sights. Its .50 caliber gun chattering, it tattooed the ground in front of them.

"I would guess you overlooked the one with the big machine gun," Yousef said sarcastically.

A second burst of fire and rounds stitched across the hood.

Blair jerked the wheel right, then left, cutting a zigzag pattern.

"Yousef, grab that sack at your feet."

He shot her a wary glance and fumbled for the sack.

When he looked inside, his eyes saucered.

"C'mon, grab a couple, they don't bite." Blair glanced at the side mirror and saw her pursuers swerve sharply behind her. "The bloody wankers are coming around on your side. When I hit the brakes ... pull the pins and toss them!"

Hands trembling, Yousef removed two grenades and sat staring. "How can I remove the pins?"

"Use your teeth, for Chrissakes!"

Gingerly, he yanked each pin.

The .50 caliber barked again.

Hot lead chewed the passenger side of the Land Rover and tore through glass and sheet metal. A shower of glass and fabric from the rear window and seat exploded.

"Now!" Blair shouted, her foot mashing the brake pedal.

Their Land Rover swerved, its four-wheel disc brakes screeching, biting hard.

With his eyes scrunched tightly, Yousef tossed the grenade. By sheer luck, it flew directly into the machine gunner's nest. Their pursuers' vehicle shot past them.

Her Land Rover spun in a perfect 180 and lurched to a shuddering stop in a roiling cloud of dust.

A booming explosion ripped the air, and the attackers' vehicle burst into flames and black smoke.

Blair fired the engine and tore out, rocks and sand spitting from the rear tires.

Yousef gulped hard and stammered. "I dropped the other bomb."

Busy with her stunt driving, Blair hadn't noticed. Because of the timing of the skid, the second grenade had hit the lip of the Land Rover's window and bounced back into the rear seat.

"Jump!" Blair shouted, shouldering her door and pulling Noor along with her as they rolled out of the vehicle, the Land Rover plodding on without them.

Scrambling to their feet, they ran. Blair shoved Noor to the ground and dove on top of her, shielding her with her body.

A blast of heat washed over them.

Blair lifted her head and turned to see an oily column of black smoke plume the sky.

"Now we're bollixed up but good," she cursed and pounded her thigh. She brushed the hair from her eyes as she stood and slapped the dust from her bush jacket.

Noor's soft voice broke her mood. "I think Yousef's found something."

Yousef! In her anger she had forgotten about him. Then it registered and she turned to Noor, hesitating and pursing her lips. "I don't think he made it, li'l one."

Like the disembodied voice of a spirit, Yousef's voice wafted from over a near rise.

"Over here … this way."

She stood rooted, puzzling over the voice.

Tugging at her arm, Noor made for the hill.

"You see, I was right … he's calling us … let's go."

Stumbling along, Blair trudged up the rise, led by the mysterious girl.

Standing at the top of the ridge, Blair looked down, blinking in disbelief and amazement.

Yousef stood waving his arms and grinning from ear to ear. "*Doktari*," he shouted gleefully, gesturing with a flourish like a stage magician who had just materialized an elephant. "Allah may have taken our Jeep, but He has gifted His servant with His winged horse!"

Behind him, blocked on a makeshift landing strip, with wind direction flags flaming from poles in the breeze, stood a vintage World War II German fighter plane.

A black swastika on a white field was painted on the fuselage. The decal of a howling wolf's head leered from the side of the engine.

Boys and their toys, she thought. *I'll bet this wannabe Nazi al-Dajjal has a few U-boats and a dozen V-2 rockets stashed away in a massive bunker somewhere.* If it wasn't so sick, it would have been almost comical.

Walking beneath a wing, Blair removed the blocks from the wheels, whose struts were canted inward like a mosquito's legs coiled to take wing. Then she hoisted Noor upward.

"It may not be as wonderful or elegant as before, but we're going to fly again, little one."

Noor reached out and softly stroked Blair's cheek.

Noting it was a two-seater, Blair figured it must have been a trainer. Pulling herself onto the wing, she crouched and called to Yousef.

"Unless you figure Allah has graced you with nine lives, you'd better haul your arse up here."

Stiff-legged and muttering to himself, Yousef made his way to the plane. As she took his nervously twitching hand and hoisted him upward, Yousef managed, "If you fly like you drive … I may need nine lives."

Blair nodded toward the dust devil streaming across the landscape toward them.

"Looks like we've got more company."

Yousef craned around to look. "Here they come again!"

Seated in the cockpit, with Noor planted in Yousef's lap in the rear seat, Blair donned the leather flying cap and matching mid-forearm-length gloves and goggles that al-Dajjal had been nice enough to leave for her.

She fired the radial engine. It sputtered and coughed, spitting a cloud of sooty smoke. She adjusted the choke, fired it again.

The engine growled.

The column of Land Rovers was coming up fast.

The bark of machine-gun fire echoed toward them.

The propeller cranked and gradually built up revs, finally spinning in a blur.

Rounds slammed into the ground, just missing the fighter.

The fighter crept forward as Blair eased the throttle. The ground beneath was cratered and the aircraft bounced as it gained speed, hurtling down the strip.

Glancing to her left and then her right, Blair saw two Land Rovers racing just off her wings on either side.

Blair flinched as another round found its mark, and the glass of the canopy to her left spider-webbed with fine cracks.

As the plane lifted off and soared into the burning sun, Blair shouted over her left shoulder to Yousef, “If you know any prayers … you’d better say them now!”

From the rear, she could already hear him praying fervently at the top of his lungs.

“’Cause if I’d had just a few more flying lessons … at least I’d know how to land this torpedo.”

CHAPTER 5

Devlin was no stranger to death and massacre, a tour in Mogadishu and Bosnia, followed by Iraq, had raised his threshold for pain. The lingering pain that resulted from witnessing firsthand the stark horrors of war. Nevertheless, his sixth sense told him this was a menace, the likes of which he had never encountered. It was something that pushed the envelope of the real world and its laws, something possibly otherworldly, demonic.

He held his KRISS .45 in a white-knuckled grip so tightly his wrist began to cramp. Sweat streamed down his spine, matting his shirt to the small of his back. His throat parched with apprehension.

The old woman's nostrils *did* flare as she sniffed the air. He wasn't imagining a damned thing.

Hunchbacked and staggering, she rose. When she turned she extended her arm, pointing it directly at Devlin.

A shriek like a giant hawk exploded from her scabbed lips.

In unison, the others rose.

Each in turn fixed Devlin with their glassy, vacant stare.

It was when they pulled back that he saw it. The body of a Syrian soldier, or what was left of it, lay obscenely on the ground. Looking closer, he saw it had been ripped to shreds as though a pride of ravenous lions had torn flesh from bone.

Limping woodenly, the mob crabbed toward him.

Some upright, others crawling.

He raised the KRISS and sighted on the first ghoul. With the first burst, the old hag's head exploded in a shower of blood and bone fragments. The duet of automatic weapons fire rang out as he and Chewie let their 45. rounds rip into the mob. They jerked and keened like wounded animals as they toppled to the ground, one by one.

CHAPTER 6

Sgt. Conners tossed the last of the wrenches into the toolbox and made for the chopper. Braxton and Scout met him halfway.

"Well … Sergeant, is she ready to go?" Braxton asked.

Tweaking the bristles of his walrus-sized moustache, Conners answered, "She was cankered up like an ol' whore, she was, sir. But now she's as fresh and clean as a new bride."

Brax shook his head and turned to Scout, who was blushing red. "Anything from Major Devlin?"

"That's a big fat negative. Reported in about ten minutes ago, but I can't raise 'im now."

Before Brax could answer, the sound of autofire crackled in the distance.

Without speaking, they rushed for the helo.

Conners drew up short. "Sir, listen."

The constant drone made familiar by a hundred old war movies now seemed unreal by its stark intrusion into the real world.

Their eyes turned to the sky, hands shielding their eyes from the harsh sun.

"Well, I'll be buggered." Conners shook his head in disbelief.

Brax chimed in. "What the bejesus is …?"

Scout's high-pitched voice cracked next. "What the fuck?"

"Not a fuck, laddy boy, she's a Focke-Wulf FW 190. Pretty li'l thing, ain't she now? Fastest little radial engine prop fighter the Luftwaffe turned out."

"Twilight Zone time," Scout muttered as the German fighter overhead howled past, tipping its wing.

In the distance, Brody and Chewie spotted a figure ducking into the doorway of an old mosque.

They made their way across the tangle of dead soldiers and ghouls.

Inside the mosque, they stood looking and listening.

Then they heard it; the steady march of shuffling footfalls coming toward them from an archway to the left. First one, then two, then a horde of zombified villagers poured through the opening, eyes filled with bloodlust, arms outstretched and pawing the air as they worked their jaws, making guttural animal-like sounds.

For an instant, the soldiers stood like stumps, too dumbfounded to move. But then Brody's eyes met Chewie's. Chewie nodded. "Run!"

They peeled out of the mosque, racing across the square, but unlike in the movies, instead of moving as a stumbling blind herd, these mutants rushed at their heels.

Chewie turned, running backward and firing from the hip as he went. Brody sighted on the nearest building. In the doorway, he could make out an old man gesturing wildly.

"This way!" Brody shouted to Chewie.

They stumbled into the building. Chewie slammed the door behind them and rammed the crossbeam into place, securely baring the door.

They stood, their backs sandwiched against the door, panting in ragged breaths, reloading their weapons with fresh mags.

Brody flinched. An old man emerged from the shadows.

It was the same figure who had been signaling them earlier from the doorway.

His long white hair spilled over his shoulders.

From his tours in the Middle East, Brody recognized that the man was a Sufi, an Islamic mystic. The coarse woolen robe, which hung from his rounded shoulders, was the clue, since *Suf* means wool in Arabic. And similar to the rough, homespun robes worn by Franciscan Monks as a sign of their vow of poverty, the Sufi Holy Men dressed in the same austere fashion.

Although the old Holy Man was brittle with age and stoop-shouldered, he gave off a sense of youthful vitality.

He slowly made his way toward them. Brody's eyes traveled from the Sufi's long white beard to his twinkling eyes, eyes that gleamed with understanding and wisdom.

When the old man spoke, his voice was deep and strong.

"Providence has brought you here."

Taken aback by the Sufi's command of English, Brody just stared.

The old man smiled knowingly. "Yes, I speak your tongue. The Creator has brought you here. Destiny is like the ebb and tide of a vast ocean. In this case, it has washed you upon my shore."

Sneaking a peek through the crack in the door, Chewie said, "There's more of them now. They're just standin' out there in a big semicircle."

The old man drew closer and placed his sun-leathered hand on Brody's shoulder. "He meant for you to witness this profanity of nature, this evil. You were brought here for a purpose. The birds will guide you … heed the ways of the cuckoos, who lay their eggs in another bird's nest to hatch."

Brody started to speak, but he couldn't find the words.

This strange old man, talking in riddles. Cuckoo was right. But there was something in his eyes that belied any notion of insanity or senility. The spark of truth shone brightly.

"Fear not, my son. You must have faith."

That's when they heard it. The uncannily familiar sound of a fighter's droning engine screaming past overhead, followed by the chatter of machine-gun fire.

As though he could read Brody's thoughts, the Sufi looked up and pointed toward the stairs. "You see, He sends his angels to protect you. Why don't you go to the roof and greet them."

With that, the Sufi turned and slowly walked away, vanishing into the shadows.

Chewie shrugged. "Whata we got to lose? C'mon!"

Glass showered into the room as a figure leaped through the window, landing on Chewie's back.

The mutant screamed and writhed as he clawed at Chewie's hair and cheeks, drawing blood. Chewie let out a war cry and whirled, viciously pitching the attacker over his shoulder and onto the floor.

In an instant, the attacker was on his feet.

He lunged, ropes of drool streaming from his mouth.

Chewie's meaty hand grabbed the man's shoulder, and he rammed the muzzle of the submachine gun into the man's gut.

As the slugs tore into him, the mutant jerked in spasms like he had grabbed a high voltage wire, arms flailing, teeth gnashing. He finally sank to the floor in a heap.

They ran for the stairs, their boots pounding as they took the narrow steps two at a time.

CHAPTER 7

Blair spotted the helicopter and was low enough to figure the men who dotted the ground next to it for Brits or Americans. Intending to wing past and circle back, she flew over the rise toward the village.

From the back, Yousef screamed, “Where are you going? Land this beast. They will help us!”

Cruising low over the village, Blair sensed something was amok. She made a wide turn and circled back over the village. Blair stared in horror as a throng of people below swarmed around a knot of fleeing American soldiers, manhandled them to the ground and began to ….

She pulled down her goggles, ripped off the leather cap, and rubbed her eyes.

There was no mistaking what she’d seen.

“No!” Yousef called from behind her, cupping his hands over Noor’s ears as he shouted. “You’ve flown us straight into Hell! Don’t land here, please. Those are the Devil’s Jinn down there. They’re eating those men! Allah, be praised, save us!”

Despite Yousef’s hysteria, Blair knew he wasn’t too far off the mark. The crowd was feeding on the men below, and she’d be damned if she didn’t stop it.

She sucked in a deep breath and steeled herself.

Banking right and making another wide turn, she came around, engine screaming like a banshee. Searching, she found the little red button on the control column. As she spiraled down from above, her thumb hit the button.

When she leveled out, the two wing guns flared as she strafed the ground below on her pass. Blair could see the line of dust puffs stitch its way across the ground and into the mass of ghouls.

The crowd reacted, scattering in a frenzied mob.

As she rocketed past, she noticed the trucks. They were caked with dust, but she could just make out a logo on the sides. Big red letters read: GENO-DYNE SYSTEMS.

She circled back for a second run.

On the roof now, Chewie and Brody looked on as the dark shadow of the fighter swept over the square below. The dull rattle of its machine guns was like the ripping of fabric. Incendiary rounds and tracers spat from its wing guns, streaking through the air and making bursts of flame wherever they found their target.

As the fighter winged past, a new sound assaulted their ears: the steady, reassuring *whump, whump, whump* of a helo's rotors.

From above, a shadow spread over them. Struggling to stand as the chopper's rotor wash buffeted them, they shielded their eyes and looked up in time to see their comrades, fast-roping from the chopper onto the rooftop.

Brody could make out Conners's fat head leaning out the side of the helo behind the machine gun, sporting a toothy grin and giving him the thumb's-up sign.

Brax ran toward them.

"If you aren't a sight for sore eyes," Brody shouted.

"Looks like you got yourselves jammed up pretty good, Brody. Any sign of the other squad?"

Brody and Chewie exchanged somber side-glances.

Chewie looked over the rooftop at the massacre below. Then he turned to Brax with a hollow stare. Always a man of few words, Chewie said, "Let's call 'em missing in action and leave it at that."

Brax looked puzzled and turned to Brody as though he were seeking a better explanation.

Brody nodded. "I'll give a full debriefing later. Let's just get the hell outta here."

At the sound of the high-pitched drone of the warplane, they turned.

The fighter's wing tipped again as it soared past them and slowly began to climb, heading due east.

Brax screwed up his face and managed, "Nazi fighters, strange lights … a whole squad gone missing. And I'll be damned if I didn't just see a good-looking redhead flying that bird as she shot past."

Chewie grunted and winked at Brody. "Or maybe she was an angel in disguise."

CHAPTER 8

LONDON

The tall priest with the ruddy complexion waited patiently behind the green line in front of the customs official. A sign over the booth read: Diplomats Only.

Noor's tiny hand gripped the priest's big hand tightly, nervously squeezing it for reassurance as she stood at his side, her brilliant blue eyes looking up at him.

Noor studied his face. It was cheesy soft and round and reminded her of a full moon peppered with craters.

The priest scratched his acne-scarred cheek and glanced down at her, his green eyes winking beneath bushy red brows. When he winked and made a funny face, the freckles on his plump pug nose and face seemed to dance.

It was their turn now.

They stood at the booth and the skinny-faced man took the priest's passport. Noor thought it was pretty. The cover had a gold seal with two crossed keys on it.

The customs official studied it.

"Father Dominic Kelly attached to the Vatican nuncio to the Court of St. James, diplomatic status."

Father Kelly gave a big smile. "That is correct, officer. And allow me to present my young ward."

As Father Kelly slid the new passport across the counter, he gently nudged Noor with his knee.

Noor got the hint and curtsied awkwardly, holding the hem of her new robin's-egg-blue dress as she struggled not to fall. The shiny patent-leather shoes pinched her toes.

Noor saw the skinny-faced man's quick smile fade to a scowl as he buried his birdlike nose in her passport. She didn't like this man at all, but she remembered the instructions Blair and her brother Father Kelly had given her before boarding the flight. She plastered a toothy grin onto her face and tried not to show how scared she really was.

"And little missy, you would be one Gwendolyn Grace Kelly," old skinny-face said, his voice filled with doubt, his beady eyes staring.

As a smile dimpled her cheeks, Noor answered, "Oh, you can just call me Wendy, sir."

"My niece, officer," Father Kelly offered.

The official's eyes ticked from the priest's full head of flame-red hair and pasty freckled skin, to Noor's flaxen, silken hair and latte-colored flesh tones.

Father Kelly learned forward like he was telling a secret, and whispered, "She's adopted."

The customs official huffed and shook his head. Prune-faced, he stamped both passports and said gruffly, "Welcome to the United Kingdom."

Seated together in the back of the shiny black limousine, Noor took in the driver's funny-shaped hat with the little red fuzzy ball on top. He'd been waiting at the curb and treated her and Father Kelly like they were a prince and a princess. She liked this man; his friendly smile and silly squeaky voice made her laugh.

She stared out the window at the passing scenery. So many cars; everything looked so clean and green compared to the streets of that city in Iraq where Blair had taken her.

She giggled to herself when she thought of the look on poor Yousef's face when Blair had finally landed the plane near Yousef's cousin's village. She remembered how the herd of goats had scattered beneath them as the plane came in for a landing, its swaying wings making her tummy ache. Then they'd clipped the thatched roof off a tiny house and somehow landed in one piece, although Blair had said the plane was a "bloody wreck."

Then Blair had gotten to a phone and called her brother. He was an important man who lived in a place called Italy, but was traveling through a city called Istanbul in a place called Turkey.

He'd sent a plane for them.

Noor had seen how much Father Kelly and Blair loved each other when she saw how tears glistened in their eyes when they finally hugged each other at the airport in Istanbul.

They'd spent a night in a fancy hotel, with slippery silk sheets and rugs on the floor so thick that Noor laughed when she rubbed the toes of her bare feet in them.

It tickled.

They'd gone shopping and Blair had bought her pretty new clothes. Noor's gleaming smile suddenly turned into a frown. Suddenly thinking of her dead parents made her sad, tormented by guilt. When Blair asked her what was wrong, she'd shrugged it off, saying she was hungry. They stopped for a snack. Blair had winked at her over a cup of hot chocolate, and then she'd told her to close her eyes.

When she opened them, a big pink stuffed animal with buttons for eyes greeted her. Blair had said it was called a Teddy Bear. Noor loved that soft cuddly bear and named him Mr. Muffins. She had not let it out of her sight, eating with it, sleeping with it and now traveling to a strange new world.

She knew that Blair was coming to join them on a separate flight.

She'd promised to follow, saying Father Kelly could work miracles, too, and got her something called a Vatican passport that was like a magic ticket. A ticket that could let her visit faraway places and come to Blair's home in London to live with her.

A tiny tear crowded the corner of Noor's eye now as she thought of Blair. She missed her so.

She squiggled around, the smooth leather seat squeaking under her bum as she moved.

Noor thought that was such a funny word when she'd heard Blair use it. Blair had pulled herself from the rocky ground after the crash landing, and rubbed her backside and said, "I won't be able to park my sweet bum in a hard chair ever again."

"Father Kelly," Noor said.

He smiled warmly. "Call me Dominic, please. How do you like London, li'l one?"

"Oh, it is so big and the buildings look old but different, like something out of a picture book."

"That's because they've been drawn in picture books so many times. Wait, I have something for you."

He leaned forward in his seat and spoke to the driver. "Father Benjamin, did you bring that book?"

"Here we go," he said as he handed a book back across the seat.

Father Kelly placed the book in Noor's lap.

She read the title: *Peter Pan.*

"It's about a girl who can fly."

"Just like me?" Noor asked, eagerly thumbing through the book.

He smiled. "And her name's the same as your new pretend name."

Noor wrinkled her nose and stammered, "You mean Gwen-dal-anne?"

He gave a hearty belly laugh. "Yes, but it's Wendy for short."

When she looked up, a frown tugged at the corners of her mouth. "But are we going to your house now? I am so tired and hungry. Maybe your wife could cook us some lamb and rice?"

Both of the priests laughed long and heartily, which puzzled Noor. She didn't see what was so funny about lamb and rice.

Following at a discreet distance, a hulking black Mercedes sedan was hot on their tail. The female passenger in the front seat was talking on her mobile, her eyes glued to the limo in front of her.

With her nineteen-thirties matinée idol hairstyle, her high cheekbones and wide-set eyes and swan-like neck, she was striking. But the white-blonde color of her wet-look hair and the hard line of her jaw exuded an inhuman brutality.

The thin lips done in a deep crimson shade of lipstick were cruel.

"We are directly behind them now," she said, speaking into the cell phone. "There will be no mistakes."

She rolled her large sapphire eyes as she listened.

"We will get the girl at any cost."

She slapped the phone shut and lit a cigarette, letting the nicotine fill her lungs. She exhaled and studied the cherry tip for a second before taking another drag.

A thin smile came to her lips. She nudged closer to the driver. Beneath the tailored gray Armani suit she wore a form-fitting silk white blouse that accentuated the mounds of her pert breasts. The top buttons were purposely left undone, revealing her swelling cleavage.

She massaged the hollow of her throat with her fingertip and sighed.

From beneath his Neanderthal brow, the driver's eyes ticked to her chest.

She felt how his eyes lingered.

She pouted her lips as her thigh rubbed against the driver's leg. Then she ran the finger of her left hand along the inseam of his trousers.

His knuckles blanched as he tightened his grip on the steering wheel, and his massive shoulders and biceps tightened beneath the bulging seams of his jacket.

As she leaned in to blow in his ear, she ground the tip of the burning cigarette into the back of his massive hand, violently grinding it deeper and deeper.

He didn't react in the least.

As his dull gray eyes stared straight ahead, he cracked an oily grin.

Still not satisfied, she raked his cheek with the long red fingernails of her hand.

As blood trickled down, he absently wiped it away with the back of his huge hand.

"*Du drecksack!* You're such a bore, Ernst," she said, sulking as she slid back to her side of the seat. She pulled a Sig Sauer from the shoulder holster beneath her jacket and jacked a round into the chamber, then stared intently at the limo, licking her upper lip with the moist tip of her tongue.

The two thick-necked thugs in the back broke out in a boisterous and taunting laugh.

She nodded over her shoulder. "*Geh fick deine Mutter*! If one of you baboons screws this up, we will see who laughs last," she warned them, her voice simultaneously laced with a seductive huskiness and unforgiving violence.

CHAPTER 9

Blair sat in coach between a guy who needed an extension for his seatbelt and a woman who insisted on telling her life story, from the beginning.

It was a long flight.

The idea of Noor, however, waiting for her in London buoyed her spirits. Flying separately was a necessary precaution, just in case someone was looking for a lone redhead and a child.

She hadn't been sure how her brother Dominic would react to her call. He was always wagging his tongue and harping about her expeditions being too dangerous.

Since their parents had passed in the motor crash, they had grown close. Dominic becoming a priest had at least fulfilled their mother's dream, although she wished her parents had been more supportive of her career choice. "Can't have it all… now can we, Blair? A career and a family …" she heard her mother's voice admonishing her for the umpteenth time. It brought a smile to her lips.

In her heart of hearts, she knew that Dominic would help them. There was no way in hell she would leave that poor child behind. Just the thought of al-Dajjal touching Noor's chin the way he did made her flesh crawl.

And somewhere down deep inside, she had the nagging feeling that this wasn't the last she'd see of the bastard.

Besides, Noor wasn't exactly just any child, now was she? She'd been amazed at the aura the girl projected.

The strength.

The calmness in the face of grave danger.

No, this li'l one was special, all right.

Her thoughts turned to her brother again. Father Dominic Kelly, the Vatican's "miracle detective," the press had labeled him after the stigmata case he'd investigated in Brazil. Well, Noor was certainly right up his alley then.

A true walking and talking miracle worker.

She would never be fortunate enough to have a child of her own. Doctors had said she couldn't. It was a big step, asking Dominic to use his Vatican clout to get Noor into the U.K.

Eventually they'd have to go through proper channels, but the immediate need was for Noor to be safe.

To be loved.

Father Kelly was reading to Noor from *Peter Pan*, the lids of her eyes growing heavier with each line. *Poor little thing,* he thought. *What an ordeal for a child.*

Blair's call had caught him by surprise. He hadn't heard from her in months. But the fear in her voice tore at his heart, and he moved heaven and earth to get her and the child to safety.

Using the old boy network that exists even within the Vatican, he'd called in a favor and secured a travel document for the girl. He, too, believed that there were forces of evil in this world. By God, hadn't he experienced them first hand on too many occasions?

As he stroked Noor's silken hair, she was lying safely curled in his lap, sound asleep. He thought of the reports he'd heard of children with strange abilities, so-called Indigo Children, which, until now, he'd dismissed as wishful thinking on the part of a demoralized culture which hoped for old-fashioned signs and miracles. He thought of his recent trip to Istanbul. His hunch had paid off. The dervishes had the Jung diary he had been searching for after all. Convinced of his sincerity and his good intentions, they'd agreed to part with it.

The secrets it contained could provide the solution to the long sought after puzzle that consumed his father's life work, and now admittedly—consumed his.

He was eager to return to London and get back to his first love, the study of the old codices of Alchemy. Had his life taken a different path, he would have gladly followed in his father's footsteps, toiling away as a poor academic at some small university that afforded him the time for his studies.

The limo pulled onto a narrow street.

Up ahead, a lorry was stalled crossways in the roadway.

Just as they came to a halt in front of the truck, he heard the roar of a powerful engine from the rear and the screech of brakes.

Dominic spun toward the sound, peering out the back window.

A black Mercedes shuddered to a stop.

The doors flung open.

A tall, lean woman, wearing oversized sunglasses and a dark pant-suit, emerged from the passenger side door of the Mercedes, and two men in dark suits spilled from the back.

The sunlight silvered her white-blonde hair.

Her fist held a pistol.

By now, the other two men bracketed the limo, their weapons pointed directly at them.

It was an ambush, plain and simple, he reasoned. But the limo wasn't armored.

Fumbling for the door lock button, Dominic screamed at Father Benjamin, "Hit the gas … they're after the child!"

Father Benjamin rammed the shift lever into reverse. The limo lurched backward, crashing into the grille of the Mercedes.

Shifting into drive, Father Benjamin floored it. The limo's big V-8 howled as the rear tires smoked and squealed. But the hulking limo was rooted in place.

The bumpers of the two cars were locked.

The driver's side window suddenly exploded in a spray of glass.

A silencer-shrouded muzzle stabbed inward.

The muffled bark of gunfire followed.

Father Benjamin took two in the chest, bucking in his seat as the rounds punched his rib cage, and then, slowly toppled over.

Dominic could make out one of the men who clutched a shiny tool snugly in his hands. He was moving to Dominic's side of the limo.

The priest threw himself across Noor, shielding her from the coming attack.

—Wham—

His side window splintered, glass rained over him.

The door knifed open.

He heard the woman's husky voice now.

"Careful, *du arschgesicht*! Don't injure the child!"

Rough hands dragged Dominic from the limo and pitched him to the pavement.

He looked up to see the men pulling Noor from the car. She didn't resist, just clutched her pink teddy bear tighter to her chest. And when her pleading eyes met his, he struggled to gain his feet.

The overpowering scent of perfume wafted down at him.

The woman's long legs stood in a wide stance directly before him, blocking his view of the girl.

"Don't get up, priest," she said calmly as she viciously drove the tip of her pointed boot into his ribs again and again. He felt the crack of bone.

He groaned weakly.

Through a bleary haze, he saw her squatting in front of him, felt her long fingers smoothing his hair, felt her hot breath on his face as she pressed closer.

"Hush now, *liebschien*. Pain is *gut, ja*?" she whispered, nuzzling his ear as she stabbed at his bruised ribs with muzzle of her pistol.

"Hans, take this one, too," she shouted to another attacker. "He pleases me."

CHAPTER 10

Brody Devlin nodded to the boyish-looking MSG, Marine Security Guard, who stood post beside the elevator. Brody and Chewie took the unmarked elevator down into the guts of the American Embassy basement complex. They made their way through a sterile, white neon-lit corridor to the communications center. In turn, they held their palm to the reader and placed their right eye into the eyepiece, which scanned their unique corneas.

Cameras tracked their movements and fed the image of their features into a Face-Ident computer program. With a sharp buzz, the heavy fire door opened and they entered.

Like the hallway, the large white bleached room was immaculate; you could have eaten off the floor. Racks of electronic equipment lined the walls. The chilled air, combined with the chrome and glistening metal and industrial computer tiles, gave the room a cold, inhuman quality.

Evenly spaced swivel chairs ringed a long conference table, which was enclosed in a thick glass shell. An LED screen hung from a metal frame at one end of the table. Next to it stood an oversized shredder and burn bag which was incinerated daily.

It was a bigger version of the "Cage," which was a high-tech soundproof and eavesdropping proof area.

It was swept constantly for bugs and when occupied, a film of one-way material lowered, shrouding the Cage.

Some had laughed at the concept of a mole within the embassy reading lips; but when it happened, countermeasures were taken.

Seated at computer consoles and workstations, techs busied themselves sorting embassy traffic.

Behind a larger console in the corner was a command and control center, which served as a multi-agency switchboard for surveillance and dignitary protection teams.

A tech who was engrossed in a cheat manual for the latest Halo computer game looked up.

"Slow day, hey Reynolds?" Brody said.

The twentysomething tech shrugged. "Comes with the job, Major. *Wazzup*?"

"Inter-agency meeting—and we'll need a conference call on the scrambler."

"Got it on the schedule right here," he said, pointing to a clipboard that hung from the console. "Sorensen's callin' in, is he?" the tech asked with a glint in his eye, which was double-speak for an ass-chewing.

The embassy was a small place and word spread like wildfire.

Brody knew that the boss, Bill Sorensen, was hopping mad about the cluster fuck in Syria. But Bill was basically a good leader and a level-headed guy.

Chewie's gravelly voice cut in. "No one likes a smart ass, son." His icy stare clearly unnerved the tech, who gulped hard and gave an exaggerated nod.

The door buzzed and Lt. Braxton entered with two men.

Brody recognized one as Chief Inspector Adam Newley of SO15, formally known as Special Branch, the division of the Metropolitan Police's Scotland Yard with full arrest powers dealing with major crime and counter-terrorism.

The other guy was short and stiff-necked with watery blue eyes that took in the whole room in a glance. His stare was deliberate and flashed intelligence. He was grossly corpulent, his layers of fat somewhat disguised by the elegant tailoring of his dark suit. He had a grub-pale, round, forgettable face. He looked old school, a member of the British "old school tie" club known as SIS. Her Majesty's Secret Service. Brody knew from working with them that most of these spooks were closer to what the other branches referred to as metro-sexuals, effete snobs in tailored suits from the elite universities, than they were to Sean Connery's portrayal of the infamous MI-6 agent, James Bond. In plain English, they were a cliquish bunch of pricks who didn't trust anyone who wasn't *their* kind.

Newley rushed over to greet him, extending his thin, pasty hand. "I say, chaps, it's been far too long since we bumped heads."

Brody noted the briefcase cuffed to Newley's left wrist. When Newley proffered his free hand to Chewie, the big lug opted for his silent Indian routine. Flinty eyed and unmoving.

Newley's brow beetled as he regarded Chewie's massive frame from head to toe. "My God, Brody, what do you feed this man?"

Brax cut in. "Major, this is Sir Nigel Cummings from …"

"Our dear friends at Legoland."

Brody used the nickname for the SIS's new HQ on the Thames, whose odd design resembled building blocks.

"The pleasure's all mine, Major Devlin," Sir Nigel said with a disrespectful smile.

Then Cummings turned to Chewie, who reluctantly extended his hand and introduced himself. With raised eyebrows, the fat man declined to shake.

Speaking as though Chewie weren't even there, Cummings panned the rest of the group. "Raindancer, eh? I say, an American redskin in the flesh, how quaint."

The jerk had just stepped on his dick, Brody thought as he winced, took a deep breath, and expelled it forcefully.

Face expressionless and jaw set firmly, Chewie said, "EE-TOH-SHNEE, WHO-HNAU-YEH."

Looking puzzled at first, Cummings's jowly face registered understanding. "Your native tongue, old boy. How charming, indeed."

Brody bit his lower lip, suppressing a laugh. Chewie had taught him enough Dakota to know he'd just called Cummings a lying bastard.

Chewie was grinning now as he mumbled, "*Te futueo et equum tuum.*"

Cummings shook his head, looking even more puzzled.

With a nonchalant shrug, his plump manicured fingers fished a chain from his waistcoat and flipped open his gold pocket watch. His gray gold-flecked eyes squinted. "I believe the briefing is scheduled for exactly fifteen-thirty hours, which gives us exactly forty-eight seconds to commence." He snapped the cover shut and made for the Cage, hands tucked neatly in his coat pockets as he sauntered toward it.

Brody turned to Chewie and whispered, "I got the first part, but what the hell was that last bit?"

With a sheepish look, Chewie explained, "Been tryin' to cut down on the cursing lately, boss. So I picked up a little Latin."

"And?"

"I told the jerk to go screw himself and the horse he rode in on."

Seated at the conference table, Brody hit the intercom. "Seal us up and lower the shades, Reynolds."

The door closed with a pneumatic hiss and the blinds trundled down.

The green scrambler phone rang.

Devlin picked up, excusing himself to the others.

He winced when he saw that Chewie had parked himself next to old stiff-neck Cummings. It spelled trouble with a capital T.

Sorensen's voice came on the line.

"Devlin, are we on the speaker?"

"No sir, but the others are here and waiting."

"Good, this will only take a moment. We don't have any more word on the missing members of the operation. Negotiating with the Syrians for release of their bodies isn't an option. Later satellite images showed that the Syrian Air Force bombed the whole region right off the face of the earth, big-time! Near as we can figure, the village was a bio-genetic experiment that went terribly wrong, and somebody wanted to cover their tracks completely."

Brody's voice hitched. "Have the families been …?"

"Made the rounds to our people in person. Wouldn't want it handled any other way."

Brody could hear the pain in Sorensen's voice. He was a stand-up guy.

"On to business. We have intercepts that place al-Dajjal in Europe and headed your way."

"Cheeky bastard, isn't he?"

"Could be his biggest weakness. Exploit it."

"Point taken, Bill. Got a strong lead on who his contact is here?"

"That's why I've arranged this inter-agency meeting. Got to keep a lid on this or the boys at Langley will want a piece of the action."

"And our guests won't?"

"Once you hear the full briefing, you'll have a clearer picture, Brody. And one other thing …"

Brody filled in Sorensen's thought. "Sir, this time I won't come up empty-handed."

"Well said. But that's not what I was getting at. Your unit will be posing as DSS agents."

"Yes, sir. We're carrying their creds, shields, and Dip passports."

The ΩMEGA Force frequently carried credentials identifying them as special agents of the U.S. State Department's Diplomatic Security Service. Aside from providing a plausible cover, it afforded them law enforcement powers in the States, entrée into and full liaison with other intelligence and security services, and the black diplomatic passports provided full immunity when overseas. Brody had a feeling he knew where his boss was going with this.

"Good." Sorensen's voice hitched slightly. "But DCM Janet Wimple and Ambassador Logan weren't too keen on my having you and your team listed on the official rolls as it were. So—"

"Keep a low profile, and don't step on any toes," Brody offered.

"Exactly," the boss added, "especially DCM Wimple's open-toed Prada high heels. "Now put me on the box."

Brody knew Janet Wimple all too well from his past life as a DSS agent. He knew that the Deputy Chief of Mission of the U.S. Embassy in London ranked "security types," as she snidely called them, somewhere bellow Neanderthals on the evolutionary ladder, while Brody and his team considered the empty suits—or diplomatic corps—to be more closely related to the reptile species, specifically—lizards and snakes. Or in Ms. Wimple's case, an Iguana, complete with bulbous eyes that glared and a wattle of chins that shook when she flew into a rage. The only thing she lacked was a forked tongue.

Now heads turned as the door hissed and Scout Thompson slinked sheepishly into the room. Late, as usual. Scout had a weakness for clubbing, and right now, his eyes looked like two burn holes in a wool blanket. But Scout was basically a good kid.

Brody shot him a dirty look just to play with him.

Sorensen's voice cracked from the speaker pod on the center of the table. "Gentlemen, let's get on with it, shall we?"

Brief greetings were said all around the table.

"As you know, both our governments have a burning interest in al-Dajjal, and we have both paid too dearly with the loss of personnel to stop now," Sorensen explained. "Our latest intel put him in Istanbul, Turkey last week. Our sources report that he was scouting for antiquities. Unfortunately, we lost his trail before a rendition team could be dispatched to grab him. And, as usual, the Turkish Secret Service wasn't overly cooperative."

"Antiquities, you say?" Cummings asked, cocking his head.

"That's correct. Seems he was interested in a map on display at the Topkapi Palace Museum, the Map of the Ancient Sea Kings. It's from the sixteenth century but was based on charts, if you believe the legend, from the time of Alexander the Great. Anyway, the point is that an NSA cellular intercept confirmed that he's headed for London, but we don't know how or when … just soon."

"Potential contacts?" Inspector Newley asked.

Sorensen answered, "Inspector, I think you can already guess based on the intel I requested for you to share with my team."

Newley nodded to himself and hoisted a Zero briefcase onto the table, unlocking the handcuff from his wrist.

"Sat recon did a number of passes over that village, Major Devlin … before it was obliterated," the boss continued. "If you'd all direct your attention to the screen now."

The secure teleconferencing capabilities gave Sorensen the tools to remotely control the digital display from miles away in Washington, D.C.

The pixels converged into the image of a column of trucks. The image zoomed into a close-up of the logo, which read:

GENO-DYNE SYSTEMS

"GENO-DYNE SYSTEMS, gentlemen," Sorensen said. "What are their trucks doing in this remote, godforsaken village in Syria?"

Sorenson paused for effect, then continued. "Mr. Cummings, would you care to brief us on the company's background, please?"

Cummings cleared his throat. "GENO-DYNE is an international conglomerate, which is headquartered here in the UK. Its founder and CEO is Heinrich von Gant."

The image of Gant appeared on the LED screen.

"Gant is a German national who immigrated to the UK after the war. He anglicized his name. His true name is Heinrich Lubendorf von Gantzinger. He is both an industrialist and an academic."

"Dangerous combination," Newley added.

Cummings rolled his eyes. "If I may continue without interruption, please?"

Brody studied Gant's image.

The man was old as sin, with long, silky white hair, swept back from a face that was all hard planes and angles. He had a high intelligent brow, razor thin lips, and small yellowed teeth. Looking closer, Brody noticed something odd.

For some reason Brody couldn't lay a finger on at the moment, the man's features seemed counterfeit, almost masklike.

Cummings's voice droned on. "Gant's formal education is in engineering, however he's a self taught polymath … schooled himself in everything from physics to philosophy, and he's fluent in six languages. His passion is history, archaeology, and antiquities, especially rare books.

"During the war, he was involved in Germany's future weapons projects. He locked horns with Werner von Braun over the immediate value of the V-1 and V-2 rocket program.

"But there's also a mysterious side. He was a member of an occult Pan-Germanic organization known as *Der Vril Gesellschaft*, the *Vril* Society, a spinoff of the infamous Thule Society, pronounced THU-LAY. This is the very same group of racist intellectuals and aristocrats who sponsored Hitler in his rise to power.

"He helped found the *Ahnenerbe* , the Nazi Occult Bureau, which fits nicely with his interest in archaeology."

Brody broke in. "Didn't Himmler send expeditions around the globe, searching for the Ark of the Covenant or something?"

"More precisely," Cummings explained, "Himmler wanted to find clear-cut evidence of the purity and ancestry of the Aryan race. They launched expeditions to Norway, Tibet, and even Syria and Iraq in nineteen thirty-eight, before the war. Al-Dajjal's parents headed up the dig in Syria."

The word *Syria* stabbed at Brody's gut. Was there some sort of connection between the Nazi's dig in Syria, and the strange happenings he'd just witnessed there?

Lt. Braxton added, "Yeah, Major, but part of their program was experimentation on live subjects, namely the poor Jewish prisoners in concentration camps."

Brax had worked for DOJ's Office of Special Investigations, the branch responsible for tracking down old war criminals, which had given him an encyclopedic knowledge of World War II. Though an attorney by trade, Brax had preferred being a field agent, much to the displeasure of his superiors who thought his time would have been better served pushing a pencil and burying his nose in dusty old files. His research skills, fluency in German and Slavic languages, and quick mind had secured him a spot with the ΩMEGA FORCE.

Brax went on. "They'd line 'em up and choose the ones whose skulls looked interesting, then have 'em shot and collect the skeletal structures for studies. Doctor Joseph Mengele's genetic experiments were part of it. To study the effect of wounds on the human body, they'd just take some poor sucker out and shoot him in the gut and study what happened as the poor bastard laid there bleeding out."

"Gentlemen, if I may!" Cummings scowled. "This perverted ideology isn't just some distant nightmare. Neo-Nazi groups and Islamic fundamentalist groups have found common ground in their hatred of the whole Jewish race, and their goal to wipe them from the face of the Earth.

"But let's get back to facts. Heinrich von Gantzinger, AKA Gant, is best known as a major arms dealer, lately specializing in Unmanned Vehicles and Weapons Systems, but he has research facilities that are exploring the frontiers of genetics.

"He has also accumulated vast wealth, ensuring him wide influence in the global banking and political arenas of many nations."

Chewie had begun squirming in his seat like a fifth-grader. Now, suddenly, he raised his hand like one.

Cummings tried to ignore him, but Chewie persisted.

"Very well, Mr. Raindancer, a question?"

Chewie puffed out his chest. "Just one. Who the hell let this *Canis Filius* into the UK and protected his ugly butt?"

Brody cringed. *There he goes with the Latin bullshit again.*

Cummings deferred to Sorensen, whose voice came from the speaker.

"Chewie, you've heard of Operation Paperclip?"

Listening intently, Chewie nodded.

Brody shook his head and answered for the big knucklehead. "Our resident 'Rhodes Scholar' is nodding in the affirmative, Bill."

Sorensen went on. "After the war it was a mad grab. The States, the Russians, and Churchill were eager to get their hands on Germany's research, top scientists, and engineers. It was a necessary evil. And yes, some—SOBs— to use your Latin phrase, never paid the piper for their contribution to war crimes.

"Heinrich von Gantzinger was sponsored by the UK and, well… the United States also helped fund his research into advanced weapons systems. That answer your question?"

Cummings's gaze slid back to Chewie, his eyes slitted and a condescending expression on his face.

Chewie wiggled around in the chair and ….

Brody buried his face in his hands when he saw Chewie raise one butt cheek to Cummings.

… squeezed out a loud fart that ripped and soured the air.

Chewie shot Cummings his *bite me* look and said, "*Fabriacate diem, caput steronis*, Make my day, Shithead!"

Laughter broke out around the table.

Cummings's face scrunched and his hand clipped his nostrils shut as he said in a nasally tone, "Lovely, so mature and just … lovely."

Cummings was standing red-faced and still as a light pole, so Newley rose to his feet.

"Thank you, Mr. Cummings. Now, where were we? Oh, yes, Gant's involvement and peculiar background. Both our export office and the American export controls security division have been trying for years to nail Gant, for the sales of controlled and classified technology and weapons.

"The Israeli Mossad has also been hot on his trail as of late. Seems he's been brokering deals with every fanatic in the Middle East. You chaps … how do you say it? Yes, think he's '*GOOD for the rap*' dealing in unauthorized plutonium shipments to North Korea and Iran.

"In short, he's become a liability and an embarrassment to the Crown."

Brax cut in. "Sounds like it may suit everyone's interests if Mr. Gant … just disappeared?"

No one spoke, but Newley's eyes locked on Cummings.

Fighting with his girth, Cummings stood and moved to the front of the table. He stuffed his thumbs into the pockets of his vest.

He sighed heavily. "Oh, the Devil take it … one of our best agents tried to infiltrate GENO-DYNE. He went missing. Last night his body washed up in the Thames."

The silence hung heavily in the Cage.

"The autopsy showed he'd suffered prolonged and gruesome torture … I'll forgo the details."

"Sorry for your loss," Brody managed, sure that he was expressing the thoughts of everyone seated around the table.

Sorensen broke in. "Major Devlin, we know that al-Dajjal is working for Gant, probably has been all along." Now Brody was getting the picture.

"We need to get the goods on him—and fast … and hopefully … snatch our target in the process."

Solemn looks washed around the room.

"I want your team to go undercover and infiltrate Gant's organization."

"What's the plan, sir?" Devlin asked dryly.

"It's twofold. You'll pose as a shady arms buyer. With your knowledge of future combat systems, it should be a cake walk."

Famous last words, Brody thought.

"And the second prong of attack?" he asked.

"His hobby, his passion … will be the bait," Sorensen explained. "Tomorrow afternoon, Gant will be attending a showing and lecture series at the British Museum. The Yale library is touring an old codex, an alchemical text known as the Voynich manuscript. I want you to be there to approach him on the weapons sham.

"Another operative will make him an offer he can't refuse."

Brody leaned into the table, his voice soft. "Who and what would that be, Bill?"

"With his father's death, Professor Dominic Patrick Kelly inherited the mantle of being the United Kingdom's foremost expert on Alchemy. Father Kelly will offer Gant the missing pages to the Voynich manuscript, which hold the key to decoding the whole damned thing."

Brody looked puzzled. "Did you say … *Father* Kelly? And how do I find him?"

Sorensen chuckled, "Yeah, he's a Catholic priest, but holds a doctorate in history. He won't be hard to find. He'll be giving the lecture."

Cummings jumped in. "Let me give Major Devlin the reason why Gant is so obsessed with the Voynich and Alchemy."

He turned to Brody. "I detected an inquisitive look on your face when I flashed Gant's photo on the screen." He tapped the keyboard and the image reappeared.

Brody said, "His face looks like a mask. Just doesn't jive, it's too symmetrical."

"Precisely, Major Devlin. Let me explain. Some time ago, Gant was severely injured in an explosion in one of his research labs. It left him terribly disfigured. Gant's intelligence is only exceeded by his vanity.

"We know he spent a fortune on reconstructive surgery; however, our sources tell us it was, for the most part, an utter failure.

"What we see here is indeed a prosthetic, a bit of make-up artistry, if you will. He hired the top make-up artists from Hollywood to come up with this face.

"What monstrous thing lies beneath it, no one has ever seen."

Chewie grunted and reflexively, Cummings pinched his nostrils. Chewie rolled his eyes and wise-cracked, "He's a regular Phantom of the Opera, then, aye?"

"Well put indeed, Mr. Raindancer."

Chewie looked surprised; Cummings finally seemed to like something he'd said.

"Your comparison of Gant to an enraged, vengeful sociopath is spot on. Now, to make matters worse, from Gant's point of view, he has no heirs to carry on the family name. His son died young in motor crash a few years back. His only living relative is his niece, Margot Gant. An attractive woman who apparently inherited the deviant tastes of her uncle." He nodded toward Newley.

The chief inspector took a deep breath. "Miss Gant is a bit of a mystery woman, with no past and no criminal record. Her file picks up with her recent arrival in the UK. But the lads at Metropolitan Police tell us Margot Gant haunts the S&M dives, gets her jollies with riding crops and hooks, she does. And she's none too particular whether her lovers are boy-toys or rent-girls, or whether they're willing partners or not." Newley blushed as he said it.

As if poked with a cattle prod, Scout finally came to life. "I'll bet Brax would volunteer to cruise the clubs and get close to her, Major."

Brody shrugged and shook his head. "I just *bet* he would."

"Get too close to a she-wolf like that and you might pull back a stump, Brax," Scout said as he hid his hand in his coat sleeve, waving it at Lt. Braxton, who brushed it away.

Cummings took over.

"If we've all quite satisfied our prurient desires and adolescent fantasies, let's proceed to the Voynich … shall we?

"Despite what many think, Alchemy is not only about the quest to turn lead into gold. It also is firmly locked into the myth of the Fountain of Youth. We know that Gant has sponsored expeditions to the Yucatan in Mexico in search of the miraculous fountain. We know that he has spent an equal fortune trying to prolong his life and restore his facial features.

"The strangest thing is this. He may very well have had some success in his search for eternal youth." Cummings paused and hit the keyboard again. The image of a yellowed document flashed on the screen.

"How's your German, gentlemen? I draw your attention to the birth date on Heinrich von Gantszinger's birth certificate."

Brax's mouth hinged wide. "That's impossible. Hell… that would make him—"

Cummings accentuated each syllable.

"One Hundred and THIRTY-EIGHT YEARS OLD."

Never one to let someone else have the last word, Chewie added, "Or the oldest living bastard on earth."

CHAPTER 11

The imposing facade of the British Museum rose like a sentinel against the gray sky.

Brody and Brax climbed the steep steps and entered the Great Court. Brody wore his favorite white twill shirt under a custom-tailored blazer. His gray slacks matched his knit silk tie. His gold Rolex Presidential winked from under the sleeve of his royal blue blazer as his arms swung at his sides. He looked the part; smelled of casual wealth.

Playing the role of legal advisor and banker, Brax wore a dark blue wool Brooks Brothers suit.

Brody looked up at the ceiling of glass overhead, which covered the whole grand foyer, and gave a low whistle. "Pretty impressive," he said to Brax, who nodded his agreement.

In the center stood a large rotunda, bracketed by sweeping staircases. Shadows from the pyramid-shaped glass tiles of the skylight above played across the white marble floor and the sides of the rotunda, etching an eerie geometric pattern.

On either side of the center staircase, like ancient landmarks, smaller versions of the museum's colonnaded facade served as entrances to exhibit halls.

"Excuse me," Brax said to a young girl manning the information booth, flashing his faultless smile. "Could you tell us where we could find Doctor Kelly, please?"

The girl looked up from the magazine she was reading, her frown transforming into a warm smile as she seemed rapt with his steely blue eyes and good looks. As she primped her hair, her eyes flashed interest. "American, eh?"

Brax shot her a wink.

She blushed and looked down, her fingers punching the computer keyboard at her station.

"There's a Doctor Kelly who's in the reading room this afternoon," she said, her puppy-love stare lingering on Brax. "Want I should show you, luv?"

Brody broke in. "I think if you just point us in the right direction, we could manage."

She wrinkled her nose, glared, and handed Brody a map.

As they walked away, Brody smirked at Brax. "Man, I've got ties older than her."

They entered the cavernous reading room and made their way to the reference desk.

A woman with red hair done in a neat bun stood with her back to them. Brax began to speak, but Brody cut him off, "Easy, tiger, I'll handle this one." He cleared his throat. "Miss, could you direct me to Doctor Kelly?"

The woman turned. Even with her red hair swept severely back and little makeup, her natural beauty took Brody's breath away. She possessed a subtle beauty with a fey quality. Her eyes, arrestingly wide in her heart-shaped face, were a shimmering, stunning color of green. When he looked closer, a twinge of familiarity needled his thoughts. He couldn't remember the time or the place, but he had definitely seen her somewhere before.

Her bottle-green eyes studied him. "Yes, how can I help you?"

"I beg your pardon?"

She shot him a quizzical look. "Why, what did you do?"

"No, I mean I'm looking for Dominic Kelly, the priest."

"Well, why didn't you say so in the first place? But who isn't?" Her brow furrowed.

Fidgeting and clearly annoyed at Brody's line of questioning, Brax cut in. "We didn't mean to upset you, miss. If you could please explain. This is important. Where's Father Kelly?"

"Like I said, that's exactly what I'd like to know. My brother's supposed to be giving a lecture…"—she glanced at the wall clock—"… in forty-five minutes, and he's not here."

The words "my brother" finally sunk in and Brody understood the confusion. She started to turn away when Brody chimed in.

"So you're *also* Doctor Kelly?"

She tapped the nametag on her white blouse that read Dr. Blair M. Kelly and turned. Without looking back, she moved away and said, "You like to overstate the obvious, don't you?"

"Miss, is it like your brother not to show for something like the Voynich Lecture?"

She stopped in her tracks and turned. "I don't see how that's any of your business. You Americans are so bloody pushy, aren't you?" Then her voice softened and a questioning look washed across her face. She regarded them both closely. "You're both pretty fit for academics supposedly interested in a lecture on ancient codices. And judging from the bulges under your arms, you both have severe deformities or you're concealing sidearms."

Smart girl, Brody thought. He gave an innocuous smile and suggested, "Is there a place where we could talk in private?" Brody's expression was serious but empathetic. "You seem worried about your brother."

She chewed her lower lip and nodded.

"Let's go to my office."

In her upstairs office now, she plunked down behind a desk littered with books and papers without offering them a seat. Brody and Brax shrugged and slouched into two faded leather chairs across from her. With a knowing look, she leaned forward. "Since you're both Yanks, that rules out the police. So who the blazes are you?"

Before Brody could answer, a sharp knock came from the door. Her brow creasing with annoyance, she rose and went to the door.

Brody's gaze followed her. His wide frame filling the doorway, Nigel Cummings nodded politely and proffered his card and flashed his credential case.

Blair read the card and gave a long sigh. "Spooks from MI-6 and rude American agents … what next?" She stepped aside and the fat man waddled past her.

Cummings looked around the small office and noticed there wasn't a seat. He cleared his throat and glared at Brax, who reluctantly stood and moved behind the chair.

The fat man slowly eased into the narrow chair and squirmed, trying to force his larded ass into a comfortable position. Brody hoped the chair would give out from the weight.

"This is about Dominic, isn't it?" Blair said, her eyes beginning to glisten. As she pulled herself back from the edge of panic, suddenly her womanly persona became little-girl fragile.

"If you would be so kind as to let me proceed, dear boy," Cummings said sarcastically, his eyes mockingly seeking Brody's approval.

Brody shrugged. "Be my guest."

"I'm afraid I have some rather troublesome news, Ms. Kelly. We found your brother's limousine in an abandoned lot this morning."

Blair's lower lip trembled slightly.

"There was a body in the trunk," Cummings added coldly.

Blair started to shake.

"There, there now, Ms. Kelly. It wasn't your brother's. It was another priest, a Father Benjamin, also attached to the Vatican nuncio."

What a flaming asshole, Brody thought as his heart began to ache for the woman, but then he saw the look of relief wash over her face.

Blair stiffened. "I don't need your condescending sympathy. How's my brother mixed up with the likes of you…"—she turned and glared at Brody—"and this American twit?"

Brody thought the fire in her eyes made her just that much more attractive.

"Father Kelly has been working with us," Cummings answered dryly. He went on to explain the trap that had been laid out for Gant, omitting the bulk of the facts surrounding Gant's present activities and focusing on his reasons for a keen interest in the Voynich manuscript.

He followed with a thumbnail sketch of Brody's and Lt. Braxton's role in the charade, including their interest in al-Dajjal.

Brody studied her, the way her intelligent eyes flashed understanding. He studied her freckled nose, the way she wrinkled it like some nervous tic now and then. When Cummings mentioned al-Dajjal, her eyes grew big with recognition, and Devlin detected an increase in her heart rate, indicated by the throbbing of the carotid artery in her lovely neck. But he also detected that she may be concealing something else, as though there were more than the understandable concern for her brother's safety tearing at her heart as she listened.

Cummings coughed into a monogrammed silk hankie and blew his bulbous nose. "I think that about covers it. Which leaves us with one burning question..."

Blair's eyes met the fat man's.

"Will you act in your brother's absence? Become our operative, and dangle the bait? You would make a lovely spy, dear girl."

Blair studied her hands for a moment, her gaze panning to the photo of her brother on her desktop. "I was making notes for the lecture, anyway." She swept her hand over the mess of papers strewn across her desk.

She skewered the fat man with her eyes. "I have some conditions."

Brody smiled to himself. *Thatta girl.*

Cummings sighed. "Very well, dear girl, but you have to—"

"NO buts! I want in all the way. I want to see this through to the end. I'm not going to sit back on the sidelines and trust that you will make my brother's safety your primary concern."

Brody cut in. "Welcome aboard, then. We'll do everything in our power to get your brother back safe and sound."

Her face finally softened, but quickly went hard as if she'd caught herself lowering her guard. "You're bloody damned right you will, because I'll be right beside your rude arse every step of the way."

Blair spun on Cummings again. "There's just one problem."

Cummings's eyebrows tweaked. "Oh, how so?"

"I don't think Dominic actually has the missing pages or the key to the Voynich riddle."

"That's unfortunate," the fat man said, his eyes twinkling slightly, "but not insurmountable."

A stoop-shouldered old man with a withered face poked his head in the door. "Begging your pardon, Doctor Kelly, but it is time for the lecture."

As they rode down the lift together, Blair was silent, deep in thought. She fought back the urge to scream. Her mind raced with images of her brother and Noor, who were probably somehow in the hands of that madman, al-Dajjal.

She had decided to keep them in the dark concerning Noor for now. She took a cleansing breath and stole a quick side-glance at Devlin. He winked and gave her a reassuring smile.

His light blue eyes were kind, she decided. They held no hint of deceit or duplicity. He was tall, over six feet, and had a strong chin. For a middle-aged man, he was fit. His healthy good looks and thick dark hair made him easy on the eyes, all right. Maybe she *could* trust him.

As for the fat man from MI-6, she didn't trust him as far as she could spit.

CHAPTER 12

Noor woke with a start. A loud clinking noise scared her. She scanned the tiny room. The walls were painted in bright blues and pinks, but there were no windows. Instead, one whole wall was mirrored.

She studied her reflection. Noticed her clothes.

She was wearing pajamas, dotted with dogs.

She crinkled her nose. *Must be a boy's.*

She raised her arm and the sleeve drooped limply over her tiny wrist. *And they're way too big for me.*

Another loud clank rang from somewhere outside the room. She thought it had kind of an echolike sound. It was spooky.

She swung her legs off the twin bed and padded to the big door. There was no knob. Beyond her reach, she spotted a tiny narrow slot in the middle of the door.

She felt the door panel; it was cold to the touch like metal.

Then she began to remember, although she was groggy and her head felt kind of like it was stuffed with cotton. The idea made her laugh to herself. Then she remembered Mr. Muffins, the pink teddy bear. In a panic, she looked everywhere.

Beneath the edge of the bed frame, one tiny fluffy pink ear peeked out. She dropped to her knees, snatched the bear, clutched it to her chest.

A tear began to trickle down her cheek as she remembered Father Dominic's warm smile and those mean men. And that poopy, creepy woman with the snow-blonde hair. The creepy lady reminded her of al-Dajjal. She had those same snake eyes and nasty laugh like Captain Hook in the Peter Pan story. *The book!* She dove under the bed and saw it just out of reach. She strained to reach for it and finally her fingertips found the cover. She pulled it toward her.

She stood and looked around again.

With a sharp metallic click, the slot in the door slid open.

A pair of dark eyes peered in at her. Then that same noisy clang and the door suddenly swung open.

A shadowy, squat figure filled the doorway, backlit by harsh fluorescent lighting that spilled from beyond the door.

CHAPTER 13

Dr. Blair Morgan Kelly absently smoothed her skirt as she stood at the podium before the group of students, historians, press, and heavy-hitter museum contributors. She tapped the microphone, leaning forward as she nervously cleared her throat. Behind her, a large, LED flatscreen displayed the image of various ancient codices, and a woodcut of an alchemist hard at work in his laboratory, surrounded by golden glyphs of magickal symbols. The title of the exhibit loomed in large letters:

Magick and Alchemy.

"The Voynich manuscript, or the *sweet enigma*, as some have called it…"—an image of the codex appeared as Dr. Kelly spoke—"… is shrouded in a tale of mystery.

"A tale of sorcerers and Alchemy, of angels and necromancy."

She paused for effect.

"A tale of spies. A tale of wife swapping, and the quest for eternal youth.

"The manuscript is a hundred and four vellum leaves, about six by nine inches, written in an unknown secret script. The ragged edges of missing pages, how many no one knows, can be seen upon close inspection.

"It is liberally illustrated with about four hundred mysterious drawings—plants, zodiacal diagrams, what have been called 'cosmological' diagrams—and is richly colored in blue, green, and red. There are diagrams of *naked* women, romping on what seems to be an intricate network of bathtubs and water slides." Blair felt the blood rising to her face.

"The Voynich was a curiosity for a while until a man named Newbold claimed he had deciphered it and pronounced that it was the work of Roger Bacon, the thirteenth-century alchemist and Franciscan monk. No one could verify Newbold's results, and he died, not from some King Tut like curse, but from shame and ridicule. He wouldn't be the first or last to seemingly become a victim of the Voynich curse. Many who have studied it closely have become mad with the obsessive belief that they have found whatever preconceived notion possessed them. The Voynich, some say, is like a funhouse mirror, which reflects darkly what lies within the onlooker's deepest thoughts, his soul."

She paused and looked toward the back of the room, her eyes widening slightly.

Brody Devlin turned and saw them entering. It was Heinrich von Gant and his niece, a tall woman who slinked like a jungle cat as she moved. They were surrounded by a phalanx of thick-necked men. *Bodyguards*, Brody reasoned, judging by their steroid-pumped physiques that bulged from beneath their tight-fitting dark suits.

Brody was startled by Gant's appearance.

The man was tall, even taller than himself. His body looked thin and seemed board-stiff, inflexible. But when the museum staffer led them to their seats, Brody realized he'd been too hasty in his judgment. Gant strode briskly with a controlled grace. The movement would have gone unnoticed by a layman, but Brody was a pro. It betrayed a hidden suppleness and muscle tone.

When they filed into their seats, Gant's gaze fell on Brody, and he could feel himself being scrutinized with cold efficiency and cunning.

He returned the stare and a sudden icy chill streaked through his veins. Inexplicably, Brody felt like he was being tugged and pulled by some unseen force into the unforgiving jaws of a bear trap; this strange man before him could seemingly read Brody's thoughts, smell his fear.

The visual umbilical was severed when Gant took his seat and Brody turned back to the podium. Brody shivered, suddenly chilled to the bone marrow.

Blair cleared her throat.

"The 'VMS,' as we abbreviate it, was found in a Jesuit monastery … in nineteen twelve by a rare book dealer, Wilfred Voynich. Wilfred was a man of mystery and a bit of a rogue. He was a Polish emigrant who had forged passports for the Polish Revolutionary party and was imprisoned in Warsaw and then—Siberia for two years in a tiny cell.

Somehow he escaped and found his way to the UK. Although penniless in 1896, he suddenly acquired substantial wealth, enough to open his antiquarian bookshop in London. Some say that Wilfred, along with his friend Sidney Reilly, was secretly an agent for Britain's Special Branch. We know that the Russian Secret Police had Wilfred under surveillance for years. Adding to the mystery, Wilfred never actually divulged where he had found the VMS. In a letter to Wilfred's secretary written by his wife Ethel, that was only opened after her death, she finally revealed that the VMS was part of collection he'd found in the Villa Mondragone, a former Jesuit College in Italy. Later, his wife—as if she wanted to be rid of it—donated it to Yale University, where it is now MS four-oh-eight, which the Beinecke Rare Book Library has been gracious enough to loan us for our exhibition.

"The claimed authors include God, Roger Bacon, Anthony Askham, the Cathars, the Illuminati … the topics: spiral nebulae, contraceptives, suicide, capsicum, sunflowers and other botanical novelties from the New World, which presents a problem with the standard dating of the VMS. Sunflowers weren't brought back to Europe from the Americas until many years afterward."

A tottering old professor with a Vandyke beard asked, "Who do you think actually wrote it … and do you think it is really a book on Alchemy?"

Blair smiled knowingly, letting her gaze briefly drift to Gant, whose face returned a grim smile.

"I think it is an alchemical text, but probably not truly the work of Roger Bacon," Blair said. "One theory is that it's likely the same book that appeared in Prague in sixteen-oh-eight. Rudolph the Second was obsessed with the occult and converted his whole castle into an alchemical laboratory, inviting alchemists from far and wide to transmute lead into gold. He bought the VMS from a pair of English sorcerers, Doctor John Dee and Edward Kelly.

"But Dee was also a man of letters and science, an English Euclidian mathematician who served at the pleasure of Elizabeth I as her court astrologer and fell under her protection."

A fresh-faced university student in the back row raised his hand. "Wasn't Doctor John Dee also accused of practicing the black arts?"

"Yes, that's where things get really interesting. Dee, although gifted, possessed no psychic ability, so he searched for a medium. Well, he found one. Edward Kelly, a criminal and a rogue who had his ears clipped for counterfeiting. Kelly claimed to communicate with angels, and, by means of Alchemy, turn lead into gold. Kelly claimed he found an undecipherable manuscript in a tomb in Wales, along with a vial of red powder he called 'the elixir of life,' after which Kelly became an adept at scrying—an old word for fortune-telling—by using a crystal ball."

Blair pointed to a raised display case next to the podium.

"Ladies and gentlemen, the amber-hued crystal ball of John Dee, supposedly delivered to him by the Archangel Gabriel."

A quiet murmur swelled, then drifted away.

Brax whispered into Brody's ear, nodding, "Check out the ice princess." Brody's eyes fell on the entourage again.

Seated at Gant's side was a striking woman whom Brody recognized from the briefing photos as Margot Gant, the old geezer's niece.

She was encased in a white form-fitting Versace pantsuit, which accentuated her ripe figure. He had to admit she was stunning, but in a dangerous way. With her close-cropped white-blonde hair, her milky, porcelain face, and her cruel lips, she was a "bad girl" from head to toe. The deep red color of her lips reminded him of the imprint of freshly spilled blood on snow, a curving thin bloodstain which was as frigid as the ice around it.

As though she sensed his attention, her gaze slid toward Devlin. He gulped hard. She stared intently, then turned away with a snap of her long neck. Brody was chilled by her pale-blue eyes. Only her eyes were alien in the frozen landscape of her face; they were alive, almost feral. They pulsed with raw, unbridled sensuality.

Despite himself, Brody was spiked with pangs of desire. The sound of Blair Kelly's voice snapped him out of his daydream.

"While in a deep trance, Edward Kelly would gaze into the crystal ball as Dee transcribed what was supposedly an angelic language called Enochian, which the Rosicrucians and ceremonial magickians still use in their rituals today. That's where the wife swapping gambit entered the picture. Kelly told Dee that the angelic hosts commanded that he and Dee share everything, even their wives. And according to Dee's notes … they did. Dee's son, John, later recalled that his father and Kelly spent months with another scrying device, called the Shew-Stone, trying to decode a mysterious book written in hieroglyphics."

Blair moved to the case, lifted the lid and hoisted a black obsidian mirror. "This was an Aztec antiquity presented to Dee by parties unknown, most likely a fellow Rosicrucian occultist like Francis Bacon."

Blair carefully nestled the Shew-Stone back into its resting place in the display case and looked toward the back of the hall.

There, standing with his pasty plump hands resting on a walking stick, was the fat man. A smirk came to her lips as she pointed to the rear.

"Ladies and gentlemen, we are graced with Sir Nigel Cummings's presence, an *old* expert on codes and cryptology from the Foreign Office."

Heads turned.

Somewhat flustered, Cummings stared daggers at Blair. Then, realizing all eyes were on him, he smiled graciously and nodded.

Brody had to give the woman credit. She had bronze balls, that's for sure.

"Sir Nigel ... could you please elaborate on Dee's involvement with Her Majesty's Secret Service?" she asked.

Cummings straightened and squared his shoulders as he hobbled down the aisle and made his way to the front of the hall. "I'd be most happy to share what ..."—he paused as though catching himself—"what I've read. Perhaps you would all be interested in a spot of trivia."

Heads in the audience nodded eagerly.

"Some would say that John Dee was the founder of the British Secret Service, or MI-6 as the public knows it. During his travels throughout Europe, he was actually reporting clandestinely back to Queen Elizabeth I by means of a secret code, his angelic language, his so-called Enochian script.

"His signature was—007—which of course, Ian Fleming adopted as James Bond's number, his license to kill. The zeros represented his preying eyes, the elongated seven, the square root sign, and also a lucky number in numerology."

Someone asked, "So the magic was a ruse, then? He was really a spy and a code maker?"

"Well ... with these eccentric types, I would hazard that the truth lies somewhere in the middle. Robert Boyle, the famous biologist and esteemed member of our Royal Academy, stated in a lecture that he knew for certain Dee's angelic script was, *in truth*, an elaborate code. But then again, in the world of spies and Alchemy, one cannot take anything at face value. Boyle, like Sir Isaac Newton, also studied Alchemy, even allegedly traveled to Istanbul and obtained *the Book of Abraham* from a Turkish secret society. Some say it was an earlier version of the Voynich and held the secret of the Fountain of Youth."

Brody saw that Cummings's eyes purposely cut to Gant as he finished, as if to punctuate his sentence.

Blair moved to Cummings's side. "There is another myth that involves a more recent historical figure. None other than Doctor Carl Gustav Jung, one of the greatest minds of our century. Jung also became obsessed with Alchemy and wrote volumes.

"As you may know, Jung was a bit of a mystic who was deeply versed in the occult. Although most of his writings are available and have been published, part of his estate has gone missing.

"His magick diary, his *Red Book*, vanished. The rumor goes that he cracked the Voynich code while in a trance, and the key to deciphering it was written in his diary. Jung reportedly told his closest friends that the VMS holds the formula for the Philosopher's Stone, the secret to eternal life."

From the corner of her eye, Blair saw Gant's eyes narrow to slits as he leaned forward in his seat, his face glowing with the sheen of perspiration.

Time to bait the hook, she thought.

"Now it sounds terribly farfetched, but I have recently been contacted by an antiquities dealer from Istanbul, who claims to have Jung's missing diary."

Her face filled with a wide grin as she noticed that Gant's face had gone stony with concentration.

The elderly professor type sporting a beret and a goatee raised his liver-spotted hand and asked, "*Mon Dieu!* I'd certainly like a sip of that elixir of life myself, Doctor Kelly." In a thick French accent, he continued. "*À vrai dire*, I rather fancy myself becoming a young master Harry Potter, *oui*?" He gave a flirting wink. "Do you think M*ademoiselle* might oblige an old fool?"

Blair laughed. “Perhaps … but then again, if you should see me fifty years from now, ladies and gentlemen, and I still have my looks, and gravity has not taken hold, well … you can assume I opted not to share the recipe.”

Laughter blossomed throughout the hall.

“That concludes our lecture for today,” Blair added, nodding toward Cummings, who bowed demurely. “If you’d care to view the VMS and the Dee exhibit, please do. Cocktails and hors d'oeuvres will be served shortly. And for those who are members of the museum’s booster club, please remember to bring your checkbooks.”

CHAPTER 14

Noor almost giggled when the figure came out of the shadow into the brightness of the room. He wasn't scary now. He was a short dumpy-looking man with what Noor thought looked like rat's fur pasted onto his head. He had apple-red cheeks, a moon face, and wore a long white doctor's coat.

She tried to look away, but couldn't take her eyes off his funny looking hat.

"I think the young lady is being a bit rude to stare so, don't you? Or perhaps you've never seen a toupee," the little man explained. He slid it off his head, revealing his shiny pate. "You see, now I look like an egghead, *ja*? His tiny eyes twinkled with laughter.

"I didn't mean to be rude, sir—"

"Please, little Miss Noor," he said, slipping the rug back onto his head. "Call me … well, how about *Doktor* Humpty Dumpty?"

"Don't call me that! My name is Wendy," she stammered.

Noor thought he was making a joke, but she didn't get it, although Doctor Humpty seemed to be having a good laugh by the way he slapped his hands excitedly, and his face bloomed from his natural pinkish-white, to red.

"Say now, speaking of eggs, I bet little Miss … Wendy, if you prefer … would be wanting some breakfast, *ja*?"

Noor's tummy rumbled at the thought of food. She was starving.

"Could we have hot chocolate and eggs and bread and porridge and butter and ice-cream and …?"

"Certainly, but I'll turn my back while you slip into these clothes. Wouldn't be ladylike to dine in your pajamas." He handed her a blouse and slacks and shoes. He pointed to the tiny sink and cupboard in the corner. "Why don't you freshen up now, too."

Noor stared blankly, then sniffed her armpits. "Am I not fresh?"

Humpty Dumpty slapped his thigh. "Oh, dear Ms. Wendy, I mean wash your face good, don't forget to wash behind those ears and then brush those pearly whites and comb that silken hair, *ja*?"

"Okay, but turn around and don't peek, Doctor Humpty."

"Tell you what. I'll wait outside, and you just call me when you're ready, *ja*?"

Noor nodded and when the door closed tight, she ripped off her PJs and made for the sink. She looked at the soap, put it to her nose and instantly pitched it into the sink. Whew, it smelled like old cheese. She turned on the faucet, wet her fingertips, and dabbed behind her ears. Next she grabbed the toothpaste. She struggled to undo the cap, and when she did, she squeezed the tube so hard that a stream sprayed through the air and covered the mirror over the sink. She shrugged and dabbed her finger in the gooey mess and proceeded to brush her "pearly whites" with her index finger.

Finished, she looked at her reflection. With her haunting indigo-hued eyes, she studied her body. Put her hands on her hips and turned back and forth. She wondered if she'd ever grow big pillows on her chest like Blair had. She tweaked at her eyebrow like she'd seen Blair do at the hotel. She cried out in pain. *Forget about that,* she thought… *let them grow as big and bushy as a nanny goat's*. Next she grabbed the hairbrush and began to run its soft bristles through her silken hair, counting each stroke, again mimicking Blair.

Outside in the hall, Dr. Craven, AKA Humpty Dumpty, quickly slipped into the adjacent room. In the dimly lit room, he stood gazing at Noor through the Mirropane two-way glass, his eyes dancing as he lit a cigarette. "Such a fine specimen, don't you agree?"

The tall man at his side turned, looming over him now. His face was expressionless. He wore khaki pants, a button down Polo shirt and loafers, and his hair was now dark and wavy.

Al-Dajjal had made himself up as a "typical American" he'd told his henchmen once he'd cleared customs at a private airfield near Heathrow and had climbed into the Mercedes earlier that day.

Ernst had taken his rightful place riding right-front in the limo, the correct bodyguard position. Now that al-Dajjal had returned, he was no longer required to be Margot Gant's driver and lap dog. He was al-Dajjal's right-hand man, a highly skilled and ruthless assassin. Ernst was known as "*der Eisaxt*" for a reason. The ice axe was his *tool* of choice, as he called it.

Copied from the British SOE's Pickett-close-combat weapon issued to commandos in World War II, it was custom tooled from a strong but lightweight aluminum alloy. Instead of a thin dagger blade on one end of a tube, it had a curved, retractable saw-toothed blade, like a mountain climber's ice axe. The reverse end was weighted with a steel ball. When the blade was retracted, Ernst could strike his victim with the heavy ball, using it like a black jack, its wrist-strap looped around his forearm. When he pulled a ring on the side of the tube, a razor-sharp wire spooled out and the weapon became an effective garrote.

Al-Dajjal thought the nickname suited the man. He was certainly as dull-witted as sack of axes, but also served faithfully as a blunt instrument, usually defeating adversaries with his stamina and seemingly limitless threshold for pain. He would sit in a bar, pick out someone he didn't like because of the way the man spoke or walked or failed to make eye contact with him. With his one good eye, that is. The other had been gouged out in a bar fight, replaced with a yellowish glass eye that made him seem cross-eyed, since the glassy orb had a slight inward cant.

One night, a well-built weightlifter type had made the mistake of staring *der Eisaxt* down instead of looking away, which was equally an affront to the man. They'd gotten into a shouting match, and the weight-lifter heaved *der Eisaxt* through a plate glass window and out onto the sidewalk. Not satisfied, the man foolishly went to get a second lick at *der Eisaxt*. As *der Eisaxt* gained his feet, the man bludgeoned him with a fire extinguisher he'd ripped from the bar's wall.

Steely eyed and showing no reaction, *der Eisaxt* wiped the blood from his good eye and shattered nose, and flicked his forearm. His "tool" flashed from beneath his sleeve, filling his hand. With a sharp flick of his wrist, the axe blade shot from the tube and locked into place, its pointed teeth gleaming. His good eye sparked and burned with a quiet rage; the other stared dully like a marble. He hurled himself across the sidewalk and slammed the attacker to the pavement.

While straddling the man, *der Eisaxt* proceeded to viciously rake the weightlifter's face with the axe's jagged claw, again and again, blood splattering *der Eisaxt's* chest and filming his face. Finally, for the *coup de grace*, he hoisted his tool high into the air and arced downward in a powerful blur of motion. He buried it deep into the weightlifter's forehead. Then he ripped it free, leaving a gaping crater as his signature.

Al-Dajjal knew that *der Eisaxt* had only one passion in life. He didn't particularly care for women, usually satisfying his needs with a cheap streetwalker who, for a little extra money or drugs, would allow for his dark tastes, which leaned toward domination; he didn't particularly care for food or drink, usually settling for fast-food, as if eating was a tiresome necessity, and he drank cheap liquor only if available. What *der Eisaxt* needed, the only thing he absolutely required of life—was to maim, torture, and kill. And as long as al-Dajjal sated his bloodlust on a regular basis, the man was as loyal and faithful as a wolfhound.

Looking down at the baby-faced doctor now, al-Dajjal said, "Let her have her breakfast with the other children now. Then begin the testing and examinations this afternoon."

Doctor Craven tore his gaze away from the two-way looking glass and met al-Dajjal's icy stare, just as Noor had finished brushing her teeth and combing her hair. "Yes, the testing. If she has these unique abilities as you say, it's a sign that the *Sonnenkinder* have indeed arrived, *ja*?" His beady eyes glistened.

In a flash, al-Dajjal's hand lashed out and grabbed the doctor by his ear, twisting hard and jerking it higher and higher. "*Verdamnt, du fette schwienhund!* Do you have the audacity to question what I have reported, *Herr Doktor*?"

The blood drained from the doctor's rosy cheeks as he grimaced in agony and rose on his tiptoes. "Certainly not, I just meant—"

Grunting his answer, al-Dajjal released his hold. The doctor made for the door on weak legs, rubbing his ear as he went.

Turning, al-Dajjal called to the brooding hulk standing behind him. "*Der Eisaxt,* fetch the priest. Take him to the interrogation room."

Ernst nodded obediently. "*Ja voll*, immediately, *mien Herr*."

As Ernst headed for the door, al-Dajjal added, “And bring your tools!”

CHAPTER 15

Chewie tugged at his necktie and unbuttoned the collar of his shirt. He never wore ties, but the limo driver's uniform was part of his disguise. To add insult to injury, he had to tuck his long ponytail beneath his driver's cap.

Outside, in the museum's VIP parking area, he made small talk with the other drivers and had just handed Gant's driver, Rolf, a steaming mug of coffee from his thermos. Knowing how limo drivers love to shoot the breeze while spending countless hours waiting for their boss to return, Chewie found striking up a brief friendship with Gant's driver was a snap. All he had to do was bitch about the long hours and how they never fed him or even sent out a cup of coffee. Chewie cinched the deal by sharing a flask of Schnapps with Rolf.

Chewie suggested they take a stroll and girl watch, explaining that a friend on the museum's staff would ring his cell when the guests began to leave. Rolf was reluctant, but after two more hits of Schnapps he agreed.

From his post in another limo, Scout Thompson could overhear their conversation, since Chewie was wired. Once he saw the coast was clear, Scout, also dressed as a driver, casually sauntered to Gant's limo. He clicked a state-of-the-art universal remote he'd improved upon since designing it in his past life, the "youthful dalliance of a child prodigy," his attorney had called it when he was busted for boosting cars. The remote did its magic, disabling the limo's alarm and unlocking the doors. When the doors' lock posts sprang up, he eased open the driver's door and slid behind the wheel.

Within minutes, he'd planted the bugs and tagged the car with a GPS tracking device. He whispered into his lapel microphone, "She's wired for sound, big guy. You and Rolfie boy can head back now." Scout went back to his limo and booted up his laptop, checking for signal strength and levels.

Scout's voice poured into the tiny earpiece Chewie wore, completely concealed behind his long, thick hair. Chewie turned to Rolf. His face tightening, he grunted, "I've gotta pinch a loaf. Let's head back."

CHAPTER 16

Gant's lean frame towered over the other guests who stood in a knot around him at the cocktail reception. At his side was Margot, looking like she was desperately trying not to show that she was bored to tears.

Blair excused herself from a sagging fleshpot of an old dowager and her thirtysomething gigolo escort and threaded her way across the room to Gant.

When Blair got nearer, she saw that Gant's eyes were plum-dark. The tall man's face was long and angular, his high cheekbones and hollowed cheeks giving it a cadaverous appearance. His nose was strong with a firm bridge. His face was taut, had few wrinkles. He seemed younger than his years and exuded a strength that belied his gaunt frame. But when her eyes tracked to his neck, she saw the ravages of age. It was so cranelike it couldn't be hidden by his collar and tie. The sight of that hollowed and creased sagging flesh made Blair twinge with revulsion.

He turned to greet her, immediately breaking off a conversation with another guest. "Why, *Doktor* Kelly, what an excellent lecture." She extended her hand, and Gant bowed elegantly and kissed the back of her hand, his scabrous lips like sandpaper against her skin.

"Although I must confess we are all a bit puzzled."

"How's that, sir?"

"We had expected your brother to give the presentation. I must admit, however, that I suspect you are much easier on the eyes." He gave the poison-wet grin of a serpent.

Blair forced a smile. "He's been unavoidably detained." She studied Gant's face, looking for a reaction, and finding none, went on. "Were you aware of the Jung diary?"

Shaking his head emphatically, he leaned in as though speaking in confidence. "Ah, the lady does not mince words. As you know, I have an abiding passion for antiquities and would be most interested to see it." He added the last words almost as an afterthought, feigning disinterest, Blair reasoned, but she saw through the ruse.

From the corner of her eye, Blair noticed Margot Gant, whose aloof expression turned to icy contempt as her uncle gave Blair his undivided attention. Blair figured she didn't appreciate the snub, since Gant hadn't bothered to make the proper introductions.

Even when Blair's gaze slid back to Gant and she maneuvered herself with her back to Margot, Blair felt the ice princess's arctic stare prickling the hairs on the nape of her neck.

Blair flirted shamelessly, laying it on thick, reaching out absently and touching Gant's forearm now and then as they spoke. "Then I guess you would be interested in seeing some of the photocopies I have of the diary the Istanbul dealer sent me?" She let her words hang out there, taunting him.

Gant's eyes saucered. "You have copies?" His voice was laced with nervous tension now, belying his earlier pretense at only a passing interest in the diary.

Blair patted the breast pocket of her suit jacket. "I keep them close to my heart," she said with a wink.

A man who introduced himself as a military attaché interrupted their conversation. To his left stood Brody Devlin and Brax. Gant sighed heavily, and turned to the attaché. "General Powers, how like you to come to an old man's rescue when you sense he is succumbing to the wiles and charms of a beautiful young lady."

Blair blushed appropriately, trying not to make eye contact with Brody and Brax because she wasn't sure she could keep a straight face if she did.

The attaché beamed and eyed Blair. Then he introduced Brody and Brax as interested parties who represented a major arms buyer.

"Excuse me, gentlemen, but I have to powder my nose," Blair said, turning.

"*Doktor* Kelly, please rejoin us, wont you?" Gant said, his silken tone almost a request, masking the demanding quality of his stare.

Gant proffered his hand to Brody, who shook and returned the hardness of Gant's vise-grip. When Brody loosened his hold, the man tightened his, held fast, squeezing with bone-crunching pressure. *Okay, if you wanna play games, old man.* Brody clamped down with all his strength, his eyes locked on Gant's now, whose dark eyes flickered with amusement.

For those few seconds, there were no secrets between them. Gant appeared to see right through him and ridiculed what he saw. Then Brody remembered it was Gant who wore the real mask. Looking intently, Brody had to admit the prosthetics and makeup were barely detectable to an untrained eye.

All at once, Gant released his hold and Brody wondered if he hadn't imagined the whole thing.

The attaché said, "Mr. Devlin represents clients who are looking for specialty UAV weapons, Mr. Gant."

Gant replied in a mocking tone. "Could we perhaps establish from the get go who these clients are, Mr. Devlin."

"I'll have to take the Fifth on that, sir," Brody said, and deferred to Brax.

"As legal counsel for the clients involved," Brax explained, "they have asked me not to divulge their identities until we are sure you can meet our needs. However, they asked me to furnish you with these letters of credit."

Gant took the folio containing the letters from Brax and handed them to the no-neck bodyguard without looking at them and waving dismissively. "I'm sure everything is in order, Mr. Braxton. I have some … new toys as I call them in my war chest." He gave a brittle laugh. Then his eyes zeroed in on Brody again. "But you are also aware of Geno-Dyne's genetic research facilities, I take it."

Brody nodded.

"Would your mysterious clients also be interested in genetic research, perhaps?" he added, raising his brows, saying the words slowly and deliberately as though taunting Brody again.

"Most certainly. Are you developing some super-soldier out there, or maybe a master race army?" Brody threw back the challenge and stood in silence as Gant's eyes narrowed, then widened suddenly.

"A bit of American humor, eh? Why don't you come out to the proving grounds tomorrow afternoon for a little demonstration?"

Blair sidled up next to Brody. "Excuse me. Am I interrupting something, Mr. Gant?" She gave her best teasing smile.

"Hardly, my dear lady. Just discussing business. But I have a splendid idea. Why don't you and Mr. Devlin and company all serve as my guests tomorrow afternoon. I am having a party of sorts for the wards under my care."

Looking puzzled, Blair asked, "Wards, Mr. Gant?"

Margot slinked into the group, drawing all eyes to her as she moved. Her haughty gaze was mesmerizing as she panned the men's faces, one by one. Blair noticed how the men, including Brody, were staring like love-struck schoolboys. To Blair, however, Margot had a stiff, lacquered appearance, like a doll with unblinking eyes from a horror movie. A doll that exuded all the warmth of a shrunken head.

"Ah, Margot. Gentlemen, allow me to present my lovely niece," the arms dealer said in a smug tone, as if mocking the men's obvious infatuation with the woman.

Margot's eyes cut to Blair. "My uncle is a very generous man. He has a school for foundlings at the estate. We call it *Eden*. Tomorrow is the school's fourth anniversary, so we are having a garden party for the little darlings."

The callous undercurrent in Margot's voice made Blair think of the witch in the Hansel and Gretel story. She pictured Gant's wards locked securely in cages suspended from the ceiling and a cackling Margot stuffing their little faces to fatten them up for the big bake-off, where she would set the whole gingerbread house on fire and roast them all alive for dinner. But it occurred to her that Margot had made a slip. She'd bet a bottle of Macallan single-malt Scotch that Eden was exactly where Noor was being held.

They nodded their acceptance of Gant's invitation.

"Excellent. Well, ladies and gentlemen, we must be off now." His eyes skewered Brody as he turned. "Have a most pleasant evening."

As he studied the retreating image of Gant's entourage leaving the hall, Brody leaned in and whispered in Blair's ear, "Penny for your thoughts?"

Blair cupped her mouth with one hand and blew out a sharp breath. Then lowering it, she turned and winked. "I don't know about you, Mr. Devlin, but this girl needs a couple of good stiff ones. What do you say?"

"Are you asking me out for a drink or trying to seduce me?" Brody teased.

She rolled her eyes. "Are you buying, Mr. Big-fat-expense account?"

"Just call me Sugardaddy Bigbucks, Little Orphan Annie," he said as he took her arm and made for the exit. Brax cleared his throat. "Oh, don't mind me. I'm going to check out the sights, mail some postcards, have a quiet dinner alone, do some crosswords."

Brody shot back over his shoulder, "Like hell you are, Lieutenant. And you're gonna stay clear of that girl in the information booth downstairs and chaperone Chewie and Scout. I want everyone clearheaded with their batteries fully charged for tomorrow, if you get my drift, lover-boy."

Brody paused and turned. "If you need me, ring my cell. Try *not* to need me!"

CHAPTER 17

They had hopped a red double-decker bus and transferred twice. Now on foot, they were a long way from the museum, cutting down narrow streets and switching back again. Brody didn't say anything, but he realized why Blair was backtracking. When they rounded a corner, Brody caught the fleeting image of two of Gant's dark-suited henchmen tailing them; one behind, who came to a dead stop and clumsily ducked into a storefront when they'd doubled back and were moving right toward him, the other goon was pacing them from across the busy street.

"Are we on a forced march, Doctor, or do you plan on taking five to put on the feedbag anytime soon? Is there a pub or something close by?"

"Call me Blair, Mr. Devlin."

"Okay, Blair. But please, it's just Brody. Hey, I'm thirsty and famished, how about it?"

"There's a pub right around the corner."

Casting his eyes around, he added, "You sure we aren't lost? Looks like the neighborhood's getting a little rough."

"Don't worry, braveheart. I'll protect you."

The sign read *Ten Bells*. Brody knew enough history to understand they'd wandered into Whitechapel, Jack the Ripper's old haunt.

They entered and were seated on hard, unforgiving wooden benches, drinking Scotch neat with a water chaser. Curious looks from the rough-looking patrons made Brody uncomfortable.

"I feel like we're on display at the zoo," Brody said, his voice low, his eyes busy.

"Not us, Brody," she said, downing another shot in one gulp and slamming the glass on the table. "It's just you in the monkey cage, luv."

"Come here often?" he added sarcastically.

"It's a tourist trap, actually, so no. But I blend in. You look like a typical mark." She nodded toward his gold Rolex and shiny loafers. "The ones who are eyeing us are trying to figure my con."

"Con?"

"Relax, braveheart. You're with me." She turned and winked at the brooding clique of men straddling the bar, as if they'd shared some private joke at Brody's expense.

"Oh, terrific. They're muggers and pickpockets."

"You wanted to eat."

"Sure, but I'd like to walk outta here with my wallet, my watch and my bridge work intact."

"Stop being such a whiny-Nelly."

The Shepherd's Pie came and Brody spooned a big slice and wolfed it down, knowing he needed food or she would drink him under the table.

Just then, a guy with eyes demented enough to make Jack the Ripper green with envy glared and pushed his heavy frame off the bar, ambling his tree-trunk sized body right toward them. He had a big beer gut that stretched the fabric of his shirt so taut that it threatened to turn the buttons into deadly shrapnel any second. But his arms and shoulders rippled with muscle. His knuckles were scarred and his hands were like sledgehammers.

He stood towering over the table now.

"I don't like yer looks, bloke. Er yea makin' a nuisance ov yerself? "

Blair cut in. "Everythin's fine here, y' big handsome lug of a man." She laughed with her green eyes, trying to deescalate the situation that was brewing.

It wasn't working.

"I don't much like that crooked grin on y' fat face, Yank!"

"My mother likes it," Brody said. "Why don't you let this stupid Yank buy you and your mates a couple pints, my friend?"

The big lug's hands fisted at his sides. Brody's offer wasn't working. He noticed the man's mates easing away from the bar, their flinty gaze boring into him as they moved slowly and deliberately closer.

Locking eyes on the man and holding his attention, Brody deftly scooped the large malt shaker from the table and tightly wrapped it into his handkerchief under the tabletop.

"I've got me a notion ta wipe that grin right offa y' ugly mug, I do." He nodded toward the door. "Why don't y' sling your hook, then. Before I snatch y' up by yer short and curlies!"

Reflexively, Brody's hand covered his crotch. But Brody Devlin was never one to resist the inevitable. "You know I'd really like to help ***you out***. Which way did you come in?"

Like he was hefting a small sack of taters, the big lug's meat hooks grabbed Brody by his collar and yanked him off the bench.

Brody twisted and spun out of his grasp, bringing the weighted handkerchief around in a swift arc that landed on the man's jutting chin with a sharp crack.

Blinking his eyes, the giant shook his head and grinned, flashing a picket fence of yellowed teeth.

Brody's jaw hinged in disbelief. *Hell! Where's Chewie when I need him?*

"Is that all y' got, m'laddo?" the big lug taunted as his sledge-hammer fist connected with an uppercut to Brody's jaw, sending him tumbling ass-over-teakettle, sprawled flat on his face.

Blair sprang to her feet, drove the heel of her shoe hard into the man's instep, then stabbed out with the fingertips of her wedged hand, sinking deep into the hollow of his throat.

The big lug choked, stumbled backward, gasping for breath.

Blair wheeled on the men, who by now stood like stumps, all of them shocked into drop-jawed silence. One must have found some courage and began to take a step toward her. She brought two fingers to her lips and gave a shrill whistle. Blair launched into a tirade. The words, uttered in some strange language Brody didn't understand, tattooed the air.

Sheepishly, two burly men helped Brody to his feet and unceremoniously dropped him into the pew as another plunked a pint of bitters onto the table in front of him. Slapping his back and raising a toast with a shot glass in his gnarly hand, he said, "Here's to our wives and girlfriends. May they never meet!"

Another smaller man strained beneath the bear's weight as he struggled to hobble-carry the ol' big lug back to the bar. He ordered two shots of whiskey, glancing around as he was downing the first one, before reluctantly planting the second in the lug's waiting meat hook.

Brody took a long pull from the mug.

Blair pointed to the foam mustache on his upper lip and laughed.

He frowned, wiped it with the back of his hand.

"What language were you speaking to those guys?" he asked, taking another slug of bitter ale and massaging his aching jaw. "Sounded close to Welsh, maybe Gaelic?"

"It's called the *Language of the Trees*, the tongue of the Druidic Bards and the old Celts, used by the artisans, the poets."

"Traveling troubadours?"

She nodded. "After the Roman invasion, the Druids were persecuted, almost wiped out. They survived as roaming minstrels, wise men or women who wandered freely, spreading the old ways through song and rhyme. I think you call them Travelers in the States. Some folks mistake us for gypsies, but they speak Romany." She blew a sharp breath, reached over, took a slug of his ale.

She'd worked up a sweat. She pulled the pins from her bun and shook out her hair, which cascaded thickly over her shoulders. She tucked her head forward, gathered her mane of red locks, and lifted it off the back of her neck, turning slightly.

Brody admired the graceful curve of her neck, and her finely sculpted, almost elfin ears. Peeking from beneath her hairline and winding down her neck where it vanished under the edge of her blouse's collar, Brody caught a glimpse of her tattoo. It was a stylized Celtic tree with three vertical lines descending below it, done in rich shades of red and green and blue.

Blair caught him staring and quickly allowed her hair to tumble back into place.

A buxom barmaid returned with fresh pints and hot food. Brody dug in.

He noticed Blair was brooding now. He put down his fork and leaned closer. "You haven't been completely truthful with me, have you?"

She looked away.

"When you spoke about Dee and Kelly swapping wives it implied that there was something more to Alchemy than two men playing with an old-fashioned chemistry set."

She nodded.

"If your brother really was dabbling with turning lead into gold, he couldn't do it by himself … he needed you. Something called the Chemical Wedding, right?"

Her face reddened. "It's complicated … but you're right. It takes two, a man and a woman. The most famous couple being Nicholas and Perenelle Flamel of Paris. In about 1382 they suddenly had untold wealth and established fourteen hospitals and numerous churches. Legend has it that they never died."

"Old wives' tales."

"Well, in 1761 they were seen attending the opera in Paris."

Brody rolled his eyes. "That would make them some four hundred years old."

"Exactly." Blair gave a knowing smile that faded quickly. "I haven't told you everything."

Brody nodded. "It's got something to do with the tattoo?"

She shrugged. "But I'm not trying to play games or conceal anything purposefully. I … well, I was afraid you might think less of me. Dominic and I are not like you, we're not what you'd call your average Irish-Welsh family. Sometimes I feel cursed." She looked away again; a slight tremor laced her voice as she went on. "The tattoo. I've had it since I was a little girl. What you saw was just the tip of the iceberg. It forms on the nape of my neck. But then it crawls over my shoulder blades, and snakes down my spine, all the way to the small of my back."

"A Celtic knot of some sort?"

"More like an alchemical symbol of sorts. Specifically, it's the sign of the Tree of Life and below it is the sigil of the Awen, which means the essence. It's the symbol of my bloodline. The Daughters of Awen. You see, the word Druid is a compound of the old words for—"

"The oak and door and wise," he offered.

She flashed an approving smile. "To the Druids, trees were gods or doorways to the otherworld. Like in Alchemy, the Tree of Life signifies, as is above, so is below. The branches or cosmos above, connect downward to the what's below, the roots. Our tongue, Ogham, is named for Ogmos, the Celtic god of writing and knowledge. So we have another parallel with Alchemy, whose father was Hermes or Thoth, the Egyptian god of writing and magick. Our tongue is what the linguists call an inner language that evolved from the secret runic language of the roving minstrels, Druid priests, and magi. It's probably Bronze Age."

Brody was all ears, hanging on every word.

"When our parents were killed in a motor crash, the Awen took us in, protected us."

"So, Father Kelly isn't just a Roman Catholic priest. He's some sort of a high priest with the Awen, too?" he asked.

She gave an indulgent smile. "No. Our ancestors were the Tuatha De Danaan, a Goddess worshiping tribe of ancient Gaels. They, like the Awen, were matriarchal."

"That makes you the High Priestess and—"

"Guardian of the doorway. As was my mother."

Brody sighed heavily and met her eyes. "Then you're in real danger, Ms. Kelly. Gant is a raving lunatic. If he's aware of this, then it's you he's after, not your brother."

"Perhaps … but more likely right now he wants the photocopies of Jung's diary that I told him I was carrying for safekeeping."

Brody stared incredulously. "You told him you had copies? And on your person?"

She laughed. "Don't be such a pigheaded worry-wart. There are no copies. There is no diary. I just made it up."

"It's no joking matter, Blair. Both your brother and al-Dajjal were recently in Istanbul, searching for antiquities."

"I didn't know that Nazi bastard was in Turkey."

"Maybe your brother beat him to the punch. Maybe Dominic

actually found it." He paused, his face dead serious. "Don't you realize you've painted a bull's-eye on your forehead?"

She stiffened. "Well … that was the idea, wasn't it?"

Brody rolled his eyes and glared. "In a word, NO!"

Blair studied her hands, then looked up, swallowed visibly. "There's more I haven't told you, Mr. Devlin."

His eyes softened. "I'm listening. But please, it's Brody."

"There's a young girl, Noor. She's a very precious little girl, with special abilities. Her father was an Irishman and her mother Syrian. They were missionaries."

"Was?" Brody probed.

She nodded, her voice hitching. "Yes … was. Al-Dajjal killed them both, right in front of her. I rescued her from his clutches in Syria. She was with my brother when he was kidnapped. I'm sure of it. You have to help me get her back." Her eyes pleaded now.

"Why didn't you tell me?" Then it hit him. "Did you say—Syria?"

"I didn't know if I could trust you. I was on a dig when…" Her voice trailed off as her gaze traveled over Brody's shoulder.

"What's wrong?"

Brody began to turn around, following her gaze.

"Don't turn around. Gant's goons just walked in."

"What are they doing?"

She hunched down in her bench. "They're squinting, trying to adjust for the dim light in here, scanning the pub. But they're definitely looking for us. We've got to make tracks."

"Head for the back door, I'll distract them," he said, rising and pitching a few notes onto the table.

Blair gripped his wrist, peeled off a few more notes, tossing them with the rest of the money.

"Big tipper, eh?" Brody said with a smirk.

"No, knuckle-head. It'll cover the breakage." She tugged at his arm, and they made their way to the bar. She whispered a few words of that strange language into the big lug's ear, who nodded. Then they threaded their way through the pub, keeping low, making for the back door.

A tall goon eyeballed them.

"Halt!" he shouted across the crowed pub and rushed toward them.

As the henchman elbowed his way past the bar, the big lug turned and sucker punched the goon hard. The man went flying backward onto a table, dowsing a brawny man and his girlfriend in ale, and rolled off onto the floor. The wide-shouldered man shot to his feet, grabbed the offending thug by the lapels, hoisted him from the floor. With a mighty heave, the man was hurled back toward the bar, where a flurry of pounding fists pummeled him to his knees.

As a second attacker ran past the bar, a wiry mutt-faced little guy in a plaid green vest and cap shot out his arm and clothes-lined the goon right across his throat. The attacker's feet flew out from under him as he landed flat on his back, the wind knocked from his lungs.

As they made their way through the back stockroom, Brody grinned at the familiar sounds of a bar fight.

The thwack of hard fists against soft flesh…

…was layered over shouting and cajoling and the crash of broken glass.

Brody struggled with the back door. "It's locked. Stand back." He took a few steps back for a running start and charged, throwing his shoulder into the door. It didn't budge.

"Men," she said, scowling. She reached on tiptoe, her fingers running along the top of the door frame.

He briefly closed his eyes as he massaged his sore shoulder. "I suppose you'll just wave your magic wand and …"

He looked up. With a click of the lock, the door swung open.

"Ever heard of a key, double-oh-seven?"

They tumbled into the alley, eyes searching, blinking hard in the harsh daylight.

They turned right and headed for the mouth of the alley and the street. Three more henchmen walked into view, blocking their path.

Brody's eyes cut in the other direction. It was a dead end, just a high, soot-grimed brick wall.

The three killers walked toward them, with slow and deliberate steps. Reaching into their suit jackets, they pulled semi-auto pistols and fitted them with sound suppressers as they moved.

"Great! Now what, Sherlock?" Blair fumed, eyeing the approaching killers.

Grabbing her wrist, Brody guided her to a fence that stretched along one side of the back of the alley. He scrambled onto a Dumpster and was greeted by a huge tomcat, who hissed sharply and bared its fangs before scampering away. He pulled Blair onto the Dumpster beside him. She turned to see the men sprinting now, their handguns outstretched and taking aim.

Brody yanked her around. “Pardon my hands, Ms. High Priestess,” he said as he planted them under her butt and grunted as he boosted her over the top of the fence.

A muffled gunshot.

Brody felt the hot lead whiz past his right ear and another round sparked off the Dumpster at his feet. He leapt and pulled himself over.

They dropped to the muddy ground on the other side.

Scanning the area, Brody saw it was a salvage yard, an automobile boneyard.

Towering before them was row after row of skeletons, a virtual labyrinth; walls composed of the rusted hulks of automobiles lay in every direction. Up ahead, in the distance, loomed a chain-link fence dotted with chrome hub-caps that winked in the sun.

From his right, Brody heard the unmistakable growl of snarling dogs, racing closer by the second. “Jeez, I hate attack dogs!”

“Run!” he shouted, dragging Blair behind him.

They ran full out, weaving around piles of bumpers, hurtling over old engine blocks.

“Over there!” Brody yelled, pointing to a bulldozer parked about twenty feet away.

From behind, the distant and excited voices of the killers shouted for them to stop.

Closer yet were the low, throaty growls and panting of Dobermans and Rottweilers.

Brody turned just in time to see the lead dog lunge and leap, arcing high—right for Blair. Ripping his.45 APC Beretta Cougar 8045 from his shoulder-rig, he shoved Blair out of the dog’s path. As the dog sailed past, Brody squeezed off two quick rounds. The Doberman’s whimpering squeal signaled that Brody had been dead on target.

Standing now, Blair stared at the dead dog lying at her feet.

The crack of gunfire drew her attention. A second four-legged beast bore down on her. When the steel-jacketed .45 rounds from Brody's Beretta pummeled the charging dog's broad chest, its front paws dug into the ground, and it tumbled head over heels in a cloud of dust.

She stood, too stunned to move, as the two-legged attackers rounded a wall of wreckage.

Brody shoved her toward the bulldozer. They dove behind the hulking blade.

"Keep your head down!" he shouted to Blair, who was peeking over the top of the blade.

She shot back, "Oh, they wouldn't dare start some Wild West gunfight in the heart of London."

"Ya think not, huh?" he said.

Sound suppressed gunfire spat as rounds beat a deafening staccato across the face of the blade.

"Welcome to the OK Corral, sister!" he shouted as he sneak-peeked over the top and returned fire.

More rounds pounded the steel, causing Brody's ears to ring now.

"So what's your plan, hotshot?" she said, her eyes burning with anger.

Waiting for the salvo to halt, he popped off another two rounds, resumed cover. He fumbled under his pants leg and pulled a SIG-P250, equipped with a laser sight, from his ankle holster. As he jacked a round into the chamber, thumbed on the laser, and tossed it to Blair, he said, "Here you go, Annie Oakley, just aim the red dot on your target and squeeze. You've got fifteen rounds, so have at it."

Without answering, she went to her hands and knees, her butt brushing his cheek as she swung around. Then she crept on her elbows to the edge of the blade.

She positioned herself and looked at Devlin. "You just draw their fire, hotshot! I'll do the rest," she ordered, her green eyes glaring daggers.

He cocked his head and shook it. Moving to the opposite end of the blade, he shrugged out of his blazer, draped the coat over a length of pipe, and waved it over the top of the blade.

Instantly, rounds tore into the fine woolen fabric, shredding it.

The volley stopped.

Blair rose, clenching the SIG in a double-handed grip, sighting the laser's red dot on one of the two killers who'd both jumped out from behind cover to kill Brody's blazer. She pumped a double-tap hit; the first slug cratered her target's forehead, the second, his chest, directly center of mass.

The second assailant just stood there, pistol in hand, frozen in shock and disbelief. Before he could react, Blair sent another high-velocity, hollow-point slug screaming his way. By then, it was too late to think. A puff of pink haloed his head, glistening in the harsh daylight. It hung there for a second, even as his corpse toppled to the ground. The .40SW rounds carried a wallop.

She ducked down, squirmed around, her back pressed against the blade. Holding the SIG muzzle-up, she sucked in deep, ragged breaths. Catching her breath, she smiled and managed, "Two down, one to go."

Brody stared in silence, his jaw dropped wide.

From behind, they heard it; an ugly snarl.

Brody spun.

A goon was directly behind them, leveling his pistol point-blank on Brody's head. *The SOB outflanked us from behind,* Brody figured.

But the snarl wasn't from the gunman. Brody's gaze ticked higher. About twenty-some feet above the killer, perched on the rusted hood of an old coupe that was tottering precariously off the edge of a stack of car husks, was a giant Rottweiler. Its eyes flashed hellfire; its lips were skinned back over its gleaming snarl of teeth. Ropes of drool hung from its incisors.

As the beast restlessly padded to and fro on the rocking wreckage, tortured sheet metal screeched.

Brody gave his best wise-ass smile. "I wouldn't stand there if I were you," he told the henchmen.

"Shut up and toss your weapons, now!" the goon said, training his pistol on Blair.

Brody shrugged and made a taunting kissing sound.

As a puzzled look washed over the killer's face, the Rottweiler's eyes sparked. He leapt. The full weight of the meaty beast hit the killer square in the back, driving him to the ground and reflexively firing off a shot. A wild round zinged past Brody's cheek, sparking off the blade near his ear.

The rusted car creaked and toppled, crashing downward onto the dog and killer below. The killer's scream came from behind a cloud of dust that roiled upward from the impact of the two and a half tons of sheet metal that became the killer's tombstone.

They rose and dusted themselves off.

The dust filled Blair's nostrils. She couldn't sneeze normally, but instead let out a muffled, demure squeak.

Brody struggled not to laugh, but he couldn't help himself.

"Laugh, will you, damn it?" But as she said it, a smile creased her face. "You could at least offer a girl your handkerchief."

He patted his pockets and shrugged. "Lost it back at the pub, remember?"

She scowled and stormed off.

After knitting their way through the scrap yard, they finally reached the front gate.

Klaxons wailed in the distance, drawing closer.

Blair proffered him the SIG pistol, butt first. He smiled and shook his head. "Keep it. You may need it."

Blair beamed and tucked the lightweight semi-auto into her coat pocket. Without warning, she suddenly grabbed him by his lapels, drew him roughly to her, and kissed him hard on the lips. Her mouth was warm and moist. Although her cheeks were smudged with dirt and her hair was a tangled rat's nest, her perfume filled his senses with the scent of rosebuds, mixed with sweat and fear.

Then she released him, tried to pull back.

But he held her tightly, gazing deeply into her eyes.

"Are you trying to seduce me, Mr. Devlin?" she asked, holding his gaze.

He stared, speechless, his mouth trying to form words that wouldn't come.

She sighed and shook her head. "There's always a moment, isn't there? And now the moment's gone." As his arms fell away, she turned and walked through the unlocked gate. Brody stood for a minute, studying her as she moved away. He knew he was falling for this complex woman, which made what he knew he had to do all the more difficult.

At the curb, he hailed a cab.

He opened the small black cab's rear door and stood.

"Hop in, Blair."

She shot him a bewildered look and stepped back. "I'm staying with you." Her tone was sharp and emphatic.

"No," Brody said, sheepishly shaking his head. "Here's where we part company."

"So what just happened back there … didn't mean a thing to you," she said, brushing the hair from her eyes and glaring at him. "You've got a girl in every port."

Brody swallowed hard. "It's because of what happened, because of what I felt, that your part in this is over. You're going to hustle back to your flat and bolt the door. I'll send someone to watch over you."

He motioned for her to get in.

She took another involuntary step back from the curb. "Don't flatter yourself, Mr. Devlin. That kiss was just an impulse. It didn't mean a bloody damned thing."

Brody stared for a moment, then climbed into the cab. "C'mon, I'll drop you at your apartment."

She wheeled around and marched off down the sidewalk.

A light sprinkle started to fall.

The cabbie said, "The meter's runnin', guv'ner."

Brody sighed, cursed himself under his breath, slammed the door.

As the cab pulled from the curb, the driver said, "'ad a bit of a row with the ol' ball and chain, did y'?"

Brody sat silently brooding. He felt like a heel but also knew that he was doing the right thing. From the start he'd been uneasy about Cummings's scheme to use Blair as bait to lure Gant. And now that he realized he was falling for her, he just couldn't risk involving her any further. The painful memories of the last woman he'd allowed to be used as a decoy on a sting operation, the memories of the woman he'd loved so dearly, the images of her brutal murder, her crumpled body lying in a lake of blood, were all still fresh in his mind.

The voice of the cabbie jolted he from his reverie. "Best ta let the lassie stew a while, she'll come 'round, you'll see. Soon you'll be given 'er a bit ov the ol slap and tickle."

Blair stopped and turned; her cheeks were dampened by a mixture of tears and the warm rain. She stood staring longingly at the retreating cab and the rude American who'd just driven out of her life.

She stomped her foot. "Bloody Yank. So full of himself, he is."

It began to rain in sheets. Lightning streaked, followed by the booming clap of thunder.

Hunching her shoulders and pulling up the lapels of her jacket, she thought, *So what now?* Then her thoughts turned to her brother and a cold chill ran through her.

Putting two fingers to her trembling lips, she gave a shrill whistle and flagged down an approaching cab.

As she ducked into the back seat and closed the door, the cabbie said, "Where to, missy?"

She heard herself answer, "The British Museum—and be quick about it!"

CHAPTER 18

A thick blanket of London fog had set in. It coiled its way over the façade of the British Museum as Blair approached in the taxi.

She had asked to be dropped at the side employee entrance.

As she fished her pass card from under her blouse and pulled the lanyard from her neck, she hesitated and turned. The employee parking lot was mostly empty now. The lamppost's sodium-vapor lights were haloed by the mist and their jaundiced glow dyed everything in a sickly yellowish hue.

Hidden by shadows and fog, a figure slowly made his way toward the entrance. Blair felt more chilled than the October evening could explain.

Sliding her card through the reader, the lock gave a solid clunk. She stepped into the welcoming warmth of the building. Instinctively, she turned and made sure the door was locked firmly behind her.

Her footsteps echoed eerily as she went down the hallway toward the elevator. At this hour, the corridors were virtually deserted.

As she approached an intersection, she heard a distinctive scuffling sound and raspy, labored breathing coming from around the corner, drawing closer.

She drew up short. Shaking her head, Blair chastised herself under her breath with a firm, "Get a grip, you silly bugger!"

When she rounded the corner, she almost collided with the man.

The wizened security guard gasped and lurched back, clutching his heart. He stared, his eyes wide as saucers, magnified by his coke-bottle thick eyeglasses.

"Blimey, Doctor Kelly, gave me a start. You did."

Blair blew a sharp breath. "I guess we're both a little jumpy, Mr. Spivey."

"You're suppos' to hit the intercom when you come in after hours," he added sternly.

"Guess I forgot. But where is everyone? It's barely seven o'clock."

"Exterminator's comin' in tonight. We'll be shuttin' 'er down tight. Didn't you get the memo?"

She shrugged.

"Well, don't be long, Doctor."

"I won't."

"I'll be on my way, then." He tipped his watchman's cap and ambled away, dragging his clubfoot as he went.

She exited the creaking old elevator and made her way down the dimly lit corridor to her office. A heaping pile of mail lay on the floor outside her doorway. She fumbled for her keys, but when she stuck the key into the lock, the door swung open.

I always lock the door. Well, at least I thought I did.

She plunked into her chair, began reading her mail by the light of her desk lamp, and only then noticed an object that caught her eye and caused her breath to catch in her throat.

She pitched the letters, mostly junk mail, and pulled a package toward her. She was right; the front of the oversized airmail envelope was postmarked Istanbul, Turkey.

The sight of the package not only obstructed her breathing, but it filled her with a sudden sense of excitement, mixed with terrible danger.

Her gaze cut to the door. She rose and went to it, peeking down the hallway in both directions before locking it and returning to her desk. She took a scimitar-shaped dagger from the desk blotter and cut open the seals.

Hesitating for an instant, she eased the contents out and onto the desk.

There were two books.

A well-worn diary with a faded red cover … and a hardback novel.

She gawked in sheer disbelief. Dominic had found it, the magickal diary of Carl Gustav Jung. He must have decided to airmail it rather than risk carrying it on his person, knowing that she would instantly recognize it and hold it for safekeeping. She laughed to herself at the irony of it. *Like the diary would be safer with me. What a joke!* She picked it up.

The alchemical legend that consumed the life of her father and now her brother stared back, taunting her. And now, it had weaved its mysterious web and had ensnared her, too. She thumbed to a page in the diary marked by a rubber band and read Jung's words.

Like Madimi, Dee and Kelly's angelic guide, I, too, have my own angelic host to steer the way. She comes to me in my dream-working. A white dove drifts down from above, gradually transforming into a young girl. Her cherubic face beams with innocence. She stands before a gleaming Emerald Tablet and points to an Angelic Script that shimmers and dances with a brilliant light.

Blair studied the strange letters that she recognized as Dee's Enochian script. She decided to translate them later and read on.

The girl smiles demurely and says, "We are coming."

As she put down the diary, her gaze panned to the hardback. She studied the cover. *The Midwich Cuckoos* by John Wyndham. It didn't ring any bells. She snatched it up, looking for a summary blurb, but it had no dust-jacket.

She eased back in her chair, kicked off her shoes, massaged her aching, swollen feet. Deep in thought, she absently played with a lock of her hair. She reached for the diary, then, noticing her soiled sleeve, thought otherwise.

From a small wardrobe in the corner of her office, she took out a change of clothes and went to the adjoining sink to freshen up. She shrugged out of her clothing and laid her things neatly on the arm of an overstuffed leather couch. Working late, she frequently slept at the office instead of going back to her tiny, empty flat. Staying close to her work somehow made her feel less lonely.

She felt the heft of the handgun, snagged it from the jacket pocket, and placed it on a table next to the sink. She couldn't help thinking of that stubborn Irish-American who had given it to her. Couldn't help thinking of his broad shoulders, his piercing gray eyes, and his thick, dark hair. Couldn't help but feel drawn to that—pigheaded loon. She shook it off.

Dressed only in her panties and bra, she opened the taps wide and let the water steam. She lathered a washcloth with soap and scrubbed her face raw. Bending, she cupped her hands and rinsed her face.

When she straightened, she studied her face in the mirror. She let her fingertips wander over her lips, imagining his kiss. The smell of his cologne …

… the lights suddenly winked out. The room was plunged into total darkness.

She stood rigid, half-naked, vulnerable and trembling like a frightened child.

CHAPTER 19

Brody nodded at the doorman dressed in a gray top hat and matching coachman's long-tailed coat, who flung wide open the entry doors of the Dorchester Hotel as the major approached.

After stopping briefly at the front desk to check his messages, he made for the elevator.

As he stepped out onto his floor, he opened the envelope the clerk had handed him and read the invitation for the party at Gant's estate. The top of the stationery was embossed with a coat of arms and the words RAVENSCAR leered back from below it in dark black ink. He had to admit Gant had a flair for the melodramatic.

Inside his room, he ripped off his dusty blazer and shrugged out of his shoulder holster, tossing it on the bed with his cell. He went to the bathroom, took a hot shower, and slipped on a thick terry cloth robe with the Dorchester's crest prominently displayed on its breast. *Nice souvenir.*

At the mini-bar, he poured himself a tall single-malt Scotch, took a long pull, and topped it off. He padded across the room and plopped onto the bed, exhausted, and wishing he had some ice for his drink. The last time he'd rung room service for ice, they'd delivered a small saucer with two cubes, half-melted. *Europe. Go figure*.

He snagged his cell phone from the bedspread and punched in the speed-dial.

Scout Thompson answered on the second ring.

"Hey, fearless leader."

"Where's she now?" Devlin asked, craning the kink out of his neck and taking another slug of the amber liquid.

"Looks like she headed back to the museum, boss."

When they'd kissed at the salvage yard gate, Brody had tagged Blair with a GPS transmitter, a remote tracking device that allowed Scout to get an exact fix on her location. It showed as a tiny blip on the grid of an ever-changing map of greater London, which Scout could pull up with the software on his field laptop.

"Workaholic, I guess. Have Brax get over there and eyeball her, make sure she's safe. If she changes her outfit, we'll lose her."

"Want him to pull an all-nighter?"

"Yeah, if he's not too busy sightseeing or hitting on chippies, that is," Devlin added as a jibe. "Put Chewie on, willya?"

Over the cell phone, Brody could hear a loud distant groan.

"He's in the crapper. Says this Limey food doesn't agree with him."

"Maybe if he didn't wolf down the whole dessert cart every chance he gets … oh hell, you pick up anything interesting from the bug in Gant's limo?"

"Not much. He got a call, sounded pissed, big-time. Didn't use any surnames but referred to a *dear Isaac*."

Brody sighed. "He's speaking German, Mr. CALTECH. It's *der Eisaxt*, the Ice Axe. Probably some sort of code name. Go on … what else did you get?"

"Told someone to have … the Ice Axe dispose of the package where the …" Scout's voice trailed off, sounding puzzled. "Something in German again, I guess."

Brody bolted upright in bed, spilling his drink in his lap and cursing himself as the expensive Scotch bathed his balls. "Play the damned file for me, now!"

"Figured you'd say that. Here it is."

Brody chewed his lower lip, listening intently to the sound of Gant's voice.

"Zum Teufel! Have *der Eisaxt* dispose of the package where *das Luder* will get the message. After he witnesses her reaction to his artistry, bring her in."

The words made Devlin's neck go cold. The quiet evil in Gant's voice when he referred to someone as a package and a—*slut*—was unnerving.

And Brody's gut told him that *someone* was Blair Kelly.

Leaping to his feet, he started barking orders into the phone. He dashed to the closet and began dressing hurriedly. When he yanked up the zipper on his slacks, he snagged a short hair and bellowed, blinking back tears and doubling over in pain.

In his mind, in his heart, he reasoned that it served him right for letting Blair out of his sight. *Stupid. Just stupid!*

CHAPTER 20

After gorging herself with a heaping plate of hot pancakes and bangers drowned in honey and butter and maple syrup, followed by two bowls of porridge and a pile of cinnamon-raisin toast drenched in butter, Noor found herself outside in the play area.

She'd seen the boys filing out of the cafeteria just as she'd entered. The boys were bland colorless clones, all dressed in typical English schoolboy fashion: gray blazer with school badge and gray short trousers, knee-length gray socks with gray shirt, striped white-and-gray tie and white-and-gray peaked school cap.

A boy with a pixielike widow's peak of sandy-colored hair covering his forehead paused and turned at the door. Deep indigo eyes studied her with keen interest. As he cocked his head and swiveled it side to side like a parrot, Noor noticed his sideburns, which tapered to a point near his elfin ears on either side of his face. But when their eyes met, he blushed, causing the cinnamon dusting of freckles to fade into his rosy cheeks. He shrugged and disappeared out the doorway.

In the playground, he knelt in the center of a small knot of boys who were playing with something.

He looked up and flashed a gapped-toothed grin this time, then looked down, eyes set in deep concentration. Another boy, with a dark complexion like Noor's, shot to his feet and yelled, "You missed me by a mile, Peter. Raji is the winner and champion!"

The boy called Peter frowned, his face knotted with anger. He ripped off his tiny cap and pitched it to the ground. A younger, smaller boy at his side reached out and gave him a reassuring pat on the back.

As she drew closer, a hush fell over the boys.

She looked over the top of their heads.

It was the strangest and most beautiful sight she had ever seen. Multi-colored glass balls hung suspended in midair, about two feet off the ground, forming a circle that resembled some miniature solar system, its tiny planets sparkling in the rays of the sun. Abruptly, as though the mysterious force that held them in place was interrupted, they fell to the ground.

The one called Peter gained his feet, brushing mud and dried grass from his knees, and looked directly at her.

His tiny hand clenched tightly in Peter's, the younger boy stood stapled to his side, his eyes bright but timid. The others followed his gaze and stood staring.

Here goes nothing, Noor thought. She gulped hard and flashed her dimples. "They call me Wendy. What are you boys doing?"

A small titter of laughter erupted from the gang.

Noor shrunk back.

Peter scowled and hushed them. He nodded for her to come closer. With small steps, she made her way to his side.

He swiped his nose with the back of his pale, freckled hand. "Name's Peter," he said and nodded toward his smaller twin. "This is Gabriel."

The little guy gave a shy smile and said aloud, "Hi, Wendy." Now his lips weren't moving, but she could still hear his tiny voice just the same, only it was coming from inside her head. His small voice whispered, "Are you our mother?"

I must be imagining things, she thought.

But his face was so sincere it tugged at Noor's heartstrings.

In turn, Peter introduced the other boys—Michael was skinny with a big Adam's apple protruding from his pencil neck, but he was handsome and his face was like an angel; his blond hair shimmered in the sunlight; Raji was the darker one, with thick waves of black hair and a gleaming smile; Johnboy was slightly chubby and wore thick horned-rimmed glasses and had a goofy habit of sucking in giant breaths and blowing them out, his lips motorboating. Peter said Johnboy did it whenever he was nervous or scared. And right now, he was doing just that, his cheeks filling then exhaling like a human fireplace bellows.

Noor figured Peter and Michael and Raji were about twelve. Johnboy was about eight and little Gabriel was the youngest, maybe five or six, she couldn't say for sure.

But Noor noticed they all had something in common. Like her, they each had deep indigo-colored eyes.

Peter told her that they were playing a game called marbles. As he and the other boys busied themselves colleting their marbles and tucking them into leather pouches, Peter paused and held a big one up to the sun.

Like a diamond, the sunlight was captured and bent and twisted into a rainbow of colors. "This is my lucky shooter," he said proudly.

"Can I hold it, please?" she asked.

He smiled and gently placed it in her hand. When his fingertips touched hers, Noor felt a tiny flutter in her chest. It was a strange feeling, but a good, warm feeling, like the first time she held a baby lamb.

"It's so pretty… but here," she said, proffering the marble. Peter's eyes narrowed as he stared at her hand. At first the marble grew warm, then tingled in her palm. Slowly it began to rise, gradually floating through the air, finally falling into Peter's full pouch with a click.

For a while, she joked and laughed with the gang. *I think they like me,* she thought. Eventually, the other boys made for the swings, and she and Peter strolled in wide circles, just talking. As she walked it occurred to her that she'd never really talked to a boy like this before. She wasn't sure how to act. *Just be yourself*, a tiny voice whispered in her head.

She was having a good time, but knew that something was wrong. When she tried to ask Peter questions about the place, and how he'd made the marble fly, he would get really quiet and repeat, "Eden is a special place, a good place."

She learned that this place was a school called Eden. Peter and his little brother had come here from an orphanage in Bristol about four years ago. He said their parents were killed in a plane crash. The other boys came from all over, but they were orphans, too.

When Noor tried to ask about that hospital-like smell she noticed when she was walking down a hallway near her room, Peter's face went white. Then he glanced around nervously and looked her straight in the eye, and whispered, "If you tell, you go to the *Dark Room* and sometimes … you never come back."

Noor didn't know why she said it, because it just popped out of her mouth. "I think you're all Lost Boys like in the book Father Dom gave me. It may look nice here and the doctor and teachers may show smiley happy faces, but it's a phony Never Neverland. And that mean blonde lady scares me the most."

"You mean Cruella De Vil?" Peter said, a laugh brightening his face.

She gave a tiny, thoughtful sigh. She couldn't understand these English people. They laughed at odd things. She had so much to learn in this strange new world. She wondered if she could ever be like them. Did she even want to be like them? Then she thought of Blair and her heart sank a little.

In a firm voice, she said, "We have to get out of here, Peter."

He chewed his lower lip for a moment and nodded. "You're right, Wendy. But how?"

They spoke in hushed whispers, laying out a plan.

Raji strolled up to them and chatted a while. "The old witch will be calling us …"—he glanced at his wristwatch, closing his eyes as if he were picturing it in his mind—"… right about now." When his eyes opened and met Noor's, he held them, telegraphing grave concern. "She will pull you out of line. Try to be brave, Wendy."

Puzzled, Noor started to ask, "But how do you know…?" A loud clanging noise drew Noor's attention. A thin woman with a hawkish face appeared near the school entrance, beating a large metal triangle with a rod.

"That's Ms. Baylock," Peter explained. "Don't get on her bad side or she'll sort you out. She's a mean old witch."

Noor spit on the ground at his feet. "I'm no scaredy-cat!"

But as they filed past Ms. Baylock, Noor remembered Raji's warning. She tried not to look the woman in the eye, only sneaking a peek from the corner of her eye. A cigarette dangled from Ms. Baylock's thin, cruel lips, the smoke curling upward. From behind her pointy tortoise-shell-framed eyeglasses, Ms. Baylock's beady eyes glared.

"You there," the witch said, calling to Noor. Noor averted her eyes and kept moving, praying silently to herself that the old hag wasn't talking to her. Suddenly, Ms. Baylock's shadow swooped down on her like a hawk. Skeletal fingers clawed at Noor's shoulder and spun her around. "You're new here, so I'll let it go this time. But when I call you, you'd better come on the quick, missy."

Too afraid to look up, Noor nodded humbly.

"C'mon along, then. *Herr Doktor* Craven wants to see you immediately.

From the corner of her eye, Noor caught Peter's wink and forced smile. He reminded her of her mother when she used to lie with her eyes, pretending something bad was good so that Noor wouldn't be frightened.

In the building, the door creaked open and Ms. Baylock shoved Noor into the room.

Squinting, Noor looked around. The room was tomb-dark and spooky. Shadows pooled like coagulated blood. It took time for Noor's eyes to adjust. Noor blinked as a harsh light suddenly blazed from above and stabbed downward. Sitting at a desk under a bright cone of light was Dr. Humpty Dumpty. A weak smile split his doughy face.

"Little Miss Wendy, do come in."

Her stomach tightened with fear. Sick with terror, her heart pounding, she inched forward. In a flash of insight, she suddenly realized …

This is the Dark Room!

He motioned to a small padded chair and Noor slumped into it. She hugged herself and shrank back.

"We are going to play a little game now. You like games, don't you, Miss Wendy?"

She nodded reluctantly, her eyes wide with apprehension.

But suddenly her face tightened and she leaned forward, gripping the armrests. Her knuckles whitened to points and in a small, quavering voice, she said, "No!"

As Dr. Craven rose and moved around the desk, he clicked a small box in his hand. It looked like the TV remote Noor had seen in the hotel. Metal bands suddenly looped over Noor's delicate wrists, pinning them to the armrests of the chair. She went stiff with terror as the doctor pulled a syringe from his lab coat pocket; the needle's thin sharp tip glinted as he moved to her side.

She broke out in a cold sweat as he rolled up her sleeve, the touch of his clammy hands raising gooseflesh on her forearm. The alcohol felt ice-cold as he swabbed her upper arm.

"You will feel a little prick, *ja*..." he explained. "There we are, not so bad, *ja*?"

The doctor released a lever on the side of the armrest. The chair's back lurched downward with a jolt, while her feet were simultaneously hoisted level with her body.

Noor lay strapped to the torturous Barcalounger. She felt her eye-lids begin to flutter, and as her head lolled to one side, the world turned a bright pink color; her stomach knotted and rippled, making her feel all queasy in her tummy. A loud buzzing sound droned in her ears. Darkness crept over her.

As she drifted on black waves, a distant voice seemed to call her name.

Wendy ... Wendy. Don't worry, we're with you, darling. Don't be afraid, child. In her foggy dreamscape, Noor thinks the voice sounds motherly and kind, no more like a grandmother's soft and slightly withered voice. Noor pictures a round, wrinkled face ... wet, kind eyes.

We're here, child. The Awen are waiting for you.

A loud buzzing drowns out the woman's voice.

Another voice, distant and fuzzy, floats through the static. Strange at first, the voice gradually becomes clear and recognizable. It's Peter's voice.

Wendy, hold on. It won't be long now. It's like you said, we all have special powers. Wendy thought of his whispered words earlier on the playground. I can move things with my mind, little Gabriel reads people's minds, Raji can see the future, knows what will happen in the next few minutes ...

Peter giggles gleefully. Johnboy is the bestest ever, Wendy. He's a regular Doctor Doolittle. Gets it from his granny. Speaks to the birds and the insects and the squirrels...

The buzzing becomes a roar and Peter's voice becomes remote.

From the darkness, a new voice called her name.

"Little Miss. Wendy. You-hoo ... jeepers creepers, open those peepers."

She began to awaken, realize she wasn't dreaming anymore.

Noor squinted against the glaring light. The doctor's maggot-pale face came into focus. Hot tears were tracking down her soft cheeks. Through her tears, he shimmered and blurred again, seeming to lean back.

"There, there, now. Doctor Humpty Dumpty didn't hurt you." She turned toward the sound of his voice. His hands were covered in old-fashioned thick, rubber surgical gloves; he held a test tube between two fingers.

He leaned over her, pressing closer, his watery eyes busy and searching. With his fingertip, he swabbed a tear from her cheek. Pursing his lips, as if his finger was dipped in the rarest chocolate, Dr. Craven slowly brought his tear-filmed fingertip to the bud of his tongue and licked it. Eyes closed, he took a deep breath and sighed. "Exquisite, the pure nectar of virginal innocence," he said softly.

When they finally opened, his heavy-lidded eyes made him seem piggish and mean. He was glowering at Noor now. "Let's see if we can fill this tube, shall we, dear?"

Then his face transformed into a sickly, expectant grin. "Think … sad thoughts."

Puzzled, Noor wrinkled her nose in confusion.

Lips forming an exaggerated pout, he added, "Maybe sweet Ms. Wendy needs a little motivation, *ja*?"

Craven raised his other hand and dangled her pink teddy bear.

A smile flew to Noor's lips as she cried, "Mr. Muffins!" She struggled desperately to reach for Mr. Muffins, but she was still manacled to the chair.

He turned and placed the test tube in a rack on a roller cart and picked up a scalpel. Facing her again, light glinted off the razor-sharp edge of the stainless steel.

Noor's face went ashen as she began quaking with terror.

In a slow, deliberate motion, he brought the gleaming scalpel closer and closer to the little bear's face. Suddenly, he plunged the tip into Mr. Muffins' eye, twisted it violently, and ripped the shiny button from the fabric.

Her voice was strangled with fear. A soft keening sound, like a wounded sparrow, escaped from Noor's lips as tears flooded from her eyes.

Craven smiled sinfully and said in a voice of quiet evil, "Good girl." With a flourish of distaste, he tossed the stuffed bear to the floor and reached for the test tube.

While he held the test tube to the corner of her eye, catching her spill of tears, his icy laugh taunted her and shivered the air as she made broken bird sounds and feather-soft sobs.

CHAPTER 21

Mr. Spivey completed his rounds and headed down the corridor to the security control room. Hobbling along, his rubber-soled shoes squeaking on the highly polished tiles, his thoughts were on the dinner the missus had packed: a tin of freshly baked biscuits, a bit a' brisket, a hot thermos of tea.

Up ahead, beneath a pool of dim light, Spivey saw two men dressed in coveralls with the words "Flea Circus Pest Control" embroidered across their shoulder blades. Their backs were to him as they faced the control room door. One was hoisting a spray can and painting the overhead surveillance camera.

"Bloody exterminators, going ta nix me dinner, they are," Mr. Spivey grumbled to himself.

The old night watchman raised his long, bony finger. "Say 'ere, now. I 'elped you lads once tonight … wot's this 'bout, then?"

They slowly turned in unison and tipped their caps.

Mr. Spivey, eyes squinting from behind his thick lenses, his face turning even more pallid, managed, "Wot the bloody hell?"

The light caught their wiry red fright wigs.

Two devilishly white clown faces leered back at him. The watchman's stare tracked from the broad, crinkled forehead to those hollow, coal-black eye sockets, to the snarl of pointed yellowed teeth beneath a red nose, its nostrils wide and flared. His heart hammered in his chest, threatening to explode.

"Ol' Horns and Hoofs 'imself!" Mr. Spivey muttered, his breathing ragged and labored now as a hand came from behind and clamped a damp cloth to his face. As the distinct, overpowering odor of chloroform filled his lungs, his knees buckled.

The leader of the demented clowns snagged a ring of keys from Spivey's belt. With a long, graceful stride, the leader stepped over the old man's comatose body. While tossing the keys to the waiting accomplice, the leader's muffled voice floated from behind a gas mask. "Open it."

As the door knifed open, one clown pitched a canister into the room and leaped to the side. A bright flash and cloud of smoke followed, boiling out of the doorway and into the hallway.

The leader pounced into the control room.

Through the fog of smoke, the leader could make out two more security guards cowering in the corner, backs pressed to a large console. One guard's hand gingerly reached for a red phone, his panicked eyes large as a clock face, and locked on the intruder.

A huge pistol fitted with a sound suppressor filled the leader's hand.

The pistol recoiled. *Phutt … Phutt.*

Two silenced rounds whispered death. One cratered a guard's forehead. When his head slammed against the console, the exit wound haloed it in a red mist. The other round caught the second guard's throat. His hand flew to his ruined neck, blood oozing red and hot from between his fingers as he made a strange wheezing, gurgling sound. Then he went limp and sagged to the floor.

As the air began to clear, Margot Gant ripped off her gas mask.

She studied the bloodbath, drinking it in through her eyes.

Breathing heavily and shuddering with sexual arousal, she moaned deeply. She was climaxing, deriving a sick, sensual ecstasy from killing. For Margot, sex and violence were one and the same.

She sighed and palmed a hand-held. "Kill the power grid, now!"

The lights dampened, then went out.

Margot wheeled on the other two men. "Hey, you two *clowns*. Get your bloody arses in here now and kill the alarms, the cameras, the phones, and back-up generator." She placed the pistol on the console to free her hands.

Stepping out of her baggy coveralls, Margot stood and kicked them aside. Her firm body was encased in a black jump suit with thickly knitted fibers so form-fitting it resembled a diver's wet suit. She holstered her

Desert Eagle Mark XIX .44 Magnum in a low-riding combat rig strapped to her muscled thigh and donned a pair of night vision goggles.

Slinging a large black canvas bag over her shoulder, Margot brushed past the clowns, headed for the stairs.

Behind the steamed windows of the Mini Cooper, which sat rocking in the museum parking lot, Lt. Braxton was way past third base. Breathing heavily and tangled in a knot of arms and legs in the cramped car, Brax felt the hot breath of the girl from the information booth panting against his neck. He pressed his hips closer.

"Jeez! It's vibrating," she said in a heated whisper.

"I know, baby. I know. I'm tingling, too!" Brax boasted.

She wiggled free of his arms and pushed him off her.

"C'mon, Cindy. Don't stop now."

She sat up, tugging at her skirt. Straightening her mussed hair, Cindy pointed to his lap.

Brax smiled sheepishly. Then it dawned on him. His cell phone was thrumming in his pants pocket. He fished it out and answered.

Cindy's shrill scream made him drop the phone. Cursing, he bent and fished around the floorboards. He found the phone, led by the bluish haze of its LED screen. When he sat up, he saw what had spooked her. The parking lot, the museum, and as far as the eye could see, was suddenly pitched into total darkness. A black out. As the full moon shone down, it lightly filigreed the slanting rain.

Scout's voice barked from the cell.

"Devlin wants you to babysit Doctor Kelly. She's back at the museum. Couple of Gant's goons tailed her and Devlin this afternoon and got trigger happy."

His eyes searching the blackness around him, Brax asked, "Anybody hurt?"

"Just the shooters. But we think Gant may try to snatch Doctor Kelly tonight."

Alarm bells sounded in Brax's mind. He turned to Cindy without lowering the phone. "Gotta run, baby. Be a good girl and get on home now."

In a puzzled voice, Scout asked, "Baby? You callin' me baby now?"

Cindy glared as Brax tore out of her Cooper, hiking up his trousers and fastening his belt as he dashed through the pouring rain and across the lot to his waiting car. Fumbling for his keys, while still holding the cell in his other hand, he found them and popped the trunk.

Tires smoking on the wet pavement, horn blaring angrily, Cindy's car screamed past, ripping through a deep puddle and drenching him with the spray. She'd barely missed hitting him. He stared at her fading taillights, brushed his wet trousers, and smiled.

Scout's voice shouted from the cell, "Hey, numbnuts! What the hell's goin' on?"

In his excitement, Brax had forgotten that Scout was still holding. "Looks like something's goin' down over here. Get on to Chief Inspector Newley. Have him send a SWAT team to the museum, ASAP!"

"Hey, I know you're already on site. Got your GPS blip on my screen. But—"

"The power's out here. Looks like the whole grid's down. Be sure to tell Newley's guys that I'm on site and dressed in civvies. Don't wanna get plugged by friendly fire."

"Roger that. Chewie's picking up Brody and headed your way. I'll advise."

Brax hung up, ripped off his suit coat, shrugged into a tactical vest. Snatching a Zero case, he slammed the trunk lid and made for the museum, his soaked shoes squishing with each stride.

CHAPTER 22

Behind the wheel of the gleaming liquid-silver Jaguar XF, Chewie poured on the gas, racing toward the museum.

The Jag's rear end fishtailed as the twin-turbo V-8 screamed.

Chewie smiled, noticing Brody's ashen face. "Hey, chill out, Brody. Put on some driving music. Maybe it'll soothe your nerves.

Brody nodded as his eyes searched the dash. With its sleek phosphorous –blue lighting system and myriad of gauges, it looked more like the cockpit of a jetfighter than a car. "Okay, I give. Where's the damn radio?"

Chewie shook his head as he reached over and punched the CD player icon on the dash-mounted LED screen.

The lilting sounds of Strauss's *Blue Danube* purred from the speakers, which transformed Chewie's mad chase into a finely choreographed waltz as he slalomed recklessly through slow moving traffic, screaming around corners.

The rain-slick pavement reflected the shimmering forest of taillights and headlamps. Tearing through a deep puddle, water sprayed from the fender wells and sluiced down both side windows.

Brody Devlin was whiplashed from side to side, thankful for the seatbelt. He tried to focus, to put Blair Kelly out of his mind, but right now she took center stage.

Until Brody saw the traffic light—

"Red light!" Brody shouted to Chewie, whose bear claws held the leather-gloved steeling wheel in a white-knuckled grip. Chewie sat stone-faced, eyes glaring straight ahead, peering through the beating windshield wipers.

—then a hulking red double-decker bus.

Brody's eyes went wide as he saw the bus on their right, seconds away from the intersection.

Chewie tramped the pedal and the Jag lurched, barreling up and down the hilly roadway.

The waltz played on, hitting a rising crescendo just as the Jag dipped, nearly bottoming out. Its engine howling, it crested a hill and slingshot into the intersection; almost airborne, the Jag skirted past the nose of the bus, missing it by inches.

When they came up on the next cross street, Brody shouted frantically, "You gotta hang a right ..."

Cranking the wheel hard, Chewie power skidded around the turn at almost a ninety-degree angle.

The Jag's ass end whipsawed violently, spewing jets of water as tortured rubber screeched.

Up ahead, glaring headlamps bore down on them and an air horn blared its frenzied warning as they rocketed down the right side of the street.

"For Chrissakes, man. You're in the wrong damned lane!" Brody screamed, his fingers digging into the dashboard.

With a casual shrug, Chewie spun the wheel and raked into the left lane. "Limey drivers, *qualem biennium*."

His face twisted in anger, Brody shot him a hard glance.

Chewie winked and translated. "What a doofus."

Then the big guy's gaze shot to the rearview mirror as blue and white strobe lights pulsed through the back window of the Jag. "Looks like we got ourselves a police escort," Chewie said with a wicked grin. "Let's rock and roll." His meaty finger pressed the touch-screen again and Steppenwolf's *Born to be Wild* blasted from the speakers.

Craning around, Devlin counted three BMW police cruisers hot on their butt, their high-pitched sirens serving as a wailing accompaniment to the driving heavy metal thunder coming from the speakers.

Brody swallowed hard as his eyes ticked from the rear window and back to Chewie's leering face. Brody knew that look. The shit was about to hit the fan.

Brody's eyes lowered to the speedometer as Chewie manually climbed through the gears using the wheel-mounted paddle shifters.

The needle shivered to seventy ... eighty-five ... ninety.

The hulking Easy Rider behind the wheel just grinned as he warbled, "Like a true nature's child … we can climb so high, I never wanna die …"

"What the hell are you doing?" Brody challenged. "Those coppers are driving TROJANS, souped-up pursuit BMWs. And that means they're armed to the teeth."

Chewie winked at Brody as he kicked the throttle. The twin-superchargers gulped air, the thrust slamming Brody back against his bucket seat. "Always wondered whether a Jag XF could outrun the 'Ultimate German Driving Machine.' This new 4.2-liter V8 pumps out 420 horses, boss."

They rocketed through another red light, narrowly missing a diaper service van with "WE DO … *DOO-DOO*" painted on its side. Squirming in his seat, Brody's butt cheeks puckered as he wondered if he might have "crapped 'is bleedin' *trousers,"* as Sgt. Conners would have said in his thick Scottish brogue.

Brody turned and glared. "Fine! Just as soon as I change my diaper, I'll have them carve 'World's Fastest Indian' on your tombstone!"

In her pitch dark office, Blair managed to wrestle into her clothes and pocket the SIG. Siphoning the darkness, her arms stretched out in front of her, taking baby steps, her big toe slammed into the edge of her desk. She bleated in agony and frustration, hopping on one foot and falling flat on her bum in the process. A knifing pain stabbed her already bruised tailbone. "Bloody hell, that smarts," she cried, then began laughing at her clumsiness.

She struggled to her feet. Using the edge of the desk as a reference, she skirted around to the back and began searching the drawers.

Her fingertips found something. "Ouch, a razor blade."

She winced, sucked her finger and resumed her search. A familiar shape. Cardboard. Small. She brought it to her nose and sniffed. Yes, it was a matchbook. Her spirits buoyed.

The match lit on the first strike. *Thank god they're dry. Now what?* By the weak light of the guttering flame, she found the phone. The line was dead.

The flame burnt her finger. She cursed again, tossed it and struck another. She made for the door, stumbling over her chair. With unsteady hands, she struggled to unlock the door. She slowly creaked it open, peeked out, and stepped into the cold stillness of the corridor.

The battery-powered emergency lights filled the hallway with a weak light. She looked toward the elevators. *No good, they'd be out of commission, too.*

Turning, she went to the emergency stairs, the cold floor leeching into the soles of her bare feet. She'd forgotten her shoes. *Brilliant, Blair. Just brilliant.*

She shouldered the door and it burst open, slamming against the other side. The loud thud echoed in the hollow cavern of the stairwell. Hesitating briefly, she stepped into the stairwell. She squeezed herself into the corner of the landing, peering at the railing along the far side of the steps. A single naked bulb burned in a wire basket overhead. To her left and right, flights of stairs led up and down into inky shadows before coming to the dull light of other landings. The only sound was her own ragged breathing as she stood deliberating … *up or down?*

Gray cinder block, looming shadows, the air musty and cool. These things seemed to shrink down upon her.

She stood shaking. She was chilled to the bone. Not solely from the fear of the unknown, but because her blouse was drenched with sweat and matted to her back. And worse, the ripening scent reminded her that in the darkness she'd mistakenly donned her same soiled outfit.

Move, Blair. Put one foot before the other and move.

She steeled herself and took a step.

From below she heard the rasp of un-oiled hinges as a door opened into the stairwell.

A dry sound, like something scraping along or being dragged across the concrete floor, snaked up the stairwell toward her. She stole a quick peek over the edge of the rail. About four floors down, a shadow crept across the landing below, dragging what looked like a sack—no, it was a body. Instinctively, she shrunk back, pressed herself into the corner. With her back sandwiched against the cold cinder block, she sank to her knees.

The hollow, steady trudge of footsteps echoed and re-echoed, floating upward toward her. As they grew closer, she could hear heavy breathing between each footfall.

Her gut knotted with tension. Her throat was parched. She looked down at her trembling hands, realizing that her fingernails were dug deeply into the fabric of her slacks.

With each beat of her pounding heart, the footfalls grew louder, closer.

She was possessed by the irrational fear that some stuffed, scabrous creature from an exhibit, some tattered mummy, had come to life and was slouching toward her, about to pounce.

CHAPTER 23

Margot glided across the exhibit hall, masked in shadow.

Moonlight struggled through the huge louvered skylight above, banding the floor. Rain beat a steady rhythm against the roof above.

She reached the end of the Enlightenment Room and stood before Case Number 20: Magic, Mystery, and Rites.

Encased behind glass were the Voynich manuscript and Dee's Aztec obsidian mirror, and a wax-covered tablet decorated with impressions of strange symbols and glyphs.

Time was the enemy. She needed to act quickly. Since the alarms had been silenced, there was no need for finesse.

Margot snaked a spring-loaded steel baton from her bag, and with a sharp flick of her wrist, she smashed the case. Glass dissolved under the force of the blow, erupting in a glittering spray.

She bagged the items and moved on, padding quickly across the room to another exhibit.

A towering totem stood before her.

Dyed in the ghostly green hue of her night vision goggles, the gruesome face of Quetzalcoatl—the feathered serpent god of the Aztecs—leered, staring starkly down at her. His snarled lips and elliptical snake eyes seemed to mock her.

Margot glared back. "Bite me!" she taunted.

She painted the figure with the beam of her torch and panned to a crystal skull resting on a Lucite pedestal nearby.

The crystal skull caught the flashlight's glare and refracted it like a diamond. The skull seemed to glow from within, blinding her.

She peeled off the light sensitive NVGs and rubbed her eyes. Her vision gradually cleared.

A throbbing blue-white light pulsed from the skull's wide-set eye sockets. Margot blinked. For a moment, Margot could have sworn the skull's glassy jaw hinged wide, then snapped shut.

One of the clown-faced bug killers sidled up next to her, taking her unawares. She flinched and glared at him, her white-blonde hair luminous in the weak moonlight. "*Sheistkopf!*"

Then she cursed herself under her breath and plucked the crystal skull from its perch. Beside it, on lower glass pedestals, were two more skulls. Like a Dutch girl picking tulips, she plucked them one by one and whistled for her accomplice to bring the brushed aluminum case.

She nestled the skulls into the pre-cut sockets in the foam lining and added the items from John Dee's case, securing them snugly with Velcro fasteners before lowering the lid and snapping the latches of the small trunk.

"*Ja ... zer gutt*!" she whispered with a sigh.

Bringing the hand-held to her lips, she said, "Hans, now we grab *das Luder*. Where is she?"

The radio squawked. "I checked the bitch's office. She's not there."

She lowered her radio, spun on the clown holding the case, and scowled. He shrugged.

She jacked the radio back to her mouth. "Fine, then we'll bait the hook. *Der Eisaxt,* get the priest out of the van and drag him in here, now!"

Two sharp clicks from *der Eisaxt's* radio signaled that he understood.

Blair had moved to the next landing. She crouched against the railing, breath held tightly, threatening to burst from her lungs.

Below, the footsteps paused.

He was on the landing.

The only sound was his ragged breathing and her thundering heartbeat pulsing against her eardrums.

She held the SIG in a two-handed grip before her and leaned her forehead against the cold steel of the slide.

Squeezing her eyes tightly and concentrating, she focused her will on the invisible attacker just a few feet below her. *There's no one here, go to her office*, Blair's mind telegraphed.

Scuffling feet moved, then stopped.

Haunting silence hung thickly in the chilled air of the stairwell.

With every fiber of her being, Blair willed the attacker to exit the stairwell. Then, suddenly, the emergency door creaked noisily and slammed with a hollow thud.

Wasting no time, she shot to her feet and climbed to the next floor.

She eased the emergency door open and stepped into the corridor.

When she reached the center of the hallway and stood approximately over the entrance to her office one floor beneath her, loud noises erupted from below. Furniture scraping across the floor, the crack of broken glass. *He must be searching my office.*

By now, she had removed the hall air vent and had hoisted herself into the ductwork. The space was narrow, but large enough for her to maneuver.

On hands and knees, she made her way through the duct, moving as fast as she could.

After a few minutes, she came to a sharp turn and paused. Then it hit her. She'd forgotten to replace the vent grate. If her invisible stalker found it lying there, he could track her. But would he bother? She doubted it.

She crabbed along for what seemed like hours in the claustrophobic confines of the ductwork, but in reality only minutes had passed. Her knees ached and her palms were covered in dust and rat droppings and only God knows what else.

Just then, something skittered across the back of her hand. Reflexively, she jerked back her arm and slammed her elbow against the side. She cursed herself for being such a weak Nelly.

A muffled sound floated toward her. She quickened her pace, following the sound through the maze of ductwork.

As she got closer, she realized it was a voice.

No more like voices.

Loud and harsh.

Followed by a soft whimpering sound.

They were the anguished pleas of someone who had been pushed beyond the normal threshold of pain, beyond human endurance. Someone who was hanging on to life by their last thread.

Her neck went cold.

She would have recognized his voice anywhere.

His tortured cries for help.

It was Father Dominic.

Her brother's voice snaked up from the mouth of the dark, endless shaft in front of her. It was a sheer, blind drop to the ceiling of the room below and through it to the floor below. Calculating the distance and location in her head, she figured it to be about twenty feet and most likely the Enlightenment Room. Her heart was knocking, knocking so hard that her vision pulsed in sync, dimming at the edges with each beat.

Her sixth-sense had guided her to this point. Now it was up to her to take the—plunge.

CHAPTER 24

Brax was making his way down the corridor, running from pool to pool of light, which fell across the gleaming white tile in intermittent cones from the emergency lighting. Earlier, after loiding the entrance door's lock with a thin plastic shank, he'd popped the Zero case and emptied its contents. Now he held a palm-sized LED readout computer in his outstretched hand. Scout had downloaded the schematics of the museum's layout. The blip from Blair's GPS tracker was a small, green dot pulsing on the screen.

Slung around his neck was the CORNER-SHOT. Crafted by the Israelis, it could be fitted with a pistol or assault-rifle pistol or .40 mm grenade launcher. It was basically a rifle with a hinge in the middle and a remote trigger mechanism.

Slotted into its grip was the APR assault pistol.

The mechanism bent at sharp angles, up to sixty degrees right or left, allowing the shooter to poke the weapon around corners, without exposing himself to the line of fire.

The business end was fitted with a micro video camera, whose wide-angle lens displayed imagery on a small high-resolution screen. The micro-camera incorporated crosshairs, auto-focus, and an infrared filter, allowing the shooter to see in low light. His model also had a laser designator mounted beneath the assault pistol's muzzle.

Brax drew up short at a corner.

Pounding footfalls raced toward the intersection from his right.

Stabbing the muzzle around the corner, he studied the small display screen.

He jolted at the sight. A ghoulish stark-white clown face with blood red lips filled the screen, almost floating in the darkness as it moved.

He wore coveralls.

A pistol clutched in his fist.

Definitely a hostile!

The evil clown was tearing down the corridor toward him.

Sighting the crosshairs of the LED screen on the charging clown's knees, he squeezed off two rounds, then two more for good measure.

The clown's eyes went wide.

A shrill cry echoed toward Brax as he saw the man pitch headfirst to the unforgiving floor; his handgun ripped from his grip and went spinning down the polished tiles, hurtling past Brax's post at the corner.

Checking for more targets and finding none, Brax stepped around the corner, secured the lost pistol, and went to the man.

Brax jacked the fore grip and the CORNER-SHOT snapped back to its straight position. Brax snatched plastic riot cuffs from his vest, and after planting his knee deeply into the small of the clown's back, cuffed him securely. Twisting around, his knee still planted in the creep's back, he ripped a second pair from his tactical vest and banded the clown's ankles firmly together. He gained his feet and looked at the hogtied schmuck.

Beside the groaning clown, Brax dropped to one knee. Roughly, he grabbed the finger of the man's cuffed hand, bent it back with a sharp twist. The man squealed like a stuck pig.

Brax bent over him, whispered into his ear. "Want some more, asshole?" The clown violently shook his head.

"How many more and where are they?"

No answer.

Brax jerked a second finger, causing it to crack.

The clown's feet drummed the floor.

Before the guy could finish his howling plea for mercy, Brax rose and planted the heel of his shoe hard against the back of the man's neck, mashing his face against the floor.

As he carefully shifted his weight to his right leg, careful not to lose his balance, Brax said from between clenched teeth, "Last chance, Bozo."

Bozo grunted and squirmed.

Brax released his foothold.

"I'm listening."

Bozo managed between gasps, "Four more … on the third floor."

Snatching a third finger, Brax barked, "Where on the third floor? And weapons, Bozo. What are they carrying?"

"Enlightenment Room … semi-autos. I swear, that's it."

Brax studied Bozo a moment, then switched the APR's fire-selector to full auto. "Bozo, I think you're full of it."

Stooping lower, Brax gagged Bozo with his handkerchief.

Brax spun and raced off, palming the note-pad and scrolling until he found the Enlightenment Room on the display as he ran for the stairs.

On the third floor, he spilled into the corridor.

Eyes searching for targets as he ran, he froze as two more Bozo-faced attackers rounded the corner.

They came out fast, and the tall one swung a sawed-off toward Brax. *Just handguns, eh!*

There was a flash. Brax was sure he'd been hit. Shotgun pellets stung his cheek. The shooter had fired high and to his left.

Instinct took over.

Brax dove for the floor, somersaulted, skidding along the highly-polished floor on his butt, legs curled, squeezing off bursts as he went.

As if in slow motion, hot shell casings hung in midair and rained to the floor; one slipped down his shirt collar. He hated it when that happened, 'cause it burnt like hell.

The 5.56 mm rounds punched into the taller Bozo's chest, and the second burst exploded in the shorter attacker's face.

He staggered, slumped to his knees, blood spurting from the mask's blackened eye socket where the round had augured its way into his brainpan.

Brax shot to his feet.

The sound of hammer blows against metal rang out. Then a tortured scream wailed toward him from the direction of the exhibit hall.

CHAPTER 25

Blair's passion, aside from archaeology, was rock climbing. And now she was putting her skills to the ultimate test.

She was employing the reverse Chimney Climb. Using opposing counter-force, she placed her right foot about knee high on the duct's wall in front of her and placed her back foot behind her, her foot mashed to the rear wall under her butt. With her arms extended and palms pushing against the opposite walls, she alternated the positioning of her hands and feet as she crabbed downward.

Her calves and thigh muscles burned with a glassy pain, stretching past their endurance point. Her arms were beginning to cramp from the strain. She was about halfway down when her footing gave way.

The ductwork buckled noisily as her foot slipped.

Hands flung over her head, she rocketed down the shaft toward the fog of light below.

Margot nervously paced back and forth across the floor, her eyes darting around the room expectantly.

Der Eisaxt's tool clutched firmly in his fist, he pounded large spikes through the soft flesh of the man's hands.

With each strike, Margot swooned and groaned her pleasure as she watched, enthralled, studying the pain-racked face of the priest with detached but keen interest.

She paused.

She never saw it coming.

From above, Blair's body dropped through the vent and slammed into Margot like a sack of anvils, knocking the wind from her lungs and driving her to her knees.

Blair rolled across the cold tiles. Her ankle twisted on the impact and she howled in pain.

Coughing and gasping for air, Margot struggled to her feet. Disoriented, she slowly regained her senses and her hellish gaze fell on Blair. "You slut!"

Margot stood staggering, her eyes filled with murder and rage.

Clutching her bruised ankle, Blair looked past Margot and screamed.

On the far wall, behind *der Eisaxt's* hulking frame, her brother, Father Dominic, hung suspended by six-inch spikes driven through his open palms and the tops of his bare feet. The nails looked like they'd gone deep into the Sheetrock and into the wall's studs.

His blood was still dripping, tracking down the white wall, pooling darkly on the floor beneath him.

Father Dominic's head hung limply against his chest. Because Blair could just barely make out a slight rise and fall of his chest, and because she could hear his faint, labored breathing, she knew he was still alive. Her gaze cut to *der Eisaxt*, then to Margot, holding her with its force.

"You crucified him, you sick bastards!" Blair screamed.

"Ernst does such marvelous work," Margot said, pasting on her hostess smile. "Looks like a living sculpture, don't you think?"

Blair cursed her and slowly eased her hand toward her coat pocket, where the SIG lay waiting.

Ernst grinned, clicked his heels smartly, and made an exaggerated bow.

"An art critic, Ernst," Margot taunted.

Blair turned away in revulsion. Reflected in a glass case, Blair caught a glimpse of her own shell-shocked face.

A voice floated through the darkness from behind Ernst and drew her attention.

"Everybody, hold it right where you are. Easy with that axe, asshole."

* * *

Outside, Scout Thompson, surrounded by a knot of tense officers, stood speaking with Inspector Newley. The loud thrumming sound of an approaching helicopter drew his attention.

The bright cone of the chopper's searchlight swept across the ground.

Gazing up and pointing toward the onrushing chopper, Newley explained to Scout, "That would be our SFO boys, our version of a SWAT team. They'll do a rooftop entry and we'll storm in from here with the rest of the CO19 officers." An ARV, an Armed Response Unit Command and Control Van, pulled into the lot as he spoke. The doors swung open and Newley nodded toward the van, indicating they should enter.

As they made for the van, a cacophony of sirens shrieked the arrival of Brody and Chewie.

The Jaguar jumped the curb and sped full throttle toward Scout and the inspector, with three BMW police cruisers in hot pursuit.

"Looks like Chewie's got himself a fan club," Scout said, shaking his head.

The Jag power slid to a lurching stop a few feet from where the inspector and Scout stood.

When the Jag's doors popped wide, Devlin and Chewie spilled out.

Behind them, the police cruisers screeched to halt.

"Bloody hell! Looks like I'd better sort this out. Those are TROJANS, armed response vehicles," Newley said as he dashed toward the police units.

The pursuing ARV officers leaped out, HK-MP-5s and Glock-17s drawn, barking commands for their captured quarry to raise their hands and drop to their knees.

Newley intervened, holding his warrant card high as he and a senior uniformed officer positioned themselves between the drawn weapons and Devlin.

The situation handled, Newley joined the ΩMEGA team in the Command and Control van, his face flushed red with anger. "You bloody Yanks like to raise a ruckus."

Brody Devlin smiled sheepishly and turned to Chewie.

"Brought the cavalry," Chewie offered, nodding toward the police units.

"Indeed," Newley replied. "Here's the situation. We have shots fired. Probably your man Braxton engaging the intruders. We should have the power grid back up shortly."

A tech sat at a console punching up displays on the video screen. Newley pointed toward the schematic of the museum's interior. "The airborne SFO unit will burst in here ... from the rooftop. I have all the street level exits covered."

Brody nodded his understanding and turned to Scout. "Have you heard anything from Brax since he entered?"

"No, his imaging signal from his CORNER-SHOT cut out almost as soon as he entered, and I didn't want to hail him on his cell because it might put him in jeopardy, give away his position."

Brody bit his lower lip, turned to Newley. "So we're literally in the dark. Don't know how many hostiles are on site or their weaponry."

Newley nodded glumly. "That's correct. We found a pest control company's van parked around the side, so my hunch would be that the hostiles, as you call them, gained access disguised as exterminators and then overpowered the security staff." He pointed toward the screen. "We'll send in two teams. Here and here."

The tech at the console put his hand to his headset, nodded acknowledgement, and cut in. "Inspector, the Air-One team reports that they've spotted a second helo approaching fast from the north."

Newley ripped the headset from the tech's head, crammed it onto his, and shouted, "Air-One, this is Inspector Newley of SO15. I didn't requisition a second air-support team. Is it that damnable tabloid press chopper?"

Exchanging worried glances, Brody and Chewie leaped out of the van. Chewie brought a pair of digitally enhanced infrared binoculars to his eyes that he'd snatched from the van.

"Any markings?" Brody asked.

"No ... wait a minute, looks like a TV station's call letters."

From the van, Brody heard Inspector Newley shouting into the headset. "Approaching helicopter. This airspace is restricted by police order. You will identify yourself and turn about immediately!"

After several attempts, Newley said, "Air-One, from Newley. They're not responding. Get up and rout those bastard newsies the bloody hell out of here!"

Within seconds, Brody saw Air-One lift off the roof and engage the oncoming chopper, painting it with its spotlight and barking commands from its PA speaker.

The mystery chopper didn't slow or change course. Instead, it made a beeline toward Air-One.

Chewie shouted. "Jeez! I see rocket pods on that whirlybird! Tell 'em to pull back."

A bright flash and the flaming exhaust stream of a rocket shot across the night sky.

Air-One took a direct hit in the rear rotor and began spinning downward like a dog chasing its tail.

It pitched nose-down into the massive skylight of the museum's Grand Court, its rotors still churning and chewing through the glass ceiling, finally sinking below the roofline. A shuddering blast and then an oily plume roiled skyward.

Brody and Chewie watched helplessly as the marauding chopper banked and winged low to the rooftop where Newley had indicated the other entry team was positioned, waiting to pounce.

The deafening chatter of a chain-gun assaulted Brody's ears, as red and orange tracer rounds fired by the mystery chopper stitched their deadly path across the rooftop.

Moments earlier in the museum, when he stepped out from the shadows, his weapon trained on them, Blair saw that it was Lt. Braxton.

He glanced toward her. "You okay, Doctor Kelly?" Then his eyes cut back to the others. He grimaced and wretched when he saw Father Dominic.

Blair nodded weakly. "I'll be fine. But Dominic needs immediate …" She let out a shrill cry as she was trying to make it to her feet, using a nearby case for support.

A bright burst burned through the skylight, bleaching the room in hot light, igniting the night sky above them. An explosion boomed loudly, shaking the walls, followed quickly by the deafening chatter of machine-gun fire from the rooftop.

Carelessly, Brax cut in front of Ernst, rushing to Blair's aid. A flash of metal and the axe's claw arced downward in a blur of motion and snatched the weapon from Brax's hand. It went clattering across the floor.

Brax lunged out, but Ernst deftly reversed his tool and drove the steel ball fitted to its handle into Brax's solar plexus, causing him to double over in agony.

With Brax defenseless now, Ernst used the tool like a black jack, bludgeoning Brax's skull and mercilessly pounding him to the floor with blow after blow.

Blair ripped the SIG from her jacket.

But Margot's reflexes were too fast; she had already closed half the distance before Blair cleared her pocket.

A violent side-kick tore the SIG from Blair's grasp.

Screaming with an animalistic rage, Margot grabbed Blair by her lapels, hoisted her in midair, her feet dangling off the ground, and hurled her across the room with an inhuman strength.

Like a stunt woman on wire rigging in a movie, Blair sailed through the air and crashed back-first into a large display case.

Razorlike shards stabbed at Blair's back as she lay in a heap of splintered wood and glass.

As she began to lose consciousness, a second blinding light poured through the skylight from above.

She heard the pounding beat of rotor blades churning overhead. She drifted deeper and deeper into blackness.

Glass rained down from the broken skylight above as a black clad figure came crashing through.

Ropes snaked down around Margot.

Scooping Blair into her arms like a rag doll, Margot shrugged into a harness. With Blair draped over her hip, the helicopter's winch hoisted Margot into the air and up into the glaring rays of its searchlight.

Ernst followed suit when a basket was lowered, disappearing into the light and through the skylight, with the night's spoils tucked safely within the case in his grip.

The interior lights suddenly blazed.

Alarms bleated and red lights pulsed in hallways.

The elevators hummed, climbing steadily upward.

Boots pounded up the stairwell.

But in the silence of the exhibition hall, Brax lay limp and lifeless beneath the figure of the tortured priest.

CHAPTER 26

The front of the British Museum was a spectacle of devastation swathed in the white-hot beams of huge spotlights and the flashing strobes of an army of emergency vehicles. Sawhorses and crime-tape closed off one of the largest crime scenes since the London terrorist bombings.

Row after row of TV vans had taken up residence behind the barricades, their long microwave antennas beaming the live reports of perfectly coifed but frenzied news correspondents back to the networks.

The fire brigade was quenching the inferno in the Grand Hall where the helicopter had sawed its way through the expanse of skylight.

Inside, FISCD technicians, the CSI unit of the Specialist Crime Directorate, were combing for evidence, while body bags were stuffed with the remains of the fallen guards, the SFO teams on the rooftop, and intruders after the MEs had completed their preliminary examinations.

Chief Inspector Newley and Brody Devlin were standing in the outer hallway of the Enlightenment Exhibit Room.

The paramedics were hurriedly wheeling Lt. Braxton and Father Kelly on gurneys into waiting elevators.

In a glum voice, Brody Devlin asked the doctor, "Prognosis, Doc?"

Skinning off his latex gloves, the ME met his stare. "Lieutenant Braxton has suffered a severe concussion, but God willing, he may have been spared permanent brain damage." He bit his underlip. "Only time will tell."

Inspector Newley cut in. "And Father Kelly?"

The doctor gave a heavy sigh. "Aside from the wounds to his hands and feet, I saw evidence of brutal abrasions and lacerations. There was the tell-tale spotting of electrode burns on his thighs and genitalia. Probably administered by a stun-gun."

Newley grimaced and swallowed hard. "Any chance he'll be able to tell us who did this to him?"

"Barring any psychological blocking, maybe as soon as forty-eight hours. It's bloody hard to tell in these cases, Inspector. You see, the psycho-trauma can play an even larger part in the victim's recovery than the actual physical injuries themselves."

"Of course," Newley said. "Thank you for your efforts."

"Very well then, gentlemen," the doctor said, turning and heading for the elevator. "I'll leave you to it."

They turned and headed back into the exhibit hall.

Chewie was down on one knee, carefully examining the floor. His eyes panned across it, then looked upward to the shattered skylight above.

Teams of technicians were laying out a crime scene zone.

Scout Thompson sat perched in one corner, his field laptop balanced on his knees.

Standing over Chewie with Newley at his side, Brody asked, "What do you have for us, big guy?"

Chewie's hawk-eyed stare surveyed the room. Pointing toward the wall, he explained, "Brax entered from behind them, probably had the drop on them." He nodded toward the floor near a large dried pool of blood. "There's a boot mark impression in the bloodstain, size twelve I'd say. Not Brax's, he was wearing a size ten loafer. I checked." Chewie rose and gingerly hauled his large frame across the hall. "There's Brax's CORNER-SHOT, lying over there. From the tool markings on the barrel, I'd say the booted attacker ripped it out of Brax's hands with some jagged-edged instrument. Forensics will sort out just what it was."

Newley and Brody nodded.

"Don't stop now, old man," Newley prodded.

Chewie took a deep breath and expelled it sharply. He pointed to the opening in the ceiling where the vent had been and now lay on the floor a few feet away. "Someone came crashing down through that duct and landed on top of the second perp right beneath it."

"How the devil …?"

Chewie went on. "There's a palm print on the floor right here and a spot of blood on some shards of glass. And here … two equally distant circular marks, probably from the perp's knees."

Newley waved a forensics tech to Chewie's position. "See that you get photos and mark it well, young man."

Then Chewie strode across to a shattered display case.

He studied the case and looked back toward the spot where he'd been standing. "The second perp threw her victim across the room. And she landed here." He pointed to the demolished case.

"Now hold on a bloody minute, old man," Newley cautioned, ripping his hand from the pocket of his trench coat and wagging his bony finger at Chewie. "You referred to the perpetrator as *her* and then to the victim again as *she*. How the deuce do you know they were women? And how can you venture a guess that she hurled her some twenty feet? Bullocks!"

With an exaggerated wave across the floor around him, Chewie explained. "No signs of a struggle, but there's a trail through the glass where the woman was dragged away."

"Oh, very well. I'll concede your hypothesis about the lack of a struggle … but your absurd conjecture about their sex is preposterous!"

Chewie turned to one of the lab techs. "Show him."

The pencil-necked tech lofted two evidence bags, his face beaming. "Mr. Raindancer here spotted these hair strands, sir." He lifted one bag. "White-blonde follicles were found over there, near the palm print, along with a woman's earring, and…"—he hoisted the second bag—"… a chipped, polished fingernail and a redhead's blood-matted hair strand was found lodged in a splinter of wood in the display case."

Brody's neck went cold at the words *redhead's blood*. In his mind's eye, he pictured Blair being flung across the room and crashing into the display case, glass flying everywhere.

Newley gave a loud whistle. "Next you'll be telling me what perfume they were wearing and their measurements, I suppose."

Chewie smiled thinly, shook his head.

"No … but I can tell you their names."

Newley's jaw dropped.

Knuckling his chin, Brody cut in. "The blonde is Margot Gant, I'd bet my pension on it. And the redhead…" His voice hitched slightly now. "The redhead is Dr. Blair Kelly. We know she was here and there's no trace of her."

Chewie winked. Then, suddenly, his clear, keen eyes sparked. He dashed back to the center of the hall, beneath the skylight, like a hound that had caught the scent of a raccoon.

He drew up short in front of Chief Inspector Newley. "Hey, give me your shoe."

"What? I most certainly will not…"

Dropping to one knee and grabbing the inspector's ankle, Chewie lifted the right foot. Newley struggled to keep his balance, vehemently protesting being manhandled.

Chewie said gruffly, "Hold still and stop wiggling, Inspector."

To the tech, Chewie shouted, "Hand me some tweezers, quick."

Brody couldn't help it. The sight of Newley balancing like a cow with a crutch, while the big Indian grappled with his leg, was too much. He burst out laughing. A welcome comic relief to the evening's violence. But when Brody composed himself, he looked closely. Stuck to the edge of the sole of Newley's shoe was a fiber.

Gingerly plucking the fiber with the tweezers, Chewie dropped it into the plastic bag the tech held out before him.

Chewie turned to Scout. "Hey, Mr. CALTECH. You still got that mini-electron microscope thing-a-ma-jig hooked up to your hundred-K Game Boy?"

Huddled around Scout, they looked on in silence as the techno-wizard loaded the fiber lifted from Newley's shoe into the scanner of the high-tech laptop.

"Holy shit!" Scout said, his eyes bulging from their sockets. "Sweet!"

On the LED screen, the magnified image of the fiber's strands danced like tiny microorganisms.

Brody looked puzzled. "Okay, what the hell is it?"

"Somethin' Future Combat Systems and the Natick Soldier Center have been workin' on for years, but so far, it's only a pipedream."

"Looks like nanotechnology to me," Chewie said matter-of-factly.

"Give that man a cigar," Scout said. "The concept is to incorporate nano-fibers into a combat suit. When a soldier flexes his biceps or legs, the 'exomuscle' or nano-enhanced fabric would multiply the force of the muscular system by as much as five to twenty times."

"A Superman suit?" Brody said, incredulously. "That would explain how 'Blondie' could toss Blair across the room like a bag of woodchips."

From behind them came a caustic voice. "Well, if it isn't Sherlock Holmes and the boyish Doctor Watson explaining the crime scene to the doltish Inspector Lestrade, while Tonto looks on."

Brody turned.

Sir Nigel Cummings, obese and petulant as ever, waddled toward them. Brody's gaze tracked from his buttery neck lying in folds over his stiff collar to his cold gray eyes. He held a book in one hand and a letter in the other.

As he stood in front of them now, he craned his fat head around the hall. He sighed and locked eyes with Devlin. "Well, Major Devlin. I see that you and your American 'cowboy-bravado' have botched your assignment once again. You must be so proud, eh?"

Chewie nudged forward, his hands fisting at his side, but Brody grabbed his arm and held him back.

In measured tones, Brody answered, "I may have lost a good man here tonight. The stench of blood here and above us on the rooftop is still fresh in my nostrils, Sir Cummings. Your snide humor dishonors the brave men who gave their lives in the line of duty."

Cummings gave a dismissive wave of his pudgy hand. "Be it as it may, I meant no disrespect." He turned to Chief Inspector Newley and planted the letter forcefully against his chest. "Your walking papers, Inspector. The Home Secretary has decided that I am to clean up your mess here. Her Majesty's Secret Service will bc taking over from here. Your paltry services, as they are, are no longer required."

Newley read the letter, his face twisting in anger.

He stiffened and neatly folded it, then tucked it into his breast pocket. The inspector turned and nodded weakly to the ΩMEGA team. Then his head swiveled on Cummings. "To hell with you, you pompous cheeky—twit." Then he spun on his heels and marched off.

Cummings shrugged and gave a blubbering chortle.

His face grew stern, eyes narrowing. "Major Devlin, might I have a moment in private, please?"

At the far end of the outside corridor, away from the foot traffic and prying eyes and ears, Brody stood facing Cummings.

"Major, we need to put our little schoolboy squabbles aside for the time being. This matter has gotten royally out of hand."

Brody started to speak, but the fat man cut him off.

"Furthermore, I understand you were involved in a gun battle earlier this afternoon. I had to do some fancy footwork to keep the Metropolitan Superintendent of Police and the Home Secretary from hauling your pink arse over the coals."

"Gant's henchmen were after the girl. It was kill or be killed."

"By the girl, I take it you are referring to—"

Brody shook a crick out of his neck and cut in. "Doctor Blair Kelly. And now she's gone missing. Most likely abducted by Margot Gant."

Cummings jutted his three chins and studied Brody in silence before speaking. "And since you have taken your blasted sweet time to inform me of these escapades, I take it that you had the foresight to at least keep your superiors informed, eh?"

Just then, Devlin's cell rang.

Cummings gave an oily, knowing grin as he nodded toward the chiming cell phone. "Hah! It would appear that you haven't. I suggest you take that call, Major Devlin. And if you haven't been busted to Corporal Devlin after finishing, please be so kind as to meet me in my car downstairs. It will be the big black one, Major…"—he crinkled his bushy brows, leaned in and whispered—"with the tinted windows."

With that, Sir Nigel Cummings fought to maneuver his fat ass and thunder thighs down the hallway, leaving Devlin to take his call.

He answered the cell. "Devlin."

He wasn't surprised to find it was Bill Sorensen's angry voice on the other end.

"Jeezus H. Christmas, Devlin! What the hell's going on over there? You've got me ducking pot shots from Capitol Hill and the White House. Langley is laying it on thick. Telling the NSC what a bunch of loose cannons ΩMEGA is, and how we're stomping all over London, running rough shod over the Brits. And Ambassador Logan and DCM Wimple are ready to skin you alive…something about a high-speed car chase through London?"

"Brax is in intensive care," Brody broke in. "He may have permanent brain damage, Bill."

"Oh, hell! Okay, take it slow and fill me in. I want to hit the ground running soon as I touch down at Heathrow."

"You're hopping the pond?"

"En route as we speak, kiddo. Bringin' some reinforcements, too. We've got to get a handle on this before it's too late, Dev."

Succinctly and briefly, as he'd been trained, Devlin told Sorensen what had transpired.

Scout rushed to Devlin's side, an eager puppy-dog look on his face. Brody tried to wave him off, but Scout persisted.

"Hold on, Bill. Thompson's got something urgent."

Catching his breath, Scout managed, "You took off before I could tell you. I got a fix on Doctor Kelly. The GPS tracker plotted her movement. I had to expand the grid you see and—"

Brody felt his heart lighten, then he glared. "For God's sake, Scout. Just tell me where the hell she is!"

"Area called North Devon. Hoity-toity old English countryside. Big estates, castles and horse farms. She's somewhere near the coast."

Devlin's mind plunged down the rabbit hole. He pictured the embossed invitation to Heinrich von Gant's little party at RAVENSCAR—his estate—that he'd received at the hotel, then he pictured the address … North Devon.

Turning his attention back to his boss, he said, "We've got new intel, Bill. I'll brief you when you come in. It's a fix on Doc Kelly's location."

Downstairs, amidst the tangle of police cars and fire trucks, with Chewie and Scout at his side, Devlin searched for a glimpse of Cummings's black sedan. Giving up and frustrated, Brody turned to his men.

"Scout, get your butt over to the hospital and check on Brax," Devlin said. "Chewie, you get out to Heathrow and pick up the boss. It's gonna be a long night."

Chewie nodded and pointed. "Looks like we've got company, Brody."

A thin little man in a bowler hat and a long gray-tweed double-breasted overcoat threaded his way toward them. He looked like a character out of a '40's spy film.

"Major Devlin, sir?" the little man inquired.

“You one of Sir Nigel’s cloak and dagger boys?” Devlin asked.

The man in the bowler looked around furtively and nodded. He pressed a hardcover book into Devlin’s palm.

Devlin pulled back, reluctantly taking the book.

“Sir Nigel asked me to send his regrets, but he has been called away. He asked me to inform you that he is organizing a raid on the North Devon estate at dawn. He asked me to collect you in the morning, sir. Would that be at the Dorchester, then?”

Dumbfounded and speechless, Brody Devlin just nodded.

“Very good, sir.” The little man in the bowler turned spryly and sauntered off.

Devlin hoisted the book and shouted to the man’s back. “Hey, I didn’t get your name, pal.”

Tipping his hat and glancing over his shoulder as he ran, the man answered, “I don’t believe I gave it, sir.”

Devlin stood on his tiptoes, peering over the crowd, trying to keep the little man in sight. “What’s with the book, then?” he shouted back, confusion filling his voice.

“A little light reading, Major. Something Doctor Kelly left for you, I believe.”

Devlin shook his head and blew a sharp breath from puffed cheeks. He glanced down at the book, read the cover.

THE MIDWICH CUCKOOS

CHAPTER 27

In her room at Eden School, Noor lay curled in a tiny ball, her legs tucked closely to her chest. She'd stopped whimpering now, but her lower lip still trembled slightly.

Clutched tightly in her tiny hand was Mr. Muffins's button eye, the only part of the stuffed animal that she'd been able to retrieve from the *Dark Room.* She'd pretended to fall, feigning wobbly legs when she slid from the chair. Unseen by Dr. Craven, Noor had scooped the button from the cold floor as she rose.

She rolled onto her back in the bed and rubbed the button back and forth between her thumb and finger. For her it was a kind of magic touchstone, a bond with Blair, her only link with hope.

And Noor made a decision. From now on she would think of herself only as Wendy, putting the name Noor and all the bad memories associated with it, the loss of her parents and her previous life, behind her forever.

Footsteps echoed down the outer hallway, coming closer, and halting abruptly at her door.

Wendy popped the button into her mouth and lay frozen with fear.

The lock clunked and the door swung inward.

Ms. Baylock was standing in the doorway, her skeletal frame backlit by the harsh light of the hallway.

"Time for dinner, missy," Ms. Baylock said, her forgotten cigarette hot beneath her hawkish nose, a scrim of smoke coiling before her glasses.

In the dining room, Wendy slid her tray off the carrier and made her way to the table where the Lost Boys were seated.

She sat next to Peter and studied the boy's faces.

Averting their eyes, they sat silently, looking down. They were staring at their plates like they'd never seen lima beans and roast beef before.

Wendy looked down at her plate, but after her earlier experience in the *Dark Room*, she didn't have an appetite.

When Ms. Baylock left the cafeteria, Peter glanced around warily and finally spoke. "You okay, Wendy? We were worried."

Absently, pushing the beans around on her plate with her fork, Wendy sniffled. "Sure, but what's wrong, Peter?"

A member of the staff walked by and Peter hunched over his dinner again. When the man had passed, Peter turned to Wendy. "They took another boy to the *Dark Room*." Simultaneously, the other boys raised their heads and nodded their agreement.

Around a mouthful of potatoes, Johnboy said, "They nicked Michael from the telly room. I've got a god-awful bad feeling about it."

"He never misses dinner, does he?" little Gabriel said to Peter, his voice hitching.

Peter nodded glumly, then affected a brave smile. "Eat your vegetables, Gabe."

Gabriel scrunched up his face and reluctantly spooned the lima beans into his little mouth, spilling half of them onto the table on purpose. "Oops!" he said, giggling.

Raji, who was seated on Wendy's left, leaned in closer. "Wendy, you must leave tonight. I overheard them talking about you. Doctor Craven was chatting with that witchy Cruella De Vil."

Puzzled, Wendy asked, "You mean Doctor Humpty Dumpty?"

"Old piggy-face … his real name's Craven," Raji explained.

"He's a meanie and he hurt Mr. Muffins," Wendy added, scowling. She fished the shiny button from her pocket where she'd tucked it and showed it to Raji.

Raji's face tightened and his eyes radiated sadness as he spoke. Wendy studied him in silence, her eyes beginning to glisten slightly because she knew what he was saying was true, and because she knew she would have to leave the Lost Boys behind. Her hand fisted around Mr. Muffins's button-eye as she listened.

Raji explained that Wendy was different than the other children, more important to the doctor and Cruella, Margot Gant. Raji had thought that they'd said something about Wendy being the key, the one with the second sight that could open the door.

When Raji finished, Peter explained the plan. "Ms. Baylock goes home every night at lights out. Johnboy and I will make a big ruckus and Raji will sneak you out. Since Raji can see what's going to happen a few minutes into the future, Raji can predict what the guards will do before it happens. He's the devil to beat at hide-and-seek."

Just then, Wendy's attention was drawn to Johnboy. Something coppery-colored scuttled out from inside his shirt, over his shirt collar, and down his arm. She flinched. It was a huge cockroach.

Johnboy noticed her reaction and gave a belly laugh. "Hey, don't be a fraidy-cat, Wendy." The roach was sitting on the back of his hand now and he was cooing to it, making soft, clucking sounds. "His name's Oscar. Wanna hold him?"

Wendy shuddered, pulled back in her seat. She loved all of God's creatures … *but a roach*?

Peter chuckled. "Johnboy can speak their language. Oscar's the only pet he can hide from them."

Wendy nodded her understanding.

Peter continued. "You can hide in the boot of Baylock's car until she gets to her flat, and then pop out and … Bob's yer uncle, you're free!"

Little Gabriel chimed in, "You won't forget us, will you, Wendy?" His big blue eyes peeked from beneath a shock of hair, staring beseechingly.

With a lump in her throat, Wendy managed, "I'll be back for you, Gabe. I promise."

CHAPTER 28

In her room, Wendy paced the floor. They'd taken her clothes when she returned from dinner and she now wore a nightshirt and slippers.

She heard a strange sound. A whispery hissing noise was coming from inside the wall. Pressing her ear against the wall, she held her breath and listened.

Then came a scratching sound, a furious scrabbling. Busy, industrious sounds:

Clinking.

Tapping.

Scraping.

Thumping.

Suddenly, alarms blared from the hallway.

The door opened and Raji's smiling face appeared.

"Let's go!" He took her hand and led her down the corridor that was dyed red by the flashing pulses of emergency warning lights. Wendy's short legs struggled to keep pace with Raji's long strides. Her lungs were burning with fear as they rounded corner after corner.

When they came to the elevator, Raji skidded to a halt and closed his eyes in deep concentration. Quickly, he pulled Wendy around the corner into the shadows. They huddled together, gulping short breaths, hoping their ragged breathing wouldn't give away their position.

The elevator doors hissed wide. Men dressed in black uniforms spilled out, their boots pounding the tile as they stormed off in the opposite direction.

Backs sandwiched to the wall, Raji and Wendy inched around the corner and leaped into the elevator. Raji punched the button for the lower garage level.

In the control room of the school's security center, a guard who was wolfing down a sandwich heard a clawing sound coming from the vent. His hand fell away from his mouth, and he turned toward the noise. His eyes were riveted on the vent screw. The screw was revolving, slowly coming out of the face of the vent plate.

The guard's jaw went slack.

Thinking it was a trick of light, he blinked and absently wiped the mayonnaise mustache from his upper lip with the back of his hand. But when he looked closer, he thought he could make out tiny maroon pinpoints of light that seemed to float in the dark cavity behind the grille.

The screw popped out, fell to the floor, rolled across the tiles and stopped at his foot.

Another guard was pounding away at the closed-circuit camera controls. "Hey, *wot* the bleedin' hell? I've got nothin' but black on five monitors."

The vent plate swung down, away from the ventilation outlet, hanging from the one remaining screw.

A dark ocean of fur poured out and into the room, tumbling down the wall and washing across the floor.

"Bloody rats!" the sandwich-munching guard yelped and leaped onto his chair.

The second guard spun toward the onrushing vermin. He fumbled for his sidearm as wave after wave of rats spilled from the ductwork and surged across the floor, up his pants legs and over the consoles and TV monitors.

The guard screamed as a brown and black mass of fur cloaked his chest and arms and tiny razor-sharp teeth gnawed at his hand, forcing him to drop his handgun.

The other guard's hand reached out to slap the master alarm button, but a large rat sank its teeth into the meaty palm of his hand, and he howled in terror.

Outside the control room, an army of roaches and centipedes gushed through the air vents of every corridor. They flooded down the outer corridors and painted the walls and security cameras black. They were a slimy, glistening mass of wiggling legs and bodies.

Johnboy and Peter had pulled the last of the fire alarms and were headed for the laboratory area. The sea of insects that blanketed the floor parted, clearing a path for Johnboy as he led the way, making soft clucking sounds as he went.

The massive stainless-steel lab door burst open.

A woman in a lab coat ran out, screaming and clawing at her hair. She was pawing at her shoulders, trying desperately to beat off the rampaging roaches and spiders that clung to her like bees to a hive. She stumbled and fell, gained her feet, and stumbled again. The heel of her shoe had broken off and she hobbled down the hallway, a glistening crust of insects covering her whole back.

The boys entered and made their way through a maze of workstations and lab equipment, eyes searching in the dim light. Peter stopped and pointed.

The sign on the door read *AVIARY.*

Johnboy nodded and they entered the room.

Birds of all species twittered and warbled and cawed from behind row after row of cages.

A brightly plumed Macaw parrot paced nervously back and forth on his perch. A nameplate on his cage read TINKER BELL. “Blimey, mates!” the parrot screeched and cawed.

Johnboy’s jaw dropped. He and Peter exchanged bewildered glances.

The parrot cawed again. “Silly bugger. Cloth-eared sod.”

“I think he’s talking to you,” Peter told Johnboy.

“Sharpest tool in the shed, that one,” Tinker Bell said, bobbing his beak. “Cat got your tongue, boy?”

“You can talk!” Johnboy stammered, puffing his cheeks and blowing a long breath.

“Crikey, guv’ner, ain’t you as clever as a bottle of chips.”

Peter moved closer. “Say, there. There’s no need to be rude. Mind your manners now.”

Tinker Bell pranced and ruffled his feathers. “Ah, sod off! Pop these cages and let’s sling a hook!”

The boys dashed from cage to cage, flinging the doors wide. The captive birds took wing and performed a swooping aerial ballet around them, chirping madly as they flew.

The boys moved to Tinker Bell's cage and gingerly opened the door.

"Caaaaw!" the parrot screeched as he burst from his gilded cage, repeating over and over, "Margot's a bleedin' *Zwitter*! I know a secret, I know a secret. *Hau ab, du wichser!*"

The boys exited the aviary room and headed for a set of double steel doors across the lab. From behind the doors came a strange laughter. It was almost but not quite human, too high-pitched and agitated.

Hesitating, the boys pushed through the doors and into a funhouse menagerie. Whooping and chortling manically, the inhabitants greeted their intruders. The boys passed rows of cages filled with sadly freakish primates and other creatures, which were barely recognizable: a ring-tailed lemur covered in scales flopped and writhed on its back for a few seconds, then the iguanalike creature rolled over and got to its clawed feet, wobbled sideways. Disoriented and sluggish, it scuttled around in a circle and chased its own barbed tail; a large hunch-backed orangutan, covered in molting feathers instead of red fur, crouched in the corner of its cage; with its misshapen head perched atop a long, thin neck, it more closely resembled a baby ostrich than an ape.

Just looking at them made Johnboy feel queasy.

With baby steps, the boys moved to another cage. Behind the bars, a chimpanzee with large deep blue eyes peered out, its expression tortured. The ape's eyes conveyed an unnerving intelligence that startled Johnboy. "He looks so sad," Johnboy said to Peter, a lump forming in his throat as he looked on.

"I think these things are mutants," Peter said, glancing around. "Somebody made them like this. It's beastly hellish."

The chimp's eyes welled with tears as a soft, barely audible keening sound came from the back of its throat, then it turned and hung its head sorrowfully.

Quaking with fear, Johnboy managed, "You think they're going to do this to us?"

Peter wrapped his arm around Johnboy and hugged him reassuringly. "Stiff upper lip now, old boy. Don't get your trousers in a Melvin. Wendy will sound the alarm and be back before you can say—"

"Tickety-boo," Johnboy answered, forcing a weak smile.

* * *

Wendy lay in the claustrophobic confines of the car's trunk, her breath held tightly and listening. She heard the hollow click of Ms. Baylock's heels against the hard concrete floor of the parking garage drawing nearer.

She heard the car door open and slam shut.

Then the engine sparked and Wendy felt the car begin to move beneath her. Moments earlier, foreseeing the exact time of Ms. Baylock's arrival, Raji had jimmied the trunk open and helped Wendy scramble into the boot of Ms. Baylock's rusted sedan.

The ride was bumpy and the air was stale. Wendy began to feel her stomach take an elevator ride to the penthouse, and she gagged back hot bile. She was a little dizzy, too.

She was shuddering now, chilled to the bone, dressed only in her flimsy cotton nightgown and slippers. Her toes felt like icicles. She tried to take shallow breaths, fearing she'd run out of air before Ms. Baylock stopped and she could escape.

She dreamt of blue skies and fresh sea breezes and Blair.

After what seemed like hours, the car began to slow and came to a stop. The car door slammed and the car bobbed slightly, signaling that Ms. Baylock had exited the sedan. Rigid with tension and biting her lower lip, Wendy waited. "Fifty-five, fifty-six," she whispered, counting to mark the time. "Three hundred and forty, three hundred and fifty, ready or not, here I come."

Scooting around in the darkness, her fingers found the emergency trunk release. She pulled.

It wouldn't budge.

She tried again, harder this time.

Nothing.

Her neck went cold. She would have given anything for a torch now; the blackness seemed to swallow her.

Using both hands, she yanked again.

With a slight popping sound, the trunk lid sprang open.

Peeking over the lip of the trunk, Wendy looked around. The coast was clear. She hobbled out and onto the sidewalk. She inhaled the sweet night air, filling her lungs and clearing her head. It began to drizzle.

Then she saw it in the distance, the bright headlights of an approaching car, snaking toward her through the slanting rain. Taking involuntary steps, she inched her way backward into the shadows. She glanced around. A large red-brick tenement building loomed at her back.

Her gaze shot back to the street.

The headlights were closing fast.

She darted out of the shadows and scurried up the front steps. In the dim glow of the single bulb over the front glass door, she tugged at the handle.

Locked.

Gooseflesh pebbled her arms as she stood shivering in the damp night air. From behind came a voice, almost making her jump out of her skin. “Could you assist me, *Mademoiselle*?” She wheeled around to see the smiling face of an elderly man, his arms filled with grocery bags. He wore a beret, old-fashioned wire-framed glasses, and had a neatly trimmed goatee.

He nodded toward the keys hanging from the fingers of his left hand that caught the light as they jangled. “If you’d be so kind as to unlock the door, *s’il vous plaît*?”

Wendy’s eyes ticked from the man to the approaching car. It was a hulking black limousine.

She snatched the keys and fumbled with the lock, her tiny hands cold and trembling.

The latch rasped and she stepped into the warmth of the foyer.

The elderly man stepped in behind her, jostling the bags as he closed the door with a labored kick.

Wendy heard the screech of brakes coming from the curb out front. As the wash of the limo’s high beams illuminated the old man’s face, Wendy noticed that his face was severely creased in wrinkles and as fragile as tissue paper. A tiny drop of rain fell from his bearded chin.

The old man slowly turned toward the sound and shook his head disapprovingly. “*Mon Dieu*! Look at the way *ces idiots* parked that automobile, blocking the whole street like that.”

The solid thud of slamming car doors came from the street.

Before the old man could turn and face her, Wendy dropped the keys and bolted for the stairwell, shouting back over her shoulder, "My mother's calling me, I've got to run."

The old man stood looking as Wendy disappeared into the stairwell. He gave a knowing smile and there was a mischievous twinkle in his eye as he whispered, "Fly away, *ma petite* bird."

Shouting voices and frantic pounding drew his attention back toward the entrance door. He turned to see two bull-necked men. Their hulking frames filled the doorway, blotting out the outer lamplight as their fists pounded violently. In an exaggerated and deliberate motion, he leaned closer and squinted.

Their muffled voices shouted for him to open the door. He glanced back toward the stairwell, turned back to the door, and shook his head no. With a shrug, he slowly turned and shambled away.

"Break it down, now!" the pursuers' leader shouted.

A booted foot kicked the door hard where the lock met the doorframe, and the door exploded inward, banging loudly against the inner wall, glass shattering, spilling across the tile floor. They rushed into the building. The leader ordered, "Grab that old fool!" just as his doddering image disappeared around a corner.

Two pursuers bolted after him. But seconds later, when they rounded the corner, they braked to a halt, the soles of their boots leaving black skid marks on the faded tile floor.

The men stood dumbfounded.

The old codger was gone, as if he'd vanished into thin air.

With her last ounce of strength, Wendy shouldered her way through the rooftop door. The steady drizzle of rain felt cool and welcoming as she pounded across the rooftop. The cold evening air poured into her lungs as she ran. *Almost there,* she thought. *A few more feet and I'll be free.*

She stopped suddenly and inched her way toward the edge of the roof.

The wind rocked her as she stood, blinking the rain from her eyes, arms outstretched and struggling to maintain her balance.

Looking down, Wendy could dimly make out the blurred afterglow of headlights. The image brought a smile to her lips. It reminded her of fireflies swarming through the night.

From behind, the door burst open, banged against the wall with a loud thud. Light from the stairwell shot across the rooftop, reaching for her.

She turned. A knot of dark figures spilled out of the doorway and stood silhouetted in the weak backwash of light.

Even in the grayness, she could recognize the outline of the tallest form, her blonde-white hair capturing the watery light. Her stature, her body language was unmistakable; it held the raw cruelty of a coiled whip. She could almost feel the black wind of Margot Gant's terror. Her tummy was sick with fear. There were tears in her eyes, and she hated that.

The sound of another familiar voice, winded from the fast climb to the rooftop, sent panic shuddering through Wendy.

"Time to come home, little one," Doctor Craven said.

She didn't answer.

Another figure at the doctor's side took a step forward.

Wendy inched closer to the edge. Then Margot's arm shot outward, halting the other man's advance.

The blinding beam of a torch seared her eyes, made her stubble slightly.

"Shut it off, *du wichser*!" Margot snapped. When she turned to Wendy, her persona transformed instantly. Feigning a sweet, motherly voice, she said, "No one's going to harm you, darling."

Oh, bullocks you won't, Wendy thought.

As she spoke in soft soothing tones, Margot's hand glided to the tranquilizer pistol tucked neatly in her waistband at the small of her back.

Somehow, Wendy sensed the weapon mean old Cruella was hiding; she could picture the cold black metal in her mind's eye. But as she stood with her arms still extended, she felt as if the wind might waft her to safety. With half-closed lips, she began singing a nursery rhyme. "Rock a bye baby, in the tree tops. When the wind blows, the cradle will rock ..."

Wendy took another step. Wind tore across the rooftop, flaming her hair.

"When the bough breaks …"

Wendy's eyes were closed tightly now, her eyelids heavy with memories that were not quite memories, dreams that were not quite dreams, as she rolled her head from side to side.

She took another step.

"NO!" Margot shouted as she dove forward.

Silent, graceful, and weightless as an angel, the eight-year-old girl disappeared before her eyes.

They stood at the edge, staring down at the street below.

Nervously peering over the ledge and shaking his head, the pasty-faced Doctor Craven at Margot's side said, "Can't make out the street from here, *ja*?" He took a step back, gave a sigh of relief. "For a moment there, I thought just maybe our little bird could actually fly."

Margot's fiery eyes glared. She spun and backhanded the doctor hard across the cheek. "She *can* fly, you fool. That's the whole damned point!"

CHAPTER 29

Blair began to awaken, her neck and back throbbing with dull aches and biting pain. Her head felt as though it were stuffed with cotton, her tongue was thick and pasted to the roof of her mouth, her throat parched. She floated upward gradually, harsh light glaring in her eyes. The muffled sound of whispering voices floated toward her. She tried to focus, to clear her head. It wasn't happening.

Images came in brief flashes: the museum, the blonde she-wolf flying across the room toward her, and then—her brother's tortured body nailed to the wall.

She wretched, but only dry heaves shuddered through her.

A hand was gently stroking her hair.

A familiar musky scent filled her nostrils.

A recognizable voice whispered softly, "There, there, Ms. Kelly."

A cold chill raced up her spine as her eyes snapped wide open.

Al-Dajjal stood leaning over her. His crooked grin mocked her.

"We meet again, Doctor Kelly."

He raised a glass and pressed the bent straw to her lips. "You're dehydrated from the drugs, Ms. Kelly. Please, take some fluids."

Her dry lips found the straw and she drank.

"Easy, now. Let's not overdo it, or you'll make it worse," al-Dajjal said, pulling the glass away. "Doctor Craven has you on an IV."

Blair's eyes cut to her arm, saw the intravenous catheter inserted into her forearm, then tracked down the length of her body. A tangle of wires attached to electrodes were pasted to various points on her body and snaked back to a bank of monitoring devices. She was strapped to a canted operating table, her feet lower than her head.

Instinctively, her wrists fought the padded leather restraints. She arched her back off the table, twisting with what little strength remained. Her feet drummed against the table, straining against the straps lashed tightly around her ankles.

A familiar icy laugh floated toward her from the darkness. "Really, Ms. Kelly. Struggling is quite useless."

With the whirring sound of an electric motor, the operating table began to recline.

Then it hit her. She was wearing a hospital gown.

Frantically, her gaze shot around the room. A figure stepped out of the inky shadows. She remembered that treacherous grin, the glassy eye that canted inward. It was the man with the axe from the museum.

Al-Dajjal said, "Ernst, are your tools ready?"

Nodding eagerly, Ernst sidled up next to al-Dajjal. His yellowish eyes danced in the bright light of the surgical lamp that glared down from overhead. "Don't worry, I've sent your clothing for dry-cleaning," he told Blair. Ernst gave a taunting laugh as his gaze flowed up and down her body, raping her with his eyes.

She quaked more in anger than terror or a little of both. "You touch me again, you bloody bastard, and I'll cut off your …" Her throat seized up, and she coughed in spasms.

Al-Dajjal had moved to the adjacent wall where a large LED screen hung. When he clicked a remote, the screen filled with a montage of flickering images. Her mind reeled at the sight.

It was her naked body, captured from every imaginable angle.

"Ernst, you've missed your true calling," al-Dajjal teased as he took a cigarette from a gold case, fastened it to a holder, tucked it between his lips and lit it. "What remarkable photos." His eyes locked on Blair, a scrim of smoke wafting over his face. "Especially this one!" As he clicked the remote, the screen pixilated into the image of Blair's back, the elaborate tattoo captured in all its glory.

"Unfortunately, though quite beautiful to behold, I'm afraid we'll need your help in interpreting the intricate design," al-Dajjal explained. "You see, we were operating under the false assumption that your brother held the key. And unfortunately for your brother, we wasted valuable time and energy trying to induce him to share his secrets. You saw the results of his bull-headed tenacity. Let us hope, dear lady, that you won't force my friend here …"—al-Dajjal nodded toward Ernst—"… to resort to such extreme measures."

Blair heard the squeak of un-oiled wheels as a rolling surgical cart came into view from her right. Ernst was positioning it at her side. He stood to one side of the cart, so that Blair could clearly see the tools laid out neatly. His hands gloved in latex, Ernst slowly and deliberately ran his fingers along the gleaming row of instruments, hesitating at a scalpel, then moving on to wicked-looking pliers, then pausing at a razor-toothed saw.

"I take great pride in my work, *fräulein,*" *der Eisaxt* explained, his glass eye struggling to focus, his lips skinned back over yellowed teeth. "It's almost like a symphony, beginning slowly, ebbing across the soft flesh of your firm body, then rising to a crescendo as I probe deeply into the interior cavities."

The blood-red drum of Blair's inner ear pounded as her raging heart sent torrents of blood coursing through her veins. A loud buzzing followed as she slowly began to slip into a dead faint.

A sharp, caustic stench assaulted her nostrils.

Her eyes fluttered open. She jerked when she saw *der Eisaxt's* false eye hovering over her like a ruinous planet. He was waving a bottle under her nose and grinning wide. "I won't let you drift off, *liebschein.* At least not until the second chorus, *ja*?"

CHAPTER 30

Ginny Doolittle spoke the language of cats. In fact, she was multilingual. She could be seen on any given Sunday afternoon ambling down Cross Road, tipping her wide-brimmed felt hat at a neighbor as she pushed her cart brimming with bottles and aluminum cans.

Ginny Doolittle never stopped to chitchat, unless a gibbering gray squirrel or warbling sparrow called her over. Occasionally, a passerby would feel cut by her lack of acknowledgment; but when she was support-hose-deep in a juicy bit of gossip with a chattering squirrel, she simply couldn't be bothered. After all, it wasn't as if her furry and feathered friends could just stroll into the corner pub for a little heart to heart with their mates over a couple pints of bitters.

The neighborhood thought her to be a bit daft. Of course, she held an equally low opinion of her fellow humans.

If you gave her a cursory glance, you might assume that any old lady who wore a moth-eaten fur stole around her neck in the heat of summer was indeed a bit off. And on this particular afternoon, a French poodle made the same wrong assumption.

Mrs. Doolittle was doing her best to console a pigeon whose Alzheimer-inflicted mate had somehow lost his way home.

"Well, I know you're simply beside yourself with worry, my pet," Mrs. Doolittle said softly. "But men are such scoundrels, always running off with some young bird. They spot a little graying of the pin feathers … and off they go."

The pigeon stared blankly.

Mrs. Doolittle shook an admonishing finger. "You're just in denial, pet. Sometimes we girls just have to face the music."

A French poodle, true to his rude countrymen's reputation, bounded around the corner and between Ginny's bandy-legged knees, knocking her to the pavement. He didn't even turn back to survey the damage.

Mrs. Doolittle shouted after him, "You bloody Frog, where's your manners!"

Suddenly, as if by magic, the scruffy stole around her neck sprang to life. Eyes popping wide and hissing, the resurrected tabby cat bolted from her neck and scampered down the street in hot pursuit of the fleeing Frenchman.

"Oswald, you come back here this instant!" Mrs. Doolittle called, pushing the brim of the floppy felt hat from her eyes and struggling to her feet.

Neither she nor Oswald saw the lorry wheeling around the corner. The loud shriek of an air horn and the squeal of brakes sealed Oswald's fate.

Finding unknown strength and speed, Mrs. Doolittle ran toward the sound.

Ginny Doolittle made a low, strangled noise in her throat as she stood, frozen, looking down at Oswald's pancaked body.

The tiny bell, ripped from his neck by the force of the collision, rolled slowly toward her and came to rest at Ginny's feet.

Tear-blinded and dazed, she stooped to retrieve the bell.

The lorry driver appeared at her side. The hard lines of the huge man's face softened instantly. "The missus has a tabby just like …"—he paused, pulling an oily rag from his back pocket and dabbing his eyes—"I swear, mum, the bloomin' lil' thing just…"

As Ginny's eyes met his, the warmth, the understanding they radiated conveyed more than any words could have. The driver nodded solemnly and walked away.

A small crowd gathered.

As Ginny kneeled before what remained of Oswald, she said more to herself than anyone in particular, "Foolish boy. I warned you, Oswald … didn't I? You're not as young and spry as you once were. And how many times have I told you that you don't need to defend my honor anymore …"—her voice hitching, she added—" my brave, valiant Sir

Oswald." Gingerly, she reached out and lifted him. His limp little body lay snuggled in her arms.

Then from behind came a child's gentle voice. "I could mend him, y' know. I'm good at mending sick things."

Turning, Ginny saw her, a young girl with eyes as piercing blue as a June sky and skin as clear as summer air, stood barefoot, wearing a nightgown. The face was angelic, her hair gossamer. Even if she had not been wearing a nightgown in the middle of the crowded sidewalk, she would have looked out of place.

The girl had a calming aura about her. She extended her arms, offering to take the cat. Hesitating at first, and then not really knowing why, Mrs. Doolittle laid Oswald in the girl's small but elegant hands.

Mrs. Doolittle smiled weakly. "I'm afraid dear Oswald is in the Lord's hands …"

Although the child was beautiful, and most young girls projected innocence, Ginny couldn't help but be taken aback by the unusual quality of the girl's face. It projected a virginal, peaceful quality you would normally find only in great works of art.

"Don't worry, Ginny. I know how to mend him good as new," the girl said softly, but with absolute confidence.

Ginny nodded involuntarily. "I believe you do, child. Do you have a name? You seem to know mine."

"Wendy … just call me Wendy."

The wailing Klaxon of an approaching police car drowned her words.

Wendy flinched.

She appeared visibly shaken, her eyes darting furtively, her voice quick and nervous. "I have to—"

Picking up on the girl's reaction, Ginny grabbed her arm, guiding her through the knot of onlookers and toward the alley. "This way, my dear," Ginny said as they ducked into the alleyway. "Discretion is the better part of valor."

Once at a safe distance, they stopped. Ginny plopped onto a crate and huffed, bringing her hand to her chest. "My old ticker cannot take all this excitement, my dear." She patted the space next to her. Wendy sat, raising her legs and curling them to her chest. She gently laid Oswald at her feet.

Scurrying sounds came from inside the crate beneath them.

The beady eyes of a rat peered over the edge of the crate.

"Well, hello, young man," Ginny said, smiling. "I hope you don't mind that we dropped in on you without an invitation, but we're in a bit of a fix." The rat wiggled its nose. "Oh, how kind of you, but I've already had lunch, and I'm not fond of Limburger anyway."

Skittering onto her lap, the rat nestled comfortably.

"I don't suppose we could contact your parents, could we, Wendy?"

Wendy bit her lower lip and shook her head, not making eye contact. "No … mum's *in hospital*," she lied.

She patted Wendy's hand. Wendy responded by gently taking Ginny's arthritis-bunched, tremulous hand in hers. Ginny's gaze turned to Oswald. "I'm afraid no hospital could help him now."

A serious look washed over Wendy's face. She stared intently at the cat as she tenderly stroked its bloodied pelt.

When Ginny withdrew her hand to fish into her bag for a handkerchief, she noticed an odd, warm tingling sensation in her hand.

Pulling her hand from her purse, she held it out in front of her, studying it. Slowly, she began to straighten one gnarled finger and then another. Soon she was splaying and flexing her fingers. The numbing pain was gone. She stared in silent disbelief, first at her hand and then at Wendy.

At first a soft purring sound, then a yawning "meow" broke the silence.

Startled, Ginny looked down.

Oswald slowly lifted his head, stretched long, and rose to his feet. He shook his head, leaped into Ginny's arms, and licked her cheek.

The rat, less than delighted by Oswald's miraculous recovery, skittered off Ginny's lap and disappeared into the safety of his crate.

Hot tears of joy crowded Mrs. Doolittle's eyes. Standing, she said, "You are a special child, aren't you?" She took Wendy's hand. "Let's get you out of those clothes and into something more festive, me bonny li'l *laeken*. We're going to have a celebration."

"*Laeken*?" Wendy asked.

"It's an old Celtic word for girl. But in your heart you already knew that, didn't you?"

Wendy nodded as the puzzled look washed from her face, replaced by a broad knowing smile.

As the old bag woman and the young girl walked hand in hand out of the alley, the shearing sound of wings filled the air as a flock of doves swooped down from above. They darted and twisted in an aerial ballet, then gathered in formation, as if leading the way. A pure white dove landed on Wendy's shoulder, cooing softly.

When they turned the corner, exiting the alley, Ginny saw that more doves lined the rooftops on both sides of the street. Looking upward and shooing them away with her felt hat, she said, "Be gone with you, me li'l darlings. You'll give us away, you will."

CHAPTER 31

Bill Sorensen sat comfortably nestled in the back of the limo, sipping a glass of Jack Daniels neat. Beside him, dressed in a tailored Anne Klein pantsuit, sat Madison Dare, gazing at the passing scenery as they sped down the highway.

Madison was also a member of the ΩMEGA UNIT. Her good looks had caused many agents to underestimate her cunning and intelligence. But Madison thought of it as an advantage. And she wasn't averse to playing that card if the situation called for it. Recruited from NSA, she held advanced degrees in math and physics and spoke six languages fluently. Her mind was a steel trap. And rumor had it, so were her thighs.

"Please convey my appreciation to Sir Nigel for having you fellows pick us up at Heathrow."

The man riding shotgun in the front seat nodded, tipped his bowler hat. "Glad to be of assistance, Mr. Sorensen. We are all on the same team. I've made reservations for you and Ms. Dare. I trust you'll find the accommodations to your liking, sir."

Sorensen leaned forward. "Say, I don't believe I caught your names." When he glanced back, he winked at Madison, who smiled.

The man in the bowler turned his scruffy neck and faced the rear. "Name's Pope, sir." He nodded toward the driver, smiled thinly, and added, "And that's Mr. Miles, your wheel man."

Sorensen eased back in the seat, glanced at his wristwatch. He thought about calling Devlin, then decided against it. Cummings seemed to have the situation well in hand and he didn't want to make any more waves at this juncture. There had been enough noses bent out of joint already.

He figured Devlin could use a little rest before the next phase of the op went down. Madison was coming in fresh, batteries fully charged. If need be, he could count on her to take up the slack. Besides, Pope had explained that Sir Nigel wanted to have a face-to-face with Sorensen without Devlin in attendance. Sorensen had chuckled at the turn of phrase *in attendance*. These Brits could waltz you around the dance floor and stick a blade between your ribs without breaking a sweat. Elegant coldhearted bastards that they were, they would smile thinly as they pumped a slug into your grandmother and made bets on which way she'd fall.

But for now at least, Sorensen would play along, not ruffle any feathers.

He glanced at his watch again and gazed out the window. "Excuse me, Mr. Pope."

"Yes sir?"

"We seem to be heading away from the city. Where exactly are we meeting Sir Nigel?"

Looking straight ahead, Pope said, "Sir Nigel has laid on a special surprise for you. As a matter of fact, you'll be the guest of honor."

Sorensen rolled his tired eyes. "I'm flattered, but you didn't answer my question, did you?"

Just as Sorensen reached for his cell, the smoked-glass partition suddenly rose.

With a loud click, the door locks engaged.

Instinctively, Sorensen's hand flew to his SIG, nestled in his shoulder rig. But gas steamed through the vents, clotting the air.

From the corner of his eye, Sorensen saw Madison drawing her weapon, but it, too, was a futile act. The limo was fitted with bullet proof glass. No way could either of them blast their way out; they'd be struck by the ricocheting rounds and the windows were sealed tight.

Madison slumped in her seat.

Sorensen cleared leather and coughed violently, the noxious fumes tearing his eyes and taking their toll. He tried to hold his breath, but as his SIG tumbled from his hand, the darkness enveloped him.

The door to the interrogation room in the main complex crashed open, and Margot Gant marched into the room, cursing with each stride. She made directly for Ernst.

"Put down the pliers, you stupid fool. I want to try drugs first. If we have to resort to your crude methods, let's wait until her Loverboy's here."

Her gaze shot to al-Dajjal, waiting for his intervention.

Al-Dajjal took a deep pull from his cigarette and nodded to *der Eisaxt*, who sighed heavily and returned the pliers to the tray table. "Not going soft on me, are you, Margot?" al-Dajjal said sarcastically.

Margot glared and crimped her lips. "Dr. Craven's hypnotics are more effective." She skinned off her leather gloves and slapped them against her thigh. "We lost the little brat, and the children created a diversion at the school, raised bloody hell," she mumbled as she turned and paced the floor. "We will deal with them later." She stopped pacing and met al-Dajjal's gaze. "The little brat snuck out in Ms. Baylock's car. I was alerted by the GPS tracker implant that Craven inserted in her forearm."

Al-Dajjal stiffened. "Heinrich will be quite disappointed in you, darling. *Mein Brüder,* outwitted by a mere child."

She wheeled on him. "She got away from you in Syria, darling *Brüderlein.* I wouldn't be so quick to judge."

Dr. Craven entered, his eyes brightening at the sight of Blair strapped to the operating table. "I see my patient awaits, *ja?*" He held a black doctor's bag.

Blair had passed out again and lay still.

The doctor brushed past Ernst, looking distastefully at the surgical instruments as he placed his bag on the table and stood at Blair's side. His gaze tracked to the monitors displaying her vital signs and he smiled. "She's a healthy girl."

Next he removed a syringe from the bag, fitted its needle into a vial, and drew the liquid into the hypo.

Tapping her forearm with his fingertips, he said, "*Ja*, healthy veins, *das ist gut*." A thin smile creased his waxen face as he plunged the needle home.

Al-Dajjal's cell phone rang and he answered. After speaking briefly, he snapped it shut and turned to Margot.

"Our guests have arrived."

Margot nodded. "No complications?"

Al-Dajjal shook his head. "None whatsoever." He turned to Ernst. "Why don't you see that our guests are made … *comfortable*."

Scout Thompson was leaving the hospital when his mobile played the theme from *Star Wars*, signaling that Chewie was on the line. He'd programmed a distinctive ring for each member of the ΩMEGA UNIT.

"Speak to me, great one," Scout said.

"Cummings's pencil-necked geeks picked up Sorensen and Madison at the airport."

"Madison's here?"

"Yeah, Bill left word with Customs. Said we should stand down until we get further word from him."

Scout detected something in the big lug's voice. "Hey, what's eatin' you? We all know you got the hots for Madison, big fellow. Just chill, you'll see her soon enough."

Chewie grunted. "How's Brax doing?"

"Doc says he'll pull through okay. But he'll be outta commission for a while. Father Kelly's out of intensive care."

"Okay, meet me at the hotel. I wanna talk to Brody. This Cummings guy is full of *bovis sterus*."

"Yeah, he's got bullshit oozing from the pores of his oily hide, all right." Scout pocketed his cell and hailed a cab.

CHAPTER 32

At the hotel, Devlin was tossing and turning in a fitful sleep when the phone rang. He ripped off the sweat-drenched sheets and blinked at the bedside clock.

6:00 AM.

He fumbled for the telephone. Ragged breathing came from the other end. Then a soft whimpering sound. Through a sleep-clouded haze, he struggled to focus.

He recognized the voice. It was a woman's voice. Blair's voice.

Devlin swung his legs off the bed and leapt to his feet. He stood rigid, felt his bowels turn to jelly.

"Good morning, Mr. Devlin. I trust you had a pleasant night?" The hoarse mocking voice of Heinrich von Gant poured through the earpiece.

"Put Blair back on!"

"Oh, you'll see her soon enough, Mr. Devlin. And your friends also."

Devlin's hands fisted at his sides.

"If you want to see Ms. Kelly … *alive* that is, you'll come to RAVENSCAR immediately … and you'll come alone, Mr. Devlin. You will not contact your associates, nor the authorities. Is that perfectly clear, young man?"

Before he could answer, the line went dead.

A sharp knock came from the hotel room's door.

Devlin's hand snatched his Beretta from under the pillow, and he padded across the carpet to the door.

He stood with his back pressed against the wall to the right of the doorframe, his .40 semi-auto at the ready, naked as a jaybird.

* * *

Chewie arrived at the Dorchester and saw Scout standing at the entrance, his trusty laptop's case gripped in his hand. He hit the Jag's power-window rocker switch and the passenger side window glided down. He leaned across the seat and shouted, "Hey, Mr. CALTECH, what gives?"

Scout ran to the Jaguar. Leaning in the window and breathing excitedly, he managed, "I just saw Brody leaving."

"Alone? Where was he headed?"

"Don't know, but two of Sir Nigel's men were with him."

"The limey with the bowler from last night?"

"Yeah. They pulled out in a black Bentley a few minutes ago. Tried to call you, but my cell's dead."

"Climb in!"

Scout barely slipped into the passenger seat as Chewie tramped the gas pedal; the door swung inward with the momentum of the lurching car and clipped Scout's shin.

The sleek Jag burned out, tires smoking and leaving a long patch of rubber, narrowly missing a doorman as it fishtailed past.

CHAPTER 33

As the black Bentley veered off A39 onto a narrow roadway, Brody Devlin peered out the rear side window. Sir Nigel's men had shared little if any information with him, only giving their assurance that they had already executed a raid on Gant's estate, and there was no longer any need for worry on Devlin's part.

It was a cold morning and the clouds hung dark and ominous against the horizon. Neither the overcast, slate-colored sky nor the intelligence men's pale and somber faces gave Devlin any solace. And Gant's threatening phone call didn't jive with the MI-6 boys' story about the raid. At this point, Devlin figured he'd have to just roll the dice.

The road snaked to the left, suddenly widening, and an ancient church greeted him. It was a gray stone structure with a high bell tower, perched on a hill in the center of a small hamlet.

As they drove, he busied himself reading *The Midwich Cuckoos.* It was the book Mr. Pope had thrust into his hand the night before.

He looked up from the novel and glanced out the window at the passing scenery. They were rolling past an isolated and serene-looking little town that reminded him of the Village of Midwich featured in the story. Turing back to the book, he thumbed back to the inside cover, where a scrawled handwritten note read:

> Dear Sis,
> Cuckoos place their eggs in the nests of
> other birds to hatch. Doing my best to take of
> your little bird.
> Love, Dominic

Devlin skimmed the book, getting the gist of the story as he speed-read through it. It may have seemed like an odd thing to do at a time like this, given the circumstances, but in a small way it made him feel less helpless, clinging to a desperate hope that some key, some magic gift lay inside those covers that he could use to rescue Blair from this impossible situation.

Basically, the theme of the story was about mutants and humanity's instinctual mortal fear of anyone who was too different. One day, all the inhabitants of Midwich fell into a deep sleep. In fact, anyone who tried to enter the village succumbed to the same fate, blacking out and dropping to the ground in a heap. The "Dayout," as the book called it, only lasted twenty-four hours. Nine months later, however, all the Midwich women gave birth. Married, single, widowed—it didn't matter. But these little "cuckoos" they'd hatched weren't average in any way. Their IQs were off the charts, and they had displayed telepathic abilities from infancy on. They could move things with their minds. But even worse, they could induce those whom they'd felt somehow wronged them to commit suicide; one with a shotgun, the other by driving straight into a stone wall.

Being pre-adolescents, the alienlike children were egocentric; they seemed to lack any conscience, any sense of right and wrong, any feelings of remorse or pity. And the "cuckoos" had a hive mind. What one learned, they all learned, simultaneously. Their sole motivation was survival.

Devlin pitched the book across the back seat in frustration. If only he could have had more time with Blair. If only she'd shared more details about the little girl, about Gant's twisted worldview. Was Father Kelly saying that the kids in al-Dajjal's clutches were somehow "cuckoos"?

He glanced out the window again. The Bentley was slowing. A grotesquely twisted tree towered beside a low stone wall; a gnarled branch seemed to point and reach its withered claw toward a grand mansion which loomed up ahead. The huge English country house surrounded by open fields fringed with thickly wooded areas was like some picturesque manor house in a movie. But the brooding gunmetal gray sea that lay beyond the house formed a dark backdrop like in a Hitchcock thriller; threatening and menacing, it sent icy chills through Devlin.

Bad omen, Devlin thought as the car sped up a long drive and slowed to pass through an enormous iron gate that stood wide open, unmanned. As they passed, Devlin noticed the abandoned guardhouse and dog kennel. Behind the chain-link fence of the dog pen, lean and muscled Alsatians padded to and fro in silence, their frosty gaze never leaving him as they paced. Devlin cringed. *Attack dogs again! Figures a neo-Nazi like Gant would have a pack of bloodthirsty German shepherds.* It wasn't that he hated dogs; it was more of a phobia. As a boy, his best friend had been mauled to death by a big German shepherd. His best friend being a doleful-looking golden retriever named Sam.

The Bentley pulled to a stop at the entrance. Pope jumped out and escorted Devlin toward the door. As they went, Devlin glanced around. There were many cars parked in the forecourt of the mansion, but not a single soul anywhere in sight.

Looking upward, menacing gargoyles stared down from the eaves. At an upper window, a loose shutter was swinging rustily in the wind. When he looked down and took a step forward, a large black cat streaked under foot, mewling eerily like an infant's cry as it darted into a hedge.

They were admitted to the house by a silver-haired servant whose features had been neutered by age; the only clue to his gender was the trousers he wore beneath a long black apron.

The whole thing was surreal; the only thing missing was a dissonant minor chord struck by some demented phantom seated at a towering pipe organ.

Standing in the grand foyer, it occurred to Brody that he could about-face, tuck his tail between his legs and race back to London to get reinforcements, and maybe, taking the haunting atmosphere of the mansion into account, a bag filled with crucifixes and wooden stakes wouldn't be a bad idea, either. But where would that leave Blair and the little girl?

Ahead, Sir Nigel was making his way down a large double staircase as fast as his stumpy legs would carry him.

Sir Nigel's hand was raised to greet him, a fat grin on his piggish face.

Catching his breath, Sir Nigel Cummings managed, "So happy to see you, old boy. I was terribly worried that I'd offended you last night. If you'd please accept my apologies."

Devlin looked around, shrugged. "No offense taken. It's awfully quiet, Sir Nigel," he said, his questioning voice laced with suspicion.

Sir Nigel smiled, his rosy cheeks blooming. "Everything is under control, Major. Things turned out quite lovely-jubbly after all."

Devlin met his gaze, frowning. "That so? Where are the rest of your boys and where's Blair?"

Sir Nigel gave a knowing wink. "She's just ducky, old man. Doctor has given her a clean bill of health."

"Then you found out what Gant was up to, the museum break-in and all?"

Winking, Sir Nigel said, "Oh, yes … but all in good time, Major. Come along now. Let's get you to Doctor Kelly, shall we?" After waving Pope off, the fat man took Devlin by the elbow and gently propelled him toward a large set of oak double doors across the foyer and down a hall. He rapped, leaned in and grabbed the brass handles. As he shoved open the doors, he indicated with a nod that Devlin should enter.

Brody Devlin halted just past the threshold and stared into Heinrich von Gant's beady eyes, too tired of the cat and mouse game to feign surprise.

"Mr. Devlin, how wonderful to see you again. I am simply at a loss for words." Gant stood before a cavernous blazing fireplace. With roaring flames behind him, Gant's body was thrown into silhouette, the outline tinged red.

Devlin gave a smug look. "I sincerely doubt that, Gant."

Brody glanced around the room. There was a familiar face and a few new ones. But all eyes were now on him, studying him intently as though he were something on display in a Cabinet of Curiosities. He felt uncomfortable.

He recognized Margot Gant seated on a rich black leather sofa that was in stark contrast to the white leather pantsuit that fit her body like a glove. She was postured like a model, with one long leg crossed over the other, absently bobbing the ankle of her booted foot. When she turned, her white-blonde hair fluoresced with red-orange highlights, reflecting the flickering flames of the fireplace.

A taller man, dressed in an elegant charcoal suit whose lines were broken by a pair of custom-tooled riding boots, moved toward him, hand extended. "I don't believe I've had the pleasure."

"And you won't," Brody said flinty eyed, his arms folded across his chest.

"Now, now, manners, Mr. Devlin," Gant admonished. "Let me introduce the man whom I believe you were sent to kill, Azrael al-Dajjal."

Al-Dajjal nodded. Then, without warning, his hand knifed underneath Brody's suit jacket and snatched Devlin's Beretta from his shoulder holster.

Devlin's arm acted reflexively; it shot out and his hand clamped down on the man's wrist like a vise.

"Release him, old boy," a familiar voice said from behind him, followed by the unmistakable sound of a revolver being cocked. Devlin froze, let go of al-Dajjal's wrist, and spun toward the voice. He was looking down the gun barrel of Sir Nigel's Bulldog .44 Webley.

Devlin smiled and laughed, nodding toward the old revolver wavering in Sir Nigel's pasty hand. "Careful where you point that antique, *old boy*. It's probably got more lead in its pencil than you do."

The fat man was leaning casually against the double doors, his free hand behind his broad back clasping the knob, as if his large bulk were a fleshy barricade should Devlin decide to break and run. Sir Nigel gave a terse but nervous laugh and seemed relieved when Devlin's gaze fell away from him.

An angry barking came from Margot's direction.

Devlin spun around. Two sinewy, sleek-coated German shepherds bounded across the room toward him, baring their fangs and growling menacingly.

Oh, hell no! Not more dogs! Devlin thought as he stood frozen in fear, his throat crimped tight with dread.

Al-Dajjal gave a shrill whistle and called to the dogs in German, "Wotan, Siegfried, heel!" The dogs skidded to a halt at his side. Nodding approvingly at the shepherds, he added, "Watch!"

With their heads lowered and shoulders hunched, they sat panting and drooling, eyeing Devlin as if he were a cut of choice prime rib.

Completely ignoring the dogs, al-Dajjal was giving Devlin's Beretta a cursory glance. He checked that the chamber was loaded with a round and raised it, pointing it at Devlin's gut.

Devlin sneered. "I know the drill … no sudden moves, right?"

The shepherds snarled.

Devlin's gaze ticked to the dogs as he tried to work up some saliva in his parched mouth.

The jack-booted thug shot Devlin his crooked smile. "Please, no heroics, Major. My hand is quite steady."

Without turning to acknowledge Sir Nigel, Devlin looked past al-Dajjal and said, "I see that the lard-assed Englishman has thrown in with you, Mr. Gant."

Gant grinned and there was a malicious satisfaction in his smile. "Indeed, Major. Sir Nigel's resources have been most helpful. While you and the others were otherwise distracted, he secured Jung's diary from *Doktor* Kelly's office at the museum. But don't be so humble, Major. Your efforts have been most helpful."

Devlin stiffened. "Helpful to you? Hell, Gant … if you were on fire, I wouldn't walk across the street to piss on you. Now where's Blair?"

"Patience, Major. And before the day is through, you and your colleagues will be most helpful, of that you can rest assured."

Dancing shadows, cast by the raging fire, played across the room's high ceiling, spawning sinister patterns which were never still.

A short, pudgy man strained as he rose from a chair.

His close-set watery eyes twinkled.

"Doctor Craven," said Gant, gesturing toward the piggish little man whose face glistened with sweat. "The good *doktor* has been conducting the most remarkable experiments in the field of genetics, Major Devlin. He's leaps and bounds ahead of anyone."

"I suppose that was your handiwork in Syria … the Zombielike villagers?" Brody asked Craven, his eyes and voice mocking the doctor. "What a boon for mankind and science."

Craven's brow creased in anger, his underlip forming a pout. "The genetic mutation we induced had an unforeseen side effect. It revved up the subjects' metabolism. Instinct, the will to survive, their all-consuming hunger for nourishment, turned them into throwbacks—wild flesh-eating beasts."

Margot Gant slowly came to her feet, brushed past Craven, and slinked to Gant's side. She stared at Devlin, her eyes soft and teasing one moment, murderous the next. In a voice husky and dripping with taunting sexuality, she said, "Enough of this charade, gentlemen. Let's let *Loverboy* here see his little Irish priestess."

"Very well," Gant agreed. He nodded to Sir Nigel. "Let the lovers have their moment. Please escort Mr. Devlin to *Doktor* Kelly's room."

Margot raised her hand as she glided across the room toward Devlin, her eyes filled with amusement and never leaving him. “No. I’ll see to him myself.”

As she approached, Devlin had to admit she was stunning. The slim heels of her boots clicked seductively on the polished hardwood floor, and her hips swayed as her long legs pranced like a leggy runway model. The way her leather suit was unzipped to a point just below the cleft of her breasts completed the image of aggressive sexuality.

When Margot and Devlin were gone, Gant stood stoop-shouldered, warming his hands in front of the fire. “Such a stubborn young man.” Eyes closed, Gant craned his neck, twisting out a crick. “Craven, please play voyeur and keep an eye on Mr. Devlin and the little Irish slut, won’t you?”

Craven nodded curtly and left.

His gaze locking on the fat man and al-Dajjal, Heinrich von Gant gave a thin smile and clapped his hands. “But we are neglecting our other guests. How rude. And to leave them with that brutish degenerate, Ernst.” Gant sighed. “*If* … Mr. Sorensen is still among the living, I have a little experiment to test his endurance for pain and bravery.”

CHAPTER 34

They'd taken an elevator and now were making their way down a hallway. Devlin was bewildered by Margot Gant's nonchalant attitude. She hadn't led him at gunpoint, and Devlin couldn't image how the woman could be concealing a weapon beneath that skin-tight leather outfit she wore.

Suddenly, she stopped and shoved him into a room. She stepped in quickly behind him and closed the door.

She was on him like a tigress, her full lips pressed to his, her tongue exploring the cavity of his mouth, her hands groping and squeezing his athletic buns as she moaned.

Despite himself, her raw sensuality stoked the flames of desire in his groin. He was getting aroused.

She began nibbling on his lip, then chewing playfully, her eyes wide open and catlike.

Suddenly she bit down hard and a pulled at his lower lip with her teeth, drawing blood. He cried out and pushed her away.

Her eyes were feral and taunting as she threw back her head and laughed.

She clucked her tongue and pouted. "Loverboy doesn't like to play rough," she said as her tongue flicked out and slowly licked Devlin's blood from her lips.

"What do you want?" Devlin asked bluntly.

"You interest me. Ruthless men are so attractive."

Then, almost gliding toward him, she unzipped the front of her pantsuit to the belt that rode low on her hips, exposing her full breasts and flat stomach.

He took an involuntary step back. "Trust me, honey. I'm not your type."

She inched closer, gazing intently. “Maybe I could help you escape.”

“Why would you want to do that?”

“If we were lovers, I might convince Heinrich that you could be trusted.”

“In your dreams!” Devlin gulped hard. She was close to him now, having indiscernibly crept nearer as she spoke. Margot’s gaze was hypnotic, drawing him in as she closed the distance and pressed her firm flesh against his chest. Her pale blue eyes gazed back at him, unblinking, drawing him down, his head bending toward her, his lips reaching.

Margot was sapping his will and he knew it. Her haunting gaze was pulling him downward into a churning whirlpool of lust and wanton abandon. She took his hand and brought it to her breast, holding it tightly to her firmness, her nipple hard and erect.

Then she jumped, locking her arms around his neck and wrapping her legs tightly around his waist, her firm thighs squeezing as his lips met hers.

Blindly, Devlin staggered across the room, Margot’s iron thighs compressing tighter and tighter as she ground her hips.

The crushing force of her legs banded around his torso was driving the wind from his lungs. He couldn’t breathe. He stumbled, managed to keep his balance, writhed and twisted and fought to break free.

Margot held tight, her fingernails digging into the nape of his neck, drawing blood.

In desperation, Devlin slammed her back against the wall, again and again, until finally, she released her vise-grip hold on him.

She groaned as her legs went limp and slid over his hips, her feet finding purchase on the floor.

Devlin gripped her by the shoulders and pinned her to the wall.

Her eyes fluttered and opened wide.

When she gave a teasing smile and contemptuous laugh, Devlin drew back his hand to slap her but paused in mid-strike. It was against his principles to strike a woman in anger. The image of his drunken stepfather batting his mother around the kitchen flashed through his mind.

“Yes, hit me hard. Make it burn!” Margot blurted between loud groans, shuddering in anticipation.

He pushed away from her, contempt and revulsion replacing the pangs of lust. "You're one sick bitch."

Her eyes slitted with rage as her arm pistoned out, the heel of her palm hitting him square in the chest.

Devlin flew backward all the way across the room, his back slamming hard against the opposite wall.

Shaking his head, he staggered forward, coughing and trying to catch his breath. "But you're one strong and crazy sick bitch."

Like a wildcat, she pounced, closing the distance in one leap. He saw the glint of a blade fisted in her hand and sidestepped. The blade's tip caught his cheek as it flashed past.

He dropped to floor and crouched, balancing himself on the balls of his feet and the palms of his hands. He twisted his body, his leg shooting out with a round kick that swept Margot's feet out from under her.

She crashed to the floor flat on her back, the wind knocked from her lungs, her neck whiplashing the back of her skull against the hard floor with a loud thud.

The blade flew from her hand and clattered uselessly across the bare floorboards.

Devlin gained his feet and retrieved the weapon. He cursed himself. He'd thought he'd felt a hard protuberance when Margot had ground her hips into him. Now he realized what it was. It was a razor-sharp, wide-bladed belt-buckle knife. The buckle acted as the knife's hilt, and the business end was concealed behind the belt's tongue when worn. It was deadly if wielded by a practiced hand. Hidden in plain sight, it was easily within the user's grasp. If Margot had caught his throat, he'd be lying in pool of his own blood, twitching spasmodically, his heels drumming the floor as he bled out. But she didn't.

He shook it off, stood over her. Her eyes opened briefly; a wicked grin filled her face and faded as her eyes rolled back into her head.

Devlin's gaze tracked to her bare, heaving breasts. From beneath the edges of the leather suit, in stark contrast to her pearlescent skin, a coarse dark-knit fabric peeked out. *The nano-fiber suit, of course. No wonder she's got thighs like an Iron Maiden.*

The door burst open and Pope rushed into the room, the spring steel shank of a leather-encased lead-weighted blackjack fisted in his hand.

The little man with the bowler struck out, but Devlin blocked the blow with his left forearm, stepped in with his right foot, and hooked his right arm around and under Pope's forearm. Wrenching Pope's arm at an unnatural angle, Devlin's free hand grabbed Pope's wrist and snapped it back. Devlin heard the brittle crack of wrist bones as the wiry little man bellowed in pain and sank to his knees. The leather cosh tumbled from Pope's fingers.

But Devlin was outnumbered. Three bull-necked guards along with Mr. Miles, the other SIS man, rushed into the room and took only three minutes to beat him senseless. Pope struggled to his feet. From between clenched teeth and nursing his sprained wrist, he said, "Get the bastard out of my sight and lock him in with Dr. Kelly."

Devlin came to and blinked, the harsh morning light from a window momentarily blinding him.

He blinked again and his vision cleared. Bottle-green eyes stared down at him. It was Blair.

He tried to sit up, but pain clawed at the back of his skull and he slumped back.

"Hey, take it easy there, Sherlock." Blair's soothing voice was like some angelic choir to his ears. She was pressing a cold washcloth to his forehead as she sat on the bed, his head cradled in her lap.

Her fingertip lightly touched his cheek.

He flinched and cried out in pain. "Hey, that smarts."

"Such a cry baby. What the hell happened to you?"

He winced and cleared his throat. Taking a glass from the bedside table, Blair gently raised his head and brought it to his lips.

When he had finished drinking, she returned it to the table and began swabbing his cheek with a clean towel.

"So?" she pressed.

"Pope and some of Gant's thugs tap-danced on my head, I guess."

She rolled her eyes. "I suppose you're here to rescue me?"

He gave a weak smile and nodded.

"Wonderful." Blair tilted his head slightly and studied his neck. "I don't know who Pope is, but unless he's a flaming transvestite with nine-inch nails, you've got some explaining to do, Mister."

Brody's hand went to the back of his neck and fingered the deep scratches that were crusted with dried blood.

Then he remembered Margot and their little S&M smack-down. Trying to feign an innocent look and failing, he explained, "Had a little run in with Margot Gant, too. Fights like a hell-cat."

Blair tugged at his collar and nodded, her eyes narrowing. "Sure, that explains the lipstick stains on your collar, you bleedin' liar!" She shoved him off her lap and shot to her feet. She stood across the room, glaring. "You're one of them, aren't you?"

Devlin struggled and managed to sit up. He felt like a complete heel. That's when he noticed Blair was wearing an old-fashioned gown, sixteenth-century he guessed. She looked so beautiful, so elegant, even with red-rimmed eyes that were glaring at him now.

But behind that Irish temper, Devlin could see the fear in her eyes. God knows what she might have been subjected to at the hands of these lunatics. Paranoia was a natural reaction for captives. Ripped from the safety of their everyday existence, they soon became disoriented—and sometimes the loathing and hate they felt for their kidnappers transferred into co-dependency, even romance. He had to reassure her that he could be trusted.

"It wasn't like I had a choice, Blair. Guess I came pretty close to being *psychically* raped. She somehow got her claws into my brain."

Blair stared incredulously for a moment, then her face softened. Her eyes began to glisten with un-spilled tears. She sank to her knees, sobbing. That's when he noticed the deep purplish bruising on her upper arms, wrists and ankles.

Brody went to her on wobbly legs and collapsed on the floor in front of her. He took her in his arms and kissed her tenderly on the forehead.

When he gently lifted her chin, hot tears ran down her cheeks. "Blair, I love you. It doesn't matter what's happened. We're together now, that's all that matters."

"But that man did things …"

Devlin softly pressed his fingertip to her lips and shook his head, his heart ripped from its root by the thought of Blair being tortured, but knowing that anything he might say in response would be appallingly inadequate. “It’s okay, these people are monsters. We’re both a little shell-shocked. But for the moment, you’re safe.” He placed a tender kiss on her bruised lip.

Then she began to laugh, even as furious tears ran down her cheeks. A tiny smile broke free and she blotted her cheeks with the back of her hand. “Guess we’re some pair, all right.” She sniffled and caressed his face. “I hate you, Brody Devlin. You’re pigheaded.”

“No, just stubborn.”

“And a lousy liar!”

“Nah, just unimaginative and just plain stupid sometimes.”

“A typical … man!” Blair smiled and kissed him long and hard. Then she snuggled close and whispered into his ear, “I’m pretty sure the room is bugged.”

Brody nodded his acknowledgement. Then he removed a small Derringer from the false heel of his shoe, careful to conceal his actions with their bodies, and slipped it into Blair’s palm.

Her eyes widening briefly, she continued to kiss him, tucking the tiny revolver into the bodice of her dress.

He pulled back and lifted her in his arms, laying her gently on the bed. He lowered himself to her waiting lips and kissed her again. She sniffled and he fished a hanky out of his suit pocket and wiped her nose.

She smiled, her eyes brightening. “At least you offered me a hanky this time.”

“That’s my girl,” he said. “If it’s any consolation, your brother’s out of intensive care and the doctors say his condition is stable. I called the hospital on the way over.”

She sighed heavily. “Thank God.”

He pushed himself off the bed. He went to the window, looked down into the courtyard below. Teams of guards with German shepherds tugging at their leashes patrolled the grounds below. *God, why attack dogs?*

“It’s locked tight and the windowpanes are made of ballistic-grade Plexiglas. I tried.” She pointed to a broken chair that was lying in the corner of the room.

He gave her a puzzled look, glanced toward the door.

Blair rolled her eyes. "Really, Brody. They've got a storm-trooper guard posted right outside the door. You truly think women don't know about such things, don't you? For your information, I had a Land Rover in Iraq once that was armored and outfitted with bulletproof windows. Satisfied?"

He turned and plopped down on the bed at her side.

"Okay, so for the moment we're stuck, Mata Hari."

She wrinkled her turned-up nose. "She was Dutch and a little plump. Besides, wasn't she killed by a firing squad?"

Brody smiled and pointed to her gown. "But at least you're dressed for the occasion. Like her, you can go out in style."

Blair scowled. "Very funny. So what's the plan?"

"Debriefing time. Tell me everything that happened. Don't leave anything out."

Her eyes widened as she whispered, "But the walls have ears."

"You won't be telling them anything they don't already know, will you?" He gave a warm smile and patted her wrist. "Why don't you start …"—he nodded toward her gown— "… with the getup you're wearing."

She smoothed the folds of her gown. "Gorgeous, isn't it? But honestly, I don't have a clue. Somehow it seems oddly familiar, like I've worn it before. Nuts, eh? Anyway, I was out cold, completely naked under the covers. The gown was draped across the chair. It was this or prance around in my birthday suit."

Devlin pictured her standing nude, her long red hair cascading over her alabaster shoulders. As if she could read his thoughts, Blair frowned and rebuked him, "You'd like that, wouldn't you? You dirty old man."

She told him about the escapade at the museum, about the man they called *der Eisaxt*, her voice hitching as she related the scene in the interrogation room. About Dr. Craven, about his and al-Dajjal's fascination with her tattoo. And finally, she told him about the little girl, Noor, who now called herself Wendy.

When she'd finished, she sat bolt upright. "We can't just sit here, damn it! That little girl needs me!"

Devlin looked around the room. He grinned wide and waved at the unseen cameras. Then he pulled her off the bed and guided her toward the door. "Don't move."

He walked to the center and began rummaging in the drawers of an old desk. His hands filled with a stack of stationery, he went down on one knee, crumpled the paper into a pile in a wastebasket and fished a lighter from his pocket.

"I'm bloody cold, but I really don't think a bonfire is the answer, Davy Crockett," she said.

Flames licked from the wastebasket as smoke plumed toward the ceiling. Devlin rushed to her side and pulled her toward the door.

His fists pounded the door panel as he shouted to the guard, "Hey, *Herr Arschloch.* Fire!"

* * *

In the adjacent room, Dr. Craven had his back to the surveillance monitor. Bored with Devlin and Blair's conversation, which was being recorded anyway, he had also removed the headphones. He busied himself by pouring a fresh cup of Earl Grey and stuffing his fat cheeks with biscuits drowning in marmalade. His face twisted and he sniffed the air. Was something burning? He glanced at the hotplate. Nothing unusual there. No frayed cord.

When he turned back to the TV screen, the cup slipped from his sausage fingers and shattered on the floor. Choking on a bit of biscuit stuck in his throat, he stumbled toward the console. The image on the screen was a thick fog of smoke. Frantically, he reached for the control joystick and panned the tiny pinhole camera back and forth across the room.

Through the dense haze he could barely make out an image. The door to the room was wide open and Devlin and Blair were nowhere to be seen.

CHAPTER 35

Ginny Doolittle and Wendy were rounding the corner to the side street where Ginny's flat was located. "There's so much I have to tell you. But you're safe now, li'l one. You're among friends."

Wendy gazed up into Ginny's warm eyes and nodded. "Friends, Ginny?"

A gleaming Rolls-Royce Phantom pulled alongside and stopped at the curb.

Ginny didn't notice, but Wendy did. She tugged at the old woman's tattered skirt and pointed to the limousine.

"Well, blimey, here's our friends now," Ginny said.

The driver, dressed in the smartly pressed uniform of a chauffeur, calmly exited the long car, opened the rear door, and motioned for them to get inside.

They climbed into the limo and the driver shut the door behind them. Then he returned to the wheel, carefully signaled, and pulled smoothly into the street.

Wendy felt so tiny seated in the plush folds of the leather seat. When she wiggled her butt, trying to get comfortable, it made a squeaking noise. She giggled.

An old couple that was sitting in the seat across from her and Ginny gave a tittering chuckle.

Wendy studied them. The couple both had snow-white hair, and clear blue eyes. They wore old-fashioned clothes. Wendy thought it was like in a fairy tale. They looked like they had stepped from the pages of a storybook, out of some old photograph and into the modern world. The old man rested his hands upon the knob of a shiny black cane that was between his knees, and the woman kept her hands folded peacefully on her lap.

"Bonjer, Mon-sher," Wendy said, struggling with her French and failing.

The old man's eyes twinkled as his long fingers stroked his goatee. "So we meet again, *Mademoiselle*."

Though now he was dressed elegantly, Wendy recognized him as the same old man with the grocery bags that she had helped enter the brownstone earlier.

Wendy looked down and then met his gaze with a sheepish look. "I'm sorry. I had to fib to you before, about my mother calling and all. My name's …"

He adjusted his beret. "An apology is quite unnecessary, dear child. And there is no need for you to introduce yourself. We know exactly who you are. But my name is Nicholas, and this is my lovely wife, Perenelle."

Wendy bowed her little head.

He winked. "As a matter of fact, we've been keeping our eyes on you for quite some time now."

Puzzled, Wendy turned to Ginny. "Is Nicholas my guardian angel?"

"Well, something like that. These are the friends I was telling you about, li'l darling. You are a very special girl and you're part of the Awen now, child."

"The A-wen?" Wendy asked.

"Yes, child," Perenelle said. "You can't have too many friends nowadays… no, indeed."

The old man leaned forward. "The Awen are a very old group of wise and gentle people, child. They come from ages ago, from an old group called the Druids. The Druids knew the secrets of nature, the mysteries of the universe. And they passed this knowledge down to the Awen. The Awen in turn know the secrets of the elements."

Wendy cocked her head. "The elements?"

"Metals and the power that lies within all of us. I understand you, too, have special gifts?"

Wendy shrugged. "Sometimes I can see things with my mind. And sometimes, when I get really scared, I can fly."

Perenelle reached down, pulled off her high-button shoe, and began massaging her foot. "With the way my bunions flare up so, I wish I could fly instead of walk."

The old man reached over and patted his wife's knee. "Such lovely dainty little feet, she has. My little ballerina."

Wendy liked these people. They were like Ginny, a little daft, but funny and kind. The old lady frowned and looked Wendy up and down. "Nicholas, my God, the child cannot be running around barefoot and in a nightgown."

"Maurice," Nicholas said to the driver. "If you would be so kind as to hand this young lady that box, please."

Wendy sat with the large clothing box on her lap.

"Go ahead, child," Nicholas coaxed. "I think you will find that the clothing fits you like a glove. Perenelle has a good eye for such things."

Wendy lifted the lid and let it drop to the floor of the limo. She peeled back the tissue paper and a beautiful white dress with matching satin slippers greeted her.

"It's like a princess's dress," Wendy said, lifting the gown.

When the old man turned to Wendy, his tone remained gentle, but she detected a new seriousness in his voice. "Child, let me see your arm, please."

She put down the dress and met his gaze.

Gently, the old man took her arm and ran his long, tapered fingers across it. "That should do it," he said. "Those beastly fools planted a tracking device in your arm, but I have rendered it useless."

Puzzled, Wendy stared at her forearm.

"You're a good girl," the old man said, smiling warmly. "Kindhearted and loving. You and your Lost Boys at Eden School are Indigo Children, all equally empowered with magical gifts. And as you all grow older, you will learn to harness your gifts. Always remember that with these gifts comes a great responsibility."

Wendy sat quietly, listening intently to his every word.

"There is, however, a potential danger. I've seen some Indigos grow big-headed." Nicholas noticed Wendy's frown. "What is it, child?"

Her beautiful eyes radiated sincerity. "Gosh, you mean my head will swell up like a fat melon?"

Nicholas laughed softly. “No, child. Big-headed means vain. You must never come to think of yourself as better than others, their superior in any way. Because the moment you open that door, the dark forces that lurk in the Creator’s universe will reach in and snatch you.”

The little girl wrinkled her nose. “So don’t be stuck-up and always keep my door locked, right?”

He shook his head and smiled. “I meant the doorway of your emotions, which unlocks your heart, your soul.”

She giggled. “Oops!”

“Really, darling,” Perenelle told her husband, scowling. “You’re confusing the poor dear.” She turned to Wendy. “You see, sweetums, there are bad old meanies in this world who would steal your gifts. Nasty people who seek only power and wealth.”

“I think I know who you mean,” Wendy said. “People like Captain Hook or Ms. Baylock at the School.”

“Yes, dearest one,” Perenelle answered. “Their souls were like all of us when they were born, brilliantly shimmering diamonds. But their evil ways have turned their souls into a lump of coal.”

They talked for some time. Nicholas explained that Indigo Children were named for the radiant bluish color of the aura that they emitted, which could only be seen by sensitive souls who possessed second-sight. He told her that these children usually displayed marvelous psychic abilities: telekinetic and telepathic powers.

The old man turned his head when Wendy slipped into her new dress. Nicholas broke out a box of éclairs and a thermos of tea for the adults and a bottle of milk chilled in a fancy silver wine bucket for Wendy. The pastry filling dripped onto the seat.

“Oh gosh, I’m terribly sorry,” Wendy said to the old woman.

“Oh, Maurice will clean that up in a jiffy. Don’t you worry your pretty little head.” The old woman struggled back into her shoe and looked out the window.

The limo coasted to a stop.

“My heavens, Maurice,” she said to the driver. “Are we here already?”

“Yes, ma’am,” the driver answered.

Wendy got to her knees and peered out the window. "Where are …?" The words stuck in her throat. In the distance, beyond a copse of oaks, lay RAVENSCAR Manor House, the black and ugly sea at its back.

Wendy could feel the blood drain from her cheeks, and her heart pounded against her rib cage.

"Oh, no need to fret, child," the old lady said softly. "Blair and the Lost Boys need your help. After all, you promised you would come back for them, did you not?"

Wendy had sensed Blair's presence before she'd escaped from Eden School. But she had chalked it up to wishful thinking. Now, however, the feeling was strong. And her fear began to melt away, replaced with the self-confidence of a little girl who possessed reason beyond her years, a little girl who knew her purpose in life.

Wendy stood beside Ginny, her hand clutched tightly in the old lady's grasp, waving at the departing limo.

"Aren't the Flamels just wonderful people?" Ginny said.

Wendy wrinkled her nose. "They're really very old, aren't they? Much older than they look."

Ginny gave a snorting laugh. "Yes, my wee li'l one, old as dirt."

Like an old hound catching the scent of a coon, Ginny craned her neck, sniffed the cold breeze, and turned her head toward the manor house. "Off we go now, luv."

With the little princess in tow, the old bag lady toddled off into the woods as fast as her support-hose-clad piano legs would carry her.

CHAPTER 36

When the guard burst into the room, Devlin was waiting, his back pressed to the wall on one side of the doorframe. Blair had lowered the bodice of her gown to reveal maximum cleavage. She stood squarely in front of the door.

The gaga-eyed goon made a beeline for Blair, and Devlin stepped out and delivered a sharp blow to the back of his head with the base of a heavy lamp.

They were running down the hall now as Blair managed, "I thought you chaps used a karate chop?"

"I've got soft hands," Brody explained.

"What if he hadn't opened the door? What was your Plan B?"

Devlin pulled her down another corridor, their footfalls sounding like thunder slapping the hardwood floor. "Didn't have a Plan B, actually."

As they spun around the corner, she almost lost her footing and Devlin yanked her arm to steady her.

"Bloody hell! Easy on the arm, Tarzan."

"Kick off those damn high heels!" he said.

She did. "You know, you're just brilliant. You show up here by your lonesome, don't tell your unit where you went, don't notify the authorities that I've been kidnapped …"

Pounding footsteps echoed down the hallway from up ahead.

They doubled back and bounded up a staircase. On the landing, a knight in a suit of armor greeted them. Devlin snatched the sword from the dummy knight's hand.

Blair scoffed. "Do you know how to use that thing?"

"Well, I saw *Braveheart* six times."

"Mel Gibson can dance. Can you?"

"What the hell has that got to do with anything?"

"Oscar Wilde said, 'In many ways, fencing is like dancing, except that fencing is harder and you might get stabbed in the face!' So… are you light on your feet or should I call a plastic surgeon?"

The sound of the approaching guard's boots pounded up the stairs from behind them.

Devlin shrugged and looked down the staircase. "Two left feet."

"Then hand it over, Mr. Fred Astaire," she barked as she ripped the blade from his hand and scrambled up the stairs.

Devlin followed after her.

When they reached the next floor, Blair's hand snaked out and grabbed him by the collar and pulled him next to her, tight against the wall.

Panting, her back pressed to the wall, she held the sword poised over her head. When the muzzle of a submachine gun stabbed around the corner, Blair sliced downward with the sword. Sparks ignited with the clash of steel on steel as the wide blade knifed the H&K MP-5 from the attacker's hands.

Dumbfounded, the attacker stood bug-eyed and flat-footed directly in front of her. Blair swung the sword back around and thumped him hard on the forehead with the flat of the blade. He sprawled out cold on the floor at her feet.

Devlin snatched up the MP-5.

"Oh, excuse me," he said, proffering Blair the weapon. "Here, you earned it."

She hoisted the Derringer. "This will do."

Stepping over the comatose guard, they bounded down the hall. In the distance, another knot of armed guards spilled into the corridor. The guards spotted them and raised their weapons.

Rounds chewed into the wall at Devlin's side and particles of plaster dusted his hair.

"Jeez, these bastards really love machine guns," he said, pulling Blair down as he dropped to one knee and fired a burst, taking out two advancing guards. He sprayed a second burst, and another attacker ducked for cover. "Get out of here. I'll cover you."

On hands and knees, the chatter of the H&K deafening in the closeness of the corridor, Blair crabbed her way back down the hall and turned at a bend. Suddenly, Devlin appeared at her side, standing.

"What the hell are you doing down there? Get up! Let's go!"

Cheeks puffed and flaming red, she gained her feet and wheeled on him. She drew back her hand and slapped him hard on the cheek. He rubbed his bruised cheek. "What the hell was that for?"

"I really liked those shoes!"

She marched off down the hall toward a large set of brass-studded leather double doors. Devlin stood, staring at her lovely retreating bum.

He caught up to her just outside the doors. "Whaddaya think?"

Blair glared and put her shoulder to the door. It opened into a second vestibule. The walls and floor were gleaming white and beyond stood a second set of stainless steel double doors.

"I don't like the looks of this," Devlin said.

Shouting voices came from beyond the doors behind them.

Without a word, they both ran toward the double doors, which opened wide with a pneumatic hiss as they approached.

Cold, antiseptic-laced air welled out as they rushed into the room.

The room was dimly lit as they ran from pool to pool of light that marked a foreboding path through the inky darkness. Devlin sensed that the room was cavernous. In the distance, he could faintly make out two figures standing at the far end of the long room, their backs to them.

As they ran, Devlin hoisted the MP-5, aiming at the backs of the men.

Suddenly, an overhead bank of lights blazed, washing the room in dazzling light. Blinking and trying to focus as his eyes adjusted to the harsh light, Devlin grabbed Blair's arm as they slid to a halt on the polished concrete floor.

The two men slowly turned.

Al-Dajjal and Heinrich von Gant stood leering at them.

"Well … Major Devlin," Gant said. "So nice of you to join us."

Al-Dajjal stepped forward, closing the distance, his arms held out at his sides, palms up as though in surrender. "Mr. Devlin, I see that you are armed. I suppose you'd like to shoot me squarely in the heart?"

"I would if I thought for a moment you actually had one, you coldblooded butcher."

Al-Dajjal threw back his head and gave an icy laugh. "Such sardonic wit, Major. I am truly going to miss you."

Devlin took aim.

From above came the chilling sound of bolts being jacked as unseen hands racked rounds into the chambers of their weapons. From the corner of his eye, Devlin saw Blair's gaze sweep upward and then back to him. She extended her hand and forced the muzzle of Devlin's weapon downward.

Devlin glanced up. Strung out across a steel catwalk high overhead, a line of guards had their automatic weapons trained on Blair and himself.

From behind, two guards rushed up and jerked the MP-5 from his grip. A sharp blow to the back of his calves sent Devlin to his knees.

A bull-faced guard manhandled Blair to her knees.

Al-Dajjal stood looming over them.

He caught Blair under her chin and roughly jerked her face upward toward his.

He stooped, pressed his nose to the long tresses of hair, which hung over her face. Breathing deeply, his eyes closed, he kissed the tip of her nose.

She pulled back in revulsion and spat in his face, cursing him from between clenched teeth.

The blond beefcake raised his hand, poised to deliver a backhanded blow, when Gant spoke slowly and forcefully, "Do not mark her face!"

Al-Dajjal stepped back, his hand dropping to his side. To a guard, he shouted, "Bring them along!" as he spun on his boot heels and marched off, his footsteps echoing in the darkness.

The guards jerked them to their feet and shoved them forward, the muzzles of their weapons prodding and stabbing at their backs as they stumbled ahead.

Under her breath, Blair taunted Devlin as they moved. "You realize we were like rats in maze. They arranged it so we'd end up exactly where we are. Brilliant, bloody brilliant!"

"You had a better plan … I suppose … and just thought you'd keep it to yourself, eh princess?"

"You pigheaded twit. Men … who needs them! Bullocks!" Blair shot back.

"Oh yeah? Well, that goes double, sister."

After losing the black Bentley in traffic, Chewie and Scout figured their best guess was that Devlin was being taken to Gant's estate in Devon.

Chewie pushed the Jaguar to its limits, breaking a new English land-speed record as he barreled through the countryside, causing heads to turn and fists to be raised in anger by motorists caught in their wake.

As they made the last turn, Scout was hunkered down in his seat, scared shitless, reciting prayers he'd thought were long forgotten, as he called off directions to the maniac Indian behind the wheel.

"How close?" Chewie shouted.

Scout gulped hard as the Jag shot through a dip in the road and then topping a hill, its chassis airborne momentarily, it crashed to the roadway, almost driving Scout's skull into the Jag's headliner. "Jeez! Turn here—that side road!"

The sleek sports car power-slid into the turn, its rear end whipping like an angry shark and then raking back into the center of the narrow lane.

"Damn it to hell, Chewie. I'm too young to die!"

A throaty pop came from the dual exhaust as Chewie grunted and backed off the gas.

Out of nowhere, two hulking Land Rovers with military markings lurched through the ditches on either side of the roadway, their large tires churning mud, and catapulted onto the road. They shuddered to a screeching stop, blocking the road. Both Land Rovers' doors flung open and soldiers burst out, taking cover and leveling automatic weapons on the charging Jaguar.

"Man, they take speeding freakin' seriously in these parts," Chewie muttered as his shovel-like hand yanked the emergency brake while his free hand cranked the steering wheel counterclockwise until it locked. The Jag's ass end whipped around, tires chewing into the asphalt as Chewie executed a near perfect 180.

"Oh, God! Don't tell me you're gonna …" Scout managed.

"Okay, I won't!" Chewie shouted as the big lug's size thirteen slammed the accelerator and the Jag charged forward, heading away from the roadblock.

Rounds shattered the rear window; shards of glass peppered the back of Scout's neck.

"Oh, hell," Chewie said in a dejected but calm voice, "This is a rental!"

Scout stared, his eyes as big as saucers, as a large black helicopter winged down and hovered over the roadway in front of them.

A burst from a .50 machine gun ripped up the asphalt, reaching for them. The rounds came within a few feet of the Jaguar's nose.

"That does it!" Chewie said, frowning and braking to a full stop. "I'll be damned if I'm gonna have to buy Hertz a brand new Jag."

The chopper touched down, and a side door popped open.

Ducking low, his thin wisps of hair and his coattails flaming in the rotor wash, Chief Inspector Newley ran toward them with two combat-ready soldiers hot on his heels.

The Jag's driver's window lowered and Chewie's toothy grin greeted the inspector. "Don't suppose you'd believe I've got a pregnant woman in the back seat who's about to pop, and Scout and I were rushing her to the hospital, would you?"

Newley stood glaring, his hands jammed into the pockets of his trench coat. "In a word, NO!"

"Yeah, I didn't think so," Chewie said as two soldiers jerked him out of the car at gunpoint.

Seated in the back of the Land Rover, their hands cuffed behind them, Scout sat shaking his head, while Chewie whistled the theme from M.A.S.H, *Suicide is Painless*.

From his position at right front, Newley turned and made a stern face. "Now, if you two chaps promise to behave yourselves, I'll un-cuff you."

Chewie nodded glumly.

Newley told the SAS officer to release them.

As Scout massaged his chafed wrists, Newley explained, "We have had our eye on Sir Nigel Cummings for some time now. We needed him to tip his hand. We have the proof, but I am afraid your unit has been caught up in the fracas. Seems Sir Nigel's boys snatched your boss Bill Sorensen last night and a Ms. Madison Dare."

Chewie shot forward in his seat. "Where is she?"

"Easy, old man, we suspect that she, along with Major Devlin and Doctor Kelly, are being held against their will at RAVENSCAR."

The Land Rover bumped across the rough field as he spoke. Scout's stomach was in his throat.

Finally, they came to a stop. An SAS captain met them and walked off with Newley. Chewie scrambled out and started to follow, but a barrel-chested soldier stepped in front of him, blocking his path.

"Move it, or lose it …" Chewie stopped in midsentence. It was Sgt. Conners. "Aye, laddy boy. I 'ear ye been makin' a regular nuisance o' yer-self."

Newley paused and turned. "Sergeant Conners, fill them in." Then he walked off.

Standing next to a briefing table covered with maps and satellite photos, Sgt. Conners proceeded to give Chewie and Scout the layout of the estate as they sipped coffee from Styrofoam cups.

Basically, two SAS squads had been called in because Heinrich von Gant was an arms dealer with access to advanced weapons systems. Conners explained that recon had shown a cave on the coastal side of the manor house with a seaward entrance. This necessitated deploying a third team from the Special Boat Services, the British equivalent of SEALS, to make a surreptitious entry. The SBS team, however, was currently tied up with another op, which meant they'd have to make do with an SAS frontal assault.

"You have any idea of what they're up against?" Chewie asked.

Sgt. Conners shook his head. His voice turned grave. "Aye, there's the rub, laddy boy. Gant's a bit o' a bleedin' Tom Swift when it comes to designin' newfangled weapons. Especially some downright nasty-assed unmanned offensive li'l beauties."

Scout glanced nervously at his wristwatch. "It's gettin' to be close to 1000 hours. When's Newley goin' in?"

Conners pulled at his walrus moustache and sighed.

"When he's damned well good and ready, sonny." Then his eyes ticked to Chewie, who met his gaze, his face stony, his jaw set firmly.

Scout knew that look. It meant Chewie's wheels were turning, and that meant a loose cannon was about to send one over the bow any second.

Conners led them up to Inspector Newley's position, where he stood with a command and communications control unit.

An ashen faced SAS man, wearing a headset, turned to his commanding officer, interrupting his conversation. Clearing his throat, he began, "Sir, begging your pardon, but—"

The captain scowled. "Out with it, man!"

"Sir, the forward observation post just reported a bogey."

"Are you telling me they've spotted an incoming aircraft, soldier?"

The young man gulped hard.

"Not exactly, sir." He flinched as if anticipating a punch. "They report that there's a child and an old bag lady who just flew over their position at treetop level, vectoring toward the school." He took a step back and closed his eyes.

The captain cursed a blue streak.

The young soldier reached over and punched up a live video feed from the forward observation sniper team's surveillance camera. The image of the girl, her white gown gleaming in the bright sunlight, holding hands with an old woman whose hand was planted firmly on top of her head as if to hold down her floppy hat, soared over the oaks and then across a meadow.

The men, jaws dropped wide, stood staring at the screen. All except Newley, Scout noticed.

Sgt. Conners gave a loud whistle. "Well, if it ain't bleedin' Mary Poppins."

The camera tracked back to ground level and zoomed in.

"Sir, something's happening!"

As though a giant mole had burrowed its way to the surface, a large clump of earth buckled and fell away as a metallic device rose from beneath the ground.

Scout said slowly, "Jeez, it's a Samsung Sentinel. And it's equipped with a rocket launcher!"

Newley blurted out, "Ah, what the devil did you say, son?"

The metallic beast rose to about five feet now, looking like some deathly robot. A large box-shaped lens stared coldly and inhumanly from its side. It began to swivel in a slow, panning motion.

Scout explained, "The Koreans developed it and just put her on the market. It functions as a robotic sentry. It's got infrared and thermal imaging and laser guided targeting … here, let me show you." Scout went to the keyboard and pulled up a web site. "Here's a video of this puppy in action."

On the screen, from the POV of the Sentinel, two men crept into view. The Sentinel's lens tracked them as they moved. A square-shaped box marked the Sentinel's target. A red light flashed in the center box of the robot's targeting imagery, signaling it had locked on.

In seconds, it took out the first target in a bright flash, locked on the second, and fired again. The voice of the Korean narrator explained matter-of-factly, in broken English, how the Sentinel never ate, never slept, never needed to be relieved. Next came a demonstration of its ground-to-air defense system.

"Oh my God!" Newley said.

All eyes turned back to the live video feed just as the Sentinel rotated its rocket pod skyward.

"Take that blasted thing out before it blows the girl and the old lady out of the sky!" Newley screamed.

Newley's attention was drawn to the loud roar of a revving engine. He turned just in time to see Chewie behind the wheel of a nearby Land Rover, waving good-bye and grinning from ear to ear as Sgt. Conners scrambled into the other side and slammed the passenger door behind him.

Newley bolted after them and shouted, "Bloody hell! Oh, no you don't, you crazy sonofabitch Indian. I've had enough of your shenanigans."

But when the Land Rover lurched forward, it fishtailed violently, its tires churning and spraying Inspector Newley from head to toe in mud.

The captain sidled up to Newley's side, handed the inspector his handkerchief, and pointed toward the man's mud-caked face.

From behind them, the young soldier called, "Sir, the Sentinel just fired a Starstreak missile!"

CHAPTER 37

The Lost Boys were huddled together, peering through the chain-link fence of Eden School's compound.

Gabriel had sensed Wendy's presence, so the boys had rushed outside to the playground.

Peter and Gabriel stood, their fingers wrapped tightly around the links, their noses pressed to the fence, desperately searching for a glimpse of Wendy.

Johnboy shouted and pointed toward the sky, "Look! Up there … she's flying."

Like spectators at an air show, the Lost Boys simultaneously looked up, shielding their eyes from the sun's harsh glare with their hands.

"I see her," Peter said excitedly.

"Me, too!" little Gabriel chimed in. "And she's flying with her fairy godmother."

Raji said in a grave voice, "Oh God, Wendy's in danger. I see a rocket being launched in a few minutes and it will blow her and the old lady to tiny bits!"

Gabriel looked up with tear-filled eyes and tugged at Peter's arm. "Do something, Peter. Use your powers."

Peter glanced down. Their eyes met and Peter nodded.

Suddenly a missile trail plumed against the blue sky.

Johnboy stammered, "Crikey! The rocket's headin' straight for 'em!"

Peter squared his shoulders and stared fixedly upwards, focusing with all his might on the streaking missile. His hands fisted at his temples as his brow furrowed in intense concentration.

As if guided by an invisible force, the rocket abruptly veered to the right, missing Wendy and the old woman by a few feet. It made a wide U-turn and arrowed downward. It slammed home into the Sentinel with an earsplitting shockwave of sound and bright flash, completely obliterating it.

Gabriel cried with glee, jumping up and down, "You did it!"

Raji slapped Peter on the back and smiled. "Good show, old man."

"Yeah, you're the bee's knees, Peter," Johnboy added.

Peter blew out a loud breath and shook his head. "Wasn't sure I could move something that big and that far away."

The piercing screech of Ms. Baylock's voice called from behind them. They turned to see her creeping toward them like a hungry jackal, murder burning hotly in her yellowish eyes. Two male staffers flanked her.

As she closed the distance, Ms. Baylock commanded, "Seize the little bastards! Take them all to the *Dark Room*."

The thick-necked staffers vaulted forward.

The Lost Boys had joined hands and stood side by side, glaring at the onrushing attackers. The shade of their eyes began turning from deep indigo to gleaming white.

A high-pitched buzzing sound filled the air as a black cloud of hornets swarmed out of the woods and attacked the staffers. Screaming, their arms flailing, the men fought in vain to swat off the marauding insects. They fell to the ground, cocooned in a mottled yellow-brown crust of hornets.

Ms. Baylock stood like a statue, her eyes wide with terror.

Little Gabriel, his eyes still shining with a blinding radiance, said quietly, "You better leave us be, old witch."

Walking slowly backward, her fearful gaze locked on the Lost Boys, Ms. Baylock started to retreat. With a yowl of frustration, she said, "I'll deal with you little imps later."

His powers allowing him to see seconds into the future, Raji shouted, "She's got a gun!"

A moment later, a revolver filled Ms. Baylock's skeletal hand.

Peter's gaze bore into the woman's, holding her with its luminous force. "Don't look until I tell you to, Gabe," he told his little brother, never taking his eyes off the woman.

"Okay," little Gabe said, closing his eyes and turning his head.

Ms. Baylock's gun hand began to shake violently and her wrist slowly turned, aiming the muzzle of the revolver at her own chest.

Peter stared, his eyes glowing with a bright blue-white color, eyes of fire and ice. In his mind, he pictured the faces of the other boys and girls that Ms. Baylock had carted off to the *Dark Room*, never to return.

In a last ditch effort to stop the inevitable, Ms. Baylock clamped the wrist of her gun hand and tried to wrestle the weapon away from her body; but it was as if her forearm were possessed, immoveable and hell-bent on pressing the revolver's muzzle to her heart.

Peter's hot gaze began to pulse, slowly at first, then rapidly like a stuttering strobe light.

The old witch's face grimaced in rage and horror as the revolver's hammer slowly began to cock.

A loud crack echoed across the playground as the handgun fired, and Ms. Baylock tumbled backward to the ground.

"Is it over?" Gabriel's tiny voice asked.

"Yes, she'll never take anyone to the *Dark Room* again," Peter answered, filling his lungs with deep cleansing breaths, the brilliance in his eyes quickly fading.

"Off we go then, chaps. Wendy's headed for the main house," Raji explained. "She needs us."

CHAPTER 38

Devlin was still seething with anger at being led into Gant's trap like some rat in a maze. His wrists were secured behind his back and snugged tight with plastic fast-ties as he sat in a stiff-backed wooden chair with two armed goons on either side of him.

He looked around.

They'd been led into a vast warehouse-sized room. He blinked. Harsh lighting partially blinded him. Scaffolding, catwalks and gangways formed a towering circular steel wall around him. Techs in long white lab coats manned sophisticated-looking electronic equipment which covered the polished concrete floor. A gaggle of cables snaked toward the center of the vast room, which was not illuminated by spotlights. In the shadows, Devlin thought he could make out that the cables were linked to what appeared to be a hulking device of some kind.

But where was Blair?

Just as they'd entered, the guards had separated them.

A bank of floodlights blazed from above, lighting up a dark portion of the room directly in front of him.

Blair was seated in a chair at an antique table with al-Dajjal standing behind her, one hand resting on her bare shoulder.

Heinrich von Gant slithered out of the shadows. "I thought you'd like to observe my little experiment first hand, Major Devlin. By now I am sure you're dying with curiosity."

Figuring it best to stall for time, Devlin said, "You certainly have gone to great lengths to achieve some purpose. They say you're a genius, Gant."

Gant shrugged his narrow shoulders and moved to a lab table. He lifted a small cage and went to Devlin, pressing it close to his face. "How do you like my little creation?"

Devlin stiffened.

Two maroon eyes stared from a misshapen, ratlike head. A forked tongue snaked from the creature's mouth, revealing tiny rows of razor-sharp teeth. The tongue was black and pebbled. But the head was connected to the body of a lizard with clawed feet and a fat tail. Its slimy skin was a mottled yellow-black color. Hideous.

"The crossbreeding of a mammal and a reptile," Gant explained. "A rat and a salamander."

Devlin smirked. "You have developed some new gene splicing method? And they said it couldn't be done ..."

"Your sarcasm doesn't become you, Major. The crossover of species was not achieved by that method. We found that DNA can be altered on a quantum level. By placing the zygote of a rodent within the laser's beam and then passing that same beam through the zygote of a salamander we get—"

Devlin broke in. "A freakish monster. Gant, if you're not completely mad, you're halfway there."

Gant glared and snapped his fingers. The guard at Devlin's side stabbed his ribs with the muzzle of his submachine gun. Devlin winced and smiled. "Okay, I get the point."

Gant lowered the cage and handed it to an assistant. "Do I look mad to you, Major? Am I raving and ranting like some lunatic? Did I amass a great fortune, or is it just some manic delusion that we both share? A delusion which your government also shared enough to send you and the woman here to steal my secrets."

"Oh, on that count you're dead wrong, Gant. I was sent here to kill you. But Doctor Kelly has nothing to do with this. Let her go. Your beef is with me."

"You are wasting your breath. You see, fate has brought Ms. Kelly to me." He turned and moved to the table, then nodded toward the guard. "Bring the major a little closer, please."

The guards ripped Devlin from his chair and dragged him to another seat near the table.

His gaze met Blair's. Her face was pale, her lower lip trembled slightly.

She looked up at Gant. In a mocking tone, she said, "I see that you've placed your collection of looted antiquities out for me to admire."

The Voynich manuscript lay open on the tabletop. Doctor John Dee's Aztec obsidian mirror and a tablet covered in wax lay between long black tapers fitted into gold candelabras.

"Oh, come now, Ms. Kelly. You are too modest. You see it is your second-sight, your inherited clairvoyance that will make use of these tools to decipher the Voynich and unlock the doorway for me."

An assistant appeared at his side, holding what looked like a picture draped in a black cloth. With a flick of Gant's wrist, the covering fell away, revealing an oil portrait in a gilded frame.

Brody couldn't believe his eyes.

Blair's face filled the portrait, dressed in a fifteenth-century gown identical to the one she was now wearing. Looking closer, however, Brody saw the tell-tale cracks that fissured the portrait, indicating that the painting was either a clever forgery or the real thing.

To Blair, Gant said, "I see by your expression that you were completely unaware of your beloved ancestor. History was unkind to her and her husband. They labeled him a thief and a forger of deeds and coin, a charlatan. They only alluded to her in the retelling of the wife swapping episode without explaining her true talents. How typically chauvinistic of them, don't you agree? Or maybe it was to conceal the true secret of Alchemy's Great Work, the *soror mystica.*"

Blair swallowed hard, then drilled him with a questioning look. "Are you saying that woman is—"

Gant chuckled and nodded. "Edward Kelly's wife. Your long lost relative, my dear. You see, in actuality, it was Johanna Cooper Kelly who was the true medium, the Seer of Mortlake, Dee's English home. It was she who could commune with the angels, not Edward. It was she who, while in a deep trance, dictated the language of the archangels to Doctor John Dee while gazing into the magickal Shew Stone. And she could do this because she was, like you, a Druidic High Priestess of the Awen."

Blair glared her disbelief. But her hand flew to her cheeks, exploring her own features as she sat mesmerized by the portrait.

Gant turned and snapped his fingers again.

More spotlights ignited behind him.

Glass pedestals ringed a large mirror that stood canted in the center. The surface of the mirror was faceted like a diamond. A crystal skull was perched atop each pedestal.

"The Twelve Lost Skulls," Gant said in a half whisper. "The magically fossilized skulls of the Ascended Masters, the high adepts of the Secret White Brotherhood of Shambhala." Then he went to the center of the circle where he was joined by Dr. Craven, who proffered a metal briefcase.

Gant snapped the latches and opened the case. He took out another crystal skull and held it aloft for Devlin and Blair to see. As he turned and gingerly fitted the skull into a socket in center of the large mirror, he said, "There, and that makes thirteen. A perfect *coven* of skulls."

Blair's eyes widened. So the legend of the Thirteen Crystal Skulls was true? She remembered that legend had it that when linked together and placed in a circle, with the thirteenth skull resting in the center, they gave their owner the power of the gods.

Gant made his way back to her, his eyes gleaming with satisfaction at Blair's apparently renewed interest. "I went to great lengths and expense to retrieve these sacred totems from the far corners of the Earth. They had been taken from a Tibetan monastery high in the Himalayas and hidden for safekeeping at sacred sites around the world. The booty from last night's Museum raid completed the set.

"Unfortunately, *Doktor* Jung's diary only provided part of the answer. You, however, must fulfill your destiny and guide me. Only you can translate the Voynich with the aid of that lovely tattoo on your back, my dear. I have no second-sight abilities; therefore, it is you who will act as my *soror mystica*, my womanly gatekeeper to the other side."

Blair's gaze softened as she nodded for Gant to come closer.

When he leaned across the table, she spat in his face. "You can go to hell, you bloody wanker!"

Al-Dajjal grabbed a fistful of her long hair and yanked her head back. Moving to Blair's side, he bent over her and kissed her hard. Blair struggled and squirmed, gasping for air, but al-Dajjal's free hand pressed on her shoulder, pinning her to the chair, as his other hand tugged forcefully at her hair.

Brody shot to his feet, but a rifle butt slammed into his right cheek. He sank back into the chair and looked up at his attacker. Margot Gant's leering smile taunted him. After making kissing sounds with her lips, she said, "Poor baby. Did that hurt? I hope so. You had it coming, Loverboy."

Brody winced and met her stare. "That's no way to treat a guy who knocked you off your feet, sweetheart."

Her eyes narrowed and she cuffed him hard across the face, knocking his head back and splitting his lip.

Al-Dajjal pulled back and Brody saw that the creep's lower lip was bleeding. Blair had bitten him.

Fury burned in Blair's eyes as she spat the bastard's blood from her mouth.

Brody squirmed in his chair when he saw that the creep was getting his rocks off.

Al-Dajjal grinned and wiped his swollen lip with the back of his hand. "I like a woman with fire in her loins. We'll continue this later."

Shaking his head and sighing heavily, Gant's gaze panned from Margot to al-Dajjal. "That's enough of your horseplay!" Like shamed children, they lowered their heads and took a step back.

Then he turned to Blair. "Ms. Kelly, I see that you will need some motivation." Gant nodded to Dr. Craven, who held a large industrial remote in his pasty hand. Craven gave a devilish smile and punched the button.

Floodlights ignited in sequence.

And what Devlin saw turned his stomach.

CHAPTER 39

The SAS squads had stormed the manor house and were engaged in a firefight with Gant's guards. Newley and Scout were pinned down behind an out-building, taking heavy fire.

They'd taken out a good share of Gant's henchmen, whose bodies lay strewn around them. Muzzle flashes spat from the mansion's roofline as snipers kept most of the SAS troops locked down tight in positions around the courtyard. Newley sneak-peeked around the corner of the building. Rounds chewed the brickwork, spraying his face and dusting his hair with pulverized chips of mortar and brick.

"Bloody hell!" he shouted as he jerked back behind cover. "Hell's bells, I wish we could've waited for the cover of darkness. Bastards have us outgunned and they have the high ground."

Another SAS squad lay prone behind a long stone wall to their right.

Newley barked into his handheld, "Have the helo take out those wankers on the roof. Our bleedin' arses are hanging out to dry here!"

"Roger," the captain's voice squawked from the radio.

Scout heard the steady drone of beating rotors as the helicopter churned overhead. Its guns blasting .20 mm rounds, it winged toward the mansion like an angry hornet.

The SAS men cheered as hot rounds chewed their way up the face of the manor house, window glass exploding as the chopper's chain-gun climbed. Then it began strafing across the roofline. Bodies pitched over the side and plummeted to the flowerbeds and turf below.

The troops vaulted the stone wall as other squads laid down a blanket of suppressive fire.

From the rooftop, a missile streaked wildly.

"Oh, God! It's a shoulder-launched Stinger," Scout shouted.

Within seconds, the missile connected with its target. The helo took a direct hit and exploded in a fireball as shrapnel and debris rained down onto the courtyard.

For the moment the gunfire ceased.

A shrill metal-on-metal shriek ripped the air. Scout spun toward the sound. In the distance, he saw the doors of a Quonset hut; its corrugated steel was buckling under the power of some unseen force. The doors suddenly burst wide and a tanklike vehicle sprang out.

The tank-thing was low-slung, its front wedge-shaped, with three oversized earthmoverlike tires on each side. It roared toward them, headed for a stone wall. It plowed through the wall as easily as if it were a papier-mâché movie prop.

Emerging from the cloud of dust, the behemoth monster made a hard left turn, then a sharp right, like it had been knocked senseless by the head-on collision. Straightening, it tracked across the outer perimeter of the courtyard.

It rolled up and over a big black sedan, crushing it like a garbage compactor. Then it slammed headlong into another vehicle, reversed with a sudden jolt—and rolled right over the top of a tall truck, squashing it. But when it trundled down, as if it were still punch-drunk, it canted sideways and flipped over. Magically, its wheels moved to the underside of its body and then, like an angered beast, it charged forward again.

Newley shouted to a squad of troops huddled behind another wall, blocking the tank's path. "The thing's gone berserk! Get your bleedin' arses outta there!"

The other troops sprayed the rooftop with cover fire as the endangered squad hightailed it to safety.

The tank-thing crashed through the second wall just as the last SAS man slipped away.

The mechanical beast came to a shuddering halt in the center of the courtyard. With a piercing whine, a gun turret emerged and slowly swung toward Newley and Scout's position.

Frozen with fear, Scout managed, "We're goners!"

Newley stammered and said, "Look! It's turning."

The turret crawled around a full 180 degrees and stopped. Hydraulics purring, its gun climbed steadily upward, aiming for the rooftop.

A deafening blast shattered the air as the tank-thing fired its big gun. The turret panned and the gun fired again, smoke wafting from its muzzle.

Scout shouted, “I don’t know who’s driving that thing, but I reckon they’re on our side, after all.”

Still crouched behind cover, Newley shook his head and corkscrewed his ears with his fingertips. “What’s that? Can’t hear a blasted thing.”

The front door of the mansion flew wide open and a stream of Gant’s men spewed out, tossing their weapons and raising their hands.

The SAS squads stormed in, their submachine guns trained on the henchmen, shouting for them to drop to their knees.

Newley gained his feet and squared his shoulders. He was straightening his tie as he marched toward the tank with Scout at his side.

An SAS man was standing on top of the tank-thing with a puzzled look on his face.

The captain sidled up to Newley and called to the soldier, “What’s the problem?”

The SAS man shook his head and waved his hand in a broad gesture over the top of the vehicle. “There’s no entry hatch on this thing.”

“You chaps,” the captain shouted to another group of SAS men, “check the sides for doors. And be sharp about it.”

Scout cut in. “I don’t think that’ll be necessary. She’s a CRUSHER, a UGCV, and weighs in at about six and half tons.”

“A what?” Newley snapped.

“An Unmanned Ground Combat Vehicle,” Scout explained. “I wasn’t sure at first, but when I saw how erratic its movements were … well, it seemed logical. You see, she’s a different model than ours but has six all-wheel independent drive and is robotically …”

The captain spun on Scout, cutting him off. “If it wouldn't be too much trouble, son. Would you mind tellin’ me … *who* the bloody hell was driving this beast?”

An SAS squad leader ran to the captain’s side. “Begging your pardon, sir, but …”

The captain glowered. “What now, Sergeant Peters? Is the area secure or not? Damn it, man.”

Peters turned and pointed to a troop of boys being led by two stern-faced soldiers.

As the boys stood in front of them, Newley’s jaw hinged wide.

One boy with horned-rimmed glasses was smiling from ear to ear. In his hand he held an over-sized remote control with toggle switches and a small LCD screen. The boy saluted the captain sharply. “Johnboy reporting for duty, Admiral.”

A taller boy corrected him. “They’re SAS, you wanker. Which stands for Special *Air* Service.”

“Ah, shucks, Peter. I was hoping they’d have some battleships, too.”

Scout reached out and took the remote from the boy’s hand. “You drove the tank with this?” he asked incredulously, examining the device.

The boy gave a sheepish look and shrugged. “Guess I kinda got a li’l carried away.” His voice begging a negative response, he asked, “Hope that wasn’t your car, mister?”

Scout laughed and patted the boy on the back. “You did just fine, kid.”

Beaming, the boy said, “That was the bee’s knees. Beats HALO hands down, it does.”

“What the deuce is he talking about now?” Newley asked.

“Latest computer game,” Scout explained, smiling.

The taller dark-skinned boy stepped up. “Sir, my name is Raji. We escaped from the Eden School, and we’re here to save Wendy. I can’t explain how I know, but she and your friends are in grave danger. We need to hurry.”

The Lost Boy’s faces grew suddenly solemn as they turned in unison and headed for the front door of the mansion.

“Now hold on there, lads,” Newley shouted. “You can’t go in there, it’s too dangerous. Leave this to—”

“Us professionals, boys,” the captain broke in.

Little Gabriel paused and turned. He stood staring directly at Inspector Newley. The inspector tried to speak but stammered as though he had lost his train of thought.

His eyes fluttered and then went wide, like he'd had a sudden brainstorm of an idea. He cleared his throat and stiffened. "Captain, see here now. These boys can lead us directly to Major Devlin and Gant."

The captain's gaze tracked from the inspector to Gabriel, whose unblinking gaze now held the captain with its intensity. In contrast, the captain's eyes became dull and unfocused, then blinked rapidly.

Swallowing visibly and nodding woodenly, the captain said, "Capital idea, Inspector." Then he signaled his troops and shouted, "Let's move out."

Wendy and Ginny were nestled safely in the boughs of a towering oak, gazing down at the rooftop of the manor house where they decided to wait until the fireworks were over.

Shivering, Ginny pulled at her shawl. "Bloomin' cold up here, it is." She gingerly reached down and tugged at her support-hose. "This pair is simply ruined. Scraped them on a branch when you set us down."

Wendy was staring intently at the scene below.

The bough beneath Ginny creaked and moaned under her weight. She held tighter and looked down. "Heavens, I simply must lay off those macaroons."

The tree limb buckled, jolting Ginny, who was fighting to maintain her balance. Absently, she patted her head with her free hand. "Land sakes, I've lost me bloomin' hat, too."

Wendy reached out and took Ginny's hand. "It's time to go."

Ginny nodded. "Your Lost Boys are here now."

"Uh-huh. You could feel 'em, too."

Ginny gave a warm smile. "We can sense these things can't we, me darlin'?"

Wendy shrugged. "Seems like they came to save me."

Chewie and Conners had skittered the perimeter of the manor house and had abandoned the Land Rover. They'd made their way through the woods on foot and were now ducked down behind a stone wall at the rear.

The gunfire which had roared from the front of the mansion had now ceased entirely.

Chewie's hawkish gaze surveyed the scene. "Too quiet."

"No bleedin' guards, either," Conners agreed, scowling and tugging at his walrus moustache. "Maybe the bloody fools hightailed it."

Chewie grunted and shook his head.

Conners shrugged. "'ere goes nothin', laddy boy," he said, scrambling to his feet and running serpentine toward an unguarded side door.

Chewie covered him, his steely eyes quick and alert.

Inside the manor house, they made their way through a dimly lit and deserted passageway that was as silent as a tomb; the heavy plod of their footfalls was the only sound as they inched their way down the hallway.

A shadow, something faintly metallic, streamed across an intersecting hallway in front of them.

Chewie went low and Conners went high as they trained their KRISS submachine guns on the fleeting target.

Breath held tightly, sweat streaming down his face, Conners whispered, "You hear that?"

The sound of a whining servomotor faded in the distance, then grew louder. It was as if something had jerked around, somehow sensing their presence, and was now making its way directly toward them.

The droning noise grew louder by the second, seemingly building up speed.

Behind them, suddenly, the door sealed tightly with a pneumatic hiss. Conners glanced back and cursed. "Booby-trap! And we walked right into it." Then he heard a rushing sound like running water. An oily liquid sprayed from nozzles in the baseboard, flooding across the floor.

The stench of smoldering rubber assaulted his nostrils.

He looked down and saw that the soles of his shoes were smoking as if being eaten by acid. His gaze flashed to Chewie, who was struggling to lift his foot, to move, but couldn't. When he raised his foot, gooey rubber strings, like melted cheese on a pizza, clung from the sole of his boot to the floor, immobilizing him.

Chewie made a sour face. "Some sort of a Supercaustic, probably C-plus. It's melting the rubber on our boots. We'll have to shuck 'em off!"

They did.

The nozzles spurted again, dispensing a soapy foam.

"What now?" Conners complained. "They tryin' to wash us to death?"

"Anti-traction foam," Chewie said and gave a brittle laugh.

A loud thud drew their attention. They looked up.

A robotlike thing jolted mechanically around the corner, colliding with the side of the wall and ripping off a chunk of plaster as it went. But then it straightened itself and whirred directly toward them. Its motor was revving wildly as its tracks churned like a tank. Chewie noticed that the foam only covered the immediate area around them, so as not to inhibit the robot's progress. *That Gant's one clever sonofabitch.*

It was about fifty feet … closing fast.

Streaming laser beams shot out from lantern-shaped lenses mounted high on its metal torso, lancing green rays of light helter-skelter down the hallway, reaching for them.

"What the bloody hell?" Conners managed.

"It's a RAD, Robotic Area Denial," Chewie explained hoarsely, sighting his weapon on the charging beast.

Twenty-five feet and closing.

Chewie's sweaty paw tightened on the handgrip of his KRISS as he blinked the streaming perspiration from his eyes.

"Okay, laddy boy. Let's blow that fugitive from the junk yard to bloody bits!" Conners said.

Fifteen feet …

Then, abruptly, the RAD ground to a halt.

For a moment, silence dropped like a curtain.

Without hesitating, they let loose with their weapons, the muzzle flash stuttering with each burst, the sound deafening in the close confines of the corridor. But their .45 rounds sparked uselessly off the outer shell of the metallic beast.

It stood silent and enigmatic, like it was mocking them.

Smoked curled from their muzzles as they stopped their torrent of lead and lifted their weapons.

"Didn't even faze the bugger!" Conners fumed, his cheeks flaming red.

As if to answer him, a hollow *phufft* sound, like a tennis ball being shot from a tube, burped from the RAD. Then a projectile rolled to a stop at their feet.

Before they could react, vents slitted open on the sides of the stainless-steel ball and gas hissed out.

They'd forgotten to carry gas masks.

The RAD abruptly reversed and spun around, buzzing away in search of new targets.

Chewie sucked in a deep breath as the greenish mist floated toward him. He was an ex-SEAL and had placed with the U.S. Olympic swim team. *The next Jim Thorpe* some had said. He'd set a record for the breast stroke and held an unofficial record for holding his breath under water.

Conners, on the other hand, was a heavy smoker, and his only claim to athletic prowess was his ability to wrestle a grizzly bear with one hand while downing a Guinness Stout with the other. And Chewie could see the gas was already taking its toll on him.

And from the symptoms, Chewie realized the gas contained a psychophysical agent.

As Conners's face went chalky pale, he began to stumble about—his eyelids fluttering—and then he doubled over, vomited a gusher and started walking in lazy circles.

Squinting, Chewie looked on, his breath held tightly, his eyes tearing from the gas.

The Scotsman's expression was flat, his eyes vacant.

Like a mentally disturbed patient in a padded cell, he stood leaning listlessly against the wall, then silently slid down, until he collapsed in a drugged stupor.

Chewie figured he was witnessing the effects of a so-called calmative agent, probably a mixture of thorazine and benzodiazepines, designed to render the intruder non-combative and as harmless as a puppy.

Chewie's record time for holding his breath under water was seven and a half minutes. But he had sat motionless at the bottom of a pool. As he flung Conners over his shoulder, he figured he would deserve a gold medal if he could carry the comatose Scotsman to safety before the searing pain in his lungs forced him to suck wind.

CHAPTER 40

Wendy and Ginny had glided down and landed softly on an overhang. After climbing through an attic window, they were threading their way through the mansion, led by sheer instinct.

Ginny was busying herself by commenting on the luxurious furnishings and tapestries. Floor by floor they went. They encountered a few maids who were scurrying down the hallway, suitcases in hand, fleeing the manor house after the SAS assault.

Ginny nodded and exchanged unreturned pleasantries as they dashed past her. Breathlessly, she was stumbling along as fast as her piano legs would carry her, with Wendy dragging her by the hand.

Dusting a cobweb from her hair, Ginny said, "Now if these aren't the rudest bunch of folks. Can't even stop to say hello. Why, I asked that nice-looking butler where the loo was, and he just glared at me like I was daft as a bedbug."

When they came upon the rear staircase, Wendy suddenly stopped and doubled over in pain.

Her expression grave, Ginny wrapped her flabby arm around the girl and hugged her tightly. "Is it Blair?"

"Somebody's hurting her. And the others, too. We must hurry, Ginny."

"Well … come along then, missy…"—she took Wendy's hand in hers—"me old legs are givin' out. We'd better fly."

Wendy straightened and took a deep breath. Hand in hand they soared down the staircase and winged around a corner at the bottom.

Devlin's heart clenched. Bill Sorensen's tortured body was dangling high above, suspended by a long chain.

He hovered like a wounded angel. They had stripped him naked, his flesh battered and cloaked in dried bloodstains resembling swaths of burial linen.

Gant gestured toward Sorensen's pendulous form as it swayed to and fro, dipping in and out of the spotlight. "The device is called The Strappado. An implement of torture put to good use by the Dominicans during the Inquisition.

"It's quite ingenious, you see. They would take an infidel or a Jew, same thing in their eyes, and bind his hands behind him, wrists chained to pulleys. The nonbeliever would be drawn upward to the ceiling with weights tied to his feet."

Brody wanted to vomit. He affected a poker face. "You'll burn in Hell, Gant."

"Yes, eventually, I suppose. But not for a very, very long time, Mr. Devlin. You see, like Faust, I've made my pact with the Devil. We all make compromises, we all have a price. I am simply biding my time until the note comes due and the Devil claims my soul for the fiery Pit."

"But your friend here…"—he pointed to Sorensen and laughed wickedly—"… is already there." His hand reached down and he twisted a valve. Gouts of blue flame shot from jets beneath Sorensen. Brody looked closer and saw that the gas jets sprouted from a bed of spikes, stabbing brutally upward. If Sorensen was released from his agony, he'd be impaled in the forest of razor-toothed barbs below, where he would be roasted alive by the gas flames.

"I'd better turn this down a notch." The flames muted. "There, we wouldn't want to hasten your friend's death, you see."

Brody said, "You're such a good host."

Gant chuckled. "Ah, I see you haven't lost your spirit. Good—you'll need it. But as I was saying … the sheer weight is dislocating Mr. Sorensen's joints one by one. But that's not the half of it."

Gant signaled with a thumbs-up to *der Eisaxt,* whose hand grasped a brass lever. The lever was connected to a series of herringbone gears that controlled a spool of chain. The chain stretched upward, through a pulley, and back down to Sorensen's wrists.

When *der Eisaxt* pushed the lever forward, Sorensen's body was pulled higher and higher, chains rattling and clinking as the helpless victim rose. Gant opened his palm, signaling to stop.

His eyes flashing, Gant said, "Now, for the best part!"

He signaled again, thumb's-down. *Der Eisaxt* squeezed a handgrip on the lever. The chain poured off the spool, almost smoking. Sorensen dropped. Then suddenly, with a pull of the lever, Sorensen's body halted with a bone-wrenching jerk, bobbing in glassy, exquisite pain and torment.

Wrists snapped.

Tendons ripped. With each rise and fall. Again and again.

Brody's stomach lurched end-over-end.

Gant went on, his hands steepled in front of him as though he were praying. "You see now, don't you? It's the frightening anticipation. It strains the man's limits of sanity, which is much worse than the actual agony itself. Their minds snap before their bodies can surrender."

Blair struggled in her chair, held firmly by al-Dajjal. "You are a bleedin' sadistic sod. Let him down and I'll do whatever you wish."

Bill Sorensen's body glistened in sweat. His head hung limply, chin pressed to his chest.

A shuddering boom came from somewhere above. A guard ran to Gant's side and whispered in his ear. Gant rolled his eyes and sighed. "Al-Dajjal, it seems the cavalry has arrived to rescue our guests. See to it that the vault doors are sealed, would you? And make sure the area denial robotics are functioning properly."

Al-Dajjal nodded curtly and ran off, but another guard assumed his position at Blair's side.

"Oh, don't get your hopes up, Ms. Kelly," Gant said softly. "This room is quite impregnable. And I have many secret escape routes. Now, I am sure you will cooperate fully, my dear girl, but wait, there's more. Let's see the girl!"

He snapped his fingers and another overhead light ignited.

In the harsh glow of the lighting, Brody saw the other missing team member, Madison Dare. She was encased in a glass cylinder about twelve feet high. It dawned on him that it was an updated version of Houdini's infamous *Chinese Water Torture Cell.* She was hanging upside-down from her ankles a few feet from the bottom of the glass prison, her long hair dangling beneath her.

"Madison!" Brody called out.

She was facing him and Brody could just make out the expression on her face. She didn't look good. Her face was flushed. Blood had been rushing to her brain for God knows how long.

At the sound of his voice, she began twisting her body, struggling frantically to raise herself up, grabbing for her ankles. Finally, with a loud groan, she gave up and trundled back down, swaying lazily.

Gant motioned to Margot. "Bring him closer, please, so he can have a better look. And free his hands."

Margot wrenched Brody to his feet and prodded him with the muzzle of her MP-5 pressed to his spine. In her free hand, she held a switchblade. She thumbed it and the long blade snickered out. With a sharp tug of her knife, she cut the plastic cuffs. She leaned in and whispered in his ear, her voice dripping with sexual innuendo. "I think she looks kind of sexy like that, don't you, Loverboy. Are you doing her, too?"

Brody started to wheel on her, but she stabbed the submachine gun's muzzle sharply into his back. "Go ahead, Loverboy. Just try that again and a bullet will sever your spinal column. You'll be a cripple for life, if you live."

Brody stood in silence at the side of the cylinder, rubbing his chafed wrists. He noticed that a series of PVC pipes were connected at points to the bottom the giant glass tube.

He crouched, placing himself at Madison's eyelevel.

Her catlike powder-blue eyes found his. Her voice slightly muffled by the glass cell, she said dully, "God, Brody, is that really you?"

He nodded and smiled. But he knew Madison well enough to understand that comforting words were useless. Instead, he needed to spike her adrenaline with anger.

"Hang in there, kid. You okay?"

Madison grimaced and glared. "Oh, you're a riot, Brody. Do I look like I'm fucking … okay!"

Gant joined Devlin at the glass tomb. "I designed the water torture cell myself." He rapped on the glass with his knuckle. "It's bullet proof but clear as the finest crystal." His gaze bore down on Devlin. "I am a student of human behavior, Major. Like I said, we all have our price. And we all have our darkest fears. *Doktor* Craven took the liberty of placing the lovely Ms. Madison under drug-induced hypnosis. She was most talkative … isn't that so, *Doktor*?"

Craven had moved to Gant's side. "*Ja*, she shared her dreams, her sexual fantasies…"—a grin spilt his piggish face—"… and most importantly, her worst nightmares. It just so happens that as a child Ms. Madison Dare almost drowned. She also has a deadly fear of rodents and reptiles, which happens to suit our needs very well."

Gant moved to Brody. "Major Devlin, you are faced with a clear dilemma. Two of your closest friends are both facing deadly peril. You've heard of the old chestnut about who would you save first from drowning, your wife or your child. Well … luckily you will get to make such a choice today."

Blair's voice broke in. "Enough. Let them go and I'll do what want you want. Stop torturing them!"

Gant nodded to Craven, who marched to Blair's side. He stabbed her shoulder with a syringe and stepped back. "She'll be under in a few seconds," he told Gant.

Gant took a seat across from her at the table. He slid the obsidian mirror in front of her, along with the Voynich manuscript.

Blair's head began to loll as her eyes rolled back into her skull.

In a soothing, hushed monotone, Gant began to induce her into a hypnotic trance.

Some time passed until his voice rose enough for Brody to hear him.

"I am taking you back to the womb, now farther backward in time before you were even conceived, another time, another place, a past life."

Blair stirred and moaned. Then she nodded woodenly. Gant's words transported her. "The year is fifteen eighty-six. Your name is Johanna Cooper Kelly, High Priestess of the Awen. Can you hear me, Johanna?"

Blair answered in a thick, old English dialect. "I hear ye."

"Gaze deeply into the dark looking glass," Gant commanded as he slipped it into her hand. "What is the key to unlocking the code of the Voynich manuscript that lies before you?"

Her eyes opened.

Blair's heavy-lidded gaze traveled back and forth between the Aztec mirror and the book. She reached out and ran her fingers across the Voynichese text as she gazed deeply into the black mirror.

Her voice was a soft whisper. "It is the Rosetta Stone. The key to the first and universal tongue. The one language spoken before the Tower of Babel."

Gant leaned in, his voice guttural and choked with anticipation. "Where is this key?"

Still in a deep trance, Blair's fingers found the last page of the manuscript. Then, as her fingertips traveled over the script, she said, "'Herein lies the key … To me Uriel gavest the secret of the gateway.'" Her eyelids fluttered and she added, "'The Sigil of Truth conceals the key to unlock the gate.'"

Puzzled, Gant slid John Dee's wax tablet in front of her. "I have read and understood the symbols and glyphs etched into the tablet's wax surface. They are the sigils or names of angels and demons, offering nothing more than a modicum of protection to the conjurer who uses it to summon the spirits."

Her head bobbed slightly. "'*Beneath* the Sigil of Truth, lies the key.'"

Gant rubbed his chin, deep in thought. Then his eyes brightened. He palmed a knife from his pocket. As he began furiously scraping the beeswax off the tablet, he turned to Craven to explain. "I should have thought of it! In Roman times they frequently hid secret messages beneath the plain text of an innocuous looking text etched into the wax."

Finished, he held up the tablet and read aloud, "LUX … light. Of all the colors of the rainbow, gold is the most precious. Gaze upon the Rosettes to find his resting place. Enter the mirrored gate. Within the Tomb of Hermes lies the flowing fountain. The elixir of eternal youth."

He set down the tablet and carefully turned through the pages of the Voynich manuscript, stopping at the Cosmological section. "Ah, the Rosette Diagram," he said. He neatly undid a fold-out that opened into six pages resembling a map. The diagram had nine spheres resembling islands, connected by tubes or causeways. In the upper right sphere was the drawing of a castle and towers. In another was a volcano.

"Let me see the tattoo!" he ordered.

Craven hoisted Blair to her feet, spun her around by her shoulders, grasped the fabric of her gown and brutally tugged it down with his greasy hands, exposing her back.

Gant moved to her side and held the diagram next to her tattoo.

"Yes," he said excitedly. "You see, this section is almost identical. It looks like a Medieval T-O map. Side-by-side spheres which form a T-shape in the space between them." His long finger trailed across her soft skin, his long yellowish nail leaving an ugly red mark. And Blair shivered.

"The tattoo is a map, and is very similar to the *Map of the Ancient Sea Kings* al-Dajjal secured from the Turks in Istanbul," Gant explained. He traced the outline of a gold-colored sphere and pointed to an image of a tower rising out of a deep chasm in a mountain side. He read the letters beneath it and gave a self-satisfied smile. "Look at the colors, Craven. They follow the alchemical formula. It was so simple, plain as the nose on my face."

He glanced at Blair and scowled. "Craven, cover her up and set her down. I have what I need for the moment."

Craven did as he was told, placing his own sweat-stained jacket over her shoulders as he set her back down.

Suddenly, as if she were totally spent, Blair slumped in her seat. Her head bobbed forward and she swayed in her chair. Abruptly, she looked up and stared into space, unblinking.

In the voice of an elderly man, Blair said, *"Here is the wisdom of al-Jabir. I entered the hidden chamber where an old man sat upon a gold throne, holding an emerald tablet. His form was that of stone. By a vision it was revealed to me that this was the Tomb of Hermes. And the meaning of the tablet he held, the Tabula Smaragdina, became clear to me. The first passage was a dire warning to those who would enter the cave. 'Bring not to me one lacking in wisdom or weak in his purpose, for they are profane and shall suffer a terrible death.' The inscription posed a puzzle.*

"'I, who came from the land of Atlantis, I who was revered as Thoth by the Pharaohs, speak not of fictitious things, but what is true;

what is below is like that which is above, and what is above is like what is below.

"'*As all things are produced with the word of the One, the Reckoner of the Universe, the One whose father is the Sun and whose mother is the Moon, so all things are produced from the One thing by transformation; seek the prima material, for thus you will obtain the eternal flame of life, and all obscurity will be clear to you. It is the greatest force of all powers, it overcomes every Subtle thing and penetrates every Solid thing. The First matter is the source of the Philosopher's Stone.*

"'*It rises from the Earth to the heavens and descends again, conjoining with itself the powers of Above and Below. It is found everywhere, yet the world knows it not.*

"'*Those who follow the path of ambition, hypocrisy, and vice shall enter ...*'"

Blair's voice trailed off and her chin sank to her chest as she drifted off.

Gant turned and went to her. "My God, she has channeled the soul of al-Jabir, the famous Arab alchemist, the founder of algebra. She spoke of the great Emerald Tablet of Hermes Trismegistus, the Thrice Greatest. She spoke of the cave and the eternal flame of youth!"

He spun on Craven. "Don't just stand there, bring her out of it. Inject her with a strong dose of amphetamines. I need her lucid and awake."

Craven did as ordered. When she came to, Craven brought her to her feet. On rubbery legs, Blair made her way across the room to Gant, who stood in the center of the circle of skulls next to a large laser.

"*Lux,* or light, is the answer. My dear, I could kiss you."

Blair shook her hair from her eyes and frowned. "Try it, buster, and I'll smack you into next month."

Gant gave a hearty laugh. "I was speaking rhetorically of course, dear girl. But the tattoo and your channeled communication from al-Jabir made it all clear to me."

From above, Sorensen made a keening sound, like a wounded animal caught in a snare.

Brody shouted, "Hey, Gant. You promised to release my friends if she helped you."

Gant was busy with the laser, adjusting dials and programming settings with a keyboard. Without looking up, he said in a mocking tone, "Yes, Craven. Once I've passed through the gateway, you may *see* to our guests. After all, I gave my word as a gentleman."

Craven nodded and a thin smile creased his lips.

Brody noted Craven's smug expression. "Listen, Gant. You've gotten what you wanted. Let them go."

Blair added, "You gave your word as a gentleman."

Gant looked up briefly and laughed. "But I am no gentleman, my dear. You really shouldn't trust anyone who has kidnapped you and tortured your brother."

Blair puffed up her cheeks, her eyes glaring with rage, and let out a sharp breath.

The front of the laser was fitted with a polished brass tube, segmented by large rings made from different colors of gemstones. His back hunched and straining, Gant twisted an opal knurling with exact care, like he was focusing a giant telescope.

"There we are," Gant said to Craven, rubbing his palms together. "The lenses are calibrated precisely." He took a red-leather book from his pocket and turned to Blair. "*Doktor* C. G. Jung drew the design for this marvelous apparatus in his diary, which your dear brother, Father Kelly, was kind enough to procure for us in Istanbul." He ran his thin fingers over the long brass tube, admiring it, almost caressing it. "Jung said that he had read of a mysterious device which incorporated lenses and gemstones to amplify light waves. The actual design came to him in a dream. Jung called it 'Orion's Torch.'"

Gant adjusted a dial and the laser emitted a pulsing, thrumming sound. When he threw a toggle switch, it sparked to life. A thin white beam shot out and hit the first skull, which glowed crimson, then bounced to the second, which glowed yellow, then bounced to the third, which glowed emerald green. The beams refracted from skull to skull, each transforming into eerily hued colors of the spectrum.

The air began to *hiss-crackle-hiss* with the charge of static electricity.

It pulsed.

It shuddered.

Gant stepped back from the circle with Blair in tow as the light from the last skull vectored into the apex of the mirror, igniting the thirteenth skull in a pure, vibrant light.

The laser started to overheat and began smoking. It blinked out, and the dodecahedral pattern, formed by the light beams refracted off the skulls, dimmed, then vanished.

A visible surge of electrical current ran along the thick power cables. The lines' insulation started to melt, dripping thick globs of molten-hot rubber and plastic onto the group below. The cables broke free of large transformers, snaking and whipping across the floor as they spat blue-white arcs of current from their frayed ends. The computer equipment in the huge lab became overloaded. Fried, it spewed sparks over the catwalks like Roman candles on the Fourth of July. The techs and guards bolted from their stations and ran pell-mell for safety.

Brody's eyes cut back to the circle of skulls.

The giant mirror began to vibrate; it emitted tiny photons of light that floated into the air, blooming larger and fatter; faster and faster the specks of light poured out. It was as if the photons were growing, expanding with a preternatural elasticity.

Gooseflesh crawled up Brody's arms.

A thunderous clap shook the air as a churning column of light began to spin in an ever-widening vortex.

Higher and higher.

Then the light began to cloud. It turned darker and darker.

It began to take on definition, assuming the form of an oily black elliptical surface about twelve feet in diameter. Fiery sparks danced around the edges and suddenly winked out.

As if manipulated by some invisible force, the giant black lens began to rotate and wobble like a coin pitched on a marble table. Slowly, it proceeded to right itself until it stood erect. It hung suspended in midair.

Fascinated and as though pulled by the black mirror's magnetism, Blair went toward it.

Gant and Craven exchanged glances and moved closer. Craven handed Gant a flashlight, and simultaneously they swung the intense beams of their LED flashlights into the center of the shimmering black lozenge.

What had been a brilliant, gleaming mirror just moments ago was now an obsidian void.

Smooth as pooled oil.

The light from their flashlights was not reflected, but rather seemingly absorbed, like light falling into a deep well.

Gant stood trembling. But in spite of the fear that clearly raced within him, Gant seemed compelled to reach out and touch the smooth, inky surface. “It’s the First Matter, the primordial dark matter of the universe, the threshold to other dimensions, other times.”

After tucking the flashlight into his pocket, his hand crept toward the mirror.

From the deep shadows, Wendy’s voice shouted, “No, don’t touch it! Step back, Mister, please.”

Gant spun toward the sound.

Ginny and Wendy stepped into the light and stood high above on a catwalk.

Blair started to run to her, but Gant’s skeletal hand shot out, clamped down hard on her wrist and swung her around. As he held her in an armlock, his free hand dipped into his suit pocket. When he pulled it out, a dagger lanced into view.

He pressed the tip of its pointy blade to her throat.

Glaring up at Wendy, he shouted, “You cursed Indigo Child. I gave you a home, a roof over your head, and now you betray me. I could have shown you and the boys, *Mein Sonnenkinder,* how to use your powers. Your destiny was to become the fountainhead of the new master race, the *Vril-ya*. Inhabitants of the new Eden. But, no! You’re all alike. You would rather pity these wretched souls that infest the earth like vermin, these swine that breed like cattle, mixing the races.” Gant’s gaze darted around the vast room, his eyes flashing with madness.

“Try to use your powers against me …” he warned Wendy,

“… and I’ll carve up this Irish slut like dog meat.”

The razor-edged blade glinted in the harsh light as he twisted it.

Gant was pressing it so tightly to Blair’s throat that a tiny trickle of blood began to spill down her neck.

Brody’s gaze ticked from Gant to the old woman who stood at the little girl’s side high above. “If you enter that gateway, you’ll be doomed,” the old lady cautioned. “Don’t say you weren’t warned,

Heinrich von Gant. Only the pure of heart can enter. Only a just man and righteous man who understands the true goal of the Great Work of Alchemy, the purification of the soul, shall survive the trials.

"The base metal, lead, symbolizes man's baser instincts: ambition, hypocrisy, and vice. By rejecting the quest for power and riches and assisting good, by abandoning treachery and being truthful in all things, by abandoning worldly desires and seeking equilibrium, you will transmute the leaden evil that grips your soul into the purity of gold."

Gant staggered backward toward the mirror, dragging Blair along with him. "You're lying, old woman. Don't bore me with your sanctimonious dribble. I read the secret text of the wax tablet, heard the voice of al-Jabir with my own ears. On the other side of this mirror lies the Tomb of Hermes and eternal life."

While Gant ranted on, Blair reached behind, grabbed him by the scrotum, and tugged with all her strength. As he howled in agony, she spun out from under his grasp and palmed the Derringer Brody had slipped her earlier.

"You're such a bloody fool," she said, leveling the handgun at Gant. "I wasn't in a trance. My will power is greater than you could ever imagine."

"You are bluffing, too," Gant said, matching her gaze.

"No, you pigheaded sod. I lied. I only told you half of the Emerald Tablet's warning. But go ahead. See for yourself."

Margot began to inch toward Blair.

Brody shouted, "Look out!"

Blair snapped her head around and dared her. "Take another step you Amazon hussy, and I'll put a slug right between the old lizard's eyes!"

Margot froze, her eyes smoldering with rage.

When Blair took her eyes off Gant, he saw his window of opportunity and took it.

Gant snarled and lunged at her, the cold steel of his knife flashing. She reared back and fired point blank into his face. But as he fell toward her, the round only grazed his cheek.

Gant's hand flew to his face and he clawed at his bloodied cheek. The latex appliance and make-up fell away into his hand like a snake shedding its skin. He bellowed in anger and ripped away the remaining portion of his mask.

Blair grimaced in revulsion at the hideous monster that leered back at her.

Gant's face was a twisted, paste-white mass of scar tissue, veined with red and purple. His left eye was deformed, half-covered by a flap of fatty tumor. His lips looked as though they'd been sliced off with a razor, revealing rows of small teeth, forming a permanent sardonic grin.

He looked away briefly, then met her stare, his watery eyes sorrowful, almost pleading. "Now you see why I must be healed," Gant said softly.

Because she was chewing her lower lip and trembling now, it seemed obvious to Brody that Blair felt a pang of sympathy for the demented fiend who stood before her.

Brody could see that she was dropping her guard as the Derringer began to waver, then lower. And Gant was inching closer almost within arm's reach.

Brody leapt forward. But as he ran past Margot, her arm pistoned out, and she clothes-lined him across the neck. He fell to his knees, coughing and clawing at his throat.

Again, Blair turned away, distracted by Brody's failed attempt.

Spider-quick Gant's hand flashed out and batted the Derringer from Blair's grasp. It clattered harmlessly across the concrete floor. He grabbed her wrist and yanked her toward him. He shouted to Craven, "Kill them all!" as he turned and leapt into the flawlessly black portal.

As his body passed through, the blackness claimed the first half of his torso so completely that it appeared as though he had been sliced in two. A truncated body, half in this realm and half in the next.

With his exposed hand, he pulled Blair into the black quicksilver as he disappeared.

She, too, appeared momentarily segmented as she slipped through the oily surface.

An inky rippling and she was gone.

***

As Gant dragged her toward the black mirror, Blair twisted and pulled, but Gant's fingers dug cruelly into the flesh of her wrist, his strength inhumanly potent.

She felt her hand, then her forearm, then her shoulder begin to sink into the black lens as if they were sinking into a pool of arctic water, the coolness closing around her skin with a slick, remorseless pressure.

Because of the weight that crushed from all sides, she could no longer feel the distinct pressure of Gant's grip on her wrist. It was like being sucked into oblivion by the undertow of a deep wave that was receding from some hellish shore.

Thrashing wildly, Blair felt her shoulder slipping in rapidly. She felt the frosty kiss of the shimmering glass against her cheek. Immediately, her mind was flooded with crippling terrors of being smothered, of blindness, of being buried alive in a molten glass tomb.

She tucked in her chin, squeezed her mouth and eyes tightly shut, but the cool insistence began to creep over her lips, her forehead, over her scalp, over her eyes. Then, suddenly, she felt the icy lick of the quicksilver against the back of her neck, and she knew she had been completely devoured by the mirror.

In the split second before her head submerged, she'd gulped one last mountain of air.

Her breath held tightly, her lungs burning, she floated in dead silence. A slight tickling teased at the corners of her eyelids, but when she tried to open her eyes, she couldn't. It was as if they'd been glued shut.

Dizziness drifted over her as a loud buzzing rang in her ears. She knew she was about to pass out. With a silent prayer, she opened her mouth and the cool, metallic taste of the black quicksilver flooded into her mouth.

She was gagging, choking.

She spit. Tried desperately to rid herself of the foul tasting liquid as the glassy waters entombed her.

High above on the catwalk, Ginny's face went white. She turned to Wendy. "You're the only one who can save her, li'l *laeken*. Your innocence and purity will safeguard you. Although Blair is strong willed and knows the ways of the Awen, she too will perish."

Wendy smiled and nodded. "Don't worry, Ginny. Wondergirl is here."

Although Wendy was trying to be brave, her voice was thin and choked. And as Ginny helped Wendy mount the railing, the girl shuddered uncontrollably.

Ginny consoled her. "Don't fear, li'l darlin'. Follow your heart, let that wee voice in yer head guide thee."

Wendy closed her eyes and took a deep calming breath. *I can do this*, she thought. *I'm just as brave as Wendy Darling and a lot braver than silly old Peter Pan.* Her tiny hand was fisted around Mr. Muffins's button eye, her umbilical to Blair.

She looked down. As if drawn to the little girl's aura, everyone below looked upward.

Swaying slightly and fighting to maintain her balance, Wendy stood perched on the narrow railing, her hands at her side, her little face stony with grit.

Wendy stole a quick peek over her shoulder, seeking one last reassuring look from Ginny, but the kind old lady was gone. It was as if she were a fairy godmother, who having fulfilled her purpose as mentor and guide had flicked her magic wand and vanished into thin air.

In her mind's eye Wendy pictured Ginny Doolittle's softly seamed and gentle face, her warm smile and kind eyes that radiated love. And then, like a guardian angel whispering in her ear, she heard Ginny's ethereal voice.

Follow your heart, follow your heart.

In her white gown and satin slippers, she resembled an angel. "I'm coming, Blair," she shouted. With the natural grace of an Olympic high diver, she dove off the catwalk. Her arms were flung back at her sides like a freefalling skydiver. She swooped down, building speed as she flew.

Al-Dajjal raced out from the shadows, a machine pistol in his hand, taking aim at Wendy as he ran. But the little angel saw him and barrel-rolled like a fighter jet just as he fired. His rounds went wild, missing her and sparking off the steel girders of the scaffolding.

He cursed and in a pointless gesture of rage, he threw his weapon at her as she flew round and round in a tight circle high above him.

Suddenly, Wendy banked hard to her left and soared past Brody, effortlessly gliding through the black looking glass and into Wonderland or whatever lay beyond.

CHAPTER 41

With the SAS men taking point, Scout and Newley and the Lost Boys knitted their way through the manor house.

"Which way now?" Scout asked little Gabriel, who could sense Wendy's presence.

"We're almost there," Gabe answered. "Around this corner there's a hidden stairway. Behind a big bookcase." The boy's brow knitted in concentration. "Yeah, you gotta pull out a big book … I can see the name, it's Mine Cuff or somethin' like that."

Puzzled, Scout shrugged. "We'll figure it out when we get there."

Raji broke in. "In a second, a fat man will come around the corner."

The captain and Newley snapped their heads toward Raji.

"I can see what's going to happen," Raji offered sheepishly.

"The lad says we've got an X-ray moving toward us, boys," the captain warned the forward squad, using the SAS term for a hostile.

Sir Nigel Cummings came limping around the corner, his suit torn, his face bloodied and bruised. He was waving a white handkerchief and coughing in spasms.

"Thank heavens you're here," Sir Nigel managed as he staggered toward them.

The SAS men kept their MP-5s trained on the fat man.

"Secret Intelligence Service, lads. You can lower those blasted weapons. I am one of the hostages."

They didn't.

Newley stepped up. "Where are your lackeys, Mr. Pope and Mr. Miles?"

"Bloody traitors, the both of them," Sir Nigel said, coughing into his silk hanky. "They were on Gant's payroll, leaking intelligence all this time. When I realized what they were up to, I made my way here to intercept them."

Newley smirked. "All by your lonesome, I suppose. You were going to singlehandedly take them into custody and take down Gant's operation?"

Sir Nigel scowled and shook his head. "Don't be impertinent, Newley. We at the SIS prefer to wash our own dirty laundry. And you have no business meddling in this case. I had your bloody arse thrown off it. You're a damnable loose cannon."

The fat man spun on the SAS captain. "I outrank you all. Captain, take Inspector Newley into custody immediately! I've learned that he too is a mole and a traitor to the Crown."

In the lab below, Brody stood awestruck, still blinking his eyes, not believing he had just seen a young girl fly.

Margot ran past him to the side of the cylinder. She nodded to Craven, who twisted a valve. Water gushed from the pipes fitted to the sides of the glass cell that held Madison Dare.

She'd passed out, but the roar of rushing water stirred her awake. Brody saw her panic-driven eyes and flinched. The water was rising rapidly. In a matter of minutes, Madison would be submerged.

"Over here, Major," Ernst called.

Brody Devlin's eyes ticked to the killer, who still manned the Strappado. Ernst flicked a switch and the flames flared, reaching for Sorensen, who still dangled from the chains above.

Craven stepped away, then turned and ran off, vanishing into the murky shadows.

Devlin's gaze flicked back to Margot who was calling him.

"What will you do, Loverboy? Save the bitch or your friend before he falls into the flames and the bed of nails?" Then she nodded to Ernst, who pulled a lever, and the chain slowly spooled off the winch, lowering Sorensen's tortured body closer to the flames below.

As Devlin's gaze ticked back and forth from Madison to Sorensen, Margot taunted, "Tick tock …tick tock. Time's running out, Loverboy. Better choose." She ripped the mag from her MP-5 and tossed them both away. Her empty hands extended palms-up, she beckoned to him. "C'mon, you wanna knock me off my feet again, darling?"

Ernst flicked open the curved blade of his ice-axe "tool" and pitched it toward Devlin. The wicked-looking weapon skidded across the polished concrete and slid to a stop a Devlin's feet.

Margot teased seductively, "Go ahead, pick it up, Loverboy."

"*Ja*, don't just stand there, *Herr Arschgesicht,*" *der Eisaxt* taunted, tilting his head to one side so that his glass eye stared blankly.

Devlin's gaze cut back to Madison. The swirling water had risen to Madison's eyebrows as she hung upside-down in the chamber of death.

The captain stood staring at Sir Nigel and shook his head.

"Sir Nigel, are you about through?" Newley asked sarcastically.

Puzzled, Sir Nigel puffed up his chest and tried to push past the captain. It didn't work. "Get out of my way you fool. I'm calling the PM and then the Home Secretary and have you busted back to a fry cook, you lout!"

Newley reached out and spun the fat man around. The captain bound Sir Nigel's wrists with fast-ties.

Sir Nigel struggled and bellowed, "This is an outrage. You're making a terrible mistake!"

Just then an SAS man shouted, "We've got two men down over here."

With the fat man in tow, Newley and the captain went around the corner. On the floor lay two bodies. Newley went to them and went down on one knee. "Gunshots to the head." He rolled them over.

It was Mr. Pope and Mr. Miles.

Sir Nigel stammered, "I had no choice. It was them or me."

Newley shot to his feet, dashed to the fat man's side, and dipped his hand into Sir Nigel's suit coat pocket. He pulled out a Webley Bulldog revolver and sniffed the muzzle. "It's been recently fired. And I bet when we check the ballistics we will find your gun's slugs buried in their brainpans, you lying sod."

Grabbing Sir Nigel by the lapels, Newley almost hoisted the blubbering man off the floor.

The captain put his hand on Newley's shoulder. "Easy there, old chap."

Newley, his face still flaming red, glanced briefly at the captain and released his hold.

Sir Nigel gave a condescending laugh. "By the time you get to them, there won't be anything left."

Newley calmly opened the revolver's cylinder and took out all but one of the remaining rounds. He spun the cylinder and clicked it shut. Then he jammed the Webley under Sir Nigel's chin and cocked the hammer. Around him, the captain and his squad stared, mouths gaping. A soldier started to move, but the captain waved him off.

"You like games of chance, Sir Nigel?"

The fat man shook his head, his eyes glazed with fear.

Newley glared at him. "You're going to tell me exactly what you meant by that, or I am going to pull this trigger. It may fall on an empty chamber, or it may not. But I'm going to keep pulling the trigger every time you lie to me. Eventually your luck will run out, and the walls will be covered with your brain matter, you fat, arrogant bastard."

Sir Nigel gulped hard. "You wouldn't dare, not in front of all these witnesses."

"Look away for a second then, lads," Newley said, jabbing the revolver deep into the fleshy wattle of the fat man's double chin. They did.

Sir Nigel's eyes went wide and he blurted out, "Al-Dajjal and Margot are pure sadists. They're going to torture and kill the whole ΩMEGA team if you don't stop them."

Newley's cheeks flamed. "Bullocks!" The Webley clicked. "I see in your beady little eyes that you're hiding something."

The fat man shuddered in terror, his eyes closed tightly.

When Newley cocked the hammer again, Sir Nigel wet himself.

"Open your eyes, you bloody arse," Newley commanded.

He did and shouted, “I set a bomb. To hide the evidence. That cheating bastard, Gant, stiffed me. I never got my fair cut. He threatened to expose me.”

The captain shouted, “How long have we got?”

“Have you got the time, sir?” the fat man managed sheepishly.

The captain shoved his wristwatch in Sir Nigel’s face.

Newley carefully lowered the revolver’s hammer.

“Well … I would say about ten minutes.”

The Webley’s hammer cocked again.

“Okay, about twenty minutes tops, maybe a little less,” Sir Nigel blurted.

Spinning him around and shoving him forward, Newley barked, “Then you better get your fat arse in gear. You lead on, and I hope you know a short cut.”

An SAS man broke in. “Captain, those boys and the American chap ...”

“What about them?”

“They’re gone.”

CHAPTER 42

Standing in front of the bookcase, Scout searched the shelves for something that sounded like *mine cuff*. "Do you see the book, little buddy?"

"I am too little, Mr. Scout," Gabriel said.

Peter stooped down and lifted him up in his arms.

"Jeez, that's better," Gabe said, scanning the titles. He nodded. "That one, on the end."

Scout's gaze locked on the book. "*Mein Kampf*," he said, laughing. "Well, you were darn close." He reached up and pulled down the book. The hulking bookcase creaked toward them. Scout opened it the rest of the way and they dashed through the space behind it.

An elevator greeted them.

But there was no call button, only a handprint recognition sensor plate mounted on the wall.

Scout fumbled in his vest for a screwdriver.

Peter stayed his hand. Staring at the elevator door, his eyes glowing white, the door suddenly pinged open. Casting a puzzled look at Peter, Scout shrugged and, shaking his head, he shepherded them inside.

He turned to Peter. When the boy blinked at another palm-print sensor on the car's interior panel, the doors hissed shut, then the elevator lurched and rocketed downward.

Devlin's gaze cut to Sorensen, who now hung only a few feet above the inferno, tongues of flame licking at him. The image of his face was blurred by the heat shimmer.

The only sounds were the crackling flames and the droning rush of water.

Snatching the ice axe from the floor, Devlin ran for the Strappado. He figured he could possibly revive Madison with CPR, but Sorensen would be a goner any second.

A shrill war cry cut the silence.

Swinging from a dead power cable, Chewie swooped down from a catwalk, his size-thirteen boots hitting Margot square in the back, driving her to the floor where she cracked her head hard. He swung past her prone, comatose body and let go of the cable, landing between Devlin and Ernst.

"Where the hell have you been, you big lug?" Devlin asked, grinning broadly as he made for the glass tube and Madison.

"Long story, just toss me that hatchet."

He did.

Catching it in his meaty hand, Chewie spun on the Ice Axe, whose expression changed from an oily grin to fear in an instant. He started to walk backward, distancing himself from the meanest-looking Indian he'd probably ever seen.

Suddenly, the Ice Axe's practiced hand flew behind him to the small of his back as he palmed a SIG.

But Chewie's reflexes were razor sharp. Even as the pistol rose toward him, Chewie had already drawn the axe back like a Tomahawk. When his arm shot forward in a silken motion, it flew from his grasp, churning end-over-end through the air. Its blade connected and sank deeply into the Ice Axe's forehead. *Der Eisaxt*, felled by his own tool, sank to the floor, blood spraying from his forehead like a fountain.

Chewie sprinted to the Strappado's controls and killed the flames. Then he found a length of pipe and shoved the bed of spikes out from beneath Sorensen. He lowered the wounded agent and undid the chains. Once he had him on the floor, Chewie checked for a pulse. It was fairly weak, but at least Bill Sorensen was alive. Bill's eyes fluttered open. He looked up at Chewie and with watery eyes, managed a weak smile, then groaned in agony before passing out again.

Chewie pulled a field syringe from his tactical vest and shot Bill Sorensen up with morphine to ease the pain.

Meanwhile, Devlin was struggling with the water valve of the glass cylinder. It wouldn't budge and Madison's head was submerged.

Worse, something black and slimy streamed into the glass tank from the rushing water inlets, snaking through the water toward Madison.

Devlin looked on in horror as the water became black with Gant's evil creation—the rat-headed mutant salamanders. Their ratlike heads bobbed above the surface and they bared their hungry teeth as they swam.

Chewie shoved him aside. As his ham-sized hands grappled with the valve, the massive muscles of his arms and shoulders flexed beneath his shirt. His face bright red, he said, "It's frozen tight. Won't budge." Tears filling his eyes, Chewie shouted, "Madison, hold on!"

"Hell!" Devlin shouted as his eyes cut to the glass tank. A mutant lizard was gnawing at Madison's hair.

In sheer desperation, Chewie rushed to the side of the glass tube and began punching it with his fists until his knuckles were raw and bloodied, screaming at the top of his lungs.

From behind them came a small voice. His lips motorboating, Johnboy stammered, "Name's Johnboy, sir. I can make them stop." He pointed to the mutant lizards. "And Peter here can handle the water."

After having just seen a little girl soar like a bird, Brody Devlin was beginning to believe anything was possible with these Indigo Children.

He pulled Chewie aside and they stepped back.

Johnboy dropped to his knees, and planted his palms on the sides of the glass cylinder. He whispered softly … talking to the lizards was Brody's best guess. It apparently worked, because, one by one, the mutant lizards turned away from Madison and swam to the side of the tank, their maroon eyes locked on Johnboy.

Then the taller boy, Peter, stepped up to the tank and stared fixedly at the frozen valve. Slowly the valve began to turn; the water stopped rushing into the tube.

Then Peter turned and focused his eyes on the water. He extended his hands palms-up and as he raised them higher, the water defied gravity and rose past Madison's head, up her torso to the very top of the tank, where it stayed suspended.

Peter was holding one hand up as though by doing so he was commanding the water to remain in position. With his free hand, Peter tapped the side of the cylinder with his index finger. As the glass began to crack, tiny fissures cobwebbed out from the point where Peter had touched it. The cracks grew wider until Peter finally said, “Turn your heads, it’s going to burst.”

Tiny shards of glass exploded outward, along with a torrent of water, but with a quick snap of his head, Peter held them and the water suspended in midair. He blinked his eyes and the shards dropped harmlessly to the floor just as the water rained down, pooling at their feet.

Devlin glanced at Chewie, who shrugged his broad shoulders and ran to free Madison.

“Excuse me, gentlemen. But there’s a rather pressing matter,” said a dark-complexioned boy.

Chewie was busy administering CPR, so Devlin answered the boy. “If you’re wondering about your friend Wendy, she flew into that black mirror over there. What’s your name, son?”

“Raji, sir. Oh, I knew about Wendy, but I was speaking about the bomb.”

Devlin’s jaw dropped.

“Up here, Brody.”

Devlin looked up to see Scout waving at him from a walkway. At his side was a small boy who smiled and gave a tiny wave.

“This thing is countin’ down fast, boss. It’s right next to some major gas lines.”

Devlin sighed heavily and finger-combed his hair. “A bomb. Jeez, what’s next? Can you disarm it?”

Peter moved to Devlin’s side. “Major Devlin, if Scout can tell me what to do, I could use my telekinetic abilities to disarm it.”

Brody asked, “How’d you know my name?”

“I gave the boys a full briefing, boss,” Scout shouted. “But we got a big problem. Even if Peter could help, I don’t have a portable x-ray to look inside this sucker. If I can’t see inside, I can’t tell the kid what to do.”

Little Gabriel tugged at Scout’s pants. Puzzled, Scout looked down. “What’s up, little buddy?”

“Mister Scout, I can see inside it with my mind. Then I can tell you and Peter what I see.”

Major Devlin threw up his hands. “Go for it, Scout. But you realize … these kids are gonna put us out of a job when they grow up.”

Madison coughed, spat up some water, and vomited.

Chewie gently wiped her mouth and cheek with the back of his huge hand. With his sleeve, he blotted her chin and then stroked her hair lovingly.

She looked up at Chewie's smiling face, then down at her wet unbuttoned blouse. "Oh, God, no," she managed, her voice hoarse and weak. "Please … don't tell me you gave me a lip lock!"

Chewie nodded and gave a sheepish grin. With that, Madison fainted dead away in his arms.

CHAPTER 43

An explosion rocked the laboratory, its thundering boom echoing through the vastness of the room, followed by shrill screams.

Smoke churned toward the ΩMEGA team from the direction of the catwalk above, where Scout and the Lost Boys were working feverishly to disarm the bomb.

Brody Devlin thought the worst as he bolted for the stairs, imagining that Scout and the boys had been torn limb from limb. His heart thundered in his chest as he took the stairs two at a time, struggling to breathe in the smoke-clotted air.

On the other side of the looking glass, Blair and Gant stood side by side. They were gazing upward at a tower that resembled a minaret, capped in gold, which climbed out from a wide chasm in the rocky terrain. They had been transported to some distant landscape and were high on a mountainside, another dimension where time thickened and slowed.

While the biting breeze flamed Blair's red mane, the scorching sun beat down from above. Blair looked down at her hands, her torso, then patted her chest.

Satisfied that she was still in one piece and unharmed, she moved to the lip of the chasm and peered over the edge. It seemed bottomless, reaching to the center of the Earth. The ground beneath her feet began to crumble and she leapt back.

Gant's taunting laugh came from behind her and she turned. "Watch your step, *Doktor*. After all, I don't think you can fly like the girl."

Blair's face set in a grim frown. Hands on her hips, she surveyed the surrounding scenery.

"Have you deduced where we are yet?" Gant asked smugly, his twisted grin mocking her.

She blew out a sharp breath. "Judging by the terrain, my guess would be somewhere in the Middle East, but the tower is strange, half Byzantine and half Islamic in appearance."

"Close enough, my dear. Now, shall we proceed?" He began working his way around the edge of the gorge. "If my memory serves me well, I believe there's a staircase carved into the side of the rock face over here."

Blair stood her ground, her arms crossed on her chest, her lower lip protruding.

He looked back. "Be a good girl and don't pout."

"You dragged me into this nightmare, and I'm not taking another step until you tell me just how the blazes you plan on getting back to the other side of the mirror."

"It's a bit complicated, but in order to go back, we must go forward. The portal lies below. Now come along, you're trying my patience."

Blair studied her surroundings. Climbing down the mountainside wasn't a viable option. She had no water, no idea where she was, and had no idea what, if anything, lay in the valley below. At this altitude, a thick cloud cover ringed the mountain and obscured her view. But there was no sign of life or civilization.

She marched after Gant.

They had made their way down the steep stone staircase and had come to a bridge that emptied into the tower on the other side. Once they'd crossed, they passed through a large archway; Blair blinked and stood awestruck. From their earlier vantage point, Blair could only see one side of the tower. It now dawned on her that it had been merely a façade, concealing the real structure that lay beyond its walls.

A long sloping staircase climbed up the front of a giant ziggurat. Its edges were no longer crisply defined but rounded and weathered with age. All in all, it was still a remarkable sight. She'd visited the one in Tallil, Iraq and the oldest known ziggurat in Sialik, Iran, but this was like nothing she'd ever seen.

It was gleaming white and indigo in color, and when it caught the sun, it glistened.

Blair knew that ziggurats were temples believed to be a cosmic axis, a vertical gateway and bond between Heaven and Earth, and the Earth and the underworld, and a horizontal bond between the lands of the Earth.

She didn't need any more coaxing from Gant; she ran for the stairs and started to climb. The archaeologist in her was enthralled by this once-in-a-lifetime discovery.

By the time she reached the top, she was winded and stood with her hands on her knees, panting. An ethereal voice called to her, "*Blair, of the Awen.*" She wheeled around but saw no one. "*Do not be seduced by the hunger for knowledge.*"

Despite his decrepit appearance, Gant's strength and endurance was that of a young man. He bounded up the stairs and was soon at her side. She studied him. There was something different about him. He looked fit, more toned.

Despite the warning of the otherworldly voice, she turned and dashed into the gaping mouth of the entrance.

Two passageways confronted them. She said, "This one appears to lead to the outer face of the structure which loops upward. The other—"

As Gant strode toward the second entrance without looking back, he said, "—leads downward to the portal." His hand fished inside his coat pocket, pulled out a flashlight, thumbed its switch.

Blair hesitated and sighed before she took off after him. She followed the pendulous beam of his light as he led the way. She had to lengthen her stride to keep pace with him.

They'd entered a narrow passageway, whose floor gradually slanted ever downward as they went. Blair tried to make some sense of the stonework and architecture, gain some clue from its style. In some places, however, it looked to be Sumerian, in others it appeared closer to Babylonian. Either way, her imagination conjured visions of what lay ahead: images of a brimstone underworld with bubbling pools from which the pungent stench of sulfur gas steamed; or perhaps a crystal-walled cave that glimmered with the colors of the rainbow.

The grade became increasingly steeper as they descended deeper and deeper into the bowels of the ziggurat.

Finally, as they reached what seemed to be the lowermost level, the passageway leveled off.

Faint light pulsed green then white from the yawning maw of cave that loomed before them.

Devlin pounded down the catwalk toward Scout and the boys, the honeycombed steel floor beneath him echoing with each footfall. He skidded around the corner of a large bank of equipment.

He heard shouting voices as dazzling shafts of light stabbed helter-skelter through the thick smoke. Something slammed into his chest and he fell backward on his ass.

When he looked up, the muzzle of a submachine gun fitted with a blinding LED light was trained at his head. A familiar voice said, "He's a Yankee, lads, stand down." The weapon lowered and a hand reached out. Brody took it and was yanked to his feet. Chief Inspector Newley's smiling face greeted him.

As the air started to clear, Brody looked past the inspector. A knot of men in black Nomex-3 and tactical gear, SAS men he figured, were securing the immediate area. And behind them stood Scout and the boys.

He breathed a sigh of relief. "Shit! I thought the bomb went off."

Newley shook his head. "Oh, we had to come in noisy, Major. The explosion was from us breaching the door and a few flash-bang grenades the lads tossed in for good measure."

Brody rubbed his chest.

Newley shrugged sheepishly. "I'm afraid they tagged you with a rubber slug, Major."

"Guess I'm lucky it wasn't a double-tap of 9 mm. rounds instead."

Scout and the captain appeared at Newley's side.

The captain had a puzzled look on his face. "Damnedest thing I've ever seen."

Scout held up an LED timer that was attached to the lid of a black toolbox. The numerals were frozen at 00:04.

Brody's gaze traveled from the box to Scout and then back to the box. He gave a low whistle. "Four seconds to spare. That's cuttin' her awful close."

Peter's head peered around Scout's shoulder, then he stepped out smiling.

Brody nodded to Peter. "More of your handiwork, I take it?"

Peter studied his shoes for a moment, then looked up and winked.

Brody turned to the captain. "I've got two agents down below that need immediate medical attention. And a crazy Scotsman who's doped-up on thorazine and cooling his heels in the mansion somewhere."

The captain nodded and spoke into his headset mic. "Status on the Yankees?" he asked, using the SAS term for hostages.

After a moment, he took a deep breath and met Brody's gaze. "Already got two medics attending to them. They also found Sgt. Conners having a little nappy in an upstairs bedroom."

Brody chuckled, picturing the big walrus curled up snuggly on a mountain of pillows like sleeping beauty. Chewie had filled him in about the robot's attack. But then his face went hard. "How are the other two?"

The captain nodded. "The woman's in fair shape, but the man's hanging on by a thread. We're calling in a Medevac chopper and putting the hospital on emergency standby notice." He reached out and put a reassuring hand on Devlin's shoulder. "Chin up, Major. We'll get them out of here ASAP."

An SAS man escorted Sir Nigel toward them, his hands still cuffed behind his back.

Brody grinned and gave a chuckle when he saw the paunchy man's soot-covered face and dour expression. "Well, *old boy*. Looks like you've had a really bad day."

He turned to Inspector Newley. "Do they still send traitors to the pillory at the Tower of London these days?"

Newley shook his head. "I only bloody well wish. Staked out in the courtyard with his pants around his fat ankles and the ravens feedin' at his prick and tiny balls would be too bleedin' good for the likes of him."

The captain cut in. "Major, we've rounded up most of the technicians and what was left of Gant's guards, but there doesn't seem to be any sign of Mr. Gant and—"

Now Brody cut him off. "Captain, trust me. You wouldn't believe me if I told you." With all the turmoil, Brody hadn't thought of Blair until just now. A sharp pain stabbed at the lining of his gut as he pictured her slipping through the black mirror.

"I was about to add that there's no sign of this al-Dajjal character or Margot Gant."

Brody spun and leaned over the railing. He spotted Chewie at Madison's side as an SAS medic attended to her. Next to her lay Bill Sorensen. A field IV was feeding his arm with badly needed fluids, and an oxygen mask covered his face.

He called to Chewie. "Hey, you big lug. Let 'em do their job. Margot and al-Dajjal are bookin' out on us."

Chewie looked up, came to his feet, and pounded his chest as he let out a blood-curdling war cry.

Brody turned back to Newley and the captain. In unison, their eyes tracked to Sir Nigel, who gulped hard and said, "Don't look at me. I haven't a clue as to their whereabouts … truly, gentlemen."

Newley cuffed the fat man's ear and he yelped loudly. Then the inspector reached under his jacket and pulled the Webley revolver from his waistband.

Puzzled, Major Devlin noticed that the captain's face went white as he and the other SAS men turned away.

Sir Nigel shuddered. "That won't be necessary, Inspector. There's a hovercraft docked at the seaward entrance to the manor house. I would suspect that they're making for it as we speak."

"Captain," Brody barked. "Do you have a helo on site?"

An SAS man looked over from his position and offered, "Sir, the helo's topside on the roof."

Sir Nigel cleared his throat. "There's a secret express elevator that goes to the rooftop helo pad."

The inspector studied him warily. "If you're lying …"

A small voice said, "He's not fibbing, sir. But you better hurry, 'cause old Cruella and that other meanie are loading the boat right now."

Brody looked down at little Gabriel, then shrugged and turned to Scout.

Scout went down on one knee, facing the boy. "Little buddy, can you see into their minds and tell us where they're going?"

Gabriel squeezed his eyes tightly shut for a second and then opened them. "It's a big black boat and it's under the water."

The men exchanged bewildered looks.

Then Brody, even though in his heart he already feared what the boy was going to say, asked slowly, "You mean a submarine, little man?"

"Uh-huh … and it's got kind of a crooked black cross painted on the side."

Scout shrank back in surprise. Then he stared up at Brody Devlin with a wise-assed *I-told-you-so* look.

Brody shook his head and raised his palm. "Don't even say it."

With a shit-eating grin filling his face, Scout said it anyway: "A freakin'… U-boat with a swastika painted on the side."

Chief Inspector Newley grabbed the fat man by the elbow and nodded toward the exit. "Okay, *ducky*. Off we go then."

As Brody and a cadre of SAS troops fell in behind them, Scout ran to Brody's side and tucked a pistol-like Taser gun into his coat pocket. Brody shot Scout a puzzled look. The techno geek quickly whispered an explanation into the major's ear.

Grinning broadly, Brody slapped him on the back. "That should cook her goose … but good."

CHAPTER 44

Blair and Gant had entered the cave where they came upon a box-shaped entrance.

"Doric columns," Blair said. "A Greek or Macedonian tomb would be my best guess."

On either side atop a pedestal sat a green glowing globe. Blair moved closer and held her palm a few inches from it.

"It doesn't give off any heat." She reached out and lifted the glowing sphere. As she was rolling it carefully back and forth in her hands, she noticed that within it an iridescent liquid sloshed from side to side.

When she held it out before her and swung it back and forth like a child with a new toy, she was awed by its subtle beauty.

Before her, a stone figure seemed to dart and feint as the globe's radiance swept past it. The statue was that of a man, life-sized, with a flowing beard. His robes were decorated with alchemical symbols: the sun, moon, and stars; sulfur, salt, and mercury. His right hand was raised palm out in a gesture of warning, while his left hand beckoned them forth.

"Astounding," Gant said, "the Thrice-Great Hermes."

Blair had to admit to herself that Gant was right, but the hairs on the nape of her neck bristled.

Her gaze panned the Greek inscription above the opening and she read it slowly: "The Gateway of Awareness. The journey begins with knowledge, but ends with faith. V-I-T-R-I-O-L." She paused. "Does that last bit mean anything to you, Gant?"

"*Vista Interiora, Terraie, Rectificando, Inveniens Occultum Lapidem,*" he answered in a soft whisper. "'Visit the interior parts of the earth, and by rectifying you will discover the hidden stone.'"

They entered and found themselves in a large hall with no exit. Reliefs that represented an alchemical process were set into the sides of an alcove, dominated by cylindrical furnaces, or athanors, and alchemical glassware: the alembic, a type of retort; the matrass, a round-bottomed flask.

Blair looked down. The floor was made up of an interlocking mosaic of eight-sided stones. Each stone had one of the signs or alchemical symbols of the seven visible planets or the signs of the zodiac carved upon it. The stones, like the walls around them, appeared crystalline. But instead of being clear, they were clouded with milky strands, as though a spider had woven its silken web while trapped within a block of ice.

"Well, off we go then. Let's start with Taurus, the earth sign." Blair inched forward and took a step. Suddenly, the stone under her foot began to crumble, then broke free and plunged beneath her. As Gant caught her by her arm and hauled her back, the globe tumbled from her grasp.

The missing stone left a man-sized shaft. Blair peered over the edge, watching the glowing sphere grow dimmer and dimmer as it fell into the bottomless murky depths of the shaft, finally winking out.

"This is bloody insane!" she said.

"Do you want to find the portal or not?" Gant chided her.

Blair sucked a deep breath and stood thinking for a moment. "Obviously, Astrology isn't the key. Let's stick to Alchemy. Can these alchemical ciphers or symbols represent something besides the planets? A different progression or order we could use as a path?"

"Indeed," Gant said. "The alchemical sequence. Each planetary symbol stands for a corresponding step of the process and an element or metal. It was called the Ladder of the Planets."

Blair turned and studied him. "Okay, then. Let's take it in that order."

"Calcination is first," Gant said. "That would be Saturn."

Together they stepped onto the stone with the sign for lead. The entire floor shuddered as it sank, leaving the stone they were standing upon a foot above the others.

Looking around warily, Blair managed, "What's next?"

"Dissolution. Jupiter."

They stepped down onto the sign for tin. The stones rumbled and sank another foot, leaving Jupiter halfway between the floor and Saturn at the threshold to the rear.

"It's forming a stairway down," Blair said excitedly.

They moved in sequence: Mars for iron and separation, followed by Venus for copper and conjunction. Then came Mercury for quicksilver and the Moon for silver—fermentation, distillation—and finally the Sun, for gold and coagulation. The floor was now ten feet below the threshold, and the top of a doorway appeared above the floor.

As they crowded together back-to-back on the last stone, they were still too low to proceed. "Now what?" Blair said, scanning the remaining stones. "We've run out of planets." She could hear Gant's labored breathing coming from behind her; feel his shoulders shivering with panic.

Finally, he said, "I have it! What symbol contains all the other ciphers of alchemy?" Blair's leg began to cramp, and she struggled to maintain her balance. "For Chrissakes! This is no time for riddles."

Without warning, Gant jumped to the next stone and shouted, "The egg that gave birth to the cosmos—the Monad."

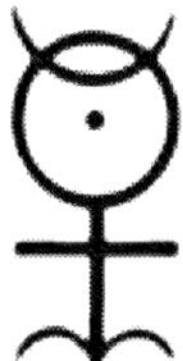

Blair now stood with Gant on the last stone as it slowly began to shudder, then creep upward. When it stopped, the doorway was fully revealed, and they were level with it. Blair glanced behind her. The seven milky stones, which had been selected, remained at various heights, stair-stepping their way back up to the entrance behind them.

"It's fabulous," Gant said. "The proverbial stairway to Heaven."

"Or … Hell," she said, looking up nervously. "And I don't like the inscription above the door: 'The Trial of Chaos.'"

As they brushed the thick cobwebs from the entrance and stepped through, a huge spider crabbed toward her. She ducked and bolted ahead into a long narrow passage. The walls were also crystalline and smoldered with a fiery orange-red hue. The passageway turned, then sloped downward, then turned again. They wound their way ever downward.

"This reminds me of the Great Pyramid's passageways," Blair told him.

"It is an inverted pyramid, my dear *Doktor*. It should end at its apex. That Which is Above … is as Below."

By the crimson glow of the walls, Blair noticed something unusual. "There are deep gouges in the walls. See how they're blackened, suggesting something sizzling hot etched them into the stone. Curious, don't you think?"

"It's puzzling, I agree," he said.

With her fingertip, she explored a groove in the wall. "They look relatively recent, but seem to have been gradually deepened. It's like something repeatedly dug out these gouges over time."

When they rounded a corner, the passage abruptly ended in a blank wall. Blair ran both hands along the wall, searching for a seam. She rapped it with her knuckles.

"Ouch," she said. "Solid." She looked closer. "What's this powdery residue clinging to the wall?"

Gant studied it with his torch. When he lowered the flashlight, it glowed eerily green. He panned its beam to the floor, then hooded the lens with his hand. "There's a pile of it on the floor, too."

He went to one knee and scooped it into his hand, letting it drain out between his fingers. Then he tasted the residue that clung to his fingertips. "Calcium. Phosphorus, hence its iridescence."

Blair felt every hair on her body stiffen, a coldness running up her back and clamping itself against her neck. "Powdered bone." She nudged the pile on the floor with her toes, and the mound shifted and became smaller, draining through a funnel-like opening in the floor.

"Quiet," Gant whispered as he cocked his head.

A loud rumbling came from behind them.

The floor quivered and quaked.

They spun around. Some unseen terror was scraping and grinding down the corridor, the terrifying sound of rock pulverizing rock.

They stood riveted, staring at the last corner they had turned.

The vibration was so strong that she felt it resonate in her bones as dust showered from the low ceiling above. The air became stifling hot, as if she were being roasted alive. The searing air burned in her lungs.

They crept to the corner and dared a glance. An enormous, rounded stone filled the passageway. Crawling toward them, inch by inch, the stone glowed red-hot like lava.

"Damn you, Gant," Blair said tersely as she ducked back, perspiration pouring off her face now.

Gant was frantically searching the walls. "This isn't supposed to be happening. There must be a hidden lever here, something. Don't you understand? This is the Calcination stage of Alchemy. We're trapped. Our bodies are about to be reduced to bone by burning!"

The earsplitting sound of the creeping stone was explosive now.

The helicopter rose off the rooftop in a nose-down attitude and churned over the manor house. The sky was sinister and brooding and darkness was beginning to fall.

Brody Devlin shouted to the pilot through his headset. "Over there!"

Newley and Brody looked on as Chewie climbed through a window and ran across the roof of a lower level of the mansion, illuminated by roof-mounted floodlights. He turned, looked up, and waved his hands madly.

"Pick him up," Brody ordered.

The chopper banked and plunged downward. As it hovered over him, Chewie jumped up and hooked his arm around the helo's modified skid rail.

"We've got him," Brody said. "Take her up."

With Chewie holding fast to the skid, the chopper rose and winged over the manor house, headed for the channel and the roaring sea.

As they soared at treetop level over the towering oaks and elms, the wind whipped the big Indian's ponytail.

Looking down, Brody searched for a sign of the hovercraft and al-Dajjal.

Suddenly, the hovercraft shot out from behind a rocky breaker.

Brody had ridden in a smaller version in Vietnam, where they were used to patrol the Mekong Delta, but he'd never seen anything like this.

Two large pontoons fitted with fat rubber skirting were attached to either side of a wedge-shaped cabin above. Beneath its skirting, a big fan sucked in air, compressed it, and blasted it out from under the hovercraft. It skimmed over the water on a cushion of air as large twin fans propelled it over the choppy water. He estimated she was doing better than seventy knots.

The captain, who was seated next to Newley, advised, "I already notified the Royal Marines. They're sending in an SBS team with another helo."

"And here they come!" Newley shouted into his mic.

A second chopper flew toward them, banked sharply and swooped downward after the hovercraft. It ducked in low behind the racing boat, skimming the waves.

Two inflatable rubber fast-boats tumbled out, splashing into the surf, followed by the British SEAL squads. In moments, they'd climbed into their fast-boats, their outboards roaring, charging in pursuit of their prey.

"Get us down closer," Brody shouted to the pilot.

He did. But just as the fast-boats were closing on the hovercraft, two wedge-shaped boats catapulted out from the stern, headed for the advancing SBS teams.

"Jeez!" Brody said, peering at the sleek boats through binoculars. "Those are PROTECTORS!"

"Bloody hell," the captain snapped and radioed a warning to the SBS helo.

"What the deuce are you saying?" Newley asked.

Brody explained. "Unmanned Surface Vehicles, robotic patrol boats, equipped with a 7.62 mm. machine gun, a Typhoon-Station. Its Toplite optical system allows automatic target tracking and acquisition with laser range finders. They're fast as hell and deadly."

"Israelis developed them, Inspector," the captain added. "We're just starting to put them into service. Nasty buggers. Our boys will be cut to ribbons."

Like hungry sharks, the PROTECTORS circled and then knifed across the waves, closing at high-speed on the fast-boats from both sides. Muzzle flash from chattering machine guns greeted the SBS teams.

"Oh God," the captain cried in anguish.

"Take us down now," Brody ordered the pilot. "It's our only shot. Put us right over the bridge of that fucker while those beasties are busy feeding on the fast-boats!"

Like a gooney bird, Wendy had crash-landed on the other side of the mirror, bruising her shoulder. She came to her feet and dusted herself off. Her sixth sense siphoned the air for Blair.

She spun and ran to the edge of the deep chasm. She took a deep breath and steeled herself. Arms out before her, she swan-dived off the ledge, caught an updraft, and soared across the deep gorge to the tower.

Without stopping, she winged her way through the stone puzzle box and sailed up and over the steep steps leading to the entrance of the ziggurat.

Like a homing pigeon, she was being guided by sheer instinct as she flew, winding her way through the dark passageway that spiraled deeper and deeper before her.

Blair sensed it before she heard it: a presence in the narrow passage, just off her shoulder. She wheeled around and saw a shadowy form. It began to take shape, pulsing with a blue-white aura. It was an old bag lady.

An old woman's kindly voice called to her, the same voice she'd heard before.

Blair, darlin'. The wise man welcomes death, only the fool fears it.

The radiant apparition vanished.

Blair called to Gant, "If you want to live, follow me." When they rounded the corner, the giant stone was only about three yards away and rumbling toward them. On their right was the corridor they'd just come from.

Blair took a few steps back and examined the back wall at the sharp bend, rubbing her hands over it. "It's smooth. No grooves. This is the only spot where the stone hasn't scraped these walls." She examined the floor. "No bone dust, either."

She stiffened. "We'll stay put. Face death head on."

"I think we should go back to the wall at the very end of the passage," Gant argued.

"I'd say suit yourself, but I need your bloody arse to get me to and through the portal, so stand your ground, you old lizard."

The giant stone had passed the edge of the corner.

Three feet and closing.

Two feet.

Gant was shifting nervously.

One foot … and Gant tried to slide out of the way, but Blair grabbed him by the arm and held him fast.

The stone was inches from their chests, and what began as smoldering heat quickly became an unbearable furnace. Blair turned her face, and the scalding surface of the stone almost kissed her cheek. She pictured a grotesque burn scar that disfigured her face.

"This may have been a bad idea," she managed.

With a thunderous boom, the wall at their backs began to ease away, allowing them a few precious steps backward and relieving the torturous heat on their chests. As though the Devil himself were manipulating their fate by sliding the moveable slats on some giant Hellraiser puzzle box, the stone shuddered and instantly vanished into a new opening in the wall, falling away from them into darkness.

Blair felt a cool breeze at her neck and she turned. Where the wall had been was now a passage that sloped gently downward. From somewhere deep within, the sound of running water drifted toward her.

They emerged from the passage into a chamber. The architecture was that of a Greek temple. A large, luminous pond lay before it. From its center sprouted a pearlescent fountain shaped like a tree; its clear blue waters flowed over the lips of clamshells that ringed the center shaft.

Gant ran to the edge of the pond and dropped to his knees. He began scooping water into his hands and drinking it. Then he buried his face in the radiant water and pulled it out, the water spilling down his cheeks.

When he turned and looked at Blair, she gasped.

The scar tissue, the ugly veining, the fatty tumors, had been magically healed. Blair could see Gant's youthful vitality emerge from beneath the ruined mask of age and deformity. The face of a young man in his twenties smiled back at her. He was handsome, with dark wavy hair and bright, clear blue eyes.

He rose and came to her. He stood erect, no longer stoop-shouldered.

"The Fountain of Youth. The primordial waters of creation. You see, I was right all along."

"I guess you were," Blair said begrudgingly. "Was it worth it, though? All the pain and suffering you caused, all the blood on your hands?"

He sneered and made a *tsking* sound. "My dear, the end always justifies the means. And the meek shall inherit nothing but the lash of the whip. It has been so, and always will be."

"So, your gods are still ambition, hypocrisy, and vice?" she asked.

He gave a wicked laugh.

"Yes, I regret nothing."

From the corner of her eye, Blair saw Wendy on the other side of the pool.

Gant turned, following her gaze and frowned. "I warned you to keep away from me, you insolent child."

Blair noted a tiny tremor worm its way through his cheek, and his skin seemed to lose its youthful sheen.

As she floated across the pond, Wendy's eyes were locked on Blair. Her face was so serene, her eyes so radiant and filled with life that she looked like a cherub.

When she reached Blair, she glided down and leaped into her waiting arms.

Blair felt a mother's love, a mother's solace as she clung to the little angel, hot tears streaming down her face. Blotting her tears with the back of her hand, she told Wendy, "You shouldn't have come, sweetie pie. I don't know if we can ever get back."

Wendy traced the outline of Blair's face with her finger, then leaned in and rubbed her turned-up nose against Blair's and winked.

She lowered Wendy to the floor and held her hand.

Gant had turned and was wading across the pool. Although the pond appeared to be shallow, the farther Gant went, the deeper the water became. The water began to change. Its luminosity faded and the clear blue color became increasingly greenish, then blackened until it looked like pooled oil. By the time he'd reached the middle, the oily-looking liquid was up to the middle of his chest.

Blair stared intently. Then she noticed the inscription of the Latin phrase IMMCISTINANTUR on the stone slab at the far end of the pond. And next to it was the acronym: VITRIOL.

Looking closer, she saw that beneath the slab was a large-mouthed pipe. A torrent of viscous, emerald colored liquid was flooding into the pool. There were a series of similar pipes with corresponding inscriptions, which read: NATRON, LIQUOR HEPATIS, RED PULVIS SOLARIS …

Her gaze flicked back to Gant, who seemed to be struggling as though the water had become thick as tar. His arms held above him, he began to twist and turn violently.

Tiny blue flames spouted out from the corners of the oily pool. They grew larger, licking higher as they began to race across the surface.

At first the odor of coal tar assaulted Blair's nostrils. But then Blair heard a hissing noise. Steam that had become a yellowish gas rose from the surface of the inky water. The air now reeked of rotten eggs.

The words on the slab flashed in her mind's eye.

IMMCISTINANTUR … was a decoded phrase from the Voynich, which she remembered channeling while in her trance. It was written in Voynichese below the pictures of naked women bathing in a pool that was fed by multiple tubes or *pipes*. In English it simply meant—*they are mixed together!* Her neck went cold in a flash of intuition. And the next word on the slab was …

VITRIOL … sulfuric acid.

She realized that the healing waters of the pool were created by an ongoing process of combining a series of *deadly* chemicals.

She snatched Wendy into her arms. "We've got to get out of here. Do you know where the portal is?"

Wendy screwed up her nose. "Whew, sure is stinky in here. Did you cut a stinker like the boys or somethin'?"

"Sweetie pie, how did you get in here?"

"Ah, that's easy peasy. You just go right through that wall over there." She pointed to the other side of the blazing pool.

But by now the flames were leaping off the oily surface of the water and a thick yellow cloud hung over it. "Okay, let's give her a go," she told Wendy, coughing. Still clutching the little girl firmly to her chest, her eyes closed tightly, they flew upward and sailed through the inferno.

Instead of the sweltering heat that she'd imagined, Blair felt a cool breeze as they soared through the blaze. And again, she thought she heard the kind old bag lady's voice whispering in her ear:

Have faith. The child will guide you.

Wendy held out the heel of her palm in front of her like a charging halfback as they flew, and she hit the lower part of the wall at full speed. That section of the wall was cantilevered and the upper half swung inward and down with the pressure of her hand. They sailed through the opening.

On the other side stood an identical black mirror.

Blair went to it and looked into its surface.

Instead of her reflection, Blair saw a dim image of Gant's laboratory. Looking closer, she could make out SAS men moving about.

She looked down at Wendy, who was still in her arms.

"You ready?" she asked.

"Uh-huh."

From behind them came a piercing cry.

She turned to see Gant's charred body staggering toward them. The stench of roasted flesh turned her stomach.

Smoke poured off the tattered rags of clothing that still clung to raw flesh. His face was blistered and lobster red; his wavy black hair was singed and falling from his head in matted clumps, and his outstretched hands were swollen and the color of charcoal, the flesh dripping from his fingers like wax from a candle as he clawed the air, reaching for her.

Blair spun around and leaped into the looking glass, pulling Wendy along with her.

The surface rippled as they disappeared into the gateway.

Summoning his last ounce of strength, Gant cursed madly and flung himself into the mirror.

A loud boom rocked the chamber as bolts of lightning arced around the mirror.

Just as Gant was halfway through, the rippling black quicksilver suddenly hardened around him.

As though a guillotine's hungry blade had fallen, the lower half of his torso was literally severed from his body.

It slid down the smooth surface of the mirror with a wet sucking noise and slipped to the ground.

On the looking glass's reverse, Gant's upper torso protruded from the mirror. Like a worm half buried in an apple, struggling to wriggle free from the surface, he pushed back from the hard surface of the mirror with his charred and blistered hands. When he realized that he couldn't dislodge himself, fear gripped him.

His panic-driven eyes searched frantically.

Nothing but unrelieved blackness surrounded him.

Then he realized that he was trapped for eternity between worlds. *Nowhereland.* As he stared into the vast emptiness, maddening terror crippled his mind. Flailing his arms, he screamed, his cries swallowed by the infinite abyss.

On the other side, Blair and Wendy tumbled out of the twin mirror and rolled across the concrete floor, knocking a startled SAS man off his feet.

When she stood, Blair offered the soldier her hand and pulled him up. Wendy was at her side now. She flashed her dimpled smile. "Pardon us, please. I guess we should have looked where we were going." Then she put her hand to her mouth and giggled.

Wendy saw that a man and a woman were lying on stretchers hefted by medics at the foot of the stairs. She looked up at Blair, her eyes sad and questioning.

Blair nodded solemnly.

Wendy dashed toward the injured pair.

A chorus of voices called to her from above.

She glanced up to see the Lost Boys, who were standing above her on the catwalk, peering over the side, elbows on the rail, hands resting on their chins. "Hey, guys. Did you miss me?" she shouted back. Little Gabriel, who was peeking out from between Peter's legs, smiled and waved excitedly.

Wendy heard Gabe's sweet voice telegraph a message directly into her mind. *Hey, Wendy. Mister Scout told us that Bill, that's the man, is hurting really bad. Please help him. And the lady, Ms. Madison, swallowed a lotta water.*

A loud groan drew Wendy's attention back to the injured man. When she took Sorensen's hand in hers, he opened his eyes briefly and looked beseechingly at the little angel. His breathing was ragged and shallow, its raspy sound exaggerated by the oxygen mask that covered his nose and mouth.

A medic started to push Wendy away. "Move along now, missy. This man's in terribly bad shape."

Scout had made his way down the stairs. He put himself between the medic and Wendy. His face set resolutely, he told him, "Hey, Mac. Leave the girl alone. This man and woman are ours, and I know what I'm doing."

Then Scout turned to Wendy and gave her a warm smile. "My name's Scout. My friend Bill here needs your help badly. The boys seem to think you can fix him."

He stood, eyes probing. He blinked, because for just a moment, he could have sworn that a halo glimmered over the little girl's head. "Maybe you could fix up Madison, too?" He nodded toward Ms. Dare, who coughed.

She looked into his sad eyes and nodded. "I fixed a bird or two, but never a person." Her gaze cut back to the boys. "Listen guys, I need your help here. We're stronger when we do it together."

"Roger, Wendy," Raji shouted back. The Lost Boys, even Gabriel, joined hands, closed their eyes and bowed their heads.

Wendy noticed that Blair had moved to her side. Blair's reassuring hand nestled on her shoulder gave her added strength.

Wendy lowered her head and clasped Sorensen's hand tightly in both of her tiny fists.

Next she turned to Madison and placed her hands on the woman's chest.

Madison cleared her throat. She took a deep cleansing breath. Smiling at Wendy, she said, "My lungs don't hurt anymore. I can breathe."

Wendy asked Bill Sorensen, "Feeling a bit better, Mister?" Abruptly, his eyes popped wide open. He propped himself up on his elbows and looked around, a surprised look filling his face.

Sitting up, he stretched his arms and back.

He rubbed his shoulder. Still puzzled, he said, "No pain at all."

The two medics were so startled by Sorensen's complete and instant recovery that they nearly dropped the stretcher.

Behind her, Wendy heard a sharp gasp.

She turned just in time to see Blair swoon, weaken at the knees, and collapse to the floor.

Tears threatening, Wendy crawled to her side.

Reaching out, the little angel felt Blair's forehead.

She's burning up. Got to mend her. She remembered Ginny's warning. *"Although Blair is a good woman and strong willed and knows the ways of the Awen, she too will perish."*

She gazed into Blair's eyes. No longer a brilliant sea-green, now they were dull and vacant. The girl's gaze lowered to Blair's chest. She was struggling to breathe, making wheezing, rattling sounds with each shallow breath. Even worse, the rosiness had withered from her cheeks. She was salt-pale, but her lips had turned a sickly purplish color.

Anger welling within her, Wendy felt her face grow hot, felt tears jetting into her eyes and tracking down her flushed cheeks. "Don't you dare die on me, Blair Kelly!"

Closing her eyes again, she pictured Blair healthy and brimming with vitality. She snuck a peek at her. To Wendy's dismay, Blair remained still, unchanged.

Her brow furrowing in deep concentration, she willed her to heal.

In her mind's eye, Wendy pictured happy thoughts: sunshine, meadows blooming with wild flowers that swayed in a gentle breeze, puppies and a baby swaddled in a bright pastel blanket, being sung a lullaby as its mother rocked the pink-faced newborn in her loving arms.

Blair's hand twitched in hers. She began to stir.

Wendy envisioned a pulsing red light that rose from the base of her spine upward, changing from a brilliant orange, to yellow, to blue as it passed through her heart. It snaked upward, and when it reached the midpoint between her eyebrows it faded, then ignited into a pure white sunburst of light that arced from her head, down her shoulders, and flowed through her hands as she moved them slowly over Blair's body.

Wendy opened her eyes.

Through a tear-clouded haze, she closely examined the woman, who lay so still, so lifeless.

From the back of her throat came a soft cooing sound, like a baby bird crying for its mother.

She put her hand to Blair's cheek. It was cooler.

The color was returning to Blair's complexion.

Her chest began to rise and fall in a silken rhythm.

When Blair's eyes fluttered open and she sucked a deep breath, Wendy flung her arms around her and clung to her for dear life. Clung to the woman who had become her reason for living, the woman who had become her surrogate mother.

CHAPTER 45

Onboard the U-boat in the red glow of the subs's control room, the *obersteurmann,* or navigation officer, turned to the captain.

"Coming up to the rendezvous point now, sir," he said, speaking German.

Kapitain Gunther Hessler nodded. "Stop all. Planes and midships."

"All stopped," the watch officer confirmed.

"Planes and midships," answered the senior of two helmsman, who sat strapped into their seats, their hands on the yokes that operated the hydroplanes controlling the submarine's depth.

At three times the size of the original, this U-boat was a completely redesigned version of the old German XXI. Gant's fortune had been put to use creating a sleek, streamlined outer hull, coated with a radar masking substance, which was the latest in stealth technology. Her nuclear reactor provided incredible underwater and surface speed.

"Sonar?" the captain asked quietly.

"Picking up the signature of a hovercraft and two PROTECTOR patrol boats bearing Zero-Four-Zero. Hold on, there's a third signature. Outboard motors, something small like inflatable fast-boats, sir."

"*Zum Teufel*, damn it!" Captain Hessler hissed through clenched teeth. "Probably an SAS squad in fast pursuit of al-Dajjal."

"Periscope depth," the captain murmured, observing the hushed atmosphere of the silent-running mode of the sub.

The helmsmen caressed their aircraftlike yokes, bringing the U-boat up from the depths, then gently eased off.

"Periscope depth, sir."

"Up periscope."

The solid tubular structure hissed upward, and Hessler slammed the handles down and adjusted the digital enhancement controls. He panned around until he got the hovercraft perfectly centered in the scope's stadia marks.

Captain Hessler's orders were to provide a means of low-profile escape for Gant, his niece Margot, and al-Dajjal. But under no circumstances was he to risk the capture of his vessel. Other "Powers that Be" within the *Vril* had also instructed him to ensure that al-Dajjal was to be eliminated if his capture seemed imminent. And right now Hessler didn't like the odds. The SAS's presence meant that things had gone to hell in a handbasket.

He called off the hovercraft's bearing and distance and said, "Ready torpedoes!"

The chopper had closed the distance and was hovering over the aft deck of the hovercraft. Devlin had climbed out onto the modified skid on the opposite side of the helo from Chewie. They crouched, the wind tearing at their faces and flaming their hair. They'd agreed to jump on Newley's signal.

The helo yawed and pitched, almost causing Devlin to lose his footing and be ditched into the sea.

As Newley signaled thumb's up, they leaped off the skid in unison and fell to the boat's deck below.

Devlin felt the icy sea spray and biting wind as he came to his feet. He glanced at Chewie, who stood across from him. Then he made a chopping hand gesture for them to advance on the cabin's door.

A SIG he'd borrowed from the SAS fisted firmly in his hand, Brody and Chewie made for the door.

Suddenly the hatchway burst open. Al-Dajjal screamed, "Wotan, kill!"

As though reading each other's thoughts, Chewie leaped to the left, while Brody rolled to his right and raised the SIG.

The German shepherd sprang, snarling. As Wotan's teeth fastened on his gun arm, Brody had a fleeting view of Margot standing behind al-Dajjal, and another shepherd—Siegfried—straining at the leash.

Brody felt the tearing rip of pain as Wotan's jaws clamped onto the lower part of his arm, making the fingers of his right hand open involuntarily, so that the gun dropped heavily onto the deck.

Beyond the pain, Brody was aware of several things—Margot's raw voice shouting above the ugly snarling of the dogs; al-Dajjal cursing in German; the stale, roadkill stench of Wotan's breath on his face, and the dog's weight as he latched on—still growling fiercely—head thrashing from side to side like he was trying to wrench Brody's arm from its socket.

Instinctively, his training taking hold, he smashed his free hand with blunt force into the dog's testicles. In training it worked so easily. For one thing, your arms were protected, and the trainer hovered nearby, ready to call off the attacking beast once you'd completed the moves. But this was reality. At first, Wotan failed to react, like he had cast-iron balls. So he reared back again and punched the mutt's nuts hard, then reached out and squeezed with all his strength.

The battered dog's growl became a yelp, and for a second he released his vise-lock, relaxing his jaws.

Brody used the brief moment to roll and swing his right hand up to the animal's throat. His thumb and fingers found the windpipe, forming a claw and pressing and digging as though he were trying to tear out the dog's larynx. His left arm whipped around, catching the beast by the scruff of the neck. But desperate with adrenaline-stoked strength born of panic, Wotan worked his jaws and snapped with blind rage.

The yelp changed into a series of chilling snarls and it took all of Brody's depleted reserves just to hang on. He could feel the deepening pain where Wotan had mauled his arm, and the weakness that accompanied it.

But like the dog, he knew he was fighting for his life, and he increased the pressure with his thumb and fingers. "Devlin, you never throttle any attacker like they do in the movies, with both hands. Always use the one-handed choke hold." He could hear his scrappy Gunny Sergeant from training school as clearly as if he were standing by his side at this moment. And the Gunny's words to live by… Kill or be killed.

C'mon, screw in with your hand on the windpipe and apply all of your strength at the back of the attacker's neck with your other hand——

he put action to the thought, as Wotan thrashed around wildly, struggling to pull free.

As he fought, acutely aware of the pain, the noise, and the confusion around him, Brody's mind clung to the thing that would keep him going—Wotan wanted blood. His blood.

"Siegfried, hold him!" Margot shrieked over the din, commanding the other dog.

Still holding Wotan in a death grip, Brody glanced to his left and saw where the SIG lay, just out of reach. And beyond the weapon was Chewie, sprawled flat on his back. The meat of his brick-sized hands was gnawed and swollen, his arms slashed and wet with blood. And Siegfried was looming over him, fangs bared, salivating profusely, ready to chew into the big Indian's exposed throat if he showed any further resistance.

It was obvious that Chewie was not going to risk something as imperceptible as a twitch of his eyebrows.

His attention was drawn back to Wotan, who was beginning to lose consciousness. When Wotan's eyes rolled back into his skull, his jaws relaxed and his massive body became dead weight.

Brody knew his best gambit was to act as though he was still wrestling with the beast, which might cause al-Dajjal and Margot to drop their guard just long enough to give him an edge.

He struggled to coordinate his next moves clearly before acting, because he knew he only had one chance at this.

But it wasn't a question of waiting for just the right moment, because the right moment was right now.

Using the dead body of Wotan as a shield, Brody fought through the fire-bolts of pain that shot through his mangled arm. He rolled right, snatched up the SIG, rolled again and fired—two shots for the hovering Siegfried; he panned and fired again and caught al-Dajjal in the shoulder with the full impact of the .40 hollow-point slug that spun him around. As he fell backward, Brody pumped another round, hitting him high and to the left, just above the ribs, slamming him against the rear bulkhead.

As the rounds struck him, al-Dajjal let out a strangled scream that was a mixture of rage, frustration, and agony. Then he slid silently down the wall, sprawling onto the deck in a black heap.

Taking advantage of the distraction, Chewie scrambled to his feet and sprang for Margot.

For a second, Margot was taken unawares, but instinctively, she spun at the last second. Catching the lunging Indian's thick wrist, she jerked her arm down hard, then toward him and away, which forced the suddenly hapless giant to be hurtled across the deck, thudding into the railing with a bone-cracking crunch.

On the bridge of the U-boat, Captain Hessler stood peering through the periscope, his forearms hanging over the handles.

He asked the radioman, "Any radio traffic from the hovercraft?

"Negative, sir."

"Anything new on sonar?" the captain added.

"Nothing but … *Gott im Himmel*!" The sonar operator stopped short as a loud ping echoed in his headphones and the blip appeared on the screen. "We've got company, sir."

The captain pulled back from the scope. "How's that?"

"Bearing Zero-Six-Four. It somehow locked onto our position and she's closing rapidly. I think she's a destroyer."

"Fire Number One torpedo," Hessler commanded, "then take us down, steep and fast."

The torpedo was away, snaking toward the hovercraft. As it sliced through the water like a hungry shark, it left a deadly wake as its calling card.

Margot turned on Brody, her eyes fevered with rage, blazing like red hot coals. "You're next, Loverboy. And no more foreplay this time."

She began moving toward him, never taking her hypnotic gaze from him.

Al-Dajjal stirred and called out weakly, "Make him suffer, *Mein Brüder*. Rip him limb from limb. Feed him to the sharks."

In a flash of insight, Brody picked up on the word … *Brüder!*

But just as Brody raised the SIG, Margot leaped through the air, hitting him like a sack of bricks and driving him to the deck. His pistol flew from his hand and clattered uselessly across the deck.

She straddled him, her iron-maiden legs hugging the sides of his torso, squeezing with bone crushing force. She pressed her face closer, her feral eyes dripping with carnality and rage, the scent of her perfume overpowering, sickening.

He squirmed like the German shepherd now, the life being slowly squeezed from his lungs.

Then, just as black motes began to swim at the corners of his vision, he remembered Scout's instructions as he headed for the helicopter. *I ran some tests on those nano-fibers we found at the museum. They have a deadly reverse effect. If you apply a high-voltage charge, the nano-fibers will squeeze her like a vise.*

On the edge of consciousness, Brody fished the Firefly from his pocket where Scout had tucked it earlier. It was Scout's amped-up version of a Taser pistol.

Summoning his last ounce of strength, he pulled the trigger, causing the compressed nitrogen to deploy two arrowlike probes that shot out and bit deeply into the nano-fibers of Margot's Superman suit.

Instantly, she relaxed her legs, allowing Brody to gulp cool air into his lungs. He pulled the Firefly's trigger again and again, and Margot rolled off him and across the deck.

He rolled on his side and met her terror-glazed stare. With each pull of the trigger, the weapon sent 600,000 volts coursing through the fibers surrounding her body. Instead of amplifying the power of Margot's muscles, the high voltage made the nano-fibers contract.

Margot groaned in sheer agony as the snug body suit shrank around her, compressing her as though she were trapped miles beneath the ocean, the outer shell of her diving bell buckling inward from the sheer tonnage of the sea around her.

Margot's face contorted into a hideous death mask; her eyes, once bright and clear, were now muddy—and their strange depth, their magnetism, was gone.

Brody Devlin looked on without pity, without remorse. Although he'd vowed never to strike a woman in anger and had always taken great pains not to kill a woman in the line of duty—Margot Gant was not a woman.

She was a man.

When al-Dajjal called her *Brüder*, it hit him. Margot was his twin brother. A gender-bending transsexual. Although estrogen hormone therapy had done away with any trace of a beard, and breast implants had undoubtedly augmented her figure—she was a pre-op—who was still tooled with the sexual apparatus of a man. When she'd attacked Brody in the mansion, he had mistaken her stiff manhood for the belt-buckle dagger. And that business of calling her Gant's niece was just part of her cover story.

Chewie grabbed him by the arm and roughly jerked him to his feet. Brody protested as Chewie manhandled him toward the railing, but then he caught sight of the torpedo. They jumped.

The hovercraft disappeared in a blinding white flame turning to crimson.

A few minutes later, his charred hand, then his head broke the oily surface of the water. He sucked life-giving air deep into his lungs. Al-Dajjal swam for his life, the limp snow-blonde husk of what remained of Margot Gant cradled in the crook of his arm.

EPILOGUE

Cartago, Costa Rica:

After their plane touched down at Juan Santamaria International in San Jose, Costa Rica, Blair and Devlin collected the luggage while Madison and Bill Sorensen proceeded to the curb. They stood waiting, sweat pouring off their faces, clothing matting against the smalls of their backs in the *humedo y caliente* August air. A black Range Rover lurched to a screeching halt at the curbside. Just as Blair and Devlin appeared with the luggage, Chewie exited the Range Rover he had rented upon his advanced arrival and joined them.

Decked out in his broad-brimmed straw hat and long white shirt, he would have been hardly recognizable if not for the fact that his hulking frame towered over the *mestizo* locals.

They loaded the luggage, climbed into the welcoming coolness of the air-conditioned vehicle, and peeled away from the curb.

Chewie slowed slightly as they passed the *Mercado Central* with its sun-leathered vendors standing proudly beside their carts filled to the brim with *verduras*: chiles of every shape, size, and color; green-yellow heaps of *platanos* and avocados.

Quickly, they left the city, traveling in a southeasterly direction into the *campo*. As they drove, Madison, who was seated in the rear with Sorensen, commented on the fertile slopes of farmland with row after row of coffee fields. A patchwork of cultivation mingled with dense verdant forest.

Gripping Blair's hand, Brody asked, "Where are we headed again?"

Blair answered, "Cartago. It's a small town about twenty-four klicks from San Jose. Wendy and the Lost Boys and the others are already there."

Devlin smiled. "I don't know how you arranged this, but then again you're a mysterious woman, Blair Kelly."

He reached forward and tapped Chewie on the shoulder.

"Didn't happen to pack a cold one or two, did ya big fellow?" As he said it, he massaged his right arm with his free hand. It was still in a sling. The ravages of the dog's teeth still pained him.

Chewie answered by nodding to a cooler on the floor. Madison opened it and disbursed cold beer to the party. As they popped the bottles, they raised them in a *brindo*.

"*Salud*," Blair toasted. "May you be in Heaven half an hour before the Devil knows you're dead."

They pulled to the side of the road for a pit stop. Brody shouted to Sorensen and Madison from the vehicle, "Don't wander off you two, unless you want to get eaten by a three-toed sloth or a troop of squirrel monkeys."

Blair stuck her head out the window, and added, "Or a blood thirsty flock of Scarlet Macaws and a giant Iguana!" Blair's laughter drifted across the countryside.

"C'mon, Blair. Iguanas aren't dangerous," Brody said.

"Well, neither are sloths and monkeys, Jungle Jim."

Chewie shook his head and let out a long sigh.

Brody patted his shoulder. "Hey, why such a long face?"

Chewie shrugged, then his gaze cut to Madison, who was making her way back to the Land Rover.

"I swear, Brody Devlin, you're the most blockheaded man this side of the Atlantic," Blair said. "Can't you see Mr. Raindancer is smitten?" She nodded toward Madison.

"Oh," Brody said sheepishly, "let me give her a little nudge, big fellow." Then he jumped out and opened the passenger door for Madison and winked. Her eyes drifted from him to Chewie, who sat grinning like a schoolboy, and then back to Brody. She gave a knowing smile and climbed in.

With Sorensen sound asleep in the back and Chewie finally finding the nerve to speak to Madison about something besides shoptalk, they drove on.

Turning serious for a moment, Brody said, "You sure Wendy and the Lost boys are safe down here? And how did you pull it off? Must have cost a fortune. Or did you spin your magic compass over a map and *poof* … X marked the spot where a treasure chest of gold doubloons was buried?"

Blair laughed. "I'm a High Priestess … not a sea witch."

Brody pouted. “Seriously, where did you get the money?”

She sat smiling, twirling a lock of hair, and humming a tune to herself. Finally she said, “Well, my brother and I are alchemists, you know.”

“Oh, sure. Why didn’t I think of that before? You turned some lead into gold and …”

She smiled knowingly and winked. “Let’s just say that the Awen take care of their own. And we have some very well-heeled benefactors.”

The Range Rover rolled to a stop at the plaza and they climbed out.

Across the courtyard stood the *Basilica de Los Angeles*. Atop its towering white pillars sat angels, their wings unfurled. Watchful guardians. Sunlight shimmered off the two rose windows that flanked the front entrance.

There stood Ginny Doolittle waving madly, the doughy underside of her arm wiggling like Jell-O. The wide-brim of her floppy hat was hanging over her face.

Next to her were Father Dominic Kelly, Scout, Conners, and Lt. Braxton. Ginny was dressed like the other five bridesmaids, Irish girls of the Awen, who, although lovely, looked a bit strange dressed in the native costume of *Las Bailarinas Criollas*: white peasant blouses, billowing gold, blue, and green skirts cinched at the waist by brightly colored sashes and *Guaria Moradas*, lavender orchids, tucked behind their ears.

The Lost Boys stood side by side, dressed in suits and ties, looking like little gentlemen, but terribly uncomfortable. Gabriel was tugging at his collar as Peter wrestled with his cowlick.

Standing before them now, Devlin asked Peter, “Hey, where’s Wendy?

Peter grinned broadly and pointed to the sky.

Soaring in lazy circles above was Wendy.

Johnboy put two fingers to his lips and whistled loudly.

Wendy swooped down, almost gliding to the ground.

With her bright eyes locked on Blair, she took off in a dead run across the courtyard, all elbows and knees, with a golden retriever scampering along at her side. She skidded to a halt in front of Blair and threw her arms around her.

"Woof," barked the retriever, catching Brody's attention. As Devlin stooped to pet the dog, he asked, "And who might you be, Furface?"

Wendy stepped back and turned to Devlin. "Oh, that's Sam. Isn't he just wonderful? Mister Nicholas and Miss Perenelle gave him to me as a present."

Devlin was taken aback by the dog's name as un-spilled tears filled his eyes. He looked closer, studying the dog's doleful eyes. It was as if his old boyhood playmate, his best friend Sam, who'd been killed by attack dogs, had been magically reincarnated and was standing right there before him. The dog wagged its tail and licked his face. Like a giddy schoolboy bolting at the sound of the final school bell, Brody ran off with Sam to play fetch.

Blair looked on, hands on her hips and shaking her head. *Typical man! He's run off with a bleedin' blonde!* When her eyes tracked to Wendy's feet, Blair burst out laughing. She was dressed in a silken gown, done up with a ribbon and looking the part of a flower girl … with one exception. She was wearing red high-top sneakers with the laces untied.

"Miss Wendy Kelly, where on earth did you get those shoes?" Blair asked, frowning.

"From Ginny. She said they were like Dorothy's ruby slippers. If I ever wanted to visit her, all I had to do was click my heels three times." Then the smile faded from her face and she sulked. "I've decided I don't want to be called Wendy anymore."

"Okay, sweetums, but how come?"

She dragged the toe of her sneaker on the ground, not looking up, and offered, "'Cause I'm safe here." She raised her head and her smile returned. "I don't have to hide anymore or use that old phony, pretend storybook name."

Blair went to her knees and hugged her closely. "Okay. Then Noor Kelly it will be."

The ceremony went off without a hitch.

It wasn't a traditional wedding *per se*, but was an old Celtic Awen custom called Handfasting.

With Father Kelly presiding, Blair and Devlin shared vows, pledging to share their joys and sorrows, their love for one another. One year and a day from now, they could return to this spot and become permanently married, renew their commitment for one year, or simply go their separate ways with strings untied.

During the ceremony, Madison stood by Chewie's side. He reached down with his huge paw and gently took her small hand in his. She gave him a warm glance and sighed as they looked on.

Dressed in a kilt, Conners played his bagpipes.

Afterwards, they held a reception at the large *hacienda* which was to be their new home. Nicholas and Perenelle Flamel had donated one of their many homes as a safe haven for the Indigo Children.

Devlin drifted away from the main party and made his way to the veranda in search of Blair. As he stood looking at the little girl perched in Blair's lap, cooing softly, an intuitive understanding came to him. He understood why Father Kelly had wanted his sister to read *The Midwich Cuckoos*.

Through some strange miracle of evolution, Wendy had developed extraordinary powers. Along with her ability to fly, she had adopted some traits and characteristics of the bird kingdom. A tiny hatchling, separated from its birth mother, often imprints its emotional bond onto another, a substitute mother.

Like the fledgling of a cuckoo bird who was placed in another bird's nest to be hatched and nurtured, this little bird had found peace and solace as she lay nestled snugly, enfolded in the warm, loving wings of her new mother bird, Blair.

Blair suddenly looked up and met Devlin's eyes. Her bright smile faded into an anxious frown. "Do you really think we can protect her and the boys from … them?" And by—THEM—he knew she was referring, not to the *Vril,* but rather to his government's security services and hers. Devlin nodded, pursed his lips and said, "We can try."

oirish/scotch drivel. specially written for U.S. halfwit market***

BACKGROUND

Alchemy, the ancient science and philosophy, is the art of transforming one thing into another, changing something imperfect into perfection. The alchemical quest of the 1200's, the transmutation of lead into gold with the fabled philosopher's stone, was but one path. Fittingly, it also serves as an allegory for spiritual quest: the purification and unification of mind, body, and soul.

The historical figures of Nicholas and Perenelle Flamel, who pursued both paths in the quest, are a good example. Flamel was a penniless bookseller who gave large sums of money to charities after suddenly becoming wealthy. A stranger walked into his bookshop with a rare book on Alchemy. Its pages were made from the bark of young trees, and the cover was made of worked copper. The book's listed author, Abraham the Jew, included an ancient curse, a Maranatha, against the unworthy who might happen to read the book: "the Lord cometh to execute vengeance upon you." Being unable to decipher the text of the book, Flamel consulted a Jewish Kabbalist in Leon, Spain, who stated that the text was ancient Chaldean. So armed, Flamel was able to translate the book. Even after his death, rumors persisted that Flamel was still alive. Years later, the infamous Cardinal de Richelieu imprisoned and executed Flamel's descendent, Dubois, ransacked Flamel's home, seized his library, including the book of Abraham the Jew, and ordered that Nicholas Flamel's coffin be pried open. When they lifted the lid, the coffin was empty. The book of Abraham the Jew went missing after the cardinal's death. But images from Flamel's notebook can be seen at :

http://www.FlamelCollege.org/flamel.htm.

Present day physicists have accomplished some of the goals of the craft. Using a particle bombardment vessel, they transformed an unstable isotope of lead into a small amount of molecular gold. At the Relativistic Heavy Ion Collider at Brookhaven National Laboratory, physicists conducted an experiment to reproduce the primordial state of matter present in the first microseconds after the Big Bang. Accelerated nearly to the speed of light, gold atoms were smashed together. The result was something akin to the alchemical First Matter, a liquid of pure energy that was 150,000 times hotter than the Sun.

Although the roots of Alchemy are buried in myth and dark mystery, ancient codices show that it was born almost simultaneously in Egypt and Asia, in about 5000 B.C. The root word, from which the word Alchemy derives, however, is no mystery. The Arabic phrase *Al-Khemia*, which means "Land of the *Khem*," refers to Egypt's fertile black soil, but also alludes to the concealed "Black Arts" of the Egyptian priests. In China, Alchemy is found in Taoism. The gold and secret elixir produced by a philosopher's stone was thought to heal the sick and, more importantly, grant eternal life. The Arab alchemists spread their knowledge to the rest of Europe when they migrated to Spain. Later, the Aristotelian concept of four basic elements (earth, water, air, and fire), were added, as well as the Arabic theories of al-Jabir bin Hayyan from the 700's, who incorporated the works of Pythagoras and the Greek philosophers. Gnosticism, the path to enlightenment by personal experience, and Greek alchemical philosophy, play a heavy role in spiritual Alchemy.

Alchemy also merged with mysticism and the Hermetic beliefs of ritual magick. The "Dry Way" was practiced in India and was linked with Tantric sex rituals. It was adopted by European occult societies who sought to release the raging fires of sexual energy. This was known as the most dangerous path. Legend had it that many uninitiated, so-called dabblers in the Black Arts were driven mad by the abrupt accent of the serpent energy, known as Kundalini psychosis.

Second-century Alexandria was the international hub for Alchemy, where the secrets of transmutation were taught to the select few, a closely guarded secret controlled by the temple priests. With the destruction of the academy and great library of Alexandria, alchemists went into hiding and formed what came to known as the *underground stream* or *golden thread.* To avoid religious persecution during the Inquisition, alchemical texts were written in allegorical code and bizarre symbols, which only the highly initiated adepts could understand.

The father of Alchemy has been associated by the Greeks with Hermes Trismegistus, his Latin name. The Emerald Tablet was credited to Hermes. To the Egyptians, he was Thoth, the god of learning, writing, and magick. In 1471, the Italian astrologer Ficino translated the *Corpus*

Hermeticum, also attributed to Hermes. The actual Emerald Tablet has never been found, but the oldest documentable source for Hermes' text is a letter from Aristotle to Alexander the Great.

Although Alchemy is considered the grandparent of modern chemistry and physics, it is also an early form of the science of psychology. It realized the relationship of psychological dysfunction and chemical imbalance in the body. The symbols of Alchemy were labeled archetypical by modern psychology and mysticism. The eminent Swiss psychiatrist Carl G. Jung devoted volumes to alchemical symbols and had accumulated a vast library of texts on the subject. He realized the underlying message and power of alchemical symbolism: red dragons, green lions, serpents, pelicans with bloodied breasts, the so-called *chemical wedding* or marriage of male, the solar, with the female—the lunar—producing a hermaphrodite or *Rebis*, the double thing.

Jung found that his patients' dreams were filled with alchemical symbols, as well as his own. He had a reoccurring dream of a mysterious phantom wing adjoining his home. Exploring his dreams, he learned that Sulfur represents our passion and will, which must be combined with Mercury, the fluid river of our thoughts and imagination. The result is hermaphroditic Salt, the Philosopher's Stone, the union of will and imagination, the integration of the psyche. The Star child of the scared marriage is then simply the integrated Self.

The *Red Book* magickal diary of Doctor Jung is also a historical document, although it remains an enigmatic mystery since it seems to have disappeared from the Jung family archives. Others say that the diary is too controversial to be seen by the public. Being a true mystic, much of what is in Jung's diary was written while he was in a trancelike state. It is commonly known as automatic writing. Historians have noted that even the handwriting in the *Red Book* does not resemble Jung's. But rumor has it that the family's estate may finally release the diary for publication in the near future.

THE NAZI OCCULT CONNECTION

The Nazis launched serious investigations into turning lead into gold, and the Nazi Occult Bureau did in fact launch world-wide expeditions in search of the origins of the Aryan master race.

The secret societies mentioned in the novel actually existed: the *Vril* Society and the *Thule* (THU-LAY) Society, otherwise known as the "*Thule Gesellschaft.*" These groups practiced occult rituals based on Pan-Germanic archetypes but were otherwise very similar to the secret rituals used by those of England's infamous order of the Golden Dawn, the Tantric path of eroticism. Dietrich Eckhart and Baron Rudolf von Sebottendorf were two of the *Thule's* more notorious shadowy leaders. Adepts of the occult, these men allegedly tutored Hitler and influenced the strange occult doctrines of the Third Reich. But Sebottendorff was an alleged double agent, working for the Germans and British Intelligence. Possibly his luck finally ran out. His body was indeed found floating in the Istanbul's Bosporus Strait in 1945. Some believe that he was killed by Turkish Intelligence agents.

The *Sonnenkinder* and *Vril-ya,* the mythical children of the master race, were indeed a demented dream of these groups. An 1870 science fiction novel, *Vril-The Power of the Coming Race*, by Edward Bulwer-Lytton, told of a subterranean master race that lived in the Hollow Earth, who were descendants of Atlantis and called *Der Vril-ya*. It was accepted as gospel truth by occultists, including the Theosophists. And the true origin of the word *Vril* was explained by a group of long-haired female mediums connected with the *Thule* Society, who claimed to have channeled communications from aliens who visited Earth and settled in Sumer in the ancient past. The word *Vril* was formed from the Sumerian word Vri-ll—like God. Legends abound that the Nazi scientists harnessed the *Vril* force to create inter-dimensional gateways as portrayed in the novel.

THE VOYNICH MANUSCRIPT

The Voynich, or VMS, is known as the world's most mysterious manuscript, the elegant enigma. For years, various psychics, scholars and code breakers have tried in vain to solve its mystery. Even the Cray Red Storm supercomputers of the United States' top code-breaking organization, the National Security Agency, have been stymied. Research by cryptologists has offered numerous models: a polyalphabetic cipher, invented by Alberti in 1460's; a code book cipher, requiring a corresponding key book; a visually encoded Hebrew cipher. Others claim that it is written in an exotic language with a fabricated cipher alphabet or *cipherbet*, a term coined by researcher Nick Pelling.

The plain truth is that no one knows who wrote it or when. And no one can actually say with certainty what the text says or what the diagrams mean. The VMS is currently kept in the Beinecke Rare Book Room at Yale. Its actual market value is dubious at best, since Ethel Voynich, the widow of its finder—Wilfred Voynich a rare book collector—willed it to a book dealer, who later donated it to the library after failing to sell it.

The history of the VMS is related accurately in the novel. Many outlandish theories as to what the VMS actually is have been offered. One of the more fanciful claims was made in 1921 when William Newbold shocked the world with his claim that the manuscript was the work of Roger Bacon, and that the letters should be ignored since he had discovered tiny markings above them, which were the actual key. He also claimed the VMS's illustrations portrayed images, which could only be viewed with the inventions of the microscope and telescope a century before they were invented. This, like much of what Newbold claimed, was simply not true. And other researchers debunked the markings.

Here is an image of the Voynich Tube from folio-f88r, along with a computer-generated 3-D replica.

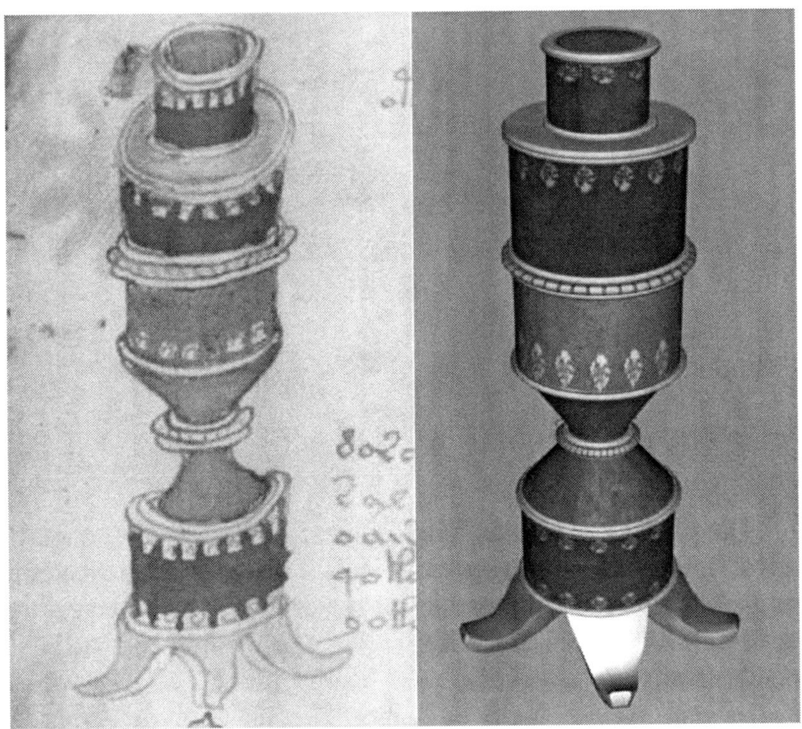

Now compare this with the images of microscopes from the 1600 and 1700's.

The English occultists John Dee and Edward Kelly are real historical figures who often appear in occult histories. Dee created the *Hieroglyphic Monad* mentioned in the novel, which he believed had the secret of transformation. Since Kelly, like many criminals, had a purposely murky and checkered past, history is not clear as to whether his birth name was actually Kelly or Talbot. The tale of Kelly persuading Dee that the angel Uriel commanded that Dee share his twenty-three-year-old bride with Edward is also factual. The Shew Stone, the Sigil of Truth, and Dee's crystal ball are real artifacts, currently housed at the British Museum along with small amounts of gold that were allegedly made by English alchemists. Historical evidence puts Dee and Kelly in Prague during the time that the VMS was purchased by Rudolf II. A letter attached to the first page of the VMS, written by the scientist Johannes Marcus Merci in 1666, tells of the purchase of the VMS for 600 ducats. The angelic or Enochian Language of the Archangels, channeled by Edward Kelly, is a complex working alphabet used to this day by ceremonial magickians. Dee, having lost his patronage with Queen Elizabeth's death, died in poverty at Mortlake. Kelly, having found disfavor with the king when he killed a member of the court in a duel, was imprisoned in Hněvín Castle of Most. Due to complications from a broken leg he suffered while attempting to escape, he was in great pain and ended his life with a draft of poison.

John Dee: the Sigil of Truth, and Enochian Script.

Edward Kelly: alchemist, necromancer, and charlatan.

In the novel I mentioned the VMS's Rosette Page, which the characters in the novel believed to a map.

One possible explanation is that it is in fact the rendering of diatoms, single-celled algae like plankton, as viewed through a microscope.

Here is an image of diatoms seen through a low-powered microscope:

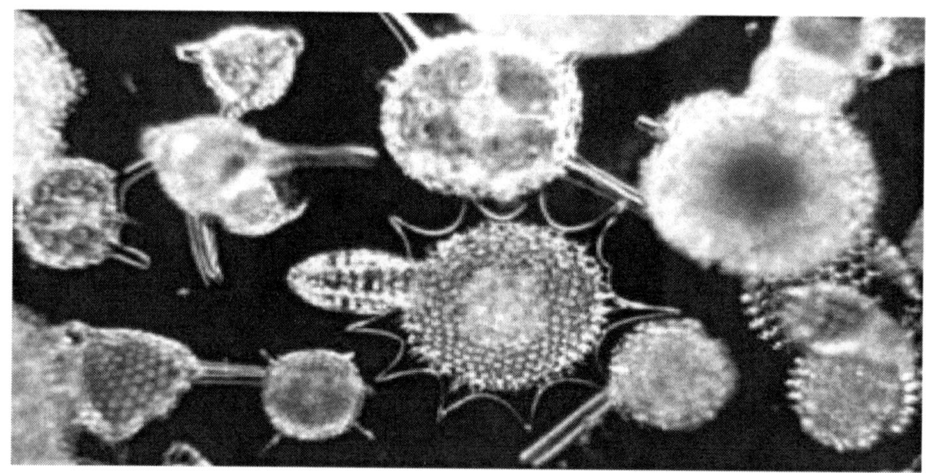

Now compare this with the Rosette diagram from the VMS: Images of the VMS can be found Online at:

http://beinecke.library.yale.edu/dl_crosscollex/SearchExecXC.asp?srchtype=CNO

This would be a plausible explanation if not for the towers, walls, and castles depicted within the spheres as mentioned in the novel. Some have suggested a link with Bacon's New Atlantis and Thomas Moore's Utopia. They were both thought to be high-ranking Rosicrucians and possible alchemists.

Here is Moore's image of Utopia and his cipher on the facing page:

VTOPIAE INSVLAE FIGVRA

VTOPIENSIVM ALPHABETVM.

a b c d e f g h i k l m n o p q r s t v

Tetraſtichon vernacula Vtopienſium lingua.

Vtopos ha Boccas peu la chama polta chamaan

Bargol he maglomi baccan

foma gymno ſophaon

Agrama gymnoſophon labarembacha bodamilomin

Voluala barchin heman la lauoluola dramme pagloni.

Horum verſuum ad verbum hæc eſt ſententia.

Vtopus me dux ex non inſula fecit inſulam

Vna ego terrarum omnium abſq; philoſophia

Ciuitatem philoſophicam expreſſi mortalibus

Libẽter impartio mea, nõ grauatim accipio meliora.

A more recent assertion to solving the riddle of the VMS has been postulated. It claims that by use of a tool known as a Caradon Grille, which involves putting the Voynich script in a table formula, then placing a template—a card with holes cut out—over the table to form words Dee and Kelly could have easily concocted a hoax. The templates with varying numbers of holes to form words with varying numbers of letters could produce page after page of something that resembled a real language.

The theory states that the VMS is just so much gibberish, made to appear all the more mysterious due to its unbreakable code.

For those interested in reading a detailed account of the symbols and theories concerning the VMS, I suggest *The Voynich Manuscript: An Elegant Enigma*, by Mary D'Imperio, a report commissioned by the National Security Agency. Unfortunately, like all those before her, Ms. D'Imperio's only conclusion is that the VMS remains a deep mystery.

FUTURE WEAPONS FROM THE NOVEL

The Protector: Unmanned Patrol Boat with mounted machine gun.

The Crusher … Unmanned Ground Combat Vehicle.

The Corner Shot

Nano-Fiber Exomuscle Suit

KRISS SUPER V .45 SMG

Lightning Source UK Ltd.
Milton Keynes UK
14 November 2009

146213UK00002B/99/P

9 789608 317680